SHADOW OF THE WINDSLAYER BOOK 1

BLOOD HERALD

ABIGAIL LINHARDT

Shadow of the WindSlayer
Book I

Abigail Linhardt

CONTENTS

CONTENT WARNING

This book contains themes and depictions that might be distressing to some readers, including: sexual assault, physical and mental abuse, suicide, and heavy violence. You have been warned. Please read at your own discretion.

PROLOGUE

Trylian galloped up the hill on his black mare toward his commanding Archon Knight and their Clarets. Smoke began to fill the air as their legion moved into the village just outside Emberforge. Snow also drifted down through the air and it was hard for Trylian to tell what was snow and what was ash. A fresh blanket had fallen the night before and made his horse pant as it ran through the ever-deepening drifts. Up ahead, he spotted his Archon Knight, the man in charge of the first column of Knights of the legion. Monguard was a tall man with blood-red hair. He was imposing to even Trylian, who had known him all his life. Monguard was the sort of man others followed without question. Trylian hoped to one day be that sort of man. But for now, he had to answer to Monguard and give his report.

"Sir," he called, catching his breath. Despite the snow, sweat trickled down his scalp, making his long black hair stick to his neck beneath his black armor. "The Elsarius are on the run. Second column has moved in from the east as planned and surrounded the village. They joined the third column and the soldiers and have crushed the Elsarius. The Knights and their Clarets are laying waste to the village. We should have it by sundown."

"Praise the Modeus," Elendir, Trylian's Claret, said softly. "The Knights have performed well."

"Not without their Clarets," Monguard said steadily, his violet eyes never leaving the fray beneath him. "Without that bond between Knight and Claret, we'd not have the magic we wield." He glanced sidelong at his Claret, Daenys. "You prayed this morning? Did the Winds hear you and bless our crystals?"

Daenys nodded wordlessly. Trylian eyed the silent Claret. Something about the man put him on edge. Daenys was loyal on the outside, but his silence often unnerved Trylian.

"I have used the crystals today," Trylian said. He drew his blade and inspected the orange spike of crystal embedded in the hilt. It was paler than it had been before he'd used it, showing the depletion of magic. He looked up at Elendir. "Thank you for your bond, as always."

Elendir smiled weakly at his Knight. "Without it, we die. But I feel blessed to be bound to you."

Unlike other Clarets, Elendir hadn't had a choice when he'd been bound to Trylian. "I still value your loyalty," he said.

Elendir nodded toward the battle unfolding below. "What's next?"

Trylian looked back down at the legion of Knights and watched as sparks of color splashed up here and there, showing where a Modeus Knight used a spell of fire, ice, or lightning to attack one of the Elsarius Knights. The Elsarius in turn flung their own spells. He could smell the lightning mingling with the fire and the tangy scent of blood. He loved the smell of blood mixing with the earth. He inhaled deeply and closed his eyes.

"Scenting the smell of victory, are you, old friend?" Monguard asked with a smirk. "Don't get drunk on it yet. We're not finished. And there is still Emberforge to conquer. We're only halfway there."

"Once we have the village," Trylian said, "we'll have an easy path to Emberforge. The Sactrium is in the middle of the city and not surrounded by walls."

Elendir frowned. "Emberforge has no walls?"

"None," Trylian answered. "And their Sactrium, the most holy of places, is made of wood. It will burn easily. They do not have the stone walls we do in Aatheria."

Trylian expected Monguard to reply with something cutting here, but the big man kept his lips pressed together.

"It will be a slaughter," Daenys whispered, his face drawn in sorrow.

"And this saddens you?" Trylian cut back.

"Shut up," Monguard snapped, stopping the argument before it began. "We must finish the village off first. We will not get to Emberforge today."

Trylian readjusted in his saddle. "We could have gone around and attacked the city directly. Why waste time and men on the village?"

"The Scion of the Elsarius," Monguard replied darkly. "He's the reason we are here."

"The what?" Trylian asked, looking back out over the village as it burned. "There hasn't been a Scion in a hundred years. Not one of the Modeus nor the Elsarius."

Monguard met Trylian's eyes, his dark and serious. "There was a prophecy given to us by the Winds. The Arch Claret himself saw it."

"The Arch Claret in Delsinor?" Trylian asked. "He's an Elsarius. Of course he'd say that."

"He has no reason to lie," Elendir reasoned with his Knight. He turned to look down at the village, and beyond it, to Emberforge. "A real Scion?"

"Yes," Monguard said solemnly. "He could be anywhere. So we must check every village and city between here and Delsinor. He will be a child of seven as of now, according to the prophecy."

"We'll slaughter every child, then," Trylian said eagerly. He gripped the reins harder, and a bloodlust rose in him. "We won't suffer a Scion of the Elsarius. The religious zealots have ruled over us long enough with their songs and prayers. The time of Elsarius is nigh. Let the Modeus rise up and take our rightful place."

"And the Scion of the Modeus?" Elendir asked. "Has one been seen in prophecy?"

Monguard shook his head. "Thus, we must search every village and city."

Trylian nodded. "Seems like a waste, but you are the Archon Knight, and I am tasked with following you. We will not stop until we find the Scion."

"*If* we can find the Scion," Daenys said, his face still dour, "we can then go home. I miss Aatheria."

"As do I," Monguard sighed.

Trylian felt the shift in the conversation as the battle raged on below them. His heart twisted a little in his chest. "I want to see my sons. Alyah died giving birth to them and I've only seen them once. They're alone and so young. I've missed almost their entire lives."

Monguard gave Trylian a sympathetic look at this. "I understand. My son Roan will be seven soon and I haven't seen him since he was five. And I miss Juliana." He blinked, keeping the emotion at bay.

"I will never forgive her for leaving me for you," Trylian laughed, trying to make light of the conversation. "I would say she chose the worse man, but seeing as you made Archon before me, I must be wrong."

Monguard finally smiled and a light laugh escaped his chapped lips. "She never regretted her decision, if it makes you feel better."

Trylian let the jab roll off him. "She's a wise woman. I trust her judgment. But at least you know what your Roan looks like. I can only imagine my boys. Twins, Monguard. I am a father of two. Winds, I miss them and I hardly know them."

"Soon," his old friend replied. Monguard drew his sword. "It is time. To arms!" he shouted, and the Knights behind him drew their blades.

Trylian looked behind them at the legion. The legion was made up of four columns of Knights, and each column held twenty-five Knights. Only first column Knights had the magic they wielded. Below them, other legions and swarms of city soldiers fought. Aatheria's military was weak compared to the Knights, he thought. The Knights were the elite.

"Daenys," Monguard said, "keep yourself and the Clarets here. If the Elsarius break our lines, run for the camp. Do you understand?"

"Yes, sir," Daenys replied. "And, Monguard? Keep safe. I couldn't bear it if you died."

"You'd be dead, too," Trylian reminded the Claret. "Eventually."

"Don't joke about that," Elendir warned his Knight. "Come back to us." He leaned over his horse and embraced Trylian before pulling his horse back and taking a few steps away to safety. "May the Winds be ever at your back."

Daenys mimicked the motion, embracing Monguard for several seconds. "Watch out for one another."

"Pray for us," Trylian replied.

"Men!" Monguard shouted, raising his blade. "Onward!"

The most elite of Knights, and those bound to Clarets, thus possessing the ability to wield the magic the crystals offered, were the first column, and those were the men that followed Monguard. Though the other columns were already deep into the fray, they were not bound to Clarets and therefore could not cast the magic like the others. It was time to unleash the power of the Modeus onto the Elsarius.

Trylian kicked his horse hard in the sides and yelled, calling on all his strength. He felt the power flow from Elendir into him as he parted from his Claret. The heat from the fire crystal in his pommel flowed through him. He flexed his fingers and a ball of fire erupted in his palm, already snapping and crackling. He homed in on one Knight of the Elsarius and locked his gaze on them. With a war cry, he hurled the ball of fire at the enemy Knight. The fire crashed into him, heating the metal of his armor. The force more than anything knocked the Knight over. Trylian stayed on his horse and used his long blade to hack at the fallen Knight.

Easily decapitating the man, he whirled around, using the purple crystal in his gauntlet to hurl a man across the battle-field with an invisible force. He watched as the dark purple crystal turned to more of a violet color as the power was drained from it. One Knight of the Elsarius, far away from him, gathered his own magic and threw a snapping web of lightning toward him. Trylian wheeled around and ducked, the electric missile missing him. He glared at the offending Knight and used his purple crystal to snap his neck. The Elsarius were weak, he thought. Relying on their prayers and ways of compassion. They had been the dominant faith long enough. It was time for strength and domination, the way the Modeus taught. Magic was to be wielded by the strong only.

"Stop that man!" one of the Archon Knights of the Elsarius cried, pointing at Trylian.

Trylian pulled hard on his reins, swinging his horse around to gallop away from the immediate threat. He hacked his way through several more men before he came to the center of the village. Others fought around him, the mayhem deafening him. Magic flew across the battle ground and blood seemed to be raining from the gray sky above. The winter clouds obscured the sun and made the late afternoon feel dark.

A ball of fire raced toward Trylian as he maimed his way deeper into the ranks of the Elsarius. Behind him, Monguard rode up, kicking at a man who tried to unseat him from his horse.

"It's like they were expecting us," Trylian called to Monguard as he hurled another ball of fire, draining the crystal in his pommel. "The Knights of the Elsarius should not have been here. The winter attack was our best strategy, but they were ready."

Monguard threw a blast of wind from his own gauntlet at a man rushing them and then faced Trylian. "We ransacked every village between here and Aatheria. Of course they knew we were coming."

Trylian didn't believe that. "How could word have traveled so fast? We struck without warning. Not even the king in Delsinor knew we were on the move. Someone among us is a traitor, Monguard."

Just then, another wave of Knights spilled over the hill behind the village. These ones wore different colors and rode under a different banner. A flag with a red river on it flew above the reinforcements.

"Redwater!" Trylian cried. "What are they doing here?"

Monguard didn't answer. He hit a man coming at them with the flat of his sword and rushed into the new fray, rallying men with him. Trylian followed his old friend into the masses and hacked away at them.

"Archers, on the hill," he called. "Shields!"

No sooner had he called than a mist of arrows rained down on them. Some used walls of magically-summoned wind to blow away the projectiles and others ducked behind round silver shields. Trylian raced behind Monguard, who threw his hand out, creating a massive wall of wind that stopped the arrows.

"You didn't bring any wind crystals?" Monguard asked.

Trylian smiled. "I have you, don't I? I'll be fine."

Monguard shook his head and raced to the other side of the village to attack one of the Archon Knights that commanded the Knights of the Elsarius. Trylian turned and used his purple crystal to lift a man off the ground and spear him on a pike.

Then something hot hit him from behind, scorching the back of his neck and burning his long black hair. The force of the fireball knocked him off his horse and into the bloody mud. He landed hard, his armor not helping in the least with the blunt force. Trylian moaned and pushed himself up. As he did, a silver sword came down toward his face. In a panic, he raised his arm and the sword crashed into his metal gauntlet, destroying the purple stone there. Growling, Trylian leapt up and quickly dispatched the one who had broken his crystal. Despondently, he glanced down at it. It was useless now. Broken. No amount of prayers from Elendir would mend it.

A woman ran past him weeping, calling for her child. Being inside the village now, he saw more citizens mingling with the Knights. They no doubt had tried to remove the innocents, but some still lingered. Trylian easily cleaved at the woman, splintering her nearly in two as he walked by. Her cries instantly stopped. A child screamed and dashed from his hiding place upon seeing it. Realizing this was the child's mother, Trylian conjured up a fireball in his palm and threw it at the child. It hit him square in the back, setting him ablaze. The child screamed and fell to the ground, trying to stifle the flames. But it did no good. In a matter of seconds, the child's crying ceased and his body lay still.

Satisfied, Trylian turned. Any who worshiped the Elsarius, the aspects of the Winds that some prayed to, deserved death. The Modeus were the only true aspects and were the teachings that should be followed. Strength above all, and victory by subjugation.

A shadow passed over him.

Trylian looked up, wondering what sort of large bird had blotted out the sun for a moment. But then he saw it. Flying not too high above the burning village was a white, leathery-winged dragon. The thing was small, young, but still belched fire into the Knights of the Modeus and the army of Aatheria, setting them ablaze. Dragon fire burned hotter and spread faster than regular flames. The men hardly had time to scream before they were lying on the ground smoldering. Dozens of them went down at once in the wall of fire created by the young dragon.

"We must turn back!" Monguard shouted from a great distance away.

"Wait!" Trylian shouted. He ran to Monguard, who was also no longer seated on his horse. "The dragon is the sign. The Scion of the Elsarius is here. Monguard, the boy is here!" This was their chance to find and kill the Scion. He'd only be a boy. Small. No different from the one he'd already killed.

"Look," Monguard called back. He pointed over the hill.

Trylian squinted into the distance and took in a blue and silver mass moving toward them. A banner with a silver anvil fluttered over them. "Emberforge is here," he breathed. If the city was answering this quickly, they had to have known in advance. This only proved to Trylian that what he had said before was true: someone in their ranks had warned Moralan that they were coming.

Trylian turned, ready to argue with Monguard, ready to stay and find the young Scion. But when he turned, he saw something that made him go still. Monguard quickly stabbed one of their own Knights who was about to cut down a weeping woman. Behind them, a small hovel of a home burned. Trylian blinked, not believing what he'd seen. Monguard ran into the house then, sheathing his blade.

Curious what his friend and commander was doing, Trylian ran in after him. Monguard heaved a fallen, flaming beam out of the way and reached down to pull up a boy of about seven. Monguard gripped the boy's shoulder and told him to run out the back of the house toward the Elsarius from

Emberforge. He turned then and froze when he saw Trylian. The boy's eyes went wide and he ran.

"Trylian," Monguard began, "listen to me now—"

"Was it you?" Trylian gasped. Something in his chest stung and his eyes watered, but not because of the flames.

"My old friend," Monguard said again, "long have I been deceived by the teachings of the Modeus. Just like you. They are foul, evil teachings. What we do is wrong. Think of Elendir and his forced servitude."

"I have not been led astray," Trylian barked back. "*You* have. You are the traitor, Monguard? You told Moralan we were coming. The men are dying because of you. This was my chance to make Archon Knight. I will fail because of you. Our men will die because of you!"

"Because of the Modeus!" Monguard tried again. "They filled our heads with lies, Trylian. We are no better than the Elsarius. Their way of peace and love is what I want now."

The betrayal hurt. Never had Trylian felt the emotions that whirled inside him now. He didn't care about the Modeus or their rivalry with the Elsarius. Monguard had wounded him.

"What would you have done with me?" he asked, his voice thick. "If we had fallen here today? Would you have spared me? Locked me in a stockade, punished me, had me executed?"

"No," Monguard quickly answered. "I had hoped to bring you with me. To convert to the ways of the Elsarius."

Trylian scoffed to hide a light sob. He blinked and the tears fell. The damn smoke drew them out. "I could never. You know that. How could you?"

Monguard swallowed hard, his face twisting in pain. "For Roan. For my son. I want him to live a better life than I did. We are slaves to the Modeus, Trylian. The abuse, the hate, the violence. I don't want that for my boy."

"Weeks of foiled plans," Trylian whispered. "Wondering how we could be so outmaneuvered. But it was you." He'd heard enough. Something in Trylian cracked and he drew his blade.

"Don't," Monguard whispered. "Don't make me hurt you. For Elendir, for your boys. I cannot bring that message home to them."

"You won't have to," Trylian growled. He charged his old friend, raising his blade.

Monguard was ready and parried the hate-driven blow. Trylian hacked madly, bringing hit after hit down on Monguard. But Monguard was a tall man, taller than Trylian. His shoulders were broader and his arms thicker. He also had a certain grace in his movements that allowed him to move quickly. Trylian danced around him, trying to find an opening. He nicked Monguard once, and that was when he realized: he didn't want to kill his friend. But the hurt boiled inside him. He didn't want to attack his friend for their shattered beliefs. He wanted to strike him down for the betrayal.

Trylian shoved hard once, their swords entangled again, forcing Monguard back. The bigger man stumbled back and tripped over the burning beam he had lifted just moments ago. He fell backward and landed hard. Trylian ran forward like lightning and kicked his blade out of his hands. Monguard reached out with a hand that bore a ring with a purple crystal in it. Understanding, Trylian screamed and brought his blade down, severing Monguard's hand.

His commander growled in pain and clutched his bloody stump to his armored chest. He looked up at Trylian. "I-Is there nothing I can say to m-make you see sense?" he asked, struggling. Sweat trickled in rivulets down his temples.

Trylian almost sauntered to his fallen friend, pressing the tip of his blade to the soft skin of Monguard's throat that was exposed above his armor. He let the weight of the sword press down on him. Trylian arched a brow.

"Nothing, old friend. But I? I will receive honors for dispatching the traitor."

"Trylian, think of Roan," Monguard tried. He didn't dare move, his eyes flitting to the fire crystal in the pommel of the blade.

"I am, Monguard," Trylian said. "Also of Juliana. Who will comfort her in her time of need?"

Monguard's blood-red brows dipped into a hard glare. His lips curved in a snarl.

"Roan will need a man to look up to," Trylian went on. "I suppose that will be me. I will mold him into the Knight you should have been."

Monguard growled like a wild animal and gripped the blade of Trylian's sword with his bare hand. He pulled, trying to rip it from his friend's grasp. Trylian held fast and instead slid the blade out of Monguard's hand, cutting his fingers. Monguard groaned and fell back, cringing away from Trylian.

Having had enough, Trylian raised his blade over his shoulder and swung. The white blade cut through Monguard's neck easily. His long red hair whipped around, mingling with the blood that flew from his neck. The body shuddered for a moment, then fell over into the fire. The smell of burning blood rose from the flames.

Outside, the other Archon Knights called for the legion and army to flee. Trylian gasped and panted, inhaling the smoke. He coughed once and ran out, taking only Monguard's sword with him. It was a unique and beautiful blade.

Once back outside, he spotted the young dragon spewing another rain of fire down, scorching a host of men. The others ran back to the west, away from Emberforge and the village. Trylian spotted bodies everywhere in the snow. The white blanket was now black and red.

Whistling for his horse, he charged back the way they'd come. This was supposed to be *his* battle. No, he was not an Archon Knight, not a commander of the legion. But it was his test. The setup was his. The charge was his. This was to be the battle that defined him. His promotion to Archon Knight would have been the next day.

But no. His friend had betrayed him. Losing him the battle. Killing countless men. Saving the Scion of the Elsarius.

Trylian kicked his horse hard, galloping away as he was chased down by the dragon overhead. The white beast glittered despite there being no sun out. He glared at it, knowing it meant that somewhere a young boy was alive and well. The Scion would grow, become a man. And all because he'd failed.

~ ~ ~

ONCE THEY CLEARED THE VALLEY, he slowed his horse. Up on a hill, the Clarets waited at a safe distance from the battle. Most of them, like their Knights, would die soon. With their Knights dead and the magic no longer shared, the power of the Winds inside their veins would overcome them and they'd die a terrible death. They needed the bond to the Knights to survive.

As he neared the group of Clarets, he heard many of them calling out for their Knights. He pushed through them, continuing on to the camp.

"Trylian!" Elendir called, riding up to him. "Thank the Winds you're safe. What happened?"

Trylian didn't respond. He'd caught the other three Archon Knights looking at him. One glared, the other two looked bemused. The horde of bloodied Knights and scared Clarets began to move at a trot away from the battle before the

Elsarius decided to follow them. They'd strike back, to be sure. Just not yet.

"Monguard!" Daenys's voice rang out from the horde. "Where are you?"

Trylian spotted the frightened Claret. His white robes fluttered in the wind, as did his long white hair. Daenys stood in his stirrups and looked around. He spotted Trylian.

"Please," Daenys called, galloping up to Trylian. "Where is he?"

Trylian blinked, staring ahead. He felt Elendir's eyes on him as well.

"Speak, Knight," one of the other Archon Knights ordered as he rode up to Trylian. "Where is Monguard?"

Trylian licked his chapped lips and tasted blood on his face. "Dead," he murmured.

Daenys gasped and let out a sob. "No, he can't be!" The Claret's eyes darted around the horde as if he thought Monguard might appear from the throng.

"I'm so sorry, Daenys," Elendir whispered, knowing the fate that was about to befall the Claret.

"Are you sure?" Daenys asked, tears freezing to his face.

The Archon Knight also locked his eyes on Trylian, waiting.

"Yes," Trylian whispered. His throat was dry. "Monguard was a traitor. He warned Moralan we were coming. This failure is his doing."

"No," the Archon Knight hissed in disbelief. "I felt they were too well prepared. The reinforcements came out of nowhere. I should have known. Are you sure it was Monguard?"

"He told me himself," Trylian replied. He glared at Daenys. "You knew."

The Claret gulped and his eyes went wide. "I... I'm sorry. I don't..."

"Is this true?" Elendir asked, aghast. Daenys and he were close, Trylian knew. Like him and Monguard.

"It..." Daenys couldn't go on.

The Archon Knight took a deep breath and looked away. "It matters not. You will be dead in a few days' time."

Daenys let out another sob.

"Leave now or taste our blades," the Archon Knight said, glaring at the Claret. "Consider this a mercy. Enjoy your final days."

"Wait!" Elendir begged, but Trylian shook his head.

Daenys's horse stopped its trot and the horde parted around him, leaving him behind.

"He'll die in the cold," Elendir begged.

"He's dead either way," the Archon Knight said stoically. "Once your Knight is dead, the Winds will consume you. There is no stopping it. Leaving him alive for these last few days is a mercy."

Trylian didn't look back. Daenys called out, begging for mercy, but didn't chase after them. It took all his strength to not turn back and look. He liked Daenys. He had loved Monguard. And they had betrayed the Modeus. That hurt more than anything. He glanced sideways at Elendir. He prayed to the Winds that his own Claret was loyal. It would destroy him to kill Elendir.

But he had other things on his mind as well. Namely Lady Juliana and her son Roan. Trylian wanted to take Roan under his wing now. He'd save the boy from his father's ideals. He'd raise Roan as his own.

After he brought them the terrible news of Monguard's demise.

CHAPTER
I

Roan planned on drowning the cat that morning, but he couldn't find the little bitch anywhere. She was no doubt hiding with her new litter of kittens under some barrel or in the hayloft. The summers in Aatheria were cool, which made the winters cold enough to freeze the fires of the afterlife. This made the animals huddle in hidden places for warmth.

It was Roan's seventh birthday, and he'd sworn as a gift to himself he'd have his revenge on the cat. She'd scratched him the other day as he'd tried to pet her kittens. She'd scampered away as he'd swung at her, dodging her due punishment. He'd never liked the cat and decided today was the best time to get rid of her. His mother, Lady Juliana, would never miss the animal. They had more than enough cats roaming the land to keep the rat population in check.

A wind picked up from behind him and blew his blood-red mane into his somber green eyes as he scanned the stable grounds in the distance. The sun shone down from above behind some white clouds. Despite this, Roan pulled his hood up over his face. His alabaster skin burned easily and the winter sun often scorched his nose. He hated being red like that. Especially since he already hated the smattering of freckles that flecked over the bridge of his too-straight nose and high cheekbones. The sun often made them more numerous.

He marched across the inner ward to the stables to continue stalking his prey. The inside of the stables smelled of horses and muddy hay. A few of the animals perked up curiously as he entered, each hoping he'd pick them to ride out into the fields.

"I'm not here for you," he said to the nearest horse that snorted a great puff of air through its long nose.

His keen eyes scanned the stables, then went to the hayloft above. He scampered up the ladder and quietly walked with knees bent into the maze of hay. Near the back was a barrel turned over onto its side. As quietly as he could, Roan walked to the barrel and looked inside.

As he'd suspected, lying on her side, kittens ravenously sucking on her middle, was the cat who had scratched him. Her yellow eyes blinked drowsily as Roan made a triumphant sound. Her sleek black body glimmered in the firelight coming from the torch above them.

"Found you," Roan muttered, reaching in. He gripped the cat by her scruff and pulled her out. The kittens mewled pathetically as they tumbled down one by one. "You'll be next, don't worry," Roan offered the frightened kittens.

The mother cat yowled in pain as he gripped her and marched back down the ladder. There was a trough of water just on the outside of the barn he'd throw her in. He'd have to make sure she didn't escape, but it should be easy. The trough was frozen over, so Roan punched a small hole in the ice just big enough to slip the cat in through.

"This is for drawing my blood," he growled.

Just as he was about to force the helpless animal under the ice, a familiar voice screamed his name. Roan turned to see his best friend Razvin, a half-Vyrkarian, come running up the muddy path from the gate. Being half-Vyrkarian, Razvin had smoky gray skin, black horns protruding from his scalp, and a long, dragon-like tail. He also had somewhat tougher skin than their human counterparts.

Razvin's long black hair whipped out behind him in a mess and a waterskin over one shoulder bounced as he ran. He panted, his little fangs showing behind his black lips. Roan noted his wide blue eyes.

"They're right behind me, hide me!" Razvin called between gasps.

The cat screamed and reached up, clawing at Roan's hand. She landed her clawed attack, scratching the back of his hand deeply. Roan cried out and dropped the animal. It scampered away, back into the stables. Roan glared after it, blood dripping down his fingers.

"This way," Roan said, motioning with his bloody hand for Razvin to follow him.

They ran around the stables and up to the back of the castle where the entrance to the kitchens waited snuggly in the stone walls behind a row of rose bushes. They crouched behind the bushes, and Razvin peeked over the branches to look back out into the street beyond the gate.

"I don't see anyone," he panted, flopping onto the ground. "I swear they were right behind me."

"What did you do?" Roan asked, already smiling. Knowing his mischievous friend, he had done something to get himself in trouble once more.

"The city guards were after me," Razvin panted. "I found the perfect stick," he began, still catching his breath. "It had a prick and balls and everything. You know that statue of Thane Mercival in the town square?"

Roan knew the old statue. It was made from stone and was old and chipped, depicting some Thane who had done some great deed a thousand years ago and supposedly deserved immortalization as a statue. He nodded.

"Well," Razvin went on, "I may have drawn on its face with charcoal and tied the prick-stick to its middle to make it look like he'd dropped his pants."

Roan laughed, trying to imagine it. "I want to see."

"Go back into town?" Razvin asked. His gray cheeks flushed red from the cold and the running. "They don't know it was me, but they could find out. I'm not like you, Roan. My father isn't an Archon Knight. I can't hide behind his rank."

"He's first column, though," Roan reasoned. "And one of the richest men in Aatheria. They wouldn't touch you."

"They would," Razvin argued back. "Married a Vyrkarian. Had a monstrous son." He sat up, his long tail whipping up behind him. "And they don't have the sense of humor we do."

"Raz," Roan smiled. "No one has your sense of humor. Or your foolishness."

Razvin smiled, lightly punching Roan in his shoulder. "If they ask, I was with you all morning."

"Of course. What were we doing?"

Razvin screwed up his face, thinking. "Stealing wine from the Sactrium?" He held up the waterskin he had slung over his shoulder.

"You didn't!" Roan laughed, taking the bag and quickly downing a swallow. He winced as the warm wine filled his belly. "But it can't be that. Stealing from the holy Sactrium is worse than giving Thane Mercival a wooden prick."

Razvin shrugged. "You think of something. You're the smart one."

Roan arched a blood-red brow and nodded in agreement. "We were hunting. But we didn't catch anything because you were too loud and wouldn't stop talking."

"Believable," Razvin acquiesced with a nod. He then took a drink of the sacred wine and grimaced.

Roan stood, holding a hand back down for Razvin. "Let's go see this wooden prick."

FORGOING HORSES, the boys trotted into the city and maneuvered the familiar streets easily. It was market day, and the square was packed. Women with baskets of goods squeezed between other patrons and merchants. A wool seller shouted through the crowd to his apprentice. Roan led the way, being taller than Razvin, even counting his horns. They pushed through, passed the wall, and found their way to the cobbled square where the statue of Thane Mercival stood. Roan pressed through one last line of peasants to find a string of city guards near the statue. The guards looked enraged.

Roan glanced up at the statue. As Razvin had professed, there was a great wooden prick-shaped stick tethered to the statue. The face was covered in black soot as well, coloring a mustache and beard onto the statue. Roan giggled and shook his head.

"You find this funny?" one of the city guards asked. He glared down at the boys. "Do you know who did this?"

Razvin immediately began to stammer and fiddle with his fingers. His face burned red. Roan stepped forward.

"I am Roan, son of Monguard, Archon Knight of the Modeus. Do not speak to me in this manner." He glared up at the guard. "Do you really think we'd be stupid enough to return to the scene of the crime if we had vandalized it?"

The guard exchanged a quick glance with his fellow before looking back down at the boys. His icy eyes landed on Razvin, who blushed and ducked his head into his shoulders.

"We need to investigate, is all," the guard said, a little put out. "Apologies, little master."

"Of course you do," Roan said, his voice softening as he took a step closer. "And I commend your dedication to preserving the dignity of our historical figures. My father often speaks of how the city watch is the backbone of Aatheria's peace."

The second guard, a younger man with a patchy beard, seemed pleased by this.

"However," Roan continued, gesturing to the busy market, "surely there are more pressing concerns than a prank? I heard whispers of pickpockets working the eastern stalls today. The merchant guild would be most grateful for your attention there."

The first guard's expression wavered between suspicion and consideration. "We can't just ignore this vandalism."

"Not ignore," Roan corrected with a diplomatic smile. "Prioritize. After all, my father contributes substantially to the guard's winter provisions. He'd be pleased to hear how wisely you allocate your resources."

The guards exchanged glances, the suggestion of Monguard's favor clearly having an effect.

"Besides," Roan added, dropping his voice to a conspiratorial tone, "between us, I overheard some apprentice boys from the tanner's guild boasting about a prank involving the old Thane. Perhaps your investigation might begin there?"

The guard's eyes narrowed, but his posture relaxed. "The tanner's boys, you say?"

"Apologies, little master," the second guard said, looking slightly embarrassed.

"Think nothing of it," Roan replied with a gracious nod. "We're all simply doing our duty to Aatheria."

As the guards nodded and turned their attention away, Razvin's mouth hung open slightly in amazement.

"We'll look into those pickpockets," the first guard called after them as they began to move away. "And the tanner's apprentices."

Emboldened, Razvin shot, "You wouldn't arrest such good an artist, anyway. Look at the magnitude of this prick.

So stout, so hard. Besides, I wouldn't do well in a city prison."

"You?" the guard dropped his crossed arms.

"Razvin!" Roan spit, glaring.

"Get them!"

Roan turned on his heel, grabbing his friend's hand, and dashing into the crowded square. The guards shouted for everyone to move, but their voices were drowned out in the din of the market. Roan and Razvin slipped through the patrons and merchants alike until they reached a back street behind a whore house. Panting, the two boys stopped and leaned up against the stone wall. The gutters smelled of piss and shit, but Roan knew the guards wouldn't follow them down this way.

He turned to Razvin. "I try and I try to keep you out of the trouble you make for yourself and yet you insist on spitting on my effort." He smiled despite himself. He threw his arm around Razvin's neck and pulled him into an embrace. "What if one day I'm not here to save you from yourself?"

The half-Vyrkarian giggled, punching Roan in the ribs to get him off. "There is no situation you cannot talk yourself out of. That silver tongue of yours is like magic from the Winds themselves."

Razvin pulled the wine off his shoulder again and offered it to Roan. He took a drink and wiped his mouth with the back of his hand. Then he handed the wineskin back to Razvin, who drowned himself in one swallow.

"Happy birthday, by the way," he said. "We celebrating tonight?"

Roan nodded. "Mother has a feast planned. I'm not supposed to know about it, but I do."

"How long have we been friends, then?"

Roan screwed up his face. "Forever, I think. I don't remember."

"And you'll have my back for forevermore, just like today?"

Roan nodded. "You know, the city guards know who I am. They'll find you."

"No, they won't, Razvin quipped. "Because you won't tell them anything."

Roan eyed his friend hard as they made their way back to his estate. "The guards answer to the capital, Delsinor. Delsinor is Elsarius. We're alone out here in Aatheria with our Modeus teachings. We wouldn't have much protection should the king decide we need to be quashed."

"That's war," Razvin suggested diplomatically. "Father says the king wouldn't dare cause a battle within Adorian."

Roan smiled. "I doubt a wooden prick on a statue of an old Thane warrants war."

The boys talked and meandered slowly over the hills back to the land surrounding Roan's estate. They followed the muddy path through the snow up to the gate where a servant waited. Roan squinted through the darkening snow in the air to the servant. The man stood with his hands clasped behind his back, clearly waiting for him.

"Master Roan," the servant called. "You are required to come to the keep at once."

"He didn't do it!" Razvin shouted quickly.

The servant smiled. "This is not about any mischief you two have gotten up to. Trylian of Aatheria has returned home."

Roan's heart leapt in his chest while a dark memory came to mind as well. "And Father?" he asked, excited. "Has he come home?"

The servant didn't reply. His eyes went dark, though.

"Who's Trylian?" Razvin asked.

Roan's mind went to the dark memory. He was five. His father had left him with Trylian to train with a bow and he'd failed to hit the target. Trylian had beaten him. Roan remembered hiding in the stables and the threat from the older man to not tell his father. Father hadn't asked about the bruises. But Trylian had never mentored him again after that.

Roan swallowed. "Is Father not with him?"

"Come inside, master Roan," the servant said instead of answering.

Something in Roan turned to ice. Something was wrong. "Raz, go home," he said softly, his eyes locking onto the keep in the distance. It was hard to see it against the dark sky now that the sun had set.

"Are you all right, Ro?" Razvin asked, lightly touching his shoulder.

"Go home," Roan repeated.

Razvin left solemnly then, and the servant led Roan up into the keep and into a room with a great hearth and a long table. Roan had rarely been in the hall as Father often reserved it for meeting with important men. His mother, Lady Juliana, stood in the room already. She was a slender, beautiful woman with long brown hair braided and clasped in rings of gold. Her elegant figure was draped in green velvet. She smiled when Roan entered.

Before she could speak, the doors on the other end of the hall opened and Trylian appeared. He looked just how Roan remembered him. Tall, black hair, keen, dark blue eyes, and a stoic face that reminded Roan Trylian was a military man. Father had a similar face, but Roan didn't remember him wearing it all the time like Trylian did.

"My friend," Mother said, holding her hands out to Trylian, who took one and kissed it. "We didn't expect you back, but are pleased you have returned." She looked behind him. "Where is Monguard?"

"Juliana," Trylian said steadily. His eyes flitted to Roan. "I have come with news from the front in Moralan."

Mother nodded and motioned for Trylian to sit. He shook his head.

"We lost the battle at Emberforge," Trylian said, his voice steely and hard. "We're pulling out before the king in Delsinor retaliates. I..." He looked to Roan once more.

Roan fought against quailing under the tall man's gaze. Something in him told him what Trylian was avoiding. He looked to Mother and saw her face go pale and impassive all at once. She seemed to stop breathing.

"Go on," she whispered. "Trylian, tell me." Her hands hung at her sides.

"Juliana, I'm so sorry," Trylian whispered, his voice gravelly. "Monguard fought with valor. He was the greatest—"

Juliana screamed. Roan jumped at the sound and took a step back. Was? Had Trylian said was? Roan couldn't stop the sudden tears that filled his eyes. He felt the blood drain from his face and neck. Even his fingers tingled with loss of feeling. The ground under him bucked and he felt dizzy as the room spun around him. Trylian kept talking, but Roan could only hear Mother's wailing.

Mother bent over, her knees giving out. Trylian dipped and caught her, holding her as she wailed. She fell into his arms and screamed again.

Roan found himself wondering about Daenys then, his father's Claret. He'd known the man well. "What about Daenys?" he whispered.

Trylian looked down at Roan. "Dead. The Winds took him soon after your father was killed."

"Why?" Roan whispered. He didn't understand.

Trylian lowered Mother into a chair at the long table and crouched before her, holding her hands as she wept. "A Claret cannot contain all the magic the Winds bless them with. It's too much for them, making them weak and fragile. Ill, almost. So they must bind to a Knight to share that burden. This gives the Knights the power to wield the magic of the crystals."

"Clarets cannot use the crystals?" Roan asked, his face feeling completely numb now. He didn't know why he was asking. He couldn't control his mind as it reeled. Father was gone? Daenys was gone?

"No," Trylian answered. "They are made to bind. So when a Knight dies, the power overcomes them, and they die."

Roan wasn't listening, though. He locked his eyes on Mother and watched as she heaved sob after sob from her chest. Tears streaked down her face.

"Take her to her rooms," Trylian called to the servants in the corner.

They rushed forward and helped Mother up, leading her out of the room. She babbled and protested, but didn't fight. Roan was left alone with Trylian. A small tinge of fear brought feeling back to Roan's feet and he glanced up. Suddenly, he wondered if this was how the black cat had felt. Scared. Cornered. He gulped.

"Roan," Trylian began.

But Roan didn't want to stay. The memory of Trylian beating him came back too strong. He turned and ran, trying to flee. Father was no longer there to protect him.

"Stop!" Trylian shouted, grabbing a handful of Roan's shaggy hair. He pulled him back, gripping his upper arm tightly. "Listen to me, Roan."

But Roan didn't want to. Snarling like a wild wolf, he twisted in Trylian's grip and bit his hand. Trylian growled and swung his other hand, backhanding Roan hard across his face. He hit Roan so hard he fell to the stone ground. Fear lanced through Roan as he looked up through tears of pain. Before he could move, Trylian stomped down onto his chest with his massive booted foot. Roan wiggled under the pressure, but couldn't throw Trylian off.

"You need a strong hand in your life, Roan," Trylian said softly, leaning down close to him. "I am sorry about your father, but this is what has happened. I will be that hand. You need me. Do you understand? We cannot have you going astray as well. I will do what I must to make sure of that."

When Roan didn't reply, Trylian pressed down harder.

"Say yes, sir," he commanded.

The sadness and hate washing over him, Roan growled instead and shoved at the boot that held him down.

Trylian clicked his tongue and shook his head. "Just like your father. Refusing to kneel to authority. He's gone, Roan. And I promised him I'd take care of you. Train you up. And I will. I won't let you fall into the wrong paths."

"I hate you," Roan snarled. He couldn't think of anything else to say. He knew he was trapped, and that feeling enraged him more than made him fearful. "I want Father back."

Trylian rolled his eyes and stood up straight. He aimed a swift kick at Roan's face and paced away. Roan yelped from the shock and quickly crawled away into a corner of the room now that he was free. He cowered there in the darkness. He pulled his knees into his chest and watched Trylian pace.

"You could be the one we need, Roan," he said, his eyes tracking Roan as he moved like a caged bear around the room. "I won't let you go to waste."

Roan didn't understand. He licked his lip and tasted blood. All the courage he had felt when talking to the city guards melted away when Trylian was near. And Father was gone.

"I want Father," Roan said pathetically before he could stop himself. He sniffled and pressed himself into the corner harder.

The door burst open behind Trylian and Mother charged in, still weeping. She flew into Trylian's arms and hugged him tight, like she was drowning and he was the only one who could save her.

"Please, Trylian," she begged. "Help us. Take care of us. I don't know what to do. I don't know what Monguard had planned. What if the king—"

Trylian shushed her gently, pressing his hand into the back of her head to hug her tight against his chest. "Nothing like that is going to happen," he assured her. "I will take care of everything."

"But Monguard spoke of the Scion," Mother said. "That could spell the end of the Modeus for us. What if they gather to strike us down?"

Trylian's eyes flitted to Roan. "We will not allow the Elsarius to wipe us out, Juliana. I won't let them."

"And Roan?" She sniffled, but didn't look at her son.

"I will train him as a Knight," Trylian said. "He will one day help us find the Scion of the Elsarius and then we will crush them. But the king has moved Knights into Aatheria to ensure we do not rise up. He is a gracious king and is allowing those in the city to remain. Others from the front, who were in Emberforge, were not as fortunate. I barely escaped."

Mother took a deep breath and sighed. "Maybe we should convert."

"Never!" Trylian snapped. "We must have faith, Juliana. We will rise again."

Roan swallowed hard and watched Trylian hold Mother. He knew then his life had changed. No more protection from Father. No more sleeping late and running around town with Razvin. His life had crumbled in one evening.

He glanced at Trylian's hand around his mother's neck and watched his blood drip down Trylian's knuckles.

CHAPTER II

The night before his seventeenth birthday, Phael had gone to bed smiling. He'd stolen honey from the Sanctuary kitchens and Lailen, the Claret in charge of the orphaned wards, had not found out it had been him. Lailen was a good man and Phael hated to hide his thievery from him, but the spring had brought many bees to their new boxes. They had more than enough honey to spare. The other wards, orphans like him, had muttered among each other, trying to figure out which of them had earned them all a stern lecture and extra chores for the missing honey. Phael didn't mind the punishment, though. He liked working the barns, herding the sheep, and gathering fish for the Sanctuary and all who lived within its sacred grounds. It had been a busy day full of hard work and helped him sleep that night. Plus, he knew the morning would bring with it a change for his life. The Winds would either bless him or pass him over with weak magic. He had hoped to be blessed with weak magic so he could follow in Lailen's footsteps and be a Claret of the Sanctuary, singing and praying all day, only going out every once in a while to bless a crop or visit a sick elder. He looked forward to that peaceful life.

But the morning brought agony.

The bells of the Sanctuary woke Phael just before sunrise, as they always had. But this time, with the ringing came a pain like he'd never felt before. Something like fire rushed through his veins, burning his insides and his brain. He woke screaming, thrashing about on the straw mattress in the dormitories. Others woke, and a few asked him what was wrong. Unsure, Phael hugged himself, lying on the bed. He moaned as the pain mounted and his eyes felt like they were melting.

"What's happened to you?" another ward asked, eyes wide as he looked at Phael.

Not understanding, Phael tried to rise. Sweat poured down his temples into his long hair and then his bones began to chill. The mix of fire and ice inside him made him want to weep.

"Your hair," one of the wards said, aghast. "It's gone all white."

Phael took up a handful of his long hair and inspected it through his tears. Where once a rich, golden yellow had flowed over his shoulders, now the strands were a stark, snowy white.

"Am I dying?" Phael gasped.

The other wards looked at him, worried, their brows pinching and eyes unsure. They had gathered around him and watched with fearful eyes as he moaned in utter pain.

"What are you boys doing?" Lailen's kind voice asked over the whispered din as he entered the dormitory.

"Lailen!" Phael cried. "Help me. I'm dying! I'm sorry I stole the honey. I won't do it again. Just please help me."

Lailen, a tall and thin Claret of about thirty with long pale brown hair, pushed through the swarm of other boys. He looked concerned until his eyes fell on Phael. "So it was you," he said with a gentle smile.

Phael nodded and clasped his hands together before him. "I'm so sorry. Please help me."

Lailen sighed and smiled down at Phael. "Boys, go about your chores," he instructed. A few of them protested, but he shooed them away. It took several minutes, but soon Phael was alone with Lailen.

"What's happening to me?" he whispered, tears trickling down his pale cheeks. "Everything hurts." He thought back to a few weeks ago when other Clarets had awoken in just as much agony. He'd thought they were dying, too. "Is it the magic?" he asked as another wave of searing heat prickled through his limbs. His eyes filled with hot tears as the wave of power scorched his insides.

Lailen smiled warmly now. "Yes, you have come into your magic, Phael. Nothing bad is happening to you. You're not dying. Not yet."

"Yet?" he yelped. "It's worse than I thought. I think—" But he couldn't go on. The surge of magic took his voice in a stab of pain.

A small laugh trickled out from Lailen's throat. He sat on the small mattress near Phael and gently took the boy's hand in his. "This is a great day for you, Phael. You have come into your magic and must bind to a Knight soon. The Winds have blessed you. They have filled you with their power and you must bind to share that power. It is too much for one man to bear. It will weaken you. Make you frail, your bones brittle. But a Knight will protect you. It's one of the most sacred bonds in the world. You are truly blessed."

Phael nodded but still held his arms around his middle. "It hurts so much. Will it ever wane?"

Lailen nodded. "But it will rise again, too. Until you are bound."

"And if I do not bind, I die?" he asked. "How long do I have?"

"Before a bond? Months, perhaps a year," Lailen said gently. "But worry not, Phael. There are many Knights of the Elsarius who need Clarets. We will have you bound in a fortnight at the most. You need not fear death. Death only comes to Clarets when their Knight dies."

"Why?"

"The Winds overpower them," the older Claret explained. "But you need not have any fear of that. The Knights of the Elsarius are brave, strong fighters. They will protect you as well as themselves. Besides," he added as an afterthought, "we are no longer at war with the Modeus. Ten years of peace, Phael. That is good. You have nothing to fear."

Phael thought. "When a Knight dies, could a Claret bind again and save themselves?"

Lailen smiled and nodded.

"And you?" Phael asked. At last, the pain began to recede, though he felt the weakness sinking into his muscles. Fatigue overtook him. "Why can I not be like you?"

Lailen's brown eyes looked away, almost ashamed. "I was not blessed by the Winds as strongly as you. I was given a drop of the magic you possess. I am suited best for praying for miracles, blessing crops, singing praises to the Winds—things of that nature. Not like you, who will give your power to a Knight who will wield the magic of the crystals."

"Can I not wield the crystals?" Phael asked. He didn't see why, if the power came through him, he should not use it.

Lailen shook his head. "Do not. You are a conduit, Phael. It is not meant for you."

"And others?" Phael asked, the pain finally simmering down to a dull roar. "What if one had no faith and they came into magic?"

Lailen once again shook his head. "The Elsarius do not reward the faithless. The Winds give and the Winds take away. Should one turn their back on them, they will be forsaken; cut off from the Elsarius. Alone. And that—a life with no faith, no protection—is a fate worse than death."

Phael went still, trying to imagine a life where he didn't

feel the thrumming of the Elsarius' love and protection in his chest. He'd always been faithful. Had been raised in the ways of the light side of the Winds. To be forsaken sounded like a death sentence.

Lailen waited a moment, looking Phael up and down, before he said, "Have you remained pure, my boy?"

Phael blushed deeply and looked away. "I have."

"Good. The Elsarius demand purity, among other things. You must remain so if you are to serve the Winds to the best of your abilities." Lailen stood. "Once you are feeling better, see to your chores. I will tell the Arch Claret that you have come into your power, and we will find you a Knight."

"A kind one," Phael asked. He didn't want to bind to a brutish man for the rest of his days. He preferred people of a softer nature, those who would find more joy in tending a garden over someone who revelled in the glory of battle.

Lailen smiled down at Phael. "You are too soft, Phael. A stronger Knight might be good for you."

Phael's face fell, and he sank a little into the sheets.

Lailen's face changed, and a slight look of regret passed over him. "But perhaps you are right. Someone who values peace over turmoil might be just the kind of Knight you need. Now..." He motioned for Phael to get up. "I want to walk you out. Come."

⚜

PHAEL FOLLOWED Lailen out of the dormitories, through the stone halls, and into the main room of the Sanctuary where the great Empyrean Core glowed. The Core, the source of all their power, pulsed and hummed. It stood many feet taller than Phael, as most things did, and was perched in a stone base with glowing runes etched into it. The nave of the inner room was vast and wide open. It was filled with other Clarets like Lailen, singing hymns to the Winds and lighting candles and incense. Phael loved this room and its colored windows, the smoke drifting slowly up. As they passed the Core, it pulsed again and a small wisp of what Phael could only assume was magic drifted out, rose, and dissipated into the air. Behind the Core, in the chancel, the Anakrite stood, pouring over an old tome.

"The magic journeying to a newborn life," Lailen sighed with a happy smile.

"Is that what that was?" Phael asked. He rubbed his chest, his heart still aching from the seizure. "How do you know which newborns have the magic of the Winds within them?"

"I can feel it," Lailen answered softly, looking up at the glowing Core with Phael. "We are present at births, or if we're not, most women bring their children to us to have them tested. When I see a new babe, I feel a surge of excitement and familiarity like a lance through my heart. That's when I know the magic in me is speaking to the magic in them." He smiled at Phael. "But not with you. We weren't there at your birth, since you were born on that pirate ship. But it's a good thing we found you as a child after your parents passed on. You were ragged and starving on the streets." His smile deepened as he looked on Phael with fondness.

Phael didn't share the smile. He hated the memories he had of living on the streets. Of being chased by wild city dogs, being threatened by merchants who knew he'd come to steal bread. "Are all children then attuned to the Core like I was?"

Lailen nodded.

"What happens if they're not?" he asked.

"Being attuned to the Empyrean Core here in Delsinor lets the Winds know you have accepted their gift, and thus they put the magic to sleep until you are older. This saves your life and makes your prayers reach the Winds when you pray for your power and for your Knight."

"And it is this way for all of us?" Phael asked.

Lailen shook his head, a sparkle in his eye. "Not for a Scion and his Claret, who are born bound. But that's another story for another time."

Phael looked up at the Empyrean Core. "Is this the only Core?"

"No," Lailen said. "Delsinor is the capital of Adorian and thus our Core sits here in the Sanctuary. We are the head of the faith, where the Arch Claret resides. Other homes of the faith, Sactriums, are built in the other cities like Caeth and Aatheria." He blanched at the name of Aatheria. "Though not all worship the Elsarius as we do. There is another Core for the Elsarius in Duskhallow in Moralan."

Phael felt reverence for his faith resonating in his chest the more he looked at the Empyrean Core. The thrumming of the Elsarius' love and protection heightened the closer he got to the Core.

Lailen tapped his shoulder. "We've tarried enough here. Let us depart and get you to your chores."

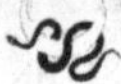

THE SPRING AIR flowed through Phael's newly whitened hair in a gentle breeze. It brought with it the smell of flowers and the crops just on the western side of the Sanctuary. Bees flitted from wildflower to apple tree, working their magic. The grass had grown long and tall and made Phael have to march with high knees through it until he got to the golden path that led from every important place in the walls of the Sanctuary. The Sanctuary was nestled in the middle of the city but had a small buffer of green pastures around it. The main gate opened right into the city square of Delsinor. The holy structure was the home of the Clarets of Delsinor and housed much of the city's crystals. The Sanctuary had many rooms for study, prayer, and even rooms where the younger Clarets and wards played. The chanting and singing of the Clarets filled the air all around the Sanctuary that morning.

Phael stopped by the kitchens first to pick up a wooden pail to take to the barn where the cows waited to be milked. Inside, he spotted a fresh pot of honey and had to fight the urge to dip his fingers into the golden magic and steal a taste. He was already on Lailen's watch list and didn't want to do anything that might stop him from attending the spring festival in the inner city. The first of spring always brought the loudest and biggest festival Delsinor ever saw. Phael often pretended the celebrations were for him since it was his birthday as well.

The cook eyed him as he picked up the wooden pail, giving him a warning glower. "You cannot fool me, Phael," the cook said with a knowing grin. "You may be sweet as the honey you steal, but there's a mischievous streak in you. I can see it."

Phael blushed and dipped his head but smiled. He grabbed the pail and quickly left before the cook could accuse him of stealing the honey the day before. He skipped happily across the ward and down to the barn. The wind picked up his long white robes and flicked them about as he made his way down. He loved the wind. It felt like a gentle hug from the earth itself. Phael craved an embrace but rarely received them.

He stopped in the doorway to the barn and looked each cow in their big, baleful eyes. "Who's first?" he asked.

One of the heifers perked up her ears and mooed loudly.

"Very well," he said with a grin.

Just as he turned to enter the long line of stalls, someone else came around the corner and bumped into him. At first,

Phael laughed lightly and stammered an apology, but then he looked up and saw who it was.

"Nox," he breathed, taking in the beautiful Claret before him.

Nox had come into his magic a week earlier. He and Phael didn't speak much, but Phael admired him from a far. Nox stirred a strange sensation in Phael's body he didn't understand. Something akin to excitement and fear all at once. It made his heart race and took his breath away.

"Hello, Phael," Nox replied with a demure smile. His hair was white as clouds and his eyes were like black pearls. "I've done this side, if you want to finish for me."

"Of course," Phael replied. He'd do anything for Nox. He wanted to say more, to keep the boy here longer and speak to him, but he wasn't sure what to say.

"Oh," Nox said, his eyes going to Phael's long, now-white hair. "When did this happen?"

"This morning," Phael answered quickly, desperate to continue looking into Nox's eyes. "It was horrible. I wish I would have known."

Nox nodded and lightly touched the ends of Phael's hair. This sent shivers of lightning up and down Phael's body. He wanted to take Nox's long-fingered hand in his and touch his soft alabaster flesh.

"It comes and goes," Nox warned him. "Be ready for it." He smiled and leaned over, picking up his own pail full of milk. "Thank you, Phael." He left, skirting around Phael to exit through the door.

Phael watched him walk away, sighing wistfully. He had work to do.

Phael did his job well, filling multiple pails and bringing them to the kitchens, one after the other. A few of the other young wards came and did their duties as well: cleaning the stalls, pitching hay, and feeding the animals. He watched them go about their chores and was pleased none of them said more than a quick congratulations on his birthday and admired his new-found magic.

While he milked the cows, he thought about what Lailen had said. Magic wasn't for him. He was just a conduit. But why? If he was the one the Winds had chosen to hold the magic, why could he not use it?

Once he was finished and the sun was high in the sky, he slinked to the smithy across the ward. The blacksmith was gone to his delight. He must have been on his way to the festival. Phael looked around the inside of the small smithy and quickly found what he was looking for. On a shelf near the forge waited several spikes of crystals. One that caught his attention was green, and another was orange. Deciding on the orange one, he picked up the spike. It was thinner than he'd thought it'd be, and short. The tip was sharp.

He gripped the crystal in his hand and took a deep breath, trying to open himself up to the sensation within him. The pain sprang up again, overtaking his entire body all at once. He groaned and doubled over but caught himself on the forge table. Something like liquid fire spread through his veins then. Phael opened his eyes and looked down at his arm. Under his white skin, his veins turned a bright, glowing orange. His skin began to burn.

"Ah!" Phael cried out, dropping the crystal. It burned his hand. But the magic didn't stop when he dropped the crystal. The ripples of heat began to encroach on his vision, making the smithy wobble. Tears filled his eyes, and they felt like they were melting.

Phael moaned and fell backward. Fire began to spirt from his fingertips. He screamed and shook his hand, but that just made the fire jump farther. The droplets of fire landed on the ground where pieces of hay lay about. One small patch caught fire, and it began to spread quickly.

"No, no," Phael groaned. He tried to pat out the fire, but the flames from his hands only caused it to grow. He flinched and pulled back, the fire burning him. But he couldn't stop producing the flames. It burned him more, coming out in a spray of flames now.

Before he knew it, the entire smithy glowed with flames roaring around him. He spun on the spot, looking around in fear, and the fire spread farther, spewing from his hands. The pain of the flames seared his flesh. He looked down and saw blisters spreading over his wrists and forearms. He screamed, the magic sapping his strength. His legs gave out and he fell to his knees. His vision was so blurred from the heat waves he couldn't see. Sweat soaked his body, and the smoke filled his lungs. The entire forge was aflame.

"Help me!" Phael screamed. He couldn't hear anything outside the smithy, the roar and crackling of the flames filling his ears.

He fell onto his belly, panting, trying to find clean air. But his body still burned, and he couldn't stop it. Finally, when he thought he'd never be saved, he closed his eyes and let the flames take him. Soon, the blackness gave way to numbness.

PHAEL WOKE to the sensation of cool water being poured over his wrists and someone wiping them down. He lay on a soft mattress and smelled the distinct aroma of the dormitories. Cracking open his eyes, he found he was able to see. The heat lines were gone and so was the pain. Lailen sat beside him, arms crossed as a healer administered cold ointment to his burns. Phael focused on the wooden rafters above, avoiding Lailen's penetrating gaze.

The healer touched his burn, making him wince and hiss.

"What were you thinking?" Lailen asked, his voice low and dangerous. "Phael!" he snapped when the boy didn't respond.

Phael quickly looked Lailen in the eyes. Tears of regret welled up there and he tried to stifle them.

"Don't give me those pathetic whimpers and tears." Lailen rolled his eyes.

I didn't mean to, Phael thought bitterly. He looked away, a small sob escaping his throat. "I'm sorry, Lailen."

"Sorry?" the older Claret asked, dropping his arms. "The smithy is burned to ash. Razed to the ground. Gone, Phael. And you—" He stopped, swallowing hard. "You could have died. Burned to cinders from the inside out."

The healer stood, drying his hands on the folds of his robes. "He'll be fine. The burns are minor. Should heal in a few days' time." He eyed Phael. "You are lucky we found you when we did, young man."

Embarrassed and distraught, Phael draped his arm over his eyes to avoid looking at the men.

"That will be all," Lailen said to the healer. He quickly snipped at a few other wards who had gathered, curious, and told them to leave. When they were alone, he sat back down next to Phael. He gently lifted Phael's arm to see his eyes. "Why? You could have died."

Phael sniffled and wiped at the tears running down his temples. "Why can't we use the magic? Why must we be only conduits?"

Lailen sighed and pressed his palms into his knees. "We cannot know the design of the Winds. We must simply have faith. The power we hold is too much for us. Summoning the fire like you did could have killed you, burned you from the inside out. It must be shared. The burden cannot be carried alone."

Phael understood that part. He just didn't know why the

Winds would curse him with magic he couldn't use. He looked over at Lailen. "I wish I was more like you."

"No, you don't," Lailen replied quickly. "You are lucky to be a true Claret. I will never bind to a Knight. Never enjoy that connection. I will ever only pray over crops, see in my dreams, and be a tool for prayer. You will see battle, Phael. You will share a bond with another that cannot be rivaled."

"I don't want to go to war," Phael said. He sat up, pressing his back into the wooden headboard. "I like the gardens. The bees. The simple life we live here."

Lailen smiled kindly at his words. "There is no war right now. Ten years of peace, we've had. Aatheria and others who fly the Modeus banner have been silent for a decade. But if your Knight was called to battle, you would have to go. That is your destiny, Phael. But you wouldn't mind. The bond between a Claret and a Knight is precious, unexplainable. You will love him and do anything for him. And he will, in return, give his life to you. You will pray every day for the Winds to bless him and recharge the crystals he uses in battle, as is your duty."

Phael sighed and tried not to think about it. "Do all Clarets come into their magic at my age?" he asked.

Lailen smiled. "Not all. There is one who might be blessed much earlier."

Phael nodded. "The Scion?"

"The Scion. He might come into his magic much earlier, having been chosen as the Elsarius's leader. They are born bound to their Claret and must find one another."

"And has that happened? Is there a Scion?" he asked, because he wanted to ensure it wasn't him.

Lailen gave him a coy smile. "Maybe. There were dragon sightings ten years ago in Emberforge. If there is a Scion, he'd be about your age now. But he must be hidden. Even the king doesn't know if the Scion has been born. But those who were at the battle of Emberforge swear they saw a white dragon that day. That it drove the Modeus back and won them the war."

"And do you believe it?"

Lailen leaned back a little. "I have faith."

Phael gingerly touched the bandages around his forearms. The burns traveled far up his arms, past his elbows. It hurt. "I'm glad it's not me. I'd hate to be a dragon."

"It would be a great honor," Lailen tried. "The Claret who is bound to a Scion can shift into one of the most powerful beasts known to our world." He narrowed his eyes playfully. "I think you'd like to be a dragon, Phael. Imagine soaring over Adorian, catching the wind under your massive wings."

"I'd rather stay with my feet on the ground," Phael shot back. "It's bad enough that I must bind to a Knight."

Seeing he'd lost the battle, Lailen nodded. "Well, you are bound for great things, whether you want it or not, my boy."

Phael's heart fell at that.

"And," Lailen went on, standing, "as punishment for burning down the smithy and almost killing yourself, you will be bound to the grounds."

"What?" Phael burst, pushing himself up from the bed. "But today is the spring festival!"

"I know. And you shall not partake." Lailen turned to leave, then whipped back around. "Don't let me catch you sneaking out. We will have guards posted at all the doors and windows." He smiled and left.

Phael sank into the bed sheets, fresh sorrow overcoming him. He looked out the window and saw the sun was past midday. The revelries would be starting soon. And he would miss them. All because he'd had to defy what the Winds had ordained.

Deciding it was the right thing, and that he had to be punished, Phael closed his eyes and prayed for forgiveness.

CHAPTER III

Roan woke early and attacked his daily training hard, like he had for the last ten years. He rode out from his home and his worrying mother to Caer Aatheria, the fort and barracks a few miles from his home inside the city walls. He'd ridden out to the caer every morning since the day he'd found out his father had died. Trylian had let him remain in his house with his mother while he was fourth column.

"Once you rise to first column, you will have to move into the caer," he had said one day. "You won't always have your mother to come home to."

Roan didn't snivel, though. Trylian was brutal to him in his training, but Roan had learned quickly to not complain about it. Ten years of hardship had made him stoic and silent. He tried not to think about those past years, however. They were dark years, lighted only by Razvin and his constant light-hearted humor. He'd never told Razvin what Trylian did to him. It wasn't his burden to bear.

This morning was different, though. It was the first day of spring, and the festivals would be in full swing by the time he was done with training. Razvin met him outside the caer on his own horse and waved Roan down.

"The best parts of the festival are outside the city walls, in the village near the water," he said once they joined up. Razvin's gray skin was pinkish from exertion and sweat made his long black hair stick to his neck. His black horns glinted in the sun, and Roan caught sight of a new notch on the side of his left horn.

"Practice was hard?" he asked. He turned his horse's head and started a slow trot down the golden road to the small village near the water's edge. He pointed to the horn when Razvin cocked his head.

"Oh, that," the half-Vyrkarian said, rolling his eyes. "Alamar. That boy never knows when to stop. He's strong and ruthless. Good thing I have my horns. Saved my life, no doubt."

"I hate him," Roan grumbled. "Thinks he's better than us because he's a year older."

"No, he thinks he's better than us because he's first column," Razvin corrected.

Roan sank a little into his saddle. "You're second column. There's almost no difference." He looked around. "Where is your Claret, by the way?"

"Atreus?" Razvin asked. "Praying. He thinks the revelries are an excuse for hedonism, sodomy, and debauchery."

"He's not wrong." Roan smiled. "He's more like an Elsarius than he likes to admit. All the talk of purity and praying."

Razvin shrugged one of his muscled shoulders. "They must pray or we lose our strength. Our magic. I don't mind what he does so long as I can do this." He raised his left hand and conjured a ball of flame there.

Roan looked at his long-time friend. Normally, they allocated their crystals to their swords, gauntlets, and armor. But right now, Razvin wore basic cotton garments that he must have been wearing beneath his armor. Then Roan spotted a thick silver necklace around his neck. Imbedded in the center of the collar-like adornment was an orange crystal.

"Clever," Roan replied. "Join me at the joust?"

"And watch Trylian unseat himself while we drink? Of course."

Roan didn't think Trylian would ever let an opponent score a point against him. But he did want to drink. He was hot and thirsty after all the combat practice, and the sun was high. Together, they rode down the hill to the village. The Northern Narrows flowed by the village in a loud, mad rush. A slight wind blew off the water, cooling the air in the village a little.

The boys meandered their way into the village and around the alderman's hall to a great opening set apart by a makeshift fence. Crowds stood around the arena watching two men on horseback in full armor stare one another down. Roan recognized Trylian's silver and blue banner on the left side. He and Razvin dismounted their own horses and tethered them to a hitching post nearby. Behind the arena, a slave market roared to life with a live auction. All around them, though, came the noise of the festival.

Coins jingled on dancers' hips as they spun with brightly colored scarves from the exotic east. Merchants called to patrons to sell their wares. Singing rose from a choir somewhere behind a small shrine to the Modeus. The smell of cooking meat and honeyed nuts roasting filled the air, as well as the smell of horses, goats, and the dust from the ground. The loudness made Roan's blood rush and butterflies fill his stomach.

They watched a few bouts of the joust (Trylian winning every one) before Razvin grew bored and wanted to go find a drink. They marched behind the arena toward the slave market where a small stall was selling sweet apple mead. Razvin stopped there to flirt with the pretty merchant girl while Roan's eyes were drawn to a cage in the slave market. He looked in and saw a girl about his age trapped and shackled inside the cage. She had long sheets of brown hair and gray eyes that shone like a storm at sea. She looked sad and scared. When she met his eyes, she glared at him despite the tear tracks down her face.

Annoyed at the gall of the girl, he picked up a rock and threw it with all his might, aiming between the bars. The rock flew true and hit her square in the forehead. She yelped and cringed away, blood already trickling down between her eyes. Roan scoffed lightly, smirking. As he watched her cower, he wondered if that was what he'd looked like that one day when he was fifteen, when Trylian had come into his room...

The memory filled his mind, blinding him to the bright, sunny day. The darkness crept in, chilling him. He remembered the stone floor under his bare feet, the dim flickering light of his bedroom...

"Oh, great," Razvin sighed, pushing a huge tankard of the sweet red mead into Roan's hands.

Roan looked up, sound coming back to his ears. Pushing their way through the crowd came Alamar and his two ever-present cohorts. Alamar was a tall boy, but not taller than Roan. Roan, as far as he knew, was the tallest boy in Aatheria, and he liked it. But Alamar came close. He was broad shouldered and handsome, with his stubbly face and long chestnut hair. He was also top of the first column. He didn't have his Claret with him.

"Look who we have here," Alamar said, tucking his thumbs into his belt and surveying Roan up and down. "How's fourth column, Blood Mane?"

Roan ignored the jibe. Alamar had called him that on their first day of combat training. Alamar had bloodied Roan so badly that he'd lost consciousness. The healer had not seen how badly Roan had bled from his scalp because his hair was the same color as his blood. He had almost died that day. But never again. Roan had trained hard and was eager for a rematch with Alamar. One day.

"Someone like you would attack a caged animal," Alamar said with a grin.

"Looking for a rematch, Alamar?" Roan shot back. He balled his fists, not having a sword at his side. Alamar didn't, either.

Alamar looked from one of his cohorts to the other. "Sounds like a challenge, doesn't it, lads?"

The other two laughed and smiled, striking poses similar to Alamar's.

"Don't," Razvin said seriously. "This is a festival day. Let's not fight. Let's drink instead."

"Try me, half-breed," Alamar snarled to Razvin. "I'll rip those horns from your skull and plow you over a barrel when I'm through."

Razvin blanched, but took a drink of the mead instead of responding.

"Just you and me, Alamar," Roan said, a devious smile spreading across his pale lips.

"Here? Now?" Alamar asked, dropping his hands.

Roan nodded. "Why not? Everyone is enjoying sport today."

The girl selling the mead quickly gathered up her bottles and hurried around her cart and out of sight. Roan watched her flee before his eyes flitted back to Alamar.

"Sure," the other boy said casually. "Come get me, Blood Mane."

"Roan, no," Razvin said sarcastically, almost bored. Then he added, "Why do you always have to show you're the boldest and strongest? Don't bother with him."

But Roan leapt like a lion at Alamar. He landed a hard punch to the boy's face and then swung his other hand, hitting him hard in the side. Alamar backed up quickly, raising his fists to protect his face. Roan smiled and casually walked a tight circle around Alamar. He heard Razvin cheering him on over the din that had started to gather around them. He waited this time, knowing Alamar would attack sloppily.

And he did. Alamar lunged, fist cocked, and stepped into a puddle of vomit from some other overly-drunk patron. He slid, and Roan took the opportunity to kick him. His heavy boot connected with Alamar's chin, making him moan and stumble back. Blood trickled down from between his teeth. Grunting, Alamar motioned to his two friends. They raced forward and Roan raised his hands, ready.

He blocked one blow but had to absorb the other to his side. The pain it shot through him was more than he'd expected. He spun to parry another punch. As he did, the boy behind him grabbed a fistful of his long red hair and pulled. Roan jerked backward and stumbled, losing his footing. Taking the opportunity, Alamar dived onto him and rained a series of punches on him with fury. Razvin shouted, "Bad form!" but didn't intervene.

Roan rolled over on the ground and kicked one of the other boys in the shin. His leg bent at an unnatural angle and a loud snapping was heard. Roan leapt to his feet and pummeled the wounded boy until he fell to the ground, weeping. Then he rounded on Alamar and the other boy. Alamar took a step back.

"No brawls in the street!" A city guard appeared with a small host of others at his back. He glared at Roan. "This may not be the city, but we uphold the laws here. No fighting in public."

Roan felt blood dribble down from his nose. He'd won the fight and was satisfied, so he nodded and turned to Razvin. He gripped his friend's arm and marched him away from the slave market. Alamar didn't even shout some cutting words as they parted. Roan smiled.

"Thanks for the help," he growled once they were deeper

into the village square, and their voices were drowned out by the singing and music once again.

"You had it covered," Razvin quipped back. "Roan, someday you must learn to drink your problems away rather than fight them."

He led the way back to the girl with her small tent over her wagon, where the mead had been replaced now that the fighting had stopped. She smiled at them and gladly took their coin in exchange for more mead. Razvin downed his in one swig and motioned for Roan to do the same.

"I can't say anything against your philosophy," Roan said, "as it seems to have worked for you. You're second column now, and they don't seem to mind that you're a helpless drunk."

Razvin smiled, his sharp teeth glinting in the sunlight. "I wouldn't drink so much if we had a war to fight. Give me battle, give me carnage. My ancestral blood demands it."

"Aha." Roan grinned. "So you do crave violence. Just as I do." He took a drink and leaned against the wagon, putting one foot up to lounge there. "Trylian says we will have war again. Soon."

Razvin looked up, hearing the despondency in Roan's voice. "You'll be first column soon, I know it. You're a strong fighter. Trylian just has to see that."

Hadn't he? He'd trained with Trylian every day for the last ten years. Roan was convinced Trylian liked to see him suffer. And holding him back from first column was just one of the ways he tortured him.

Roan was about to reply when his eyes caught a flash of gold. He looked up over his tankard and spotted the source. A beautiful woman with dark blonde hair stood across the golden path from him. She inspected a basket of flowers a street vendor held. A golden circlet around her head had caught the sun. It had three emeralds embedded in it that twinkled in the midday light. She held an orange and red rose to her nose and closed her eyes, smelling it deeply. Roan watched her chest rise, the creamy hills of her breasts catching the sun as well.

She opened her eyes and saw him staring at her. She smiled into the petals and met his eyes. When she didn't look away, courage rose in Roan. He put the tankard down and pushed himself up off the wagon. The woman's brow flicked in amusement. Roan marched up to her with confidence.

"How much for the rose?" he asked the vendor, his eyes never leaving the girl's. Her eyes were green like the gems in her circlet.

"Two coppers," the vendor said in a small voice.

Roan pulled out a gold piece and handed it to the vendor. "Pick another," he told the girl with green eyes.

She smiled and blushed. "Using your money to win me over?" she asked with a slight smirk.

"It's not about the coin," Roan said, quirking his own lips as well. "Do the flowers bring you joy?"

The girl finally broke eye contact and looked at the basket of flowers. "Hmm." She tapped her finger to her lips. "And what if that sword brought me joy?" She pointed to a makeshift smithy where a man hammered on a longsword. It had a golden hilt, and a pommel encrusted with jewels.

"Anything," Roan replied, stepping closer to her.

She smiled up at him. "I want for little. My name is Eliana, daughter of Archon Knight Thaniel. And you are Roan Red Mane."

Roan's heart fell a little at hearing the name given to him by Alamar. He looked around uncomfortably before locking back onto Eliana's green eyes. "Perhaps there is nothing I can give you that you could hold. But I could give you my heart if you gave me the chance to show you."

Eliana's face never lost its smile. She blinked slowly up at him and turned to walk away. He followed, abandoning Razvin and his mead. "Say more pretty things like that," she said.

Roan thought a moment. "I'm not a poet."

"You cannot buy words, Roan Red Mane." She giggled.

Roan stopped, moving in front of her to block her path. "We are surrounded by silks from the east, songs so beautiful they would make the Winds weep, and dancers so lovely they'd make a Claret impure. But I can't even notice those things because of you. The rose you hold is a weed compared to you. The gems in your crown don't shine near as bright as your eyes. But more than that, I sense a gentle nature in you. You are kind and giving."

Eliana nodded, her smile still glimmering over her pretty face. "I know your nature as well," she said. "You are a brute. Foolhardy. Callous. I've heard of your deeds and your ways. You are ruthless and violent."

Roan didn't stop her as she moved past him to keep walking. He turned and followed at a distance.

"But that also means you are brave and strong," she said. She glanced over her beautiful bare shoulder at him.

"I think we need to spend time together," he said. "To get to know one another better. What we've said today is all guesswork."

"Hmm," Eliana hummed, something mischievous glinting in her eye. "Perhaps."

Roan caught up to her and took her hand. He was about to speak when someone shrieked and screamed. He spun to look back toward the Northern Narrows. He saw easily over the heads of the other patrons and down the main road to the water's edge. Five dragon-headed boats floated toward them, filled to bursting with pure-blooded Vyrkarians. Their scaly skin glittered in the spring sun.

"Raiders!" he shouted. "Everyone, get back into the village!"

Eliana gasped and jerked her hand away, running into the crowd and vanishing. Roan watched her go, but he didn't dwell on his loss. The people screamed as the Vyrkarian ships rose up onto the shores and the dragon-like humanoids leapt over the sides, axes held high.

"Get everyone inside!" Roan shouted, running toward the water's edge. Sprinting past the smithy, he took up a blade and charged closer.

Razvin appeared at his side, armed as well. "Knights, to me!" he shouted. A small host of armed Knights joined them and started to line up, making a wall between the Vyrkarians and the village.

Roan knew it wouldn't be enough, though. But they had to try. The people of the village would be slaughtered otherwise. The Vyrkarians sprinted to the small line of Knights and a few other citizens who had picked up pitchforks, hammers, and swords. Roan ran out in front and clashed with a wild warrior first. They tangled swords and entered combat quickly.

All around him, a battle erupted. The singing and music gave way instantly to the clash of weapons and the screaming of the people. Somewhere, a man moaned as he was slaughtered.

The Vyrkarian Roan fought was tall and had red skin and black horns. His dragon-like face snarled and snapped. "Puny human!" the monster roared, shoving Roan back.

Roan stumbled back and fell hard but didn't let the dragonoid get in another attack. He kicked the blade that struck down toward him and rolled to the side. He slashed as he came up and clipped the Vyrkarian's chest. The monster didn't like that and struck with renewed vigor. He drove Roan back into the village where Roan spotted other wild Vyrkarians looting and ransacking the village. They took women, kicking and screaming. They gathered up jewels and sacks of gold. They even took weapons with gems in them.

"Find the crystals!" one of the monsters cried.

The Vyrkarian fighting Roan got the upper hand once again and reached out a scaly, clawed hand. It took him by the throat and squeezed. Roan tried to gasp, but his throat closed up. He swung his sword, but the Vyrkarian blocked the blow and shoved the sword out of his hand. Roan's eyes filled with tears of pain as the thing squeezed again. It lifted him up just enough so his toes scrambled to find the earth beneath them.

"Hey!" Razvin shouted from the side.

The Vyrkarian turned to look, and his yellow eyes went wide when he saw Razvin aiming at him with a bow. He dropped Roan and moved just as the feathered shaft flew past him. Roan gasped and choked but found his blade and rose up to finish the fight.

A fresh wave of Knights came around the town hall from the arena and slid to a stop for just a moment in shock. Roan motioned for them to run forward.

"They're in the Sactrium's cell!" he called, pointing to a small stone structure outside the town hall. "They're going for the crystals."

The Knights obeyed immediately, rushing in to fight the Vyrkarians who were looting the sacred building, looking for the crystals. Roan rallied the other Knights outside and slowly they were able to push back the invaders.

"Don't stop," he commanded as they neared the shore. He cut down two, three, four Vyrkarians. He aimed to maim and harm more than to kill. He wanted them to suffer. One, he cut the hands off of. Another, he severed just one leg before plucking out the eyes.

"They're running!" Razvin called, galloping up behind Roan. "They left the crystals behind."

"Push forward," Roan ordered, slashing through another invader. "Don't let them leave."

Razvin hesitated, but did as Roan commanded. So did the others. Soon, a large horde of Knights was following Roan's orders and shoving the invading Vyrkarians back. Roan caught one trying to clamber onto the boat. He reached back and took Razvin's bow from his hand and aimed. He shot the Vyrkarian in the back of his neck, killing him. He fell into the waves with a splash and floated there, dead.

Slowly, the din died down and turned to the soft moans of the wounded. Roan turned and saw the bodies strewn over the land between the shore and the village. He panted, blood smattering his face and clothes. He wiped at his cheeks and forehead, smearing the blood. It mingled with his hair, but he couldn't see it there since his hair was the same color as the blood. Razvin came up alongside him and looked out over the now-cluttered battlefield. Smoke rose from a few buildings that the Vyrkarians had set ablaze. Roan sighed and his body shook. The adrenaline pumped through him and now allowed him to take in what had happened. It was his first fray, and he'd made it out alive. A wild smile spread across his pale lips, and he couldn't stop the hysteria that pushed a laugh between them.

"Roan!"

He turned to his right and spotted Trylian shoving through the people toward him. He wore his jousting armor still, but was also covered in blood and sweat. Trylian reached him and pulled him into an embrace.

"Thank the Winds you're safe," he said. "I saw you. That was amazing. The way you took charge. The way you ran into battle."

Despite the shaking and the leftover fear, something in Roan glowed at the praise. Trylian rarely praised him. He smiled weakly. "I had to. Someone had to defend the people."

"You did." Trylian beamed at him. "A valiant feat like that will surely get you into second or even first column in no time." He clasped Roan's shoulders. "We need to get you a Claret."

The praise filled Roan, and suddenly he didn't mind that he'd been attacked twice during the festival. It had been worth it.

CHAPTER IV

Trylian stood with his back to his study, looking out the window into the dark night. The moon was out in the clear spring sky and lit up the entire ward below. The caer was silent as the men were asleep and it was late. The fire crackled behind him, softly filling the study with its warmth, orange light, and white smoke. He clasped his hands behind his back and watched Elendir in the warped reflection of the mirror. Elendir's face looked tired and dark circles surrounded his otherwise keen silver eyes. He stood waiting on Trylian's orders.

"You need rest," Trylian said softly, not turning to face his Claret.

"I will rest once our plans are fortified," Elendir said. Even his voice sounded tired, worn. "I've not heard from the Sanctuary yet, though I have been vigilant."

"Our contact is still loyal, I hope," Trylian said. He didn't trust anyone in the capital of Delsinor, let alone a Claret in the Sanctuary. But it was a fortunate alliance they had made by chance, and he was depending on it now.

"As far as I know," Elendir said. "I swear, I am trying—"

"Stop." Trylian turned now. "I know you are. I understand. Don't think I don't care about you."

"I know you do. I just want to do well."

Trylian dropped his hands and went to a small table where

a carafe of wine waited. Elendir wasn't like other Modeus Clarets. He'd been kidnapped from an Elsarius Sactrium by the Modeus and forced to bind to Trylian. It had been nearly two decades. Elendir tried his best every day to prove his loyalty. It hadn't been that way at the start. But after years of forced servitude, Trylian trusted Elendir. He just didn't want the Claret to know that. He needed him trying every day to prove himself. Keeping correspondence with their connection in the Sanctuary in Delsinor was one of the ways he showed loyalty.

He poured some wine and offered a golden goblet to Elendir. The Claret shook his head. Trylian took a sip instead. "Where are they?" he asked after a moment. "We said to meet—"

The door opened. Baelian, the Archon Knight of second column and a half-Vyrkarian with long, tangled blond hair and wild green eyes, appeared in the doorway. He was a large man and filled the frame, his brown horns almost touching the top. Unlike other Vyrkarians, he had pale, white flesh and no tail. He nodded to Trylian and entered, followed by the two other Archon Knights: Thaniel of the third column and Mathis of fourth column.

Trylian propped his hand up onto his hip and looked expectantly at Baelian. "What news from Vyrkaris?"

"The raid wasn't from Drachen," Baelian said. He took a seat in one of the red velvet chairs around the table in the center of the study. "Wyvern Shallows acted alone. And even then, the reports say it was a rogue group. Pirates, maybe."

"Drachen is primarily filled with humans," Thaniel said in his deep voice, sitting across from Baelian. "We don't think they attacked Adorian, do we?"

"Winds know what the king will think once he hears," Trylian offered, pouring the other men some wine. "All he needs to know is that Aatheria fought them off and saved the village."

"Drachen is trying to make peace treaties with Wyvern Shallows," Baelian went on. "The king that sits in Drachen's halls is half-Vyrkarian and we think the talks will go well. But the Shallows have a track record of being a harbor for such pirates. We don't know how much control the Thane will have over them."

Trylian scoffed, handing out the wine. "Peace treaties never work. They are to ensure the subjugation of one over the other. Why do you think the Atheling of Aatheria hasn't signed one with Delsinor?"

Thaniel said, "Because they are never in our favor. Aatheria is Modeus and always will be. The king wants to change that."

Trylian nodded, taking a small sip. "The king in Drachen should simply slaughter the pirates and force Wyvern Shallows to comply. If he wanted our support, that's what he'd do."

"Vyrkaris is a wild land," Baelian reminded Trylian.

"But one that could make or break our conquest," he interrupted. The other two Archon Knights nodded in agreement. "We need support if we are to move."

Baelian looked around the room, then back at Trylian. "So you are still wanting to attack Moralan?"

Trylian clenched his fist tight around his goblet and looked into the fire. He felt Elendir move behind him silently. "My defeat at Emberforge ten years ago has burned in me all these years. We were taken by surprise because of a traitor in our midst, someone who should have laid his life down for the Modeus. Someone who would have sooner seen me dead!"

Elendir's hand slipped over his shoulder, lightly touching him, soothing his heightening rage. He leaned into his Claret's hand and reminded himself to watch his emotions among his fellow Archon Knights.

"The Elsarius are weak fools," he went on. "Ones who should be wiped out to make way for strength and true rule. Their ways make us weak, simpering dogs. Harmony and balance." He spat. "They think their way of focusing magic for healing, growth, and defense only will save them? No. The magic is to be wielded by the strong. It is made to subjugate those without it. We are made to conquer. We are blessed. We are ordained by the Winds to rule." He stopped, realizing he was getting off track. He cleared his throat and ran his hand through his hair.

"If you are worried about the Elsarius," Elendir said gently, "look no further than Delsinor. The Sanctuary there is Elsarius and they sing their praises every day."

"Yes," Trylian mused darkly, tapping his finger on the goblet. Delsinor was closer than Emberforge and was the seat of the king of Adorian. Perhaps Elendir had a point. Maybe he should focus on his home of Adorian and the cities within instead of Moralan. But in truth, the entire west of Kelroth needed to be conquered, to bend their knees not just to the Modeus, but to him. After all, he had been given the blessing of magic. No. He had taken it. He wanted to take more. To rise up. He smiled at the thought. Overthrow the king? Take his place as ruler of the west? "A good thought, Elendir," he said. "Surely that will right all the wrongs of my past."

"We must move with care," Thaniel said. "We cannot be rash. We've waited these ten years in silence and submission, but we should not burn down all we've created in those years."

"I am not a rash man, Thaniel," Trylian said simply. "I am an ambitious one. But I also believe in strength above all. Do the Modeus not teach us to always strive for more? These years of quiet servitude have not been to their glory."

The door banged open then, admitting two identical giggling boys of fifteen. Trylian glared at the intrusion as his twin sons, Gareth and Tanis, entered. Their chiseled cheeks were ruddy and their eyes sparkled with drink. Gareth held Tanis up, supporting him. Tanis was panting and clutching his chest.

"You better have a good reason for coming in like this," Trylian growled to his sons.

Gareth dumped Tanis in a chair and leaned heavily on it. "We were drinking when a letter came from a rider who wouldn't say where he was from." He reached into his breast pocket and pulled out a crumpled piece of parchment with a wax seal on it. "From the Atheling of Amril." He held it out to Trylian who took it. "The letter says a convoy escorting the daughter of a Thane from Delsinor is headed to Duskhallow in Moralan. The daughter is to wed the son of a Thane from Duskhallow."

"Why?" Trylian asked, opening the letter to read it.

"Duskhallow and Delsinor are at peace," Elendir said, frowning slightly. "Why would they need marriage ties?"

Baelian sat up. "Unless they are on the move. Trying to strengthen ties with other Elsarius. Especially one from Delsinor, the seat of the king."

Thaniel and Mathis glanced at one another, brows pinching in worry.

"Does this mean war?" Mathis asked.

Trylian turned and ripped a map of the western realms of Kelroth down off the wall and spread it out on the table before them. The others stood up to see better, hunching over the map as well. Trylian pointed to Sorath, Amril, and Aatheria in turn.

"We are the only Modeus in Adorian," he began.

"What cities in Moralan fly the Modeus banner?" Elendir asked.

"Riverhaven and Lostvale," Trylian answered, pointing them out quickly.

"I agree with Baelian," Elendir said. "Marriage ties are

strong and will guarantee armies and loyalty. That could mean war. Adorian could be moving to eradicate the Modeus once and for all. This is a sign of their plans to come."

Trylian roared and pounded the table with his fist. Joy filled him. This was the excuse he needed. It was time for the Modeus to rise again.

"We will need Clarets to bind to our new Knights," Elendir said. "I will reach out to my contact at the Sanctuary in Delsinor."

"They are ready to move up," Mathis said. "Even some in fourth column are ready to fight and take on the burden of magic."

Thaniel sighed and his eyes went to Delsinor on the map. "We will have to take Elsarius Clarets. There are not enough Modeus-blessed Clarets to suit all the Knights we will need."

"We've done it before," Trylian said, aware of Elendir behind him. "It's never an issue." He turned to his Claret. "You can get us Clarets from Delsinor?"

Elendir nodded, though Trylian noted the look of sadness hidden deep behind his silver eyes. "There are plenty of Clarets who have just come of age we can take. I will arrange it."

"And the convoy with the Thane's daughter?" Thaniel asked. "We will attack and stop it?"

"Of course," Trylian said with a wicked grin. "If we kill them all, it will be some time before Delsinor and Duskhallow know what happened."

"They'll know it was Modeus," Thaniel warned.

"Not necessarily," Trylian assured him. "Could have been bandits. Highwaymen. Nomads. Who knows how people go missing on the road?"

"They will ask eventually," Mathis warned. "They may come for us directly. The king's men will find us."

"And we will be on the move by then," Trylian replied.

Elendir shifted behind Trylian. "And the Scion? One for the Elsarius rose up years ago, but the Modeus have not blessed us with one. We are at a disadvantage should the Scion of the Elsarius fight against us."

At this, Trylian leaned back in his chair, rubbing his chin in thought. "That brat bested me once before. It won't happen again. There must be a way..."

"To what?" Thaniel asked.

Trylian smiled and leaned forward onto his elbows. "The Scion is always prophesied. But one for us has not been. What if there were a way to make one? To earn the blessing of the Modeus?"

"I've heard of such things," Baelian said. "There are stories of a mountain in Vyrkaris that holds some secret of the Modeus Scion. They are cryptic and never make sense, though."

The Archon Knights looked at one another. Trylian felt their question: which of them would be worthy of becoming Scion?

"None of us," he said, cutting into their thoughts.

"Then who?" Mathis asked. "Who would be willing to bear such a burden?"

Trylian smiled. "He won't have a choice. I will make him."

The others glanced at one another.

"You have someone in mind?" Baelian asked.

Trylian nodded. "I do. And he won't be able to refuse."

CHAPTER V

Phael stood in the crowd inside the Sanctuary. The spring sunlight burst through the open windows lining the nave. The smell of incense, the wind, and flowers filled the space. Pillars lined the side aisles where depictions of famous Clarets and Knights covered the walls in tapestries. Before him, inside the chancel, the Empyrean Core glimmered. The core was a massive crystal that stood easily fifteen feet tall. It hovered inside an ornate base made of white marble. Inscriptions Phael couldn't read and runes and symbols covered the stone base, glowing even in the daylight. The Elsarius believed the Core was the source of all the magic the Winds granted them. A light thrumming and humming came from the Core at all times. It calmed Phael and made him feel safe. He loved the Sanctuary and its stone walls, its bells and songs, the peace and tranquility.

Before them, a mass of high-ranking Clarets stood surrounding one called Olenar. The Arch Claret was speaking, asking Olenar if he would be willing to take on the oaths and duties of an Emissary.

"Will you accept this promotion?" the Arch Claret said in a somber voice. He was old, but hardly looked it. The magic kept Clarets young, despite making them fragile and weak. "Will you commune with your brothers and the other Anakrites and do what is right for this Sanctuary?"

Olenar, a tall Claret with muddy brown hair and golden eyes, raised his head and his left hand. The white robes of the Clarets had long open sleeves and draped nearly to the floor. "I swear so to do," he said.

"And do you swear to uphold the teachings of the Elsarius and acknowledge that the Winds are of two natures? That the Elsarius are the way of light and peace and love? Will you bind yourself to their ways, shunning the darker messenger of the Modeus?"

"I swear so to do."

Phael sighed as he watched the ceremony play out. He had hoped to be an Emissary someday. Emissaries often traveled back and forth between the Sanctuary and Sactriums, bringing news and orders from the Arch Claret. Anakrites ran the Sactriums in groups of six or so. But he doubted he'd ever be promoted to Anakrite. Now, with his magic awakened within him, all those plans burned up. His future as a Claret bound to a Knight was written in stone. Phael idly wondered where Olenar would be sent. He didn't know the man well, and wouldn't miss him.

He glanced sideways at Lailen. He'd miss his mentor if he ever were promoted to Emissary or Anakrite. "Do you wish for such a promotion?" he whispered to Lailen as they watched the Arch Claret anoint Olenar with scented oil.

Lailen hissed at Phael to be silent before he whispered, "It would be an honor to be an Emissary. To be the message bearer between us and the divine ones in the Sactriums. But I would miss you boys."

"You'll miss me soon enough," Phael moaned. "Do I have to bind to a Knight?"

Lailen nodded. "The magic has taken the color from your hair. That means it's strong. You will perish otherwise. You know this."

"Can I not give it up?"

Lailen looked down at Phael and smiled sadly. He shook his head. "The Elsarius have chosen you. That is a great honor. You should be grateful you don't have to worry about the politics of the Sanctuary like I do. I must work and scrape for recognition to be promoted to Emissary. You will be a Knight Claret."

Phael supposed Lailen was right. He imagined the Knight he might be bound to. He hoped he'd be kind and caring. And he prayed there would be no wars. "I'd like our times to be ones of peace," he whispered. "I'd hate to go to war."

Lailen smiled. "You are a gentle one, Phael. I pray that for you as well."

"I did feel the pain again this morning," Phael confessed as the others bowed their heads in prayer as the Arch Claret called upon the Winds to bless the new Emissary. "I hope to be bound soon."

Lailen nodded. "In a few weeks' time, the Knights from Caer Delsinor will come, and perhaps many more from other cities."

Phael frowned, confused.

"The caer is the fort inside the city limits," Lailen said. "They will have the pick of all the Clarets who are ready to be chosen. You among them."

"Do you know any of the Knights?" Phael asked. "Are there any my age?"

"Some. But they are all eager for battle. I think you'd do better with an older Knight. One who is in need of a new Claret."

Phael's heart fell at this. "I don't want to be a replacement. I couldn't bear that. I want to be someone's first." He blushed and hung his head.

Lailen eyed the youth before him. "You cannot have everything you want, my boy. But know that whoever chooses you will love you for who you are. Even if it takes them time to get to know you."

Phael nodded. He didn't look up, inspecting his white boots against the stone floor instead. "I am worried, Lailen."

Around them, the other Clarets applauded and began to file out. Some moved to the chancel to congratulate Olenar on his promotion.

"About what?" Lailen asked.

Phael blushed even deeper.

"You can tell me anything, Phael." Lailen put his hand gently on Phael's shoulder and steered him back toward the narthex, away from the Core and the crowd around it.

Phael chewed on his words, thinking over what he might say. He wanted to confess to Lailen about thoughts and feelings he'd been having. But they were private emotions. Things he didn't understand. Things that gave him impure thoughts.

Lailen kept his hand on Phael's shoulder and guided him out into the gardens surrounding the outer walls of the Sanctuary. He moved until there were no human voices left, just the trickling of a small gray brook and the song of birds.

"There, we are alone," Lailen said. "Now tell me, what is on your mind? Is it the magic?"

Phael shook his head, embarrassed. "I know we are to remain pure," he said, struggling to find the words and the courage to speak to them.

Lailen stopped walking then and faced Phael. They stood under a tree with silvery bark and dark green leaves. He gently touched Phael's chin and raised his head. Phael knew he looked pathetic, pouting and simpering in worry.

"Are you having feelings for someone, my boy?" Lailen asked gently. "Those emotions are normal. But we must fight against them. Remain chaste. I can help you."

Phael sighed in relief. He was hoping Lailen would guess

the issue and that he wouldn't have to say it. But it was more than that. "I... I have feelings for another..." He gulped. He couldn't say it. Couldn't Lailen guess this one, too? The embarrassment was too much, and he cringed away from Lailen's touch, tears filling his eyes.

"Is it a boy?" Lailen asked.

Bile rose in Phael's throat, and he choked on it. His eyes went wide, and the tears fell. He held his breath and nodded sheepishly.

"It's Nox, isn't it?" Lailen asked.

Phael was shocked to see the tiniest smile ease the tension on Lailen's lips. "How did you know?"

"My boy, you are not subtle." Lailen laughed gently. "We all have seen you pining over him. Your eyes betray you. You are led by your heart, Phael, and it is loud. And it is good."

Relieved, Phael leaned into Lailen and wrapped his arms around his middle, embracing him. "I thought you'd be angry," he said, swallowing a sob. "I was so scared to tell anyone. But it was killing me."

Lailen returned the embrace, gently petting Phael's long white hair. "You cannot let your guard down, though. You know this. The Elsarius demand purity. Even in your thoughts. I am sorry, Phael."

He nodded, closing his eyes and letting another round of tears fall. He pressed his face into Lailen's chest, soaking up the comfort. "I'm sorry. I won't let my lust overcome me, I swear. I just needed someone to know."

"And I will help you," Lailen said. He pushed Phael back to look him in his eyes. Gently, he rubbed his thumb over Phael's cheek, wiping away a tear. "You cannot bear such a burden alone. But you cannot act on your feelings. Do you understand?"

Phael nodded. "Thank you, Lailen."

The older Claret smiled gently. "It is a wonderful thing to

be young and in love. More's the pity we must avoid such feelings. But you were born a Claret and must abide by the laws of the Elsarius."

"If I don't?" Phael asked. He imagined Nox again, this time shirtless and dripping in water from a rainstorm. He gasped and shook his head.

"There are punishments for a Claret who does not maintain his purity," Lailen said somberly. "I don't want any of them to happen to you. You are too gentle."

"I understand." Phael took a deep breath and sighed out the last of his sorrow. "What happens if I cannot control my thoughts?"

"You can," Lailen said sternly. "It just takes practice. If an impure thought comes to you, banish it immediately and pray to not be led astray." He looked around before he asked, "Does Nox know?"

Phael shook his head. "I was too afraid to speak to him. What if he doesn't...like boys?"

Lailen shrugged. "It doesn't matter, because you won't say anything to him. Do you understand?"

"Of course." Phael hung his head. His heart hurt. Seeing Nox and speaking to him had been the best parts of his day and now he had to quash those feelings. That longing. How could he do it? How could he bury the desire he had to be noticed by Nox? To have him turn his stormy black eyes to him? He wanted Nox's long fingers to run through his hair, to feel them on his bare skin.

Phael gasped. Lailen was right; this wouldn't be easy.

"Now," the older Claret said, gently squeezing Phael's arm. "Go to the hawk tower and check for letters. Gather them and distribute them as needed, understood? We have chores that need done and no more time to simper."

Phael nodded, hurt a little at the abrupt change in tone. He parted from Lailen and walked through the ward and around the gardens to the hawk tower at the back of the land. Climbing the stairs always made him dizzy. He was never sure if it was the tight circles that did it, or the sight of the ground below so far away that made his head spin. When he reached the top, he looked out over the ward and the Sanctuary's land.

The sun gilded the roofs below and splashed over the walls of the keep and the small building where he and the orphans slept. Beyond that was a garden and orchard where the bee boxes waited for his next heist. Around the back of the inner sanctum was a massive graveyard. He loved all the stone statues and marble headstones. It was often quiet in the graveyard, and he could be alone with his thoughts. Hardly anyone ever went into it.

Except Nox.

Before the magic had awakened in Nox, he had had beautiful, long black hair. He stood taller than Phael, but most men did. He had lithe arms and a slim waist that Phael often imagined embracing with his own arms. Nox was soft, yet outgoing. He often advocated for the younger wards and defended those too shy to do it themselves. Phael's eyes roamed over the graveyard and spotted Nox behind a mausoleum. He was a year older than Phael and his dark black eyes showed his wisdom.

Phael leaned on the open window and rested his chin in his palm as he watched Nox below. He wore the white of the Clarets, the gentle robes hanging beautifully from his hips. Phael sighed and thought back to Lailen's words. The Elsarius demanded purity of body and mind. He had to watch his thoughts and rein them in. Besides, what use was it pining over a boy?

"Duty and valor," Phael mumbled, pushing himself away from the window and the beautiful Nox below.

Just as he turned, a hawk screamed into the aviary, its talons flashing as it reached for a perch. The bird landed in a storm of feathers and shook, dislodging even more. It squawked and bobbed its head. Phael looked up and saw a small scroll attached to its leg. Gingerly, he reached up and untied the ribbon that held the scroll. The bird watched him, but did not bite.

Phael checked the name on the scroll. Olenar. The Claret who had just been promoted to Emissary.

Quickly looking at the other hawks, he saw none of them bore a message. Most of them slept, their heads tucked under their wings.

He pocketed the scroll and ran down the stairs of the aviary to the library where Olenar would no doubt be entering his name into the logs of the Sanctuary. Jogging across the ward and through the cloisters to the chapter house, he took the hallway there and ran to the library. Stopping a moment outside to catch his breath, he inhaled deeply. Then he pushed the door open and walked in as quietly as he could. The old librarian who sat near the entrance glared at him over a pair of spectacles made from refined crystals. Phael smiled at him, holding up the scroll.

"Olenar?" he whispered.

The librarian's scowl deepened at the single word. He raised one gnarled, shaking hand and pointed to the back where the logs were kept. Phael nodded thanks and skittered back behind several shelves of books and scrolls. The library smelled of dust, beeswax, and ink. Phael would have liked the silent library if the librarian didn't have some secret vendetta against him and every other young ward of the Sanctuary. He guessed it was because the librarian was not a Claret, not blessed with the magic of the Winds.

Olenar stood before a great, ornate cabinet. A small desk on hinges was pulled down and a great book lay across it. The book had wooden covers and a large lock hung off some metal latches on the right-hand side. The keys lay next to it. Olenar and a few witnesses stood over the book, signing their names. Phael waited patiently for them to be done before he politely cleared his throat.

"A missive for you, sir," he whispered as softly as he could. He held out the scroll.

Olenar thanked the witnesses and waved them away. They congratulated him once more and left the library as silent as ghosts. Olenar opened the missive and read it quickly, then he froze, his eyes unfocusing. He motioned for Phael to follow him and left out a back door into a small garden enclosed in stone walls.

"Thank you, dear boy," Olenar said with a genuine smile. "I thought it best to wait until we were out of earshot to speak."

Phael looked up. "To speak?"

"Yes." Olenar smiled and slight wrinkles appeared on either side of his mouth. His long brown hair swept down to his middle as he steered them around the small garden path. "It was you who talked all through the ceremony, wasn't it?"

"Oh, I—" Phael stammered. "I... I'm sorry, sir." Defeated, he made himself look Olenar in the eye.

"Never mind that," the older Claret said with a wave of his hand. "I wanted to speak to you."

"Why?"

"You are how old?"

"Seventeen, sir."

Olenar nodded. "And you have come into your magic?"

"I have. It hurts every morning. I had a fever last night. I don't like it."

"So you are a Knight Claret."

"Lailen says someday soon." He tried to match Olenar's long stride, but his shorter legs couldn't manage it. "I don't anticipate it with glee."

"Are you close to Lailen?" The Claret unrolled the missive again and quickly scanned it, waiting for Phael's reply.

"I think so," Phael answered.

"And has Lailen spoken about promotion for himself? To become the next Emissary?"

Confused, Phael nodded. "I think he'd make a great Emissary. He's wise, patient, and understands others before they speak."

Olenar smiled. "Lailen must think very highly of you to show his true self to such a degree."

Phael shrugged. "He's kind to me. He was the one who found me when my parents joined the Winds."

"He must know you well. What does he think of your powers?"

"Thinks I'm strong." Phael blushed at the praise he'd given himself and ducked his head down in shame. "I don't know."

Olenar stopped walking then and froze. His face turned distant again for a moment before he smiled. "Phael, my dear boy, it sounds like you have a bright future here. One where you never leave your friendship with Lailen, no doubt. He would make a great Emissary, as you said. I think the Anakrite and the Arch Claret would love to hear your testimony of him someday."

Phael almost beamed, shyly smiling. "I'd do anything for Lailen."

"I see that." Olenar rolled the scroll in his hands, tightening the bind on it. "Phael, I have to go out to a village far away and pray over the crops soon. I think I'd like you and some others to join me."

"Me?" Phael asked. "What good will I be?"

"Prayer from someone so close to the Winds and their magic will help," Olenar reasoned. "Besides, it might be the last time you see us out giving blessings. You will belong to a

Knight soon and leave us. I'd like for you to see a blessing before you go."

Phael nodded. "Of course, sir. Whatever you think is best."

Olenar reached a hand out to Phael and squeezed his shoulder. "Good boy. I look forward to it. I will let you know when the time comes."

CHAPTER VI

Roan hacked mercilessly against his opponent. His bare chest glistened with sweat and his arms knotted with muscle as he drove his opponent back farther into the training ground. The dust beneath their feet kicked up and created clouds around them. His quick footwork made his opponent wilt under the constant pressure. He took the chance to spin, his long red hair fanning out around him, and brought his wooden sword down hard onto the boy's shoulder.

"Winds, Roan," the boy moaned, dropping his blade. "I'm on your side. I'm not your enemy."

"We're all Roan's enemies," Razvin called from his perch on the stone wall surrounding the training ground. "He knows no friend. Trust me."

Roan ignored Razvin's jibe and focused on his opponent instead. He didn't remember the boy's name, but knew he was in fourth column with him. Razvin was right, though. He didn't like making friends. It made beating every opponent so much easier if he didn't recall their names. He slipped his booted toes under the fallen wooden sword and kicked it back up to his opponent. The boy caught it but looked apprehensive.

"Try again," Roan said through gathering his breath.

"I don't want to," the boy replied. "I have to run a mile still and I'm tired. You win."

"I don't want to win," Roan said. "I want to practice."

"Why?" the boy whined back, getting into a ready stance. "Not like we're going anywhere or fighting any wars."

Roan lunged at him. The boy parried the blow, and Roan followed the tip of his sword to the boy's left. "Trylian says we must always be ready."

"I am," the boy replied, annoyed. "I'm tired of drills, marching, training, the beatings. And scouting is even worse."

Roan stopped and looked the boy in the eyes. "You've been sent scouting?" Jealousy boiled up inside him. "I've never been scouting."

The boy shrugged. "It's not special or any fun. Even when I do spot something."

"Like what?" Roan pressed. "What have you seen?"

The boy screwed up his face, trying to decide to speak or not. When Roan raised his wooden blade up, he gave in. "I saw supplies coming in the last few days. Dried meat, hard bread—things they take when they travel far for days."

Roan squinted into the sun, looking up at Razvin. His friend's draconic tail twitched in thought. "Are they preparing for something?"

The boy shrugged. "What's it matter? They'll get first or second column to do their work. We'll be left here. Nothing to do. As always."

Roan felt that in his soul. Fourth column did the dirty work. While first and second got to enjoy the power of using magic, of going out on missions when they appeared—everything—they were trapped doing the chores of the caer. It was often demeaning, and the first and second column Knights bullied them mercilessly. Roan didn't understand why he wasn't first column yet.

"Don't think about it," the boy said evenly, getting back into a fighting stance. He swung at Roan and they re-entered combat. "Just do as they say and keep your head down."

Roan ducked a swing and brought his sword up, hitting the boy hard on his chin, decapitating him in theory.

"I'm done," the boy groaned. He threw his sword onto the dusty ground and turned, marching away. Roan watched him go, a little annoyed.

"Hey!"

He turned to see Atreus, Razvin's Claret, come skipping down the path. His white robes billowed around him and his long white hair whipped like a flag. "Are you two done yet?" he asked, a small smile on his face.

"We are," Razvin called back. He leapt down off the wall and handed Roan his shirt. "And we need a drink."

"Again?" Atreus asked, smiling at his Knight.

"Always," Razvin smiled. He embraced Atreus quickly and turned to leave the training yard. "Come, Roan. A drink is needed after a hard workout."

"I have drills still," Roan said, motioning to the door that led back to the barracks.

"Another time," Razvin said. "Let's go to the Willow Maid and stir up some trouble. Maybe flirt with a woman. You do know what those are, don't you, Roan?"

"Eliana," Atreus said in a singsong tone, grinning at Roan.

Roan shoved the Claret playfully, but smiled in return. "I've written her a letter, you know. So, yes, I do know what a woman is."

"But you haven't sent it," Razvin cajoled. His face fell and he looked thoughtful for the first time in almost two days. "Why haven't you?"

Roan focused on the path ahead as they pushed through the gates and out onto the road. He didn't want to look Razvin in the eye. "It's not the time. I only saw her that once. Weeks ago."

"And to see her again, you must make a move." His friend groaned dramatically, face to the sky. "Roan, you are ruthless, strong, powerful. Why are you wilting like a flower when it comes to this woman?"

The desire to punch Razvin rose up strong in Roan, but he stifled it. "I take my time. Unlike you. What happened to Violet?"

"Violet was two girls ago," Atreus offered helpfully, a little hop in his step.

"I'm more a flavor of the week kind of lover," Razvin said, narrowing his eyes and pretending to think. "There's enough of me to go around."

Roan shook his head and scoffed through his nose. "That's how you end up with spotted prick like Cayton."

Atreus laughed out loud, but Razvin blanched.

"How do you know he has spotted prick, Roan?" he asked, arching a brow and smiling saucily. "Been around his prick, have you?"

Roan wouldn't let anyone but Razvin get away with such a joke. He seethed underneath, but let the jibe go. Ahead of them, the city streets spidered out over the hills and dips of the land. Aatheria was a beautiful city, Roan thought, with its stone structures, the Sactrium in the center with its colored flags, and the great castle where the Atheling lived with his family. The streets were mostly paved with gray stone until one got to the outer rims. Shops lined the walls and alleys. Farmers came and went out the great gate that faced the southern border.

They turned down a road and headed straight for the tavern at the end. Since the sun was setting, a set of bards stood outside the doors singing and playing their instruments to gather a crowd. Inside, the great hearth glowed warm and the smell of honey and flowers permeated the air over the scent of smoke and bodies. The tavern keeper, a big round man they called Goat, was pouring drinks when the boys entered. He waved at them and motioned for them to take a seat near an open window. Goat was an older man with a black mustache shot through with white and no beard. He wore an apron around his middle that had more holes than fabric, and a smile always plastered over his ruddy face.

"What will it be, boys?" he asked, coming to serve them himself. "Haven't seen you in some weeks."

"We've been kept busy," Roan groaned, throwing his feet up onto the table and leaning back in the chair. "Trylian is running us ragged. Like we're about to go to war."

Goat stroked his thick mustache. "Any day now, I hear."

"Who did you hear that from?" Razvin challenged.

"Around," Goat said with a shrug. "He's had supplies sent to the caer recently. Looks like he's going to move. But what do I know? I'm an old man with a brain pickled in brine."

Roan smiled at the older man before ordering their drinks. He turned to face Atreus and Razvin, leaning over the table. He was about to ask them what else they knew when the front door banged open again. In the frame stood Alamar and four of his fellow first column Knights. Alamar's eyes swept the place before landing hard on Roan.

"Red Mane!" he called, a glower darkening his brow. "Outside. Now."

"No fighting in here," Goat called from behind the wooden bar. "Roan," he added pointedly.

"I wouldn't dream of it, Goat," he shouted back.

"Roan, don't," Razvin warned, taking his wrist in his hand. "Don't fight him."

"I can win," Roan said easily. "Watch me. I've beaten him before."

"But five?" Atreus asked, his pretty face pinching in worry.

"You and me, Alamar," Roan said as he sauntered over the creaking wooden floorboards to the door.

"Of course, Red," Alamar said with a sneer. He walked out into the front yard of the tavern where a few hitching posts and a trough full of murky water waited. He held up his hands to defend his face. "For the humiliation you made me suffer at the festival," he said.

"Still sore over that beating?" Roan jeered. He raised his fists too.

No sooner had he done this than the other four charged at him. One grabbed a handful of his long red hair and pulled, knocking him off balance. Two more grabbed his arms and pulled them behind his back. Roan snarled and ripped at his captors, momentarily releasing one of his arms. He got in a solid punch before a third came in and wrapped his arms around him, pinning them in place. Alamar ran up, fist cocked, and punched Roan hard in the center of his face.

White light blasted into Roan's eyes at the impact and blood trickled down from his nose and lip. He kicked out, but the three boys held him hard.

"Coward!" Roan snarled, the blood staining his teeth.

"Gullible fool," Alamar chortled. "Throw him in the water."

The three men wrestled Roan over to the trough and lifted him. He was tall, and they struggled to get him off the ground, but eventually they did. With a grunt, they tossed him into the murky hot water. He landed on the edge, bruising his side hard before he was submerged in the dark muck. He slipped as he fought to push himself up, but finally broke the surface and looked around. His hair plastered onto his face, blinding him. Alamar and his cohorts laughed uproariously as they pointed at him. Roan coughed, having inhaled some of the disgusting water, and rolled out of the trough.

Razvin and Atreus came running out, shouting at Alamar and his goons. Razvin pulled his hand back, a ball of flame appearing in his palm.

"Stand down!" Trylian's voice rang out hard.

Roan pushed himself up, seething. They hadn't fought

fairly. Of course they needed five to take him down. Alamar was strong, but not as strong or as cunning as he. Alamar had to cheat to get his revenge. Roan stood, savagely wiping his hair out of his face. Gnashing his teeth, he glared at Alamar.

One of the other boys seized Atreus and shoved him to the ground. The Claret cowered away from the attack, crawling quickly to Razvin.

"I said, stand down!" Trylian barked, his blue eyes spitting sparks at the Knight. He looked at each one in turn, daring them to move again.

Roan recognized Baelian, his Claret, and Elendir behind Trylian. They all looked somber and serious. Razvin reached down and hauled Atreus up quickly.

"Listen to me," Trylian said, his tone still snapping. "I need you all to go back to the caer and prepare to leave. Roan, Razvin, and Alamar. Get your Clarets and be ready to leave in two days' time. Do you understand?"

"What?" Alamar choked. "You want that fourth column mouse to come with us?"

Trylian's eyes flashed like the edge of a sword again. "Do as I say and respond, 'yes, sir.' Understood?"

A moment of defiant silence followed before Alamar mumbled, "Yes, sir," and turned to leave. He took the back path out, walking past Roan. He hit him hard with his shoulder and mumbled, "Of course Trylian's pet is coming along."

Roan let the insult roll off him. "Me?" he asked when Alamar and the other boys had gone.

"You heard me," Trylian said, his tone a little more gentle now. "Prepare to leave. We will be gone for some time, so get your affairs in order. Tell your mother," he added, looking Roan in the eyes. He nodded to the boys, turned, and left back down the street.

Razvin gripped Roan's shoulders. "A mission! You're going on a mission! And with us!"

Atreus smiled demurely.

"I can't say why," Roan mused, pulling his wet hair back.

"It's overdue," Razvin said on his behalf. "You heard Trylian when you fought off the Vyrkarians over the festival. It's your time to shine, Roan, my friend! This is it." He beamed, his white teeth showing bright against his gray skin.

"You could be getting a Claret soon," Atreus said. He smiled at Razvin. "It's a great bond. One worthy of a warrior such as yourself."

Roan knew he was more than ready to be promoted to second or even first column. He didn't know why Trylian had held him back as long as he had. He was seventeen; he was ready to fight. He wanted the magic. The power.

"I'll see you back at the caer," Roan said. He waved to his best friend and ran to a city stable to rent a horse instead of going back to fetch his own from the caer. Then he rode out into the farmland and down a dusty path in the moonlight. It took him some time to get to his family's estate, but he didn't care. Excitement filled him.

He burst through the gate and galloped up to the great front doors of his father's castle and shoved them open. He called for his mother, knowing it was late. A servant pointed him to the study on the upper floors. There, he found his mother drinking wine and flipping through an old tome. She smiled when he burst in and stood up to hug him.

"Roan!" she sighed, hugging him tight. She smelled of roses and wine. "It's been weeks since I've seen you."

"And it will be weeks more," he beamed. "Trylian has summoned me to go on a mission with him."

Mother pulled away and looked him in the eyes. A bit of sadness welled up there. "But I haven't seen you in so long."

She pressed her cheek against his chest, letting him rest his against the top of her head. "I miss you."

"I'll be back," he said. "And perhaps then I will be promoted. I'll have a Claret."

"Will you?" she gasped, pulling away to look up into his face. "Oh, Roan, I knew you were worthy. I knew he'd not leave you in fourth column." She stood on her toes and kissed his cheek. "What's the mission?"

"I don't know. But I will find out soon. We're to leave in two days' time." He couldn't stop the excitement that shot up in him like a geyser. "I will make Father proud."

Mother nodded, tears shining in her eyes now. "I know you will. You already have. Be careful. Do as Trylian says."

He nodded. "I will."

∽∾

TWO DAYS LATER, Roan marched down to the stable yard inside the caer's walls. There he spotted Atreus with Razvin, Gareth and Tanis—Trylian's twin sons—and Alamar with his Claret Veryl. They were all tossing their packs onto their horses and speaking in whispers. Alamar glowered at Roan, but held his tongue with Gareth and Tanis there.

"So," Razvin was saying as he helped Atreus tie down his pack, "what's the mission and why is it so secret?"

Tanis, the younger of the two twins, smiled up at his brother. Gareth was built like Roan: tall, broad, muscled, and he stood taller than Tanis, who was slimmer.

"We're going to stop a convoy," Gareth said in his deep voice. He was two years younger than Roan, but stood just as tall, and both were in third column. Neither had Clarets yet. "It's on its way from Delsinor to Duskhallow. That's all I know."

"A convoy of what?" Roan asked, knowing Gareth would know, being Trylian's son.

"We don't know," Tanis said with a wicked grin. "But we're going to slaughter whatever it is."

"You don't know that." Gareth rolled his eyes at his younger twin.

Roan didn't care. He was just excited to be on the mission. He went to his horse and saddled her up, tossing his pack on her back and fastening it down.

"This could be it for you," Razvin said to him from the next stall over. "You could get your Claret after this mission."

"Prove yourself and you all will," Trylian said, marching into the yard laden with his own pack. He carried his belt and sword in his other hand and locked his eyes on Roan. "This is your time to prove yourself to me. Don't fuck it up, boy."

Roan smiled.

CHAPTER VII

The troop was small: Trylian and his Claret Elendir led the way. Alamar and Razvin came up behind him with their respective Clarets. Alamar's Claret, Veryl, was a quiet boy with large, lake-green eyes. Tanis and Gareth brought up the rear behind Roan. They had been softly bickering for the last mile and Roan had drowned them out. A small convoy of others, including some soldiers from the city, came with them. Also a cook, a healer, and a farrier, should they need him. These three came up behind them on a large wagon that hauled their supplies.

They had been traveling for days now and had seen no action. They'd come upon a set of rogue bandits trying to ambush them in the mountain pass, but they had quickly dispatched them and moved on. The nights were quiet, with Razvin urging Roan to play his lute while he drank. Atreus sang softly along with Roan as he had the best voice of all of them.

The sun began its slow crawl down the horizon on the eighth day when they reached the forest on the other side of the mountain pass. They couldn't see it, but somewhere within a few miles of them was a small village.

"We'll make camp here," Trylian called, pulling up on his reins. "Roan, with me."

"Father," Gareth called after him, "what about Tanis and me?"

Trylian stopped and looked the other Knights in the eyes, scanning each one of them. Roan checked Alamar and saw the muscled-bound boy glaring at him.

"Shouldn't we all be in the know?" Roan asked.

Trylian looked at him with just his eyes. He scanned Roan's face for a moment before nodding. "Wise of you, Roan. Very well." He motioned them all over to the campfire the cook had set up and had them all sit around it.

Razvin and Atreus sat next to Roan and Alamar and Veryl sat across the fire. Trylian crossed his arms and looked each boy in the eyes once more.

"I picked you all deliberately," he said over the crackling of the fire. Beyond the camp, the night bugs began to sing and an owl hooted. Around them, trees sprang up, shielding them from the light of the moon. The fire danced over Trylian's stony face, igniting the few white hairs in his beard and hair.

"For our strength?" Alamar boasted, clenching his fists so his muscles bulged. Beside him, Veryl's face was deadpan and expressionless.

Trylian smirked generously. "Because I see potential in all of you. What we will do tomorrow could prevent or start a war."

At this, Roan looked up from his lute, which he'd been tuning. He shared a quick glance with Razvin, who looked worried. His black eyes pinched in concern. "Sir?" Roan asked. "What are we to do?"

Trylian dropped his arms and casually rested his left hand on the hilt of the sword at his side. "There is a convoy coming from Delsinor and bound for Duskhallow."

Roan nodded, remembering that. He didn't say anything though, knowing Trylian hated to be interrupted.

"This convoy carries in it the daughter of a Thane from

Delsinor, who is to be married to a man of some influence in Duskhallow."

Roan understood. "They could be strengthening their ties with Moralan," he offered. "What does that mean?"

"It means war!" Alamar crowed, punching his fist into the air and just missing Veryl's face. The Claret didn't even wince.

"It could," Trylian countered more calmly. "Which is why we are to stop it. We are to show no mercy. Do you understand? We are not the king's men who must abide by chivalry and law. We are Knights of the Modeus and will stop these Elsarius worshipers from strengthening their bond."

"Are we to take any prisoners?" Razvin asked.

Trylian shook his head. "Not one must walk away. No witnesses. It will be perhaps weeks before they realize something has gone wrong, and we will be long gone by then."

"What about retaliation?" Roan asked.

"We will leave no trace," Trylian answered. "They will never know what took the convoy. Is that clear, men?"

The boys nodded, mumbling a few "yes, sirs" as well.

"Get some rest, then," Trylian ordered. He took Elendir by the elbow and led him off to their tent, going inside without another word.

"This will be a slaughter," Alamar jeered, a wicked grin on his face.

Roan couldn't help but share the grin. "It will be. A rich man's convoy like that can only have a few guards at most. No Knights or Clarets, unless they hired mercenaries. This will be simple."

"Take it seriously," Gareth offered with a straight face. "Father is judging us all on this mission."

Tanis cocked his head. "What do you mean?"

Gareth looked around the fire at the other boys. "This seems like a simple mission, but there are ways to fail. I don't know what they are, but Father does. Watch yourselves. Be wise and cunning in your attacks. That includes you, little brother."

"Little by an hour," Tanis grumbled back.

Roan ignored the twins as they descended into softly whispered bickering after this. He strummed a few chords on his lute, his eyes staring into the middle distance as he thought.

"Gareth is right," he said to Razvin and Atreus, who were pouring drinks now. "I have to perform well tomorrow."

"You know Trylian better than any of us," Razvin said. "But I'm not the one on trial here. Do you know what he'll be looking for?"

Roan played a slow melody on his lute now, muffling the strings as he played. "He wants to see ruthlessness, but not unbridled savagery. He'll want to see which of us emerges as leader."

"I will," Alamar said, taking the tankard of mead from Razvin. He threw it back down his throat and wiped at his chin. "I'm the strongest out of all of us. Just do as I say and we'll all make the Archon Knight proud."

Roan glared at Alamar. "You already have your Claret. Why do you need to impress Trylian?"

Alamar gripped Veryl by the back of his neck hard. "I'm only second column, Red Mane. I want to be first. And I deserve it. You will do as I say tomorrow."

Roan sneered. "I'll do no such thing. Trylian will see me as a leader tomorrow. I'll get promoted and soon have my own Claret. Then we can have a proper duel, Alamar."

"Duel?" the other boy asked, a hint of shock in his voice. "You want to duel me, Red Mane?"

Roan nodded, still strumming his lute. "I think it's time we put our quarrels behind us and see who the superior Knight is. Don't you?"

"Winds," Razvin swore, downing his entire tankard of mead. "You two really have to fight?"

Atreus smiled and poured Razvin more mead. "Let them. We can put money on the winner."

At this, Razvin cocked a black brow. "This is why I love you, Atreus. You never let an opportunity go by." He raised his tankard to his Claret and then drank the second helping in one gulp.

"Bet on me or you're dead," Roan said with a half-serious glower. He couldn't stop the smile, though.

Razvin blanched playfully. "Bet against Roan Red Mane? Never."

Alamar scoffed and shoved Veryl up. "Get some rest, boys. We have a battle tomorrow." He grabbed his Claret by the arm and marched him to their tent where they vanished out of sight.

Razvin sighed and nudged Roan with his elbow. "Get some sleep. It may be a rich man's convoy tomorrow, but there could be guards. Knights, even. We could lose someone."

At this, Tanis looked up, his eyes rounded. "Lose someone?" He gulped.

Gareth patted his brother's shoulder. "I won't let anything happen to you. Trust me. Stick close and we'll be fine."

"We'll have each other's backs," Razvin said. "Those of us with magic will protect you."

Atreus nodded, smiling encouragingly.

Tanis swallowed hard again, his brows pinching in worry. "I'm suddenly nervous," he whispered.

Roan nodded. "Me, too. But this is our chance to prove ourselves. We can't fuck it up."

Gareth nodded once in determination. "Rest well, boys. We're going into battle in the morning."

The twins departed then, leaving Roan with his best friend and Atreus. Roan stopped playing his lute and stared into the fire. He wondered what battle was like. Yes, they had battled the bandits, but there had only been three of them, and Trylian had wiped them out with a quick wave of fire from his hand. Roan hadn't even bloodied his blade. What was battle like? Would he be able to think clearly or would the adrenaline stifle his brain?

Atreus reached out and gently touched his knee. "Don't worry, Roan. You're ready. You fought off those Vyrkarians easily."

Roan swallowed. "I wasn't being judged then. That was life or death."

"Life or death is easier than this simple convoy?" Razvin asked.

Roan met his friend's eyes. "Yes. I've trained my whole life for this. I deserve it."

Razvin smiled, showing his sharp fangs. "You do, my brother." He gripped Roan's head and pulled him in for a quick embrace, kissing his forehead. Razvin froze, smiling. "I've had too much to drink."

"You have," Roan laughed, wiping at the spot on his forehead.

"Come, Atreus," Razvin called, standing and swaying slightly. "Let us depart and leave him to his contemplative brooding."

Atreus squeezed Roan's shoulder. "We're rooting for you," he whispered before they, too, vanished into their tent.

Roan put aside his lute and picked up his sword instead. It was clean and sharp. His father's blade. He was ready to bloody it.

༄

THE SPRING AIR was cool on Roan's freckled cheeks as he crouched in the bushes just off the road. Somewhere, a waterfall roared, making it hard to hear anything coming down the road. The sun shone brightly down, igniting the golden road in a yellow light. Spots of sunlight danced between the tree branches above, laden with green leaves. The smell of earth was strong. They lay in wait along the road while the Clarets had been sent a safe distance away into the woods.

Beside him, Razvin suddenly perked up. The half-Vyrkarian nudged Roan with his elbow and flicked his horned head to the left. Without asking, Roan understood. They were coming. Roan unsheathed his sword silently and angled it to the right to catch the sun. He wiggled it back and forth, sending the signal to the others farther down the road. Then he turned back to watch the bend in the road to their left.

Just as he'd turned, four guards on horseback came around the bend. Roan swapped his sword for his short bow and prepared to aim. Behind the guards came a large ornate carriage with fringe on top and golden wheels. The curtains were drawn over the windows in the doors so they could not see in. Behind this came a wagon with cooking supplies and more on it. Two men sat atop it. And bringing up the rear came four more guards in light armor.

"Aim for the guards," Roan whispered. "Then shoot the driver of the carriage."

Razvin nodded and nocked an arrow.

Roan shot up from the foliage where they had been hiding and fired. His arrow flew straight and true, thudding hard into the chest of one of the guards. The others scattered immediately, shouting and raising shields. Razvin's bolt lodged itself harmlessly into one of the shields. Roan heard him curse before switching to his sword and charging. Following his friend, Roan dropped his bow and unsheathed his blade, charging as well.

He went for the horses' legs, cutting them and making them rear up, tossing the guards to the ground. Around him, he heard Trylian shout for the Clarets to stay back. He didn't know where they were hiding and didn't care. As he battled a guard, he heard the crackling of lightning being thrown from Trylian as he cast a bolt of it at one of the other guards. Alamar and Razvin did the same, throwing balls of fire or walls of wind at their assailants. Jealousy roiled up in Roan, but he turned that into fervor. He spun around and stopped one guard who had aimed a bow at Trylian's back, stabbing him fiercely.

Trylian spun and waved his sword in a great arc over his head. The ground behind Roan exploded at his command, lifting one man into the air about twelve feet before dropping him in a heap. Roan took the opportunity to attack the man, cutting off his head. Trylian beamed at him.

"Stop that man!" Roan shouted, seeing the driver of the carriage pick up the reins once again and prepare to drive away. But everyone was occupied. So Roan dashed forward himself, cutting the legs of the horses tethered to the carriage. The animals screamed and reared up, clawing at the air. The driver cried out when he saw Roan and leapt off the carriage, making a run for it. In that moment, Roan wished he had magic. He'd throw a bolt of lightning or a ball of fire after the man and kill him. But he didn't. So he gave chase on foot.

No witnesses, Trylian had said. He couldn't let this man get away. Pumping his long legs, he charged after him. He caught up to him faster than he expected and tackled the man to the ground. He pressed his sword into his throat and shoved down, cutting into his flesh. The man screamed and babbled for mercy, but Roan didn't hear it. With a final grunt, he shoved down and severed the man's throat. Satisfied he was dead, he leapt up and ran back.

Seeing the others were occupied, Roan ran to the carriage and threw the doors open. Inside sat two women, who screamed when they saw him. One was clearly a handmaid and the other the Thane's daughter. Their eyes went from his face to the Modeus insignia on his black armor; a snake coiled around a crescent moon. They screamed again and clung to one another.

Roan took no pity on them. He stabbed the handmaid over and over again, spurting her blood all over the other girl. He maimed her until she was almost unrecognizable. Then he grabbed the noble girl by her wrist and pulled her out of the carriage. She screamed and pulled against him, uselessly hammering on his arm. She snarled and clawed at his face. A searing burn followed her nails from his eyebrow down to his chin as she scratched him. Roan tossed her to the ground. When she landed, hands splayed, he hacked at her wrists. Her hands easily fell away from her bloody stumps and she screamed again, sobbing uncontrollably and gasping for air. She writhed on the ground, her blood smattering the golden path.

"Well done, Roan," Trylian panted, coming up behind him and clasping him on the shoulders. He didn't have long to praise him, though, as the battle still raged on around them.

Alamar leered at the girl and ignored the battle to leap onto her. He tore her skirts and unfastened his own belt. He hammered into her with abandon as the battle went on around him. Roan glared at the other boy, but defended him as he carried out the terrible act.

Roan was in combat with another, one of the last men, when someone galloped up behind them on a horse. Roan shoved the man and looked into the woods to see Atreus on his horse approach them. His eyes were wide, and he opened his mouth to speak, urgency written all over his face.

"Get back!" Trylian screamed at the Claret.

But it was too late. One of the other guards spotted the helpless Claret and let an arrow fly from his hand. Razvin shrieked. The arrow flew hard and true, striking Atreus in the throat. The Claret's head snapped back from the impact and blood cascaded down his front, staining his white robes. Razvin screamed and dropped his sword, running to his friend.

Roan had to charge the man with the bow as he was about to shoot Razvin next. Roan swung his blade with a cry, knocking the bow out of the man's hand and severing a few fingers in the process. Gareth and Tanis took down the other man he had been fighting, giving him the freedom to finish off the bowman. Roan stabbed him once, pulled his blade free, and stabbed him again and again until his face was red with the man's blood. The man finally fell and Roan gasped for air.

Behind him, Razvin sobbed loudly, calling Atreus's name. Roan slowly turned to see the Knight cradling his Claret in his arms. Atreus gargled on his own blood, his face as white as his robes. He was trying to speak, but couldn't. Tears cut clean tracks down Razvin's face through the blood.

"Why was he here?" Trylian roared. "He should have stayed—"

"Trylian!"

They all looked up. Elendir and Veryl came charging out of the bushes as well.

"What are you—" Trylian began, but Elendir interrupted him.

"Travelers. On the road," he panted. "They heard the screaming."

"Go," Roan ordered Tanis and Gareth. The two boys obeyed instantly, running down the golden path, swords drawn.

He turned back to Razvin where he knelt, Atreus draped over his arm. He wanted to stay, to comfort his friend, but knew he couldn't leave the two younger boys alone to fight whatever they might find on the road ahead.

"Stay with him," Roan commanded the others, and took off after Tanis and Gareth. Trylian watched him go.

Roan ran down the road and around a bend before he spotted the twins. They stood over two corpses on the road.

"Who were they?" Roan asked, panting.

"A pair of bards," Gareth answered. "Just on the road to the city, no doubt. Easily dealt with."

Roan nodded solemnly. "Easily, but at a great cost. Get the bodies off the road."

"Poor Razvin," Tanis said, his large eyes sad as he pulled one corpse into the bushes. "I know they were close."

Gareth punched his smaller brother once they had the road cleared. "All Knights and Clarets are close. You can't help but be."

Tanis shrugged with one shoulder. "Alamar and Veryl don't seem that close."

"That's because Veryl was an Elsarius Claret," Gareth replied.

Roan cocked his head. "What do you mean?"

The three of them started to walk back to the place of carnage and slaughter, where they could still hear the noble girl weeping.

"There are not a lot of Modeus Clarets," Gareth explained. "So we take others. Father told me. Elendir was once a Claret of the Elsarius, too."

"But they seem so close," Roan offered.

"After years of enforced proximity, I imagine it's unavoidable."

Roan frowned slightly as they hurried back. He wasn't sure how he'd feel having a Claret of the Elsarius. Wouldn't he have to watch the Claret night and day, making sure he didn't run? And how did they bind if not by will alone?

He didn't have time to think about it much more. They rounded the corner, and the battlefield came back into view. Trylian stood by and looked up, his face breaking into relief when he saw his boys.

"Don't look so worried," Gareth said in good humor, embracing his father. "Roan wouldn't let harm befall us, would you, Roan?"

Roan cocked a gentle smile and nodded to Trylian. Then he turned back to Alamar, who was fastening his pants. The noble girl lay dead on the ground, no doubt from blood loss. Roan wondered if Alamar had been plowing her while she was dead.

Next, he took in Razvin, who had stopped weeping and just sat, holding Atreus's body. Trylian walked up behind Razvin and gently laid his hand on his shoulder.

"I am sorry, my boy," he whispered. He quickly moved to Elendir and embraced him, no doubt thankful it hadn't been his Claret who had perished. "Roan, you did well. I am pleased with your performance," he said, pulling back from Elendir.

"What now?" Tanis asked. He scanned the bloodied bodies around them.

"We take everything of value and leave nothing behind," Trylian ordered. "If we're thorough, they may think bandits attacked the convoy. Then..." He smiled.

Roan looked up at Trylian, curious.

"We have one more convoy to take," Trylian said. "And that is where you boys will get your Clarets."

Gareth and Tanis whooped, jumping into the air in celebration. Roan's eye stayed fixed on Razvin and Atreus, though. Would that ever be him? Could he ever have such an attachment? He doubted it, but he wanted the magic. And soon, he would have it.

CHAPTER VIII

The sun was setting on the eighth day by the time Phael gathered enough courage to walk next to Nox. They, Olenar, and a handful of other Clarets had left Delsinor several days ago to travel to a village where Olenar was to perform blessings for the crops. Phael was eager to see what the other Clarets not bound to Knights did, and Olenar had urged him to come, saying this may be his last journey before he was bound to a Knight. The older Claret walked out in front of their small caravan, leading the way. Phael wasn't sure where they were going, but he was pleased to be a part of it.

That morning, a wave of magic had passed through him and the remnants of the pain still lingered. He'd sweat and cringed in agony as the pulse had made its way through his veins. He'd even felt like his eyes had been melting as tears streamed from them. Phael decided this was what he'd ask Nox. He had to be experiencing the same thing.

He quickened his pace to catch up to the long-legged Claret and smiled when Nox glanced over at him. To his delight, Nox smiled in greeting.

Phael's throat constricted in fear as he whispered, "Do you feel the Winds' magic in you, too?"

Nox, being a bit taller, looked down at Phael as they

marched over the forest floor. His black eyes were kind, but also held a bit of surprise at Phael's forwardness.

"Sometimes," Nox replied. "It hurts and I don't like it."

"Feels like waves of fire to me," Phael offered.

Nox pressed his lips together and tilted his head a little. "To me, it feels like being boiled alive. Like hot water is rushing under my skin. Sometimes I think I'm drowning. It scares me."

"Me, too." Phael hovered a little closer to Nox now that they were talking.

"You don't seem like the type to be scared."

"Why?"

Nox smiled mischievously. "We all know you were the one who stole the honey. And you burned down the smithy. You have no fear."

"Oh," Phael gasped. "The smithy was an accident. I shouldn't have been playing with the crystals. It's not my place. And, well, the honey was calling to me." He shared Nox's grin. A soft pink color rose in Phael's cheeks as the other boy smiled down at him. He felt his nose burn in a blush as well. "Really, I'm not as adventurous as all that."

"Neither am I," Nox admitted. "I'm afraid of so many things. Lailen says it's irrational."

"You? Afraid?" Phael thought Nox was quiet, but didn't think that silence was hiding fear. "I'm afraid of lightning and thunder."

Nox turned his face up to the sky. "That's one thing I don't fear. If it rains and the thunder comes, I'll protect you. How does that sound?"

Phael's nose turned solid red then, and he grinned so hard his cheeks ached. He knew there was nothing Nox could do about the weather, but imagining being curled up in a tent, safe in his arms and pressed against his chest, made Phael's heart flip in his chest. He imagined twirling Nox's long white hair around his finger, listening to his heartbeat, feeling his warmth.

No! he chided himself quickly. *Only pure thoughts.* A sudden melancholy poured over him. The urge to reach out and take Nox's pale, long-fingered hand overcame him. It hurt, almost like the magic was rising in him again as he watched Nox walk. His long legs made the white robes of the Elsarius swish elegantly around his ankles.

"And what are you afraid of?" he asked. "What can I protect you from?"

Nox's black eyes squinted in thought for a moment as he looked ahead. "The dark. When I was a boy, before my family was killed, my older brother used to tell me just the most terrible stories of things in the dark that would come out and eat children. I'm afraid I've never grown out of that fear."

"Well," Phael said with a soft grin, "I'll do my best to keep you safe. We can keep each other safe."

Nox's face relaxed into a wider smile. "I'd like that."

Behind them, in the wagon, a whooshing sound exploded and crackled. Two Clarets on the wagon began to giggle. Nox turned around and frowned.

"What was that?" Olenar shouted from the front. His eyes bored into Phael. "Don't tell me you brought crystals again."

"It wasn't Phael," Nox said quickly. He pointed behind them. "Jannis and Alowyn were playing with fire."

"Rat," Jannis snarled at Nox.

Olenar marched back to the other boys and held his hand out. "Hand them over."

The Claret hesitated for a moment, then sighed, rolling his eyes, and handed over two crystals. One was orange and the other green.

"I don't know where you are getting these, but this stops now," Olenar groused. "Magic is not for us. We cannot control it. It will get out of hand. You could hurt yourself or die. Do you understand?"

Nox and Phael nodded as Olenar's eyes landed on them, but the other Claret said, "Why can't we do magic? It's innate in us. It's ours. Why give it away to a Knight?"

Olenar sighed and put his hands in his long sleeves, surveying the boys before him. "Because it's too powerful for one to handle. If you do not bind, you will die from the over-whelming might of the Winds' power. The Winds designed it that way. Two there shall always be: one to protect and one to hold the magic. You might not die for some time, but one man with that much power would be a tyrant. And he would need to be stopped. Thus, two there shall always be. As it is written."

"Sounds like we're the powerful ones," Jannis said with a sneer. "The Knights need us."

"And we need them," Olenar reiterated. "The magic makes us weak, brittle, ill. Even when we share it. It prevents the excess growth of muscle and keeps us weak, burning us up. Thus, we need the Knights to protect us. My boys," he said, his voice taking on a gentler tone, "it is a good thing, the bond between Knight and Claret. Something I will never experience, for the Winds are not strong in me. But you will. And I promise you, you will love your Knight like no other. The trust you will have will be unparalleled. That bond is sacred and ordained by the Winds. Understand?"

Phael felt a rush at this. He longed for that bond. Wanted to share his magic with a brave warrior. He glanced at Nox and they shared another smile, both feeling the same way.

Olenar went on, like he was giving a lecture in the halls of the Sanctuary. "Two there always have been. That is why there are two sides of the Winds: the Elsarius and the Modeus. Two differing ideals, but only one must be followed. We must shun the darker teachings of the Modeus, who believe those without magic must be conquered."

"Why must we shun the Modeus?" Jannis asked. "If they are part of the Winds as well."

"Two aspects of the Winds there once were," Olenar said. "A Knight and his Claret. They separated after years of battling one another and founded the factions as we know them."

"Must have been long ago," Phael mused.

"Millenia ago," Olenar offered in agreement, his tone turning lighter. "Before the invention of the wheel, surely."

The boys laughed.

"Now," Olenar said with another sigh, "this place is as good as any, and the sun is getting low. Let us make camp here."

OLENAR LEFT to find water from a spring nearby and put Phael in charge of the others. The other two Clarets made fun of Phael, calling him a snitch and Olenar's favorite even though it hadn't been him who had told on them. But he tried to not let the jibes bother him. Nox told them to be quiet and mind the fire, staying close to Phael.

As they set up their tents and built the fire, Nox asked Phael, "What kind of man do you think your Knight will be?"

Phael uncoiled some rope and began to string it up between two trees. "I hope he's kind more than anything."

"You are soft," Nox said. "Gentle and sweet. You deserve someone who appreciates that about you."

Phael's blush came back at those words. "So do you, Nox. What kind of Knight do you want?"

Nox thought for a moment. "Someone brave. A real

warrior. A strong man who can protect me and won't let me down."

Before Phael could reply, Alowyn ran up to him, slapped him on the shoulder, and shouted, "You're the chaser!" before darting off into the camp.

Laughing and quickly understanding they were playing chase, Phael broke into a run and cantered after Alowyn. Nox quickly bolted in the opposite direction, smiling as well.

Phael ran after the other boy for a moment before he turned on his heel and faced Nox. Nox giggled and froze, waiting to see which way Phael would run. The fire separated them. Phael faked going to the right and Nox dashed to his left. Phael then leapt over the flames and ran after him, hand outstretched. His fingertips just grazed Nox's shoulder to tag him when their feet suddenly became entangled.

With some pain and no doubt bruises appearing on their shins and ankles, they got tangled in one another and fell to the forest floor. Phael fell face-first, but Nox twisted, landing hard on his back. When Phael hit him, they came face to face, closer than they'd ever been before. Phael could see every one of Nox's black lashes. They were so close they shared the same air, limbs entwined. Nox laughed as he wiggled under Phael, trying to disentangle himself.

"You got me," he said through his giggle. "You better run."

Phael didn't want to run. He wanted to stay like that forever. Above them, the softest rumble of thunder rolled across the dark sky. Phael flinched and looked up as rain began to fall. His hair stuck to his face as he looked back down at Nox. They both went still, looking into each other's eyes.

A scream broke the air. Both Clarets snapped their heads to look toward the fire. The other two boys ran toward them from the woods. Panic warped their faces and fear widened their eyes.

"Modeus Knights!" Alowyn screamed. "Run!"

At this, Nox tossed Phael off him and stood. Phael scrambled to his feet and looked over the flames, too. Slowly marching out of the darkness came at least six men. Behind them, looming in the darkness, stood two Clarets in white.

"They have magic," Nox called, throwing himself before Phael. "Get back!" he snarled at the Knights.

But they didn't so much as hesitate. The Knights charged into the camp. The Clarets scattered, running in every direction. Phael screamed for Nox, but bolted as one of the Knights leaned off his horse, grabbing at him. He ran, leaping over the fire, and dashed for the forest. Glancing back, he watched as one Knight grabbed Jannis and ran him through with his sword.

"Jannis!" he screamed, stopping dead in his tracks. The rain was cold and made his long white hair stick to his face. His scream made a tall Knight with bright red hair turn and face him. He marched toward Phael.

"Don't kill them, Alamar!" an Archon Knight with long black hair shouted at the one who had killed Jannis. The blue of the symbol on his cloak marked him as a high rank. "We need them alive, you fool." He looked up and saw Phael.

"Elsarius save us," Phael wept to the sky above as he turned, evading the red-haired Knight's wild grab for him. He didn't know what they wanted, if not to kill them. Before he turned to flee once more, he saw two Knights with the same face grapple Nox. This made him hesitate.

It was just enough. The red-haired Knight grabbed him hard and spun him around, grappling both his arms behind his back. Phael struggled, but it was useless against the Knight; he had to be the strongest man Phael had ever met. He couldn't budge the Knight's powerful hands on him.

"Let me go!" he cried, struggling as the Knight hauled him back closer to the fire where the others waited, also held by the other Knights. "What do you want with us?" Tears mingled with the rain on his pale cheeks.

The one who had killed Jannis sauntered forward and reached out to Phael, gripping his face in his hands. Phael felt bruises blossom under the Knight's strong fingers. The Knight forced his head left then right, as if inspecting cattle. Phael shuddered.

"Why are Elsarius Clarets so pretty?" the Knight asked, leering at him now. He made a quick, obscene gesture and snickered when Phael flinched. "They believe in purity of body, yes? We Modeus don't."

Phael writhed in the red-haired Knight's grip, finally dislodging his face from the tight grasp. "Please," he begged, "let us go."

The Knight laughed and said, "You're even prettier when you beg."

"Enough, Alamar," the red-haired Knight holding him said.

"Bring them forward," the Archon Knight with black hair said. "Let us inspect our bounty."

The Knights shoved the captive Clarets hard, forcing them to their knees between the lot of them. The Knights encircled the Clarets, all eyes piercing into them. Phael looked around and spotted Nox. His robes were torn, exposing his smooth, pale chest, and he panted. His glare would have frozen the rivers, but did nothing to deter the Knights.

"Three," the Archon Knight sighed. "We should have had four."

"That is not my doing," Olenar said, appearing from the woods. "I brought four, as promised."

Phael's heart flipped in his chest. A rush of joy shot through him at seeing the older Claret, but his words drove a stake through his heart.

"Olenar?" he whispered, his voice quivering. "What do you mean?"

"Silence, brat," Olenar snapped.

Phael glanced at Nox, who looked just as confused and frightened.

"Our deal?" Olenar asked the Archon Knight.

The Knight sighed and sheathed his blade, adjusting a silver gauntlet on his wrist where a yellow crystal was embedded. "It stands, Olenar. Despite the stupidity of my own Knight. Once I have my seat of power, I will make you Arch Claret. Though I still expect you to do my bidding."

"You give me what I want, and I am your servant," Olenar purred with a mock bow. "I give you what you want, and you make sure I am promoted."

"All in due time," the Archon Knight said. "Now, what have we here?"

Olenar motioned to one of the Knights, who was a twin with the one he stood next to, and pointed to Alowyn. The knight reached down and hauled the boy to his feet.

"Alowyn," Olenar said. "He is a good Claret but has a rebellious streak. But like all Clarets his age, he is also meek and demure when dominated."

"Perhaps for you?" the Archon Knight said, half-looking over his shoulder at a tall, gray-skinned half-Vyrkarian with black horns.

The half-Vyrkarian shook his head. "I want that one." He flicked his horned head toward Nox.

"No!" Phael gasped, realizing what was happening now. Olenar had tricked them in exchange for a promotion later when this Archon Knight took his "seat of power," as he called it. They were to be bound to the Knights. Modeus Knights.

Deciding he'd rather die, Phael leapt up and made a run for it. He shoved past the red-haired Knight and dashed toward the edge of the forest.

He didn't see it, but felt it.

A bolt of lightning struck his back, zapping through him with cracks and snaps. His body shook, and he involuntarily screamed before falling to the ground.

"Get him," the Archon Knight's voice ordered.

Before Phael had shaken the rest of the lightning from his brain, he felt those same strong arms around him, hauling him to his feet.

"Don't do that again," the red-haired Knight advised, holding him tight and marching him back to the circle. "Your life will be easier if you give up now."

Phael sobbed, fresh tears falling down his face as the Knight practically lifted him and dragged him back to the others. "You traitor!" he shrieked at Olenar when he was tossed back onto the ground, mud now pooling around his hands where they pressed into the ground. "The Elsarius will have their vengeance."

Olenar smirked casually down at Phael. "I care not. I say my prayers to the Modeus. Now, you best be on your way, my dear Trylian."

The Archon Knight nodded. "Boys, tie them. We don't want any escaping on our journey back."

Phael wept as the red-haired Knight grabbed him once again. "Please, don't do this."

But the Knight didn't stop. He pulled Phael's hands behind his back and tied his wrists tight. Gasping back a sob, Phael watched as Alowyn and Nox were bound as well. Alowyn glared and struggled in vain. Nox, defeated, hung his head as he was bound.

Above them, thunder clapped and Phael shrank away, more terror filling him than he'd ever experienced before. Just moments ago, he'd been dreaming about Nox and what his ideal Knight would be like. Now, he was captured, destined to be bound to a Knight of the Modeus. Giving in, he sobbed out loud as they were marched into the woods.

CHAPTER IX

As they traveled, Roan couldn't take his eyes off the one they called Phael. Trylian had said the night before that they'd make a good match. He couldn't imagine why. Phael was short, small, and his eyes were red from his incessant weeping. He shrank away from everything and cowered in the corner of the wagon the three Clarets had been placed in when they were not being forced to walk.

But there was something about him. Something innocent and pure that drew Roan to him. Something he wanted to destroy. The part drawn to the Claret wanted to hurt him, to make him weep again, to make him cower even more. But more than that, Roan wanted the power the Claret would bring him. This made him look with lust on the Claret. He couldn't fathom how such a frail, weak body could hold so much power.

Already once the Claret had had a fit of magic. A wave of it had pulsed through him, making his veins glow like the sun. He'd whimpered and cried out as if it hurt him, and once it had gone, he'd lain spent and exhausted on the floor of the wagon. The other Clarets couldn't comfort him, since their arms were tied tight behind their backs. Now, all three of them lay on the wooden floor of the wagon. That was when Roan realized they hadn't had a drink in almost two days.

"Stop," he called, pulling up on the reins of his horse.

"What are you doing?" Trylian asked, watching Roan dismount and go to the camp wagon.

"They're thirsty," he said offhandedly. He leapt up onto the wagon and maneuvered to the water barrel. He opened it and refilled his own waterskin before climbing back down.

Trylian looked from Roan to the exhausted Clarets to Elendir. His own Claret's face wrinkled in some concern.

"They are not our slaves," he whispered gently. "Let Roan give them water. You need them alive."

Trylian arched a brow but nodded. "Hurry. I want to reach the mountain pass by sundown."

Roan hopped up into the wagon. When he did, the Clarets tried to scramble away from him, but they were too weak. He went to Phael first and knelt by him. The Claret's lips were cracked and even bleeding a little. Roan reached down and put his hand on Phael's back, helping him to sit up.

"Drink," he ordered.

When Phael hesitated, a look of worry on his face, Roan forced the opening of the waterskin into his mouth and tipped it upward. Phael choked on it at first, but then he drank. Roan gave him a moment to breathe before giving him one more large swallow.

Then he moved on to the one they called Nox. He drank more easily and didn't shudder at Roan's touch like Phael had. The last Claret drank almost greedily, desperate for the water. Roan noted Phael's sad blue eyes on him the entire time.

When he stood to leave, the Claret mumbled, "Thank you," softly, looking away as if in shame.

Roan nodded, acknowledging his thanks, and went back to his horse.

"Couldn't have waited a few more hours when we make camp?" Trylian asked, judgment in his tone.

"We need them," Roan quipped back. "We're not here to

torture them. Isn't that right?" He looked to Veryl, Alamar's Claret, and then Elendir. "They are ours to protect."

Trylian stared at Roan for a moment before nodding. "Onward."

⁓

THEY DIDN'T MAKE it deep into the mountain pass until the sun had almost set. The path through the mountains was winding and ascended the lower parts of the mountains, making them all exhausted by the time they stopped for the evening. The cook and farrier went to work on setting up camp, and Veryl and Elendir helped. Roan didn't bother setting up his own tent. They'd only sleep here one night, and it wasn't worth it. He did remove his armor, though, and the saddle from his horse, letting it roam free.

"Tie them to the trees," Trylian ordered Razvin and Alamar, pointing to the newly captured Clarets. "Tanis, Gareth, go hunting and don't come back unless you have a buck that can feed us all."

The twins nodded and marched off into the wooded area to the north.

Roan watched as Razvin and Alamar wrestled the Clarets to the trees, tying their hands behind their backs and lashing them to the trunks.

"What are you going to do about only having three new Clarets?" Roan asked. "There are now four of us. Since Atreus."

"Unfortunate," Trylian said, not sounding emotional at all. "But Gareth had his eye on one back in Aatheria. I wasn't convinced they'd be a good match, but I may have to give in. He's a Claret of the Modeus, so that will make things easier."

Roan picked up a couple logs and built up the fire the

cook had started, then he knelt by it and jabbed at it with a stick. "How does it work? How do we bind?" He glanced at Phael, who was close by. The Claret lifted his eyes and met Roan's, listening in.

"It's a ceremony performed by an Anakrite," Trylian explained. "There's smoke and incense and prayers and all that. It's performed in the Sactrium, of course. Then, they place your hand over your Claret's, palms together, and drive a binding crystal through your hands like a nail on a cross."

Roan winced and looked up at this.

"It's quite a narrow crystal. Have no fear," Trylian reassured him. "The mingling of the blood, along with the power of the crystal, binds the two of you, channeling his power into you, and tying his life to yours. It's easier when they are willing to lie upon the altar, but we've never had a binding not work." He looked over at Elendir, who was setting up Trylian's tent. "They may resist the binding at first, but once they realize their lives are tied to yours, they come around."

Roan let his eyes shift to Elendir, too. "You two seem close."

"We are now. Weren't always. We were more like Alamar and Veryl for the longest time."

"Alamar beats Veryl," Roan added. He was shocked at the disgust in his own voice. He looked over at Phael. Hadn't he had the same intuitive feelings earlier? What was that feeling and what did it mean? Why did he want to hurt the Claret? He didn't want to be like Alamar. He promised himself he'd treat his Claret better.

Trylian didn't react, choosing instead to look up and see his sons coming back from the woods. He smiled at his boys when he saw the massive buck Gareth had slung over his shoulder.

"Sometimes, Roan, a good beating reminds one who is in

charge." He gripped Roan's shoulder hard. "You know that." He stood and moved to help the cook butcher the buck.

Roan froze, still feeling Trylian's hand on his shoulder, bruising him. His memories began to rise and consume him. Darkness encroached on his vision. He heard his own heart pounding. Heard himself screaming.

"This one looks too pretty to be a man," Alamar's voice cut into his waking nightmares.

He blinked and looked up to see Gareth, Tanis, and Alamar jeering at the bound Clarets.

Alamar ripped Phael's white robe away from his chest, exposing his pale skin. Phael whimpered and tried to cringe away but was held fast.

"No, he really is a man," Alamar guffawed. "I half-expected tits under there." He grabbed Phael hard by his chin and forced him to look him in the face. "Elsarius are supposed to be pure. I bet you're not. Face like yours. I bet hundreds of men have plowed the fuck out of you."

Phael struggled and whined but couldn't free himself from Alamar's grasp.

"I like when they struggle," Alamar growled, leaning in closer to Phael. With a sudden snap of his hand, he grabbed Phael hard between his legs and squeezed.

Phael whimpered louder and tried to sink to his knees from the pain, but his bindings held him upright. Alamar laughed and twisted his hand, pulling a sob from the Claret.

"Let him go!" Nox shouted, writhing in his own bonds.

"Enough, Alamar!" Roan found himself shouting and leaping to his feet. Razvin appeared next to him, ready to spring into action.

Alamar removed his hand from the Claret and raised them up in surrender. "Whatever you say, Red Mane. Sorry I touched your Claret." He laughed, gripped Veryl by the back of his neck, and steered him toward their tent.

"Are you hurt?" Nox called to Phael.

Phael sobbed softly, sinking down and pulling his knees together. He didn't reply.

"I knew you'd be a pair," Trylian said to Roan from over by the fire. "Something in him calls out to you, doesn't it? That's the magic. It senses the bond you two were made to have."

"I'd rather die than bind to a Knight of the Modeus!" Phael cried. He began to mumble a prayer to the Elsarius between soft, gasping sobs.

Trylian smiled darkly. "Unlike the Elsarius, we don't care what your will is. You will bind and you will not be able to stop it."

Roan watched Phael weep anew, and excitement built up in him. He was at last going to have the power he'd craved for so long. And he'd earned it.

***

ADORIAN, AATHERIA. 8TH OF CELESTRUM, 1217.

Days later, Roan finally looked upon Aatheria from the great plains that surrounded it. He was tired, felt dirty, and was ready for his prize. Razvin had been subdued the first few days, mourning the loss of Atreus. Roan didn't know how to comfort him. He didn't understand either. Atreus was just a Claret, the source of the magic they wielded. Or so he thought. The more he watched Razvin, the more he realized their connection had been deeper. He'd heard all his life about the closeness of Knight and Claret but hadn't really given it any thought.

He glanced down at Phael, who struggled to keep up with the long gait of the horses. His white robes were muddied halfway up to his knees. His white hair was ratty, and tear tracks cut through the grime on his face. Roan wanted to see defiance or hate etched into his beautiful face, but Phael simply looked broken, lost. Despair lined the corners of his delicate lips and creased his pretty blue eyes. Roan didn't want to be tied to this weepy boy. But he wasn't sure he had a choice.

Several hours later, they rode into the city, past the stone walls and guards. Trylian led them beyond the caer and straight to the Sactrium. Tanis whined about being tired and how there weren't enough Clarets for them all, but Trylian silenced him quickly.

"If we don't bind them immediately, we could lose them," he replied, his brow deeply furrowed.

"What happens once they are bound?" Gareth asked, eyeing up the one they called Alowyn.

"You acquire the ability to wield the magic of the crystals," Trylian said. He glanced at Elendir. The Claret offered him a delicate smile. "And you earn a comrade for life."

"Where do the crystals come from?" Tanis asked.

"They are mined from the most sacred of caves in Vyrkaris," Trylian explained. "Where once dragons laid. The magic is strongest there and they grow like any crystal from the very walls. You must be careful with them as we do not have unlimited supply."

"How many can I wield?" Gareth asked, his brows knitting in thought.

"Four," Trylian replied, but something in his voice told Roan that wasn't entirely true. He wondered why Trylian chose to reply thusly.

"Does it hurt?" Tanis asked, gulping.

"The binding crystal being driven through your hand?" Trylian asked sarcastically, rolling his eyes. "Not one bit."

Tanis gulped again.

"It's worth it," Alamar interjected. "Nothing compares to the first sensation of the magic flowing through you. It's divine."

"You and Veryl can return to the caer," Trylian said to Alamar. "Await a message from me for debriefing in two days' time."

"Sir." Alamar nodded and turned his horse back toward the caer, Veryl just behind him.

Roan looked ahead at the Sactrium looming up before them. It stood in the center of the city and rose up like a spike of ivory. The white stones somehow almost glittered in the sunlight. The turrets were sharp and commanded respect. The round, colorful glass on the front caught the midday sun and shot specks of rainbow light over the ground before the Sactrium. In the bell towers high above, the bells started to ring. From the inside, singing could be heard.

"Won't we interrupt midday prayers?" Roan asked, the smell of incense suddenly wafting out of the open front doors.

"What we have to do is more important," Trylian answered. He dismounted and signaled the boys to herd the bound Clarets inside.

Roan went to Phael, who looked up. Seeing the Sactrium with the Modeus symbol on the outside, he gasped. Phael turned on his heel and tried to dash away. Roan caught him easily. Phael's arms were thin, and his body felt brittle in Roan's long-fingered hands. He practically lifted the Claret off the ground and marched him into the Sactrium.

"Please, don't," Phael began to babble, trying to wiggle for freedom in his arms. "This isn't right, you must see that. Don't force me to bind, I'm begging you!"

"Shut up or I'll shut you up," Trylian hissed, his voice echoing through the stony entryway.

"Be silent," Roan urged his future Claret. He didn't want

Trylian to lose his temper and kill the frail Claret by accident. No, he was too close to lose his chance now.

The singing stopped and the crowd of Clarets in the nave turned to look at the disheveled, bloodied, and exhausted Knights behind them. The Anakrite standing behind a large stone altar in the chancel looked up. Smoke wafted all round him, scented like amber and something else Roan couldn't name. Like most Clarets, the Anakrite was older than he looked. The man was perhaps fifty years old but looked thirty. He had brown hair that was peppered with white here and there, but obviously didn't hold the amount of magic that Phael did.

"Archon Knight Trylian," the Anakrite said once the Clarets had stopped their singing. "I see you have brought us more worshipers."

At this, Nox spat on the ground and glared defiantly. "We'll never worship the Modeus."

Gareth turned around and punched Nox hard in his gut. The Claret groaned and fell to his knees.

"We were hoping you had at least one Modeus Claret who had come into his magic," Trylian said. "We're one short."

"Athael!" the Anakrite called, his eyes never leaving Trylian's.

The crowd of Clarets parted and a boy about their age stepped forward. He smiled demurely at Trylian.

"Athael came into his magic a week ago," the Anakrite said. "He is strong with the Winds. He will do nicely."

"You will bind us now," Trylian said. It wasn't a question, and the Anakrite knew it. He nodded his head in a bow.

"No, please!" Phael burst with renewed vigor. He struggled in Roan's arms, but it was useless.

Roan didn't want to squeeze him too hard, afraid he'd break the Claret's ribs. But he held fast. Trylian turned and marched the two steps it took to reach Roan and Phael. The pit of Roan's stomach dropped out as Trylian's hand shot out like a viper and gripped Phael's thin throat.

"One more word out of you and you'll wish you were dead," he snarled softly. He squeezed, and Roan heard Phael try to gasp. "Do I make myself clear?"

Phael couldn't nod, couldn't speak. He just kept trying to gasp for air.

"I'll make sure he's quiet," Roan interjected when Phael's head began to lull on his shoulders.

"You'd better." Trylian let go and Phael let out a gasping sob.

The Anakrite let out a soft exhale. Roan guessed he'd been holding his breath, hoping Trylian wouldn't kill within the sacred walls of the Sactrium. "Shall we?" he said, gesturing to the stone altar.

"Gareth, Tanis," Trylian called to his sons. "Hold that one and that one." He pointed to Phael and Alowyn. "Roan, help us hold down this one." He gripped Nox by the back of his neck and forced him across the transept toward the altar.

Roan felt Phael draw in a quick breath to protest, but he squeezed his arms. "Not one word," he reminded the Claret. Phael whimpered as Gareth took his arms from Roan's grasp.

Roan moved forward and took Nox's left hand. Razvin moved to the other side of the altar and removed his riding glove. He waited until Roan forced Nox's hand, palm facing up, onto the altar. The Claret struggled feebly in his arms. Soon, Razvin stood on one side of the altar, his hand laying palm to palm with Nox's. The Anakrite disappeared for a moment into one of the side chapels before reappearing with a silver hammer and a white, almost glowing, spike of crystal the width of an arrow. It glittered with an iridescent sheen Roan hadn't seen on other crystals. At this, Nox began to struggle in Roan's arms in earnest. But Roan held him easily.

"Struggling only makes it hurt more," Trylian drawled. He'd no doubt seen the binding ceremony a hundred times.

"This is a corrupted crystal," the Anakrite began to explain as he lit incense on either side of the alter. "It will sever your ties to the Elsarius once it pierces your hand. When your blood and the blood of your Knight mingle together, the crystal will bind you to the Modeus. You will feel the change, but do not fear. Place your faith in the Winds and they will see you through to the other side."

Nox bucked against Roan, but he held him easily. "Nothing can sever my faith," he said weakly.

"It's magic, my son," the Anakrite said. "The Modeus care only about the Knights' and their faith. The dark aspect of the Modeus was a Knight himself. You are to be subjugated. Once you are bound to a Modeus Knight, the Elsarius will abandon you for your heresy of binding to a Knight of the Modeus."

Behind Roan, he heard Phael make a sad noise in his throat.

"Now, sing the hymn of binding," the Anakrite ordered the Clarets present. "And send your prayers to the Modeus for the binding of these Knights to their Clarets."

"No, please," Nox whimpered softly, trying once again to pull his hand away from Roan's. Roan didn't budge.

The Anakrite placed the tip of the thin crystal point down on the top of Razvin's hand. Roan noticed Razvin already had a scar on the top of his hand. No doubt from the time he'd been bound to Atreus. He'd done this before. Razvin's face was impassive for once.

"Wait," Razvin said, just before the Anakrite began to chant a prayer of binding. He looked Nox in the face. "I swear to protect you. To keep you safe from every evil. To honor your life with my own. Please, do not fear me."

Nox's black eyes rounded at him and he panted, swallowing hard. "Don't, please."

"I'm sorry," Razvin whispered. He nodded to the Anakrite.

Roan regripped the Claret hard when he felt his body tense.

The Anakrite whispered:

Oh, Winds that blow through heavens high,
Thy crystals' power we glorify.
Grant us the magic of thy might,
And shield us through the darkest night.
From foes that seek to do us harm,
Protect us with thy mighty arm.
Strengthen the bond 'twixt knight and he,
That we may serve thee faithfully.
Let thy great gales our spirits lift,
And bless us with thy magic gift.
In tempest's roar or gentle breeze,
We humbly bow upon our knees.
Thy will be done on earth below,
As 'tis above where thy winds blow.
For thine the realm, power, and glory,
Forever may we tell thy story.

Without another breath, he raised the silver hammer and brought it down hard. In one smooth motion, the white crystal drove through Razvin's hand and then Nox's. Nox screamed and jerked in Roan's arms, but he was ready. Blood immediately leaked out over the stone altar, flowing freely. Roan checked and saw even Razvin winced in pain, but he held himself still.

Roan couldn't see what went on below the surface, but both Nox and Razvin panted and moaned, closing their eyes as the magic must have flowed from one into the other. Nox's veins burned a white-blue, and he groaned, almost brought to his knees. Razvin closed his eyes tight and held his breath as pain overtook him. Roan winced.

"Thou art bound," the Anakrite said steadily. He reached down, gripped the binding crystal, and pulled it out.

Roan let go of Nox and the Claret fell to the ground, sobbing. Razvin rushed around the altar and collected his new Claret in his arms, forcing him to stand.

"Take him to the infirmary," Trylian said. "And await my orders in the caer once you're finished. And, Razvin," he added, his face serious, "have them watch him. We don't want him running."

Roan watched Razvin support his new Claret as they walked down the nave and through a side door of the Sactrium.

"Roan," Trylian ordered. "You're next."

A little shaken, Roan nodded. He walked to the other side of the altar where Razvin had been standing and removed his riding glove from his left hand. Phael screamed now. He kicked his legs out as Gareth and Tanis forced him to the altar. Trylian stepped forward, seeing that his sons were both needed to hold the struggling Claret, and gripped Phael's left hand. He forced it out and slapped it down on the altar. Phael balled his hand into a fist defiantly.

Roan reached out and pried his fingers open. They were so thin and delicate he thought he might break them. He gripped Phael's hand, holding it to keep their palms together.

"It's better if you don't struggle," he whispered to Phael. "If you keep this up, Trylian will kill you."

"I'd rather die than be tied to a Knight of the Modeus!" Phael spat, tears raining down his face.

Roan shook his head. "I was wrong. He won't kill you. But you'll wish you were dead."

Phael's blue eyes met Roan's green ones. "Please," he begged softly. "Please don't do this. Let me go."

Roan shook his head. "I've waited too long for this. I've earned this."

"Is that all a Claret is to you?" Phael gasped as another sob rose in his throat. "Just magic to be used?"

Confused, Roan said, "Yes."

Phael jerked one last time as the Anakrite began his prayer over again.

Roan took a deep breath as the binding crystal, freshly cleaned in a silver basin, was placed on top of his hand. It was strangely cold.

Then the Anakrite raised the hammer and brought it down in one hard, smooth motion again. Roan couldn't stop the grunt of pain that the spike pulled from him. The sensation of the sharp crystal being driven through the back of his hand hurt more than he'd anticipated. A single tear of pain dripped down his face, but he used all his effort to keep his face impassive. Phael screamed.

Then Roan felt it.

When Phael's blood touched his on the altar, something in his veins ignited. Phael's veins turned a bright white-orange and glowed. The Claret struggled in the Knights' grip, but they held him tight. Phael screamed and cried. Something hot ignited under Roan's skin and his head exploded. His heart raced and he realized he couldn't breathe. The wind had been sucked out of him.

He threw his head back, trying to get a good breath in, but something wouldn't let him.

"Roan, breathe!" Trylian ordered.

Finally, mouth gaping, air flooded his lungs. With that, the heat inside him flared up to new heights and pain seared his every vein. Like a flame had been fanned. A roaring like that of a dragon filled his ears.

Then it was all gone in a moment. Roan collapsed forward onto the altar, gasping. Phael had passed out. The Anakrite pulled the binding crystal out and the Claret fell to the stone floor with a sickening slap. Roan watched him fall, eyes rolling into the back of his head. He was out cold.

Roan held up his bloodied, wounded hand and inspected it. It looked just like any other wound. He saw no magic. Curious, he decided to hurry back to the caer then and try his luck. He'd need crystals first, though.

"Go to the Clarets outside near the smithy," Trylian urged Roan. "The Sactrium is the only place to acquire crystals. Pay them for a few crystals—just whatever you think you want to wield. Then head back to the caer and wait for me. We'll see to your Claret."

Roan nodded, stepped over the passed-out Phael, and trotted back up the nave, out into the ward to find his first crystals.

CHAPTER
X

Every sound came muffled to Phael's ears. His entire body was sore, the surface of his flesh highly sensitive. He felt the cold ground beneath him, and it hurt to move. His head rang. He must have hit it when he fell. Phael remembered falling. Remembered the pain in his left hand. But there was something else.

There used to be a warm sensation inside his chest. Just a small one—he hardly felt it, but knew it was there. It made him feel brave when he was afraid. Gave him courage to do the right thing. Made him know when he'd done something bad. But now... It was gone. He felt empty and hallow. With his eyes closed, he tried to reach out to it. There was nothing. Just a cold, empty cavern in his chest. Had it worked? Had they severed his tie to his faith? He still felt the magic inside, knew it hummed within. But the eyes of the Elsarius were no longer upon him. Ice ran through his veins. Was this what Lailen had told him about? Was he forsaken?

His eyes flickered open and he saw his blood spattered over the stones. Someone's black boots marched toward him. A rough hand gripped his upper arm and yanked him up. It hurt, pulling a weak whimper out of him.

"Get this one settled," the Archon Knight barked to the Anakrite. "He'll spend some time in your dormitories, but I have plans for him. Make sure he stays."

Phael felt himself violently shoved into someone else's grip. He blinked several times, and his vision came back clearer each time. The Anakrite had hold of him now. He looked around. Could he run? He noticed Alowyn and the other Claret—the Modeus Claret—were gone. How long had he been out?

"Of course, Archon," the Anakrite said. His claws dug hard into Phael's arm, bruising him. "He won't so much as think about running away."

He wanted to snap that he'd do it. He'd flee the moment he had the chance. But his spinning head told him if he opened his mouth, he'd vomit over the altar.

A rough gloved hand gripped his face, forcing him to look the Archon Knight in the eye. He glared at him from beneath long black tresses. "If you so much as think about running," he growled, "I'll hunt you down. I won't kill you right away. But you'll wish you were dead. Do you understand?"

Phael took a shuddering breath and tried to nod, but the Knight's grip on his face was too strong. The man shoved him away hard, making him stumble.

"Gently, Archon," the Anakrite said, holding Phael up. "They are weak after they bind. You don't want to break him, do you?"

Phael didn't look the Archon Knight in his eyes, focusing instead on the ground. A few more words were said before the Anakrite bid the Knight farewell and pulled Phael to a door near the back.

"I will show you to the dormitories once we've seen to your wound," the Anakrite said. "My name is Halith, and I will watch over you until your Knight comes for you. You will stay here and fulfill your duties as a Claret of the Modeus, do you understand?"

"Elsarius save me," Phael whispered as Halith forced him through some torch-lined hallways.

"I am afraid the Elsarius have abandoned you," Halith said. "You will say your prayers and sing your worship to the Modeus now, the ones who will bless you every night."

Phael didn't understand. He couldn't believe the Elsarius would abandon him like this. And he'd never say a prayer to the Modeus. Not if his life depended on it.

Halith led him past the chapter house, a few cloisters, and a garden before taking a turn down another, much darker hallway. The sun had set it seemed. Outside, the bells rang midnight.

"Your duties are to provide your Knight with the magic he needs to fight," Halith said. "Every night you will pray for that bond to be strong, for the Modeus to bless you. If you do not, the magic may run weak. It is up to you to keep your Knight strong. When he needs it, you must take your Knight's crystals and pray over them, recharging them. Should you not do this... Well, I hate to think what they might do to you. Remember, child: you are replaceable. Your life is tied to your Knight's, but his is not tied to yours. If you value your life at all, you will do these things."

Phael almost scoffed into the darkness. Did he value his life anymore? He wasn't so sure. But when they turned and entered a large oaken door to their right, he changed his mind immediately. The room seemed to be some sort of infirmary. A few beds were scattered around, and shelves upon shelves of herbal remedies, potions, and other liquids lined the walls. Several Clarets moved about, administering to some lying in the beds. Others bound wounds on a few Knights. The place smelled of cold stone and something sterile, something too clean.

That's when Phael saw him: Nox sat on a table just inside the door, his hand being bandaged. Nox looked up when Phael and Halith entered. Both Clarets lit up at the sight of one another.

"Nox!" Phael cried. Halith let him pull free of his grip when he ran to Nox. Nox slid off the table and engulfed Phael in an embrace. His freshly bandaged hand went to the back of his head and pressed Phael into him. "I thought that Knight took you."

"He did," Nox said. "It seems he is to be given a residence, and I am to live with him once he acquires it."

Phael's heart fell at this. "We'll be separated?" he asked.

Halith nodded, clasping his hands before him. "The favored are often are given their own land, eventually. Trylian has had something of a soft spot for Roan and his companions for years. I suspect you won't be with us long," he said to Phael. "Once Roan, Son of Monguard, has proven himself, he may be given an estate. So long as there is one to give. But Trylian has never had an issue forcing others out of their homes."

Phael didn't release Nox's hands. He wanted to hold them forever. But his own left hand ached and still bled. Halith reached forward, forcing them to let one another go.

"Healer," he called, and a Claret rushed to them, bandages and ointment in hand. Halith guided Phael onto the table and made him sit.

Phael obeyed, his hand in pain and still bleeding. As the healer went to work on it, Phael looked to Nox. "Did you feel it?"

Nox met his eyes with his own pools of darkness. "The Elsarius are gone," he whispered. "I felt them turn their backs on me. I feel empty inside."

"How do we still have our magic then?" Phael asked.

Halith answered this with, "Your magic is a gift from the Winds. It is *yours*. The source of its power has changed is all. And you must pray to the Modeus to keep it strong."

"How?" Nox asked, disbelief twisting his beautiful face.

"Their presence in me has vanished. Like I have been forsaken."

"You have," Halith said easily. "You have done the greatest sin: bound to a Knight of the Modeus. The Elsarius will not hear you now."

Something like terror, fear, and panic rose in Phael. It was hopelessness. How could they cut him off from his faith like that? How could the Elsarius blame him for something he fought against with all his might? He didn't want this. It wasn't his fault. And yet, he knew Halith was right. He felt it. The Elsarius no longer looked upon him.

"You," he said to Nox, "must hurry to the dormitories. It is getting late, and you need to rest. No doubt your Knights will be training tomorrow. Don't forget your prayers."

Nox glared at the Anakrite but obeyed. He bowed his head and marched out, only to be escorted by another Claret waiting just outside the door.

"You steal Clarets of the Elsarius often?" Phael asked.

Halith nodded and raised his brows in mock thought. "The Modeus see fit to not bless us as often as the Elsarius. We have more Knights than Clarets. But it is of little consequence. We have you."

Phael couldn't stop the tear that appeared in his eye and fell down his bruised cheek. He looked around. Could the Sactrium be easily escaped? If it was anything like the Sanctuary he'd grown up in, the answer was no. The walls and guards would keep him in.

The healer kept up his work, cleaning the wound that penetrated his entire hand. Phael winced as the healer poked and prodded, pouring some sort of ointment over the wound before binding it.

Behind them, a man on a bed screamed. Several Clarets rushed past them and dashed to the bed behind them. Phael craned his neck around and looked. On a bed several feet behind him, a man screamed and thrashed, calling to the Modeus to save him. Sweat plastered his long brown hair to his face and his eyes rolled in his head as he gasped. The man was bound to the bed by chains. A single black vein throbbed in his temple.

"What's wrong with him?" Phael asked, never having seen such a display.

"Crystal madness," Halith said offhandedly, but his eyes turned serious and latched onto the mad man. "Not from regular crystals, mind you. No, he used corrupted crystals. Ones touched by a darkness we have never found the origin to."

"Like the one that bound us," Phael whispered, his eyes unable to leave the sight of the raving madman. "They say they do not need to be recharged. That some other power keeps them full of magic. They say they are stronger than uncorrupted crystals."

"They are. But they syphon the life essence of their users. They are addictive as well, as their use brings with them a sense of..." Halith narrowed his eyes, trying to think of a word. "They make one feel invincible. Euphoric. Unstoppable. The more they are used, the stronger they can become. This man used the fire crystal above all else. He used it until he was able to summon a pillar of fire from the sky. But that is a risk."

"Why?"

"Whatever is inside the crystals begins to whisper to the one who wields it," Halith went on. "Telling them to do things. They can be very persuasive. Especially when they promise more and more power. The only crystal that can control a man's mind is a certain corrupted crystal. This man was on a quest to find it."

"What would happen if he found it?" Phael gulped. He didn't mention that the Elsarius taught that the corrupted crystals came from the Modeus. He didn't want to argue that point.

"The man's words would become like your own thoughts. He could command you to kill your closest friend and you'd believe it was your own idea. You'd do it and convince yourself you had to." Halith quickly raised his brows and shrugged. "Every Modeus Knight has set out at least once to find such a crystal. It is a mythical quest, in my opinion."

"Why use them?" Phael asked. "If this is what it comes to."

Halith laughed out loud at this, though softly. "Humans and Vyrkarians alike all think they are the exception. They will not fall to such a fate. They will do something differently. But it is never so. The hubris of mortal kind."

Phael agreed in his mind.

"But they say there is one who could wield such crystals," Halith said, something of reverence coming into his tone. "The Scion of the Modeus."

Phael's heart turned cold at the thought. He was glad such a powerful man did not walk in the western realms.

"Done," the healer said before departing.

Phael inspected his bound hand. It hurt badly, but at least the wound was clean.

"To the dormitories, then," Halith said. He led Phael out and back into the stone maze that was the Sactrium.

They walked across a green ward and through an orchard before they came to the dormitories set apart for the Knights' Clarets.

"Sleep well, my child," Halith said, motioning for him to go inside. "Be aware that the Sactrium is patrolled. You cannot escape, so do not try. For your own good."

He opened the dormitory door and shoved Phael inside before departing.

Phael stood awkwardly at the head of the long open room. The place was lined with wooden bunk beds and filled with young Clarets just like him. Some looked older, but none as old as Olenar or Lailen. Their eyes went to him. With so many eyes on him, he withered a little.

"Phael," Nox called, running up to him. "Come here. Sleep near me."

Glad to see Nox, Phael gripped his hand and let him lead him down the row of beds. Each bed had a large trunk at the foot of it. He guessed this was where the Clarets kept their personal items. He had nothing. Not so much as something to wear to bed. And his robes were still torn from when that Knight had assaulted him. He began to shake.

"There's a cloak and some clothes in the trunks," Nox said, and relief flooded over Phael. "But there's nowhere to change."

Phael flushed red and gripped his torn robe, closing it up over his chest.

"Here." Nox pointed to a set of beds near each other and sat down. He helped Phael sit and then faced him.

Neither of them spoke for some time. Phael looked around and noticed the other Clarets hadn't stopped staring at them.

"Where are the others?" he asked. "Alowyn and that other one?"

"They will live in the Archon's estate," Nox explained. "Their Knights—his sons—live with him. And...I'm soon to leave as well, they say."

Fresh tears filled Phael's eyes.

"You are, too," Nox said, as if that were a good thing. "The rumors are that the Archon Knight favors our Knights and will give them estates of their own. We'll be able to roam the city."

Phael gulped. *And escape?* he wondered. He took a shuddering breath.

"But we can talk more later," Nox sighed. "We need rest. Winds know when the Knights will come for us tomorrow." He turned and lay down on the bed, putting his back to Phael. "Get some sleep. We'll talk in the morning."

Phael wanted to argue but knew Nox was right. He looked around and took in the eyes that still watched him. The only way to close them out was to shut his own eyes. So he did. He lay down, pulled his knees to his chest, and closed his eyes.

He was a captive. He was bound to a Knight of the Modeus. His life as he knew it was over.

He wept silently until sleep took him.

But it was not a restful night. Dreams came to him, but they were not his own. He saw a castle that he'd never been in before and felt that a monster was chasing him. He ran and hid, crying and afraid. Then he dreamed he was a Knight, marching and performing drills over and over. Then the darker dreams returned. Phael thought something evil pursued him. So he ran. He ran until his own panting woke him.

Phael sat up in the darkness of the dormitories, sweat beading down his neck. Those had not been his dreams. He knew, somehow. *Those were my Knight's dreams,* he thought to himself. *How did we share them?* Was this some Modeus magic? Or was it something else? He laid back down and curled in on himself. He closed his eyes and reached out for the Elsarius. He felt the Winds, but they were dark. He called out and the Modeus answered. A tear leaked from his eye and dribbled down his nose. Was he forsaken? He hadn't chosen to bind to the Modeus. It didn't seem fair. He'd heard of men turning their backs on their faith, but never had he heard of the faith turning their backs on their faithful.

Yes, he was forsaken.

The emptiness consumed him. He was alone, abandoned.

He went to sleep again, hoping to dream of something more pleasant, even if he did have to share it with the red-haired Knight.

CHAPTER XI

Trylian stood before the massive hearth in his library with his hands behind his back, clasped gently together. He wore a simple blue tunic tonight, foregoing his more elaborate robes and other trappings. He was to meet Gaelin Hamlin of Caeth, a fellow Archon Knight and Modeus worshiper. But tonight, he didn't want to adorn himself in the pomp and frills Gaelin had come to expect. He even took his sword off and had lain it across the library's table, along with the knife he normally kept in his boot. Tonight, he wanted to show Gaelin that he trusted him entirely. This alliance was important.

Elendir waited in a corner near a large globe that showed the conquered world. Parts of the east were filled in, as well as a few areas in the south. One day, Trylian hoped to conquer more of that world. To go farther into the east than any man ever had. To take the lands there and learn their ways. But that was in the future. The present was now. The present was whatever plan Gaelin Hamlin was bringing.

He glanced at his Claret. Elendir had been working harder than ever before and it had worn him down. He still looked tired and his eyes were surrounded by dark circles.

"The new Clarets?" Trylian asked and Elendir looked up. "How are they settling in?"

"Athael is a good boy," Elendir said softly. "He was strong

in the Modeus before we bound him. He will do well with Gareth. Alowyn is destroyed, for now. He weeps continuously and cowers in the rooms we gave them."

Trylian wasn't surprised. He'd taken many an Elsarius Claret and forced them to bind to his men. Elendir had been one of those Clarets long ago. But he was loyal now. And Trylian loved him. "I want them to share rooms. Move Tanis to his own room and have Alowyn join him. I want them together as much as possible. They need to bond."

Elendir nodded, but didn't move.

A knock sounded on the library's great oaken doors and one of them opened. A servant introduced the other three Archon Knights: Baelian, the half-Vyrkarian of second column, Thaniel of third, and Mathis of fourth. They didn't have their Clarets with them.

"I'm glad you made it," Trylian said. "Gaelin Hamlin is coming tonight with a promised plan for our next move."

"Any idea what it might be?" Baelian asked in his smooth, deep voice as he took a seat around the table near the fire.

Trylian shook his head, watching Thaniel help himself to the wine on the table. Mathis took a seat opposite Baelian and drummed his long fingers on the table. His brow furrowed a little.

"Congratulations on the killing of the Thane's daughter," Mathis said flatly. "We hear you may have started a war."

"If all goes well, we can only hope." Trylian smiled.

"Are your sights still set on Delsinor?" Mathis asked. "I cannot imagine us taking the capital. It will be difficult. Days' worth of a siege. Many lives will be lost."

"And," Thaniel put in, "who will sit on that throne once we take Delsinor? Hmm?"

Trylian heard the snark in the Archon Knight's accusation. But there was no need to cover up his intentions. Thaniel was right. "Me, of course," Trylian said simply. "With you as my council. Together we shall reign over Adorian and take it back for the Modeus."

This placated Thaniel a little. The man didn't argue back or offer another thought. He knew better.

Another knock sounded on the door. A servant began to shout an introduction before they even opened the door. "Archon Knight Gaelin Hamlin of Caeth to see you, sir."

Both doors opened and Gaelin Hamlin strode in. He was tall, but not quite as tall as Trylian, who was a giant among men. He had short brown hair and keen gray eyes. His armor, an entire set, glinted in the hearth light. He held his helmet under one arm and rested his other hand on the hilt of his sword. Behind him came his Claret. He had angled features and a permanent snide look on his elegant face. His white hair had been cropped to his shoulders, unlike others who wore it long down their backs. They entered and sauntered over to the table.

Trylian came around the table and offered Gaelin Hamlin a bow. "I trust your journey here from Caeth was a good one."

"A fine march," Gaelin said, holding his head high and not returning the bow Trylian offered. His eyes went to the other Archon Knights around the table and then to Elendir. "I wasn't expecting such a reception. Is this necessary, Trylian?"

"Is this?" Trylian gestured to the armor and sword. "I come in peace, you know." He grinned and poured Gaelin some wine.

"The road is a dangerous place," Gaelin said simply, taking the wine. He raised it and then took a quick sip. "But you are correct. I've been here two days. I don't trust you. Surely you can understand. I know what you're plotting."

"We're all on the same side, Hamlin," Trylian said darkly. "This charade is unnecessary. We all want the Modeus to reign again. To destroy the simpering ways of the Elsarius and their peaceful sympathies. They were made to be conquered."

"May the Winds be at our backs," Gaelin said in an old, traditional toast before taking another drink. He motioned for his Claret to take a seat and he did. Then he lowered himself into a chair around the table.

Trylian followed him, sitting across from him. Elendir hovered behind him, hands clasped. Gaelin's eyes went to Trylian's left hand, where a ring with an orange crystal in it waited on his finger.

"You see?" Gaelin said, smiling and wagging his finger. "You come prepared as well. We are all men of action. We understand one another. Lies are not needed. Caution is not a fool's game."

"True," Trylian said, spinning the ring on his finger. "Now, what news do you bring from Caeth?"

Gaelin leaned back a little and sighed. Then he stood and looked down at the map of the western realms on the library table before them. He pointed to a small village just south of Delsinor. "You know the Thane of this village?"

"Thane Merdoc," Trylian said. Annoyance flared up in him immediately. He hated being treated like a simpleton.

"Highly influential," Gaelin went on. "The king loves him. Often has him in court for council and even goes hunting with him."

"With a mere Thane?" Trylian asked.

Gaelin raised his brows and nodded. "But he will be away in a few weeks and his castle will be vulnerable. He and his men are traveling to Delsinor."

"And?" Mathis asked.

Trylian stopped himself from rolling his eyes. "We attack his castle," he said. "Take his land. Take his village."

"Exactly," Gaelin beamed. "When he comes back, we take him and convince him to join the Modeus. Then we have a foothold there."

Trylian slowly brought his hand to his chin and rubbed at

the stubble there. It was a stupid plan. Convince a man to join the Modeus? He couldn't imagine how to do that. Yes, Elendir had converted, but only after years of torment and servitude. They didn't have years. No, Trylian knew he was getting older. They needed to move sooner and faster.

An idea hit him, but he couldn't speak it to Gaelin Hamlin. He stifled a dark grin.

"Sounds like a good plan," he said instead. He smiled at Gaelin. "I will reach out to you when we are ready to move. Until then, wait for my word."

A few more words of pleasantries were spoken, Mathis regaled Gaelin with a few tales of their exploits, and soon Gaelin was gone and satisfied.

"You're not going through with that plan," Elendir said gently, knowing his Knight's mind.

Mathis and Thaniel looked surprised, but Baelian smirked, knowing his friend.

"You will attack the Thane on the road," Baelian said. "Take him out with no need to lay siege to his castle."

"Yes," Trylian said simply. "I will have Roan lead a column."

"Roan?" Mathis roared. "He's a boy. He's not an Archon Knight. He's not even first column."

"He's obedient," Trylian snapped. "I trust him more than I trust any of you."

"This will sour our relationship with Gaelin Hamlin," Thaniel reminded them.

"Hamlin is an Archon Knight." Trylian shrugged. "Once we have the Thane's castle, we will implement our own Thane. One of you, perhaps?" He let his eyes land on Mathis.

"That...would be agreeable," Mathis mumbled, avoiding Trylian's piercing blue eyes. "But I cannot leave Aatheria. I won't give up my place as Archon Knight. Not yet."

"Then we'll appoint a Thane of our own," Trylian said. It

didn't matter that Mathis wanted to stay. They had plenty of nobles who were loyal to the Modeus. Any one of them was as good as the next.

"Roan won't understand," Elendir offered softly.

Trylian shrugged. "He doesn't need to understand. He needs to obey. And he will."

"And when Gaelin finds out what we've done?" Baelian asked.

Trylian sighed sadly. "The actions of a disobedient Knight. Roan will be punished for his transgression."

Mathis's brow fell at this. "You will torment the boy? I thought you held him in higher regard than that."

Trylian's eyes flashed. "This is why it must be Roan. He will obey and he won't ask questions."

CHAPTER XII

Roan woke early on the second day of having his Claret. The first day, Halith, the Anakrite, had not let them spar together. He'd insisted they spend the day getting to know one another, but that had not happened. Phael was quiet and kept his eyes, often filled with tears, on the ground. He followed Roan about the caer's grounds, but didn't speak much. Roan had asked him a few questions, but was met with either silence or one-word answers. So he spoke instead. He told Phael about his father's death; being raised by Trylian; his mother, Lady Juliana; and his hopes for becoming first column and eventually being an Archon Knight.

"Because of you, I'm second column now," Roan said after he picked Phael up from the Sactrium and they both walked back to the caer to spar with Razvin and a few others on the second day. "I completely leapt over third and went right to second." He couldn't stop the grin that pulled at his face.

Phael kept his eyes on the ground. It had rained the night before, the ground black with mud and the sky gray. The spring storms had been keeping the days dreary and cool. Roan looked down and noticed Phael's white boots were covered in mud, as were the ends of his white robes. The Modeus robes had low necklines, showing Phael's delicate collar bones and part of his thin shoulders. Roan couldn't help but judge him a little. He was so thin, fragile. He couldn't imagine him wielding a sword or fighting.

"I'm not sure how this works," he confessed as they came closer to the caer and the walls surrounding it. "Halith and Elendir will be teaching us today. Telling us what we need to know. I suppose your part is simple enough."

Phael didn't give any indication that he'd heard Roan and this angered him. He gnashed his teeth as he looked at his Claret and wanted to grab his arm, swing him around, and force him to look into his eyes.

"Do you hear me?" he growled instead.

His tone must have been enough because the Claret raised his wide blue eyes to Roan's green ones and nodded silently.

Satisfied, Roan shook his head and led the way in silence. They were let into the gate and he wound his way around the ward, past the smithy, and to the training ground. It was only partially full of other Knights and a few Clarets standing nearby. Some were sparring and others were in deep conversation. Some of the Knights were much older than Roan and were watching the younger Knights work. He spotted Elendir and Halith near a small open part of the grounds, waiting with Razvin and his new Claret, Nox.

Roan noticed Phael perk up the moment he laid eyes on the black-eyed Claret. His steps grew stronger and his head no longer homed in on the ground before him. He even pulled away with his strides a little to reach them before Roan. Phael stood by Nox and the Clarets shared a glance.

"Are you working with us today?" Roan asked Razvin, smiling. "I thought you'd have better things to do."

"I do, being first column now," Razvin smirked, crossing his arms over his chest. Behind him, his tail flicked in anticipation. The way he raised his head made his horns point to the sky. "But I wanted to help train you. And afterward, I want to show you something."

"Razvin has been given an estate," Halith sighed, waving his hand in exasperation. "He's most pleased with it."

"Really?" Roan asked, a drop of jealousy splashing into his stomach. He couldn't inherit his father's estate until Trylian granted it to him, being the steward after Monguard's death. Trylian had withheld it for so long, Roan was sure he would never get it.

Razvin looked put out at his secret being told. "Yes," he snarled, glaring at Halith. "About a mile from your keep. We're neighbors." He grinned, showing his fangs. "It's not a keep like your home, but it's a good-sized manor, with farmland around it. I have my own land! There's everything I need to make Kelroth's best mead."

Roan couldn't stop the genuine smile that pulled through his jealousy. Razvin deserved the promotion, he knew that. He'd been a good Knight, and it was about time he came into his own.

"We should celebrate with a feast and revelries," Roan said.

"And mead," Razvin added with a nod.

"Out from under your father's thumb," Roan said, slapping Razvin on the shoulder. "You're a man now, my son."

Razvin laughed lightly. Before he could speak again, Halith said, "Enough congratulations, my boys. We have work to do. Roan and Phael, I want you to spar with Tanis and Alowyn."

Roan smirked with confidence. "If you insist. I'll crush that runt, though."

Just as he said this, the twins entered the yard, their Clarets in tow. Alamar came behind them with Veryl close beside him. Veryl looked just as despondent as he usually did, eyes sad and downcast. Roan had known Veryl for a few years now, since Alamar was a year older than him. He hoped Phael wouldn't be that sullen for that long. Not that he needed anything from the Claret; he'd already taken everything he needed from Phael.

"Ready yourself, boy," Roan jeered to Tanis, taking up a wooden sword with a blue gem inlaid into the hilt.

"Don't get cocky," Tanis called back. He tightened a vambrace with a purple gem inside it around his wrist.

"Clean combat, boys," Elendir said softly, hands behind his back as he backed up to the side of the yard. "Don't kill each other. Trylian will be most upset if you do."

Roan licked his lips and grinned at Tanis as he readied his stance. Tanis was two years younger than Roan, but was tall for his age. He wasn't near as broad and muscled as his brother Gareth. But Roan knew he was quick. He'd spent years training with the twins and knew their strengths. But that also meant Tanis knew his.

Roan circled Tanis and spun the wooden sword in his hand lightly. He feinted to the left and then swung from the right. As Tanis raised his sword to block the blow, Roan called on the magic for the first time. He felt a sudden connection to Phael, and a wash of emotions engulfed him. Sorrow filled his eyes, fear clenched his heart, and despair wound around his brain. But over that came a surge of strength, and he shot a blast of ice from his left hand, hitting Tanis hard in the chest.

Tanis stumbled backward but didn't let the blow stop his concentration. He raised his left hand and shot a pulse of energy behind him just as Roan moved to hit him again with the magic. Confused at first, Roan moved to hit Tanis with his sword. But the blast wasn't for him. Phael screamed and was knocked off his feet, blown backward by the magic blast. As Phael was hit, the ice storm faltered and died.

"What the hells?" Roan growled, backing away.

"If Phael loses concentration, your magic falters," Elendir said easily from where he stood a safe distance away. He motioned for Roan to go to Phael. "See that he's all right."

Glaring at Tanis, Roan shoved past him and ran to Phael. The Claret's head had hit the stone wall behind him and blood trickled down his scalp, reddening his white hair. He panted and tears crawled down his thin cheeks. He looked at Roan, confused and frightened.

"Protect your Claret," Halith called. "Keep him a safe distance away."

Roan hauled Phael to his feet and clasped his shoulders. "I'm sorry. Are you all right?"

Phael sniffled, but nodded. "I didn't know... I mean, I didn't think he'd... I'm sorry."

Roan shook his head. "Not your fault. I'm supposed to make sure you're safe." He looked around. "Stand farther back, behind that line of posts." He pointed to a set of sparring posts. To Elendir, he asked, "How far away can a Claret be before I lose the magic?"

"We've experimented with such a question," the older Claret said softly. "It seems to grow weak at a mile or so. Gone at two miles. So don't be afraid to leave him behind you, but always watch him when you do. During a battle, an enemy may send a column to find your Clarets and kill them if you cannot see them. Keep them safe."

"All they do is stand around," Alamar jeered from where he leaned against the stone wall, watching.

"We do more than that," Elendir corrected, for once sounding stern. Roan had never heard the Claret use a tone like that before. "Our magic is in our prayers. We keep you safe while you battle. We keep the magic strong."

Alamar rolled his eyes at this.

"If you don't believe me, just have Veryl stop praying for a week. See what happens," Elendir chirped easily. He was unafraid of Alamar, and Roan admired that about the frail Claret.

However, Roan didn't know how much of that he

believed, either. Yes, he believed in the Winds and the Modeus, but did prayer really have such power? And what did it matter when every Claret prayed for the same thing?

"Again," Halith called.

Roan and Tanis faced off again. Roan tried to get to Alowyn like Tanis had to Phael. He tried to get in line of sight to throw ice at him, tried to slide around Tanis to strike at the Claret, but Tanis protected Alowyn better than he had Phael. Soon, he gave up and just went for Tanis, knowing he could overpower the slighter boy. And soon he did. Using his ice magic and his own brute strength, he soon had Tanis on the ground.

"Well fought," Halith said, clapping lazily. "Now, come here." He led the boys to a table of crystals. He motioned to them all. "Mined in the mountains of Vyrkaris," he said. "Each one unique. Only the Sanctuary and the Sactriums have the authority to sell the crystals. It is against the law of the west to sell them outside the protection of our faith. If you ever see someone selling them in the darker corners of the city, they are to be reported. Understood?"

The boys mumbled understanding. Roan ran his eyes over the colorful crystals laid out before them. Phael was close by his side now. They both leaned over the table to look. Tanis and Gareth's eyes were wide with wonder and a hunger for the power. Roan picked up a purple one and noticed it was like the one Tanis had been using before.

"What we call telekinetic magic," Halith explained to Roan. "A force we cannot see. But we can feel it." He smiled at Phael and his still-bloodied head. "Fire," he said, picking up an orange one. "Ice is blue, thunder and lightning, yellow. Green will split the earth and control earthen growths. This one that looks like gold will summon the very Winds themselves."

"Are these the only kinds there are?" Roan asked.

"As far as you are concerned, yes," Elendir said stoically.

The boys all exchanged looks with one another. "What does that mean?" Gareth asked with a knowing smirk.

"Corrupted crystals?" Phael asked.

Everyone snapped their heads up at the soft voice. Roan was shocked to have heard the Claret speak at all.

"Ah," Halith sighed. "Yes. They have an opaline sheen to them. Like the binding crystal. But they are not to be used by you." He eyed the boys.

"Why not?" Tanis asked. "I've heard they don't need to be recharged with prayer." He reached down and picked up a white crystal that had the faintest orange hue to it. "This one is empty. Corrupted crystals don't empty out."

"Do you know why?" Halith asked gravely. "Because they take the life essence of the one who wields them. Killing you slowly. Draining you."

"But they're stronger," Alamar put in. "I heard a story of a Knight who conjured an entire storm with a yellow crystal because it was corrupted."

"They are dangerous," Halith snapped.

"Shouldn't that be up to the Knight?" Roan asked. He was curious about these more powerful crystals. More power couldn't be all that bad. "If one desires to wield a corrupted crystal, he should be allowed."

Elendir and Halith gave one another a sharp glance. "If you can find it, so be it," Elendir said softly. "We cannot stop you."

Roan let a smirk flick across his face before smothering it.

"What effect does it have on a Claret?" Nox asked.

"The bond will affect you," Elendir said gently. "It could take your life force as well, since your life is bound to your Knight. We don't know. We've seen the madness settle in, but not the death that can be brought by such use."

Only weak minds would let the magic corrode them, Roan thought. He'd be different. He would not let the magic get to him like that. He would not go mad. He was strong of mind and wouldn't succumb like some weakling.

"The crystals will be allocated to your weapons," Halith went on. "Choose wisely as they will be with you until a smith can remove them or replace them. Each night, your Claret will pray for the crystals to be replenished and thus they shall be." He eyed Alowyn and Phael. "You *will* pray to the Modeus to keep your Knight strong. That the Winds bless them. Do you understand? If you do not keep your Knight strong, he may perish in battle and thus shall your life end as well. You do this for yourself as much as for them."

Roan noted Phael's face fall and his eyes fill with tears, but he nodded, face downcast.

"Roan," a voice called from behind them.

They all turned to see Trylian, wearing no armor, come around the bend and into the yard. Trylian held up his hand and flicked his finger to order Roan to come to him. "Bring your Claret," he said.

Roan turned, gripped Phael hard by his wrist, and pulled him along, following Trylian into the cloisters surrounding the training yard. Phael struggled against him just once before Roan squeezed harder, warning him. Then the Claret trotted after him without pulling against him. Roan let go once Trylian stopped and turned to face them.

"I have a mission for you," Trylian said. His eyes were narrow, and his brows dipped in a slight frown; Roan could tell he was being serious. So he waited. "There is a Thane from the village south of Aatheria who will be traveling on the road between here and Delsinor in a few days' time. One of our contacts in Caeth has brought me this information and is keenly interested in his estate in the village."

Roan nodded. Often the Modeus army would siege a small keep and take the land for themselves. But it had been years since he'd heard of that happening. He wanted to ask what the plan was but knew Trylian hated being interrupted. And he had the scars to prove it. So he waited.

"I want you to find this man on the road and kill him and anyone he has with him." Trylian prodded a finger into Roan's chest. "No questions, just obedience. Do you understand?"

"Me alone?" Roan asked, eyeing Phael at his side.

Trylian shook his head. "I am giving you ten first column Knights and their Clarets. This does not mean you are an Archon Knight, not even close," he said when Roan felt his green eyes light up. "You are second column, but I trust you to do as you are told. That is why I am giving you this task. Do you understand?"

"Yes, Trylian," Roan said obediently. He didn't care that he wasn't made Archon Knight. He didn't expect it. He also didn't expect to get a mission so soon after acquiring his Claret. Excitement rose in him like a hot geyser. He clenched his fists to stop them from shaking.

"And you." Trylian turned his sharp finger onto Phael. "You do your part and Roan lives. If anything goes wrong, you are dead. You are replaceable. Roan is not. Do you understand?"

Roan watched Phael swallow hard and nod his white head silently. His Claret began to shiver, and he knew it wasn't because of the warm spring breeze. He was nervous. This would be his first skirmish.

"I'll protect you," Roan offered. "Better than I did today. I promise."

Trylian's blue eyes snapped from Phael to the blood that had dried to his forehead. "I see. Yes, you will do better. If this Claret dies, I can't get you a new one for some time."

"I understand," Roan said before Trylian could ask. "In addition to the ten Knights and Clarets, I'd like to bring Razvin with me. He'd be a great second-in-command and the men like him."

"None of them will like you after this," Trylian said with a gentle smirk. "A second column Knight, commander of first column? No." He shook his head. "They will hate you. May as well bring Alamar with you in that case."

"Alamar already hates me," Roan grinned back. "I'll enjoy ordering him around."

Trylian scoffed and smirked fully now. "I'm sure you will. Yes, bring the Vyrkarian. I trust your judgment."

"When do we leave?" Roan asked.

"In a week or less," Trylian said. "The travel time is great from here to Caeth. In the meantime: train. Get to know your Claret. Show him he can trust you. Use your magic. Just don't kill anyone."

Roan smiled. "I can't make any promises."

Trylian ignored this last jibe and said, "We will get you a map and show you where he's traveling. Roan, do this and you could be Archon Knight before your eighteenth birthday."

CHAPTER XIII

Trylian was right; the road from Aatheria to Delsinor was long, but traveling even farther south took longer than Roan had envisioned. He hoped they wouldn't miss their mark, but according to the plan Trylian had given them, they were right on time. The days of travel let him watch Phael. The Claret was quiet, but seemed to have a great fondness for his fellow Claret, Nox. They often walked side by side, speaking in whispers. Roan let them sleep apart from him and Razvin for most of the journey, not thinking it would do him any good to force Phael to sleep inside his tent.

Alamar, one of the first column Knights Trylian had picked for Roan, often glared at Phael. He made dark and rude comments about him, questioning his purity and poking fun at his slight frame. Roan saw Phael try to ignore Alamar but noticed how the Knight's words upset him and made him shrink in fear. Veryl, Alamar's Claret, didn't speak to the others, since they were not from the Sanctuary, and he didn't know them from before.

Each night, Roan would play his lute and Razvin would make the men drink just enough to get them drowsy. They often sang songs together while others patrolled the perimeter of the camp. They reported back to Roan easily, having no issue with him being the authority. Roan noted this and which

Knights seemed to respect him. Alamar, of course, did not, but he didn't acknowledge it. Not yet. He'd report to Trylian once they were back home.

One night, Roan was playing his lute alone while Razvin and a few others walked around the perimeter. Most of the other Knights had gone to bed and the evening was silent. He was plucking a melancholy tune and thinking of how his father used to sing with him. Father had taught him how to play the lute, against his mother's wishes. He was just letting himself get soaked into the memory when Phael came dashing up to him, panting. Tears filled his eyes. He didn't speak but quickly planted himself on the ground close to Roan as if he were hiding behind him. Roan looked up and saw Alamar in the distance, eyeing Phael. He glared at the other Knight.

"You can't let him know you're afraid of him," Roan said easily, stopping his plucking. He looked Phael in the face.

Phael took a shuddering breath and pulled his knees up to his chest. He looked at the lute. "I didn't think someone like you would play music."

Roan almost smiled. "Father taught me. Mother thought I should spend more time training and practicing for battle. Father said any real man who can wield a sword should know how to make music as well. 'Music doesn't make you harmless,' he used to say. 'The difference between a harmless man and a dangerous man is that a dangerous man can be gentle. A harmless man is just dangerous.' I never understood what he meant by that, but I remember it."

Phael sniffled and ran his hand under his nose, shyly looking Roan in the eyes. "It means that a man who has the ability to be dangerous is strong so long as he keeps his power under his control." He nodded to the lute. "If you can cut a man down, but those same hands have the ability to play gentle music, then you are that kind of man."

Roan shrugged with one shoulder and leaned back down

to his lute to play a few chords. "I like music. It soothes me. Being still and playing the slow melody forces me to order my mind. To rein it back under my control."

Phael swallowed and waited a moment before saying, "I can see that in you. I've also seen you during training. You're a real warrior. You're not like the others." His blue eyes darted to where Alamar and a few other men lounged, talking loudly and laughing. "You don't attack for no reason. Especially those weaker than you."

At this, Roan looked up. "Did Alamar hurt you?" He scanned Phael's body, looking for signs that the Knight had laid a hand on Phael. If he had, he'd beat the hell out of Alamar.

Phael shook his head. "Just said things to me." He avoided eye contact now, like he was afraid of Roan.

"You can tell me anything, Phael," Roan said. "I may not know you that well, but that will change. You are mine, and no one else can touch you."

The Claret gulped and nodded as though he'd been scolded. He tilted his head and pressed his cheek onto his knee, laying his head down.

Wanting to calm him, Roan said, "Tell me something that you like. Favorite song, food—anything."

Phael bit his bottom lip, and his brows pinched in confusion. He didn't respond until Roan went back to playing the sad melody. "I got in trouble more than once for stealing honey."

Roan looked up and smiled, amused at the trifling theft. Phael relaxed a little, seeing the grin. He nodded and went on.

"I love honeysuckle as well. There's a wall in the garden in the Sanctuary that's covered in it. It grows all through the spring and summer and even into the autumn. I don't know how it stays alive for so long. It smells sweet and reminds me of..." He stopped and gulped, looking away.

"Of what?" Roan pressed, changing to a more cheerful melody in a major key.

Phael's eyes flitted to Nox and back. The other Claret sat with Veryl, speaking in a low voice. Roan caught Phael's cheeks reddening, as well as the tip of his nose. He was confused at first but then understood. He glanced back at Nox. The Claret had eyes black as a starless sky that made him look sweet and innocent. Roan nodded.

"Does he know how you feel?" he asked.

Phael reddened even more and shook his head. "I don't... That is... I'm not..." He stammered, panting around his unfinished sentences.

"Forget it," Roan cut in. He wasn't that interested, anyway. He eyed Nox, though, wondering about the attraction. He'd only been attracted to women before. Like Eliana. His thoughts went to her long blonde hair and her dazzling eyes. He wondered vaguely where she was, what she was up to.

"Do you like anyone?" Phael asked.

Roan shrugged and kept playing. "I thought I did once. I don't have much time to think about it." He nodded toward Nox. "I thought Clarets of the Elsarius had to remain pure in mind and body."

Phael blushed deeply again and turned his face away. "It is the way. But all pure things must be pursued with vigilance and discipline."

Roan tilted his head to look at Phael. "Tell me about life in the Sanctuary. I've never been to Delsinor."

Phael cleared his throat gently and rocked a little before he answered. "The Sanctuary is beautiful. I was brought there as a child. I remember the first time I heard the bells, the Clarets singing inside. The smell of the incense. It's all wonderful. The sunlight plays through the stained-glass windows like fairies from stories. The smoke often filters through the sunbeams, looking like gentle ghosts." He stopped and his eyes shone with unshed tears.

Roan realized this must be painful for him. He strummed a chord and sighed. "We need to sleep." He stood.

"Can I..." Phael asked quickly, reaching up as if to stop Roan from leaving, "...sleep in your tent tonight?"

The request didn't seem that strange. Roan shrugged. "I don't care. If you snore, I'll kick you."

PHAEL SAT AWAKE, watching Roan sleep. The Knight had laid out his gauntlets and sword, which had the crystals embedded into them. Phael was to pray over them and make sure they were fully charged and ready for battle the next day. But he didn't think he could betray the Elsarius and pray to the Modeus. Despite the fact that he was forsaken. What would happen to Roan in battle if he didn't pray, though?

He took a shuddering breath and hovered his hands over the crystals. He closed his eyes and felt his hands shaking. "Please," he whispered, "forgive me." Hot tears rose up in his eyes. "I'm sorry, I don't know what to do. I cannot pray to the Modeus. Elsarius, give me strength. Bless these crystals, give them power and shine your protection down on Roan." He sniffled and took a calming breath. "Keep him safe. For me." He felt nothing.

Phael opened his eyes and looked down at the crystals. They hadn't gotten any darker in color. His heart fell. He clasped his hands together and pressed his forehead into them, rocking back and forth on his knees. The tears fell.

"I can't," he moaned softly, not wanting to wake Roan. "I cannot pray to the Modeus. Please, Elsarius, help me. Hear me. I know he's not a servant of yours, but please help me. I have faith that you won't abandon me. Bless these crystals and give them power."

He looked down again and saw there was still no change. His breath hitched in a sob. They were going into a small skirmish, that was true. It wasn't a full-on battle. Maybe he didn't need to bless the crystals? Perhaps Roan would be all right and not use them.

"Don't be a fool," Phael chided himself. He re-clasped his hands and closed his eyes, shaking. "I can do this. Just once."

He waited a moment, feeling like the Modeus looked down on him now, knowing the pain he was in. He swore he felt the aspect's pleasure. He gathered himself and stopped another sob that wanted to escape his throat. "Laugh at me all you like," he said steadily. "I am not here for me. I don't pray to you in subjugation, but out of necessity. Bless these crystals. Protect Roan, your servant. Don't let harm befall him."

Phael gently placed his hands over the crystals and found he still shook.

"Give them power and might. Fill them with your magic."

A slight wind rustled through the tent then, chilling Phael. Then he felt it in his chest. His magic ignited and heated him. He gasped as air filled his lungs, the Winds rushing inside him. He waited a moment more before he opened his eyes and looked down. Slowly, he pulled his hands away from the crystals and inspected them. They were deeply colored now, full of magic. Phael let out a breath he'd been holding and swallowed hard. He felt dirty. Like he'd done something wrong.

"Elsarius, forgive me," he whispered. He felt nothing. "Am I forsaken? Do not abandon me." Emotion rose in him, and he couldn't stop the sob that tore from his throat. That's when he felt eyes on him. He was not alone. The Modeus watched him even now. They had heard his prayers. Phael wiped at his tears and let out a defeated sigh.

Without waiting another moment, he crawled back to his

bedroll and got under the blankets, hiding himself away from the Modeus's gleeful eyes. He huddled down deep and closed his eyes, weeping and praying for forgiveness.

A THRILL SHOT through Roan as he looked back at the long line of Knights and Clarets following him. He had galloped ahead to find the trail of the convoy carrying the Thane. It had been days, and they had finally found it. He took out a brass glass and looked through it, following the dirt road that wound around the hills and valleys. Razvin rode up behind him, panting at keeping up with him.

"Not far, surely," he huffed.

Roan shook his head, sliding the glass closed. "Anyone watching from Delsinor will see us pass. Have the men wear their cloaks to cover the Modeus insignia on their armor." He pulled his own hood up over his bright red hair. "We don't want to give them any reason to follow us. Or to come to Aatheria once they learn the Thane is dead."

Razvin nodded and kicked his horse, galloping back toward the men. Roan stayed, looking out over the rolling hills to Delsinor. The city was vast, but far away. The great river that ran from the Northern Narrows all the way down past Delsinor glittered in the late day sun. Behind him, the wind ripped through the mountains, making a low hissing sound that could be heard even this far away. They had to take a long road around Delsinor. But soon they'd meet the Thane on the road. He had no doubt left Caeth some nights ago and would be closer than Roan thought.

"He'll be just on the other side by now," Roan said to himself. "The forest just south of Delsinor." He took up his glass again and looked through it. It was powerful enough to show him the small patch of forest south of Delsinor, but he knew it was there. They needed to hurry. They needed the cover of the trees to attack the Thane in.

He turned back to the road and continued to trot up the path. He was glad for the few hills that hid the road from the prying eyes of Delsinor. He hadn't gone more than a few paces before he looked back and spotted Phael atop a hill. He had stopped his horse and gazed out to Delsinor.

Roan wheeled his horse around and trotted back to Phael. "Don't do it," he advised darkly. "Don't run."

Phael didn't turn to face him, but Roan saw a tear leak out of Phael's sad eyes. "That's my home," he whispered. "Lailen is no doubt thinking we are dead." A soft sob burst out of his pale lips.

Roan groaned and reached out to grab the reins of the horse. "Don't run," he repeated. "It's not worth it. You'll be shot before you get there."

Phael turned his face to Roan; it was creased with sadness. "You'd order them to shoot me?"

"I'd have to stop you," he replied honestly. "We cannot have you giving away our secrets, our mission. I'd have no choice."

A little gasp made Phael's chest rise and fall quickly, but he nodded. He quickly wiped at the tears and followed Roan down the hill.

The next day, they came into view of the forest. "Razvin, with me," Roan ordered.

The half-Vyrkarian trotted up beside him.

"We're going into the forest to find the convoy," he explained to the other Knights and their Clarets. "Alamar, make sure they stay here." He pointed to Nox and Phael. "We'll be back once we find them, and we'll have a plan of attack. Understood?" he said, imitating Trylian's way of speaking.

The others nodded and a few added, "yes, sir," before he turned and galloped into the woods. He kept his eyes trained on the underbrush, looking for signs that a caravan had gone through. It wasn't hard to find. The Thane traveled unsuspectingly through the woods, leaving trails in the dirt and in the foliage on the side; broken branches showed where a large carriage had gone through.

"It's too easy," Razvin said with a crooked grin.

"He doesn't know his days are numbered," Roan replied. "Let's continue on foot. He's got to be close."

Together, they dismounted and wandered into the woods. Roan crouched and pulled his hood up over his head so his bright red hair wouldn't catch the sun. Razvin, being gray-skinned and black-haired, blended into the dark green shadows of the forest. Roan lost sight of him more than once. He was hurrying through the low-hanging branches when Razvin's black-clawed hand shot out to stop him.

Without speaking, Razvin held up two fingers to his eyes and then pointed forward. Roan strained his neck up to look through the trees. Not fifty yards away he spotted smoke and the colorful walls of a rich man's carriage. He dropped to his knees and peered through the leaves again. He spotted a few horses, some guards, and a few other members of the Thane's entourage milling about. They had made camp and no doubt some were out hunting.

Roan held a finger to his lips for Razvin to remain silent, then flicked his head back the way they'd come. Together, they slinked back to the edge of the forest where the others waited.

"Maybe twelve guards," he whispered to the Knights. "Several nobles, probably lords. Kill them all. Take whatever you want. Clarets." He looked at Phael and Nox leading the group. "Stay back and stay out of sight. We'll be watching you."

He noted Nox and Phael glance at one another. If they

were going to run, now would be their chance. He prayed to the Winds they didn't run. He'd hate to have to track down and kill Phael. The weepy, frail Claret was starting to grow on him. He looked at Phael until the Claret noticed and looked back. Slowly, Phael nodded.

Satisfied, Roan got back on his horse. "We'll surround them and then attack. Wait for my signal."

The ten Knights rode into the woods, splitting up and going around the path to encircle the green where the convoy had camped. Razvin stayed close to Roan and Alamar peeled off to their left with a handful of Knights. Roan got to the area where they had spotted the camp and waited. He looked into the woods and saw a flash of steel, the sun glinting off a sword. Then he shouted.

Unsheathing his longsword, he kicked his horse in the side and charged into the green. The entourage was taken by such surprise that no one moved until Roan's blade had hacked off the head of the cook near the fire. Then all hell broke loose. The men scrambled to their weapons, shouting and calling. Roan flung a spidering net of lightning out and hit two men, making them scream and shake before they fell to the ground panting. He charged up to them and lopped their heads off as well. He spun his horse, looking for the Thane.

"Find the Thane!" he shouted, leaping from his horse and landing hard on the ground.

"Get him out of here!" one of the guards shouted, motioning to a colorful tent near the edge of the camp.

Roan put his head down and dashed to the tent. A guard outside it raised his blade and blocked the first blow. Then Roan raised his hand and used the other crystal in his vambrace: fire. A wave of hot orange tongues lashed out at the man, burning his face and singeing his beard.

"Knights!" the guard shouted, shoving Roan back. "Find their Clarets!"

Roan whipped around and saw three guards and a blacksmith with a hammer run into the woods.

"Stop them!" he shouted.

Razvin looked up from where he'd just stabbed a man and dashed after them.

With him distracted, the guard backhanded Roan hard and stabbed at him. Roan clumsily blocked the blow and redirected it into his shoulder, where the blade stabbed him just under his pauldron. He grunted in pain and reeled back, away from the second attack. Flinging another ball of fire at the man, he got his feet back under him. Then he shot a bolt of lightning from his hand and it struck the man. As he screamed and jolted in a fit, Roan hacked off the hand that held the sword and then stabbed him through the throat. The man gurgled and fell backward.

The tent stood unguarded. He took one step toward it when he remembered the Clarets. He glanced back to see Razvin and a few other Knights fending off the guards who had ridden into the forest to find them. Satisfied that Phael was safe, he flung open the tent flap and marched inside. The Thane stood in the middle of the tent, a fire poker in his hands. His face twisted in fear as he beheld Roan.

"What do you want?" the Thane stammered before his eyes went to the Modeus insignia on his armor: a snake coiled around a crescent moon. "No," he gasped. "Where did you come from?"

Roan barred his teeth as he grinned maniacally and raised his sword. "As far as you're concerned, I came from the pits of hell."

He shoved the man back and called up just enough of the flames to make his hand burn hot. He tossed aside his glove and gripped the Thane by the throat. The man screamed as his skin burned and blistered in the shape of Roan's hand. He knew he was just supposed to kill the Thane, but why not have a little fun with him first?

The man screamed, his tone going higher and higher as Roan squeezed. Finally, when he thought he couldn't stand the squealing anymore, Roan let go and stood back, picking up his sword again. The man's fine tunic and cloak were spattered red from the charred blood that leaked from his destroyed neck. The Thane scrambled back, raising one hand as if to ward off his attacker.

Roan smirked and brought his blade down hard and fast. It was sharp enough to sever the man's raised hand in one hack. The limb plopped into the grass, making the Thane squeal all over again. His eyes bulged as they followed the dribbling blood down to his hand in the grass.

"Winds save me!" the Thane screamed.

Roan shook his head. "They can't hear you now."

He raised his sword like a club and swung with all his might. The Thane's head spun off in a beautiful arch of rivulets of blood, spattering the tent walls and Roan's face. He blinked as the blood dribbled down into his eyes and he looked upon his kill. He couldn't stop the wild smile that pulled his lips up into a cruel grin.

"All you had to do was kill him," Razvin said from the entryway to the tent. "All the rest of that was unnecessary."

"He's dead, isn't he?" Roan said back, panting. "The mission is done. Doesn't matter how I finished it."

Razvin narrowed his eyes a little, but didn't reply right away. "You like killing, don't you?"

Roan shrugged, wiping his sword on a bit of grass just outside the tent. "I like doing the things I've been told to do. Trylian said I could be made Archon Knight if I did this. Why not do it well and come back with a story to tell?"

His friend waited a beat, then nodded, looking away. "Well done, then, Roan."

CHAPTER XIV

The journey back was quieter than the days it took them to get out. Razvin was silent but still joined them now and then for a song and drinking. Roan had celebrated the first night they'd camped, having the men hunt a large buck and bring back several rabbits as well. They'd stayed up late, drank, sang, and had gotten a late start on their initial journey back. But Roan didn't care. Phael stayed close to Roan most nights and slept in his tent now. Roan didn't mind. Phael was quiet and meek and didn't speak much.

They passed Delsinor without incident and met very few on the road. They did run into a caravan of nomads on their way to Aatheria, and spent several days with them on the journey, enjoying their merry company before parting ways, since the nomads needed to make a stop at the village just south of Aatheria. Roan had caught the eye of one of the nomadic women, but he didn't pursue her in any way. No, he had his mind on Eliana again, since his and Phael's conversation. He wondered about her and decided when he got back, even if he didn't receive his Archon Knighthood, he'd find her and pursue her. He was almost eighteen, after all, and it was high time he found a wife. He smiled at the thought and imagined her naked before him.

When they reached Aatheria, the men departed to their estates, congratulating Roan on a job well done, and some promised to speak to Trylian on his behalf. Roan thanked them and turned his horse toward the city streets.

"We're not going back to the caer?" Phael asked. His back was bent, and dark circles surrounded his pretty eyes.

Roan took in Phael's weariness but ignored it. "We have to report to Trylian. The sun's setting and I want to get there before it's dark. I want you with me," he said quickly when Phael opened his mouth to protest.

Casting his eyes down, Phael nodded mutely.

Together, they rode through the city and out the western gate. Not half a mile from the western gate lay Trylian's land. He had a large keep with farmland around it that grew all sorts of crops. The land was quiet, though, as all the farmers had gone in for the day. The sky was purple as the sun set and torches began to ignite over the land as the firelighters got to work.

The gatekeeper let Roan in, knowing him well, and pointed him to the front gate. They passed inside and left their horses outside in the ward. They were led into the keep that was so familiar to Roan he could have seen himself up the stairs to Trylian's library.

"It's late," the servant said, glaring at Roan. "The master might be in bed."

"He's not," Roan promised. "I know he's waiting for me."

The servant shrugged and kept walking. They wound their way up several sets of stairs over red carpets and past several opulent rooms before the man knocked on two great wooden doors.

"Enter," Trylian's voice said from within.

The servant looked a little surprised, but let Roan and Phael in. Trylian sat in a great oaken chair at the head of a table, and three other Archon Knights, all of whom Roan knew, sat with him. Elendir, Trylian's Claret, stood behind him, hands gently clasped behind his back.

Trylian met Roan's eyes and smiled. "Report?" he asked, steepling his fingers eagerly before him.

Roan looked around and spotted one man he didn't know. He almost stammered but stopped himself from speaking and looking a fool before the stranger.

"Gaelin Hamlin," Trylian offered when Roan didn't speak right away. "You may speak freely in front of him." A strange, dark glint entered Trylian's eye then, but Roan couldn't guess at its meaning. "Speak, Roan."

Roan nodded and glanced at Phael. His Claret looked warier than before but held himself tall in the presence of the Archon Knights. Roan was grateful for that. He looked back at Trylian.

"We found Thane Merdoc's convoy, just where you said it would be," he began. Trylian frowned and Gaelin Hamlin stirred in his seat. Roan swallowed. Something wasn't right. Nerves bunched under his skin, and he wasn't sure why. Trylian looked pleased but livid at the same time. Quickly, Roan imparted a short and precise narrative of what they had done, the travel, the slaughter, and then held up the Thane's tabard with his house symbol on it as proof. He dropped it on the table, smattered in blood. By the time he was finished speaking, a proud grin had spread across his face. He practically beamed and looked to Trylian for his due praise.

Trylian stood and so did Gaelin Hamlin. "You did what?" Trylian asked, his voice low and dangerous. He was furious.

Ice ran through Roan's veins. He knew that tone. He'd heard it many times in his life. It was usually followed by a bloody beating and nights of licking wounds and soothing bruises. The scared child in him rose, making him almost quell under Trylian's enraged gaze.

"I-I...," Roan stammered, not sure if he should go on. Nothing frightened him like Trylian angry. "I killed the Thane," he said after an embarrassing moment of more stammering. "Like I was ordered to." He glanced back at Phael for reassurance that he had understood the order correctly. Phael had gone so pale that his skin matched his white robes.

"Killed Thane Merdoc?" Gaelin Hamlin roared. "What is going on, Trylian? Why did this whelp kill the Thane? That was not what we discussed." The man glared at Trylian.

"Guards," Trylian called. The doors burst open and a set of four guards entered. They all wore the blue of Trylian's house, hands on their swords. "Roan, what have you done?"

"What I was ordered to do," Roan pled, the fear strangling his voice. He wrestled with the fear, trying to keep it in check. But he'd been on the receiving end of Trylian's wrath too many times to know nothing good was about to come. But why? What had he done wrong?

"This is absurd," Gaelin Hamlin roared. "What is going on, Trylian? Did you order this boy to kill Thane Merdoc or not? Have you gone back on our deal, our plan?"

"Never," Trylian snapped back. "Roan, you disobeyed me."

Roan stammered again, confused and lost. Had he misunderstood Trylian? "What did I do wrong?" he pleaded.

"You killed a man we were to make a deal with," Gaelin Hamlin snarled. "That was our way into Caeth and to surround Delsinor. That was everything! It's gone now. Our chance is gone." He glared at Roan so hard, Roan thought he felt a fire sear into his face. "I demand recompense. Punishment must be doled out. This foolhardy boy disobeyed your orders and has cost us months of preparation. Cost us our chance. He must be punished."

"I agree," Trylian said. His blue eyes bored into Roan.

Roan blinked, trying to conjure rage at the betrayal, but the fear was too cold to let the fires of anger stir. He held his ground. "I swear, I did as I was ordered to."

"You misunderstood me," Trylian said in a low, dangerous voice. "How could you be so stupid, Roan?"

Roan gulped.

"Seize him," Trylian ordered the guards.

Two of them rushed Roan and grabbed his arms, pinning them behind his back. Roan struggled against them, but they pulled his arms harder, straining his muscles.

"Trylian, please!"

"He did as you asked," Phael tried, stepping forward. The guards descended upon him next, the other two easily grappling the slight Claret.

"Phael, don't," Roan interjected. "Leave him alone."

"They must be punished," Gaelin Hamlin said softly, his face red and a vein throbbing in his temple. "I want to see it. I want to make sure you are genuine in your rage, Trylian. This boy and his Claret have cost me everything. The entire plan is ruined. I want to see blood."

Roan jerked against his captors, but they held him tight.

"Yes," Trylian said after a moment of looking Roan in the eyes. "They will be flogged. Take them outside, lash them to a hitching post, and flog them."

Roan imagined these men whipping Phael. He saw the Claret's thin, frail body in a bloody heap on the ground. He was already exhausted. He wouldn't survive a flogging from these men.

They were going to kill Phael.

The men pulled on Phael to lead him out of the room and the Claret burst into hoarse sobs.

"Wait, wait!" Roan begged, digging his heels in as the men began to haul him away. "Phael had nothing to do with this. He followed me. Did as I ordered. It's my fault. Leave him alone. Don't punish him for something I did."

Trylian glanced at Gaelin Hamlin, thinking.

"Fine," Gaelin Hamlin said, a sneer pulling at his lips.

"Then I want you to endure twice the punishment. Trylian, I want this boy beaten to within an inch of his life with hot irons."

"No!" Phael cried, his knees giving out under him. He fell to the floor, still held by the guards.

Roan struggled again to no avail. "I don't understand. Please, Trylian, tell me what I did wrong."

Trylian didn't speak. He merely shook his head, then flicked it toward the door, ordering the guards to take him out.

Roan's shoulders groaned in pain as the guards forced him back down the stairs and out into the ward where the stables were. A thick hitching post stood just outside the door. Roan tried to brace himself for the punishment that was to come. He knew he'd burn from the hot irons. He'd be bruised and maybe even bleed. The wounds would be substantial. They could get infected; they could fester, and he could die from them. He wanted to beg and plead once more but knew it would do no good. And besides, he didn't want Trylian to see him weak. To see him beg for his life.

He wiped the fear from his face and turned his expression to stone instead. Behind him, Phael still wept.

The guards pulled Roan's hands up and above his head, lashing him to the post with leather strips. They took his armor and even tore away his undershirt, baring him to the cold night air. He couldn't see the men behind him, but he heard them. He saw their shadows dancing out before him in the torchlight from the stable braziers. They were long and dark. He heard a hissing and a metal clang as a cauldron of hot irons was placed behind him. He could see the heat rising from them, rippling the shadows before him. He tensed his great shoulders and waited.

"Trylian," Gaelin Hamlin's voice said from behind him.

"If what you say is true, you won't mind punishing the boy yourself. And remember: I want to see blood."

Roan braced himself as memories flooded his brain. Dark hallways with Trylian looming in them. Dark corners he scrambled away to hide in. He saw Trylian's hand, red and shiny with his own blood. Mother never cared. She never rescued him. She let Trylian do whatever he wanted to Roan, some things worse than others.

Roan clenched his eyes shut against the images. He pulled uselessly on his arms, but his wrists were held fast.

Trylian's shadow moved and came up right behind him. Trylian gripped a handful of Roan's long red hair and pulled hard. Roan yelped softly as Trylian pulled his head back so he could look up into his face.

"This is for the good of us all," Trylian whispered. He picked up a red-hot iron and pressed it to Roan's neck, searing him from his jawline to his collarbone.

Roan couldn't stop the scream that tore from him at the pain. His flesh sizzled and he could smell it in the cool night air. Somewhere, Phael was babbling and begging. He wanted to tell the Claret to shut up or this would be him. And he'd not survive it.

Trylian pulled the iron off Roan's neck, dropped it, and grabbed another fresh one. It glowed orange in the night. Trylian stepped back then and swung. Roan gasped as the blow fell. It knocked the wind out of him while at the same time burning him. He felt a welt rise up on his back. But before he could recover, Trylian struck him again. And again. The blunt object hurt more than the burns and soon he was gasping for air. His ribs ached, and he felt bruises on his very bones. Trylian didn't spare him. He never did. He struck Roan over and over until dizziness overcame him. He couldn't breathe. His vision swam as tears drowned his eyes and then leaked down his cheeks.

More blows fell, stopping his lungs. His heart hammered. Blood heated the burning wounds on his back. Would the punishment never end? What had he done wrong?

Soon, he couldn't even hold up his head and it lolled back on his neck. His knees became weak and he would have crumpled to the ground had he not been hanging by his wrists.

"More blood," Gaelin Hamlin said.

Other voices spoke and there was a moment of reprieve when no blows fell.

Roan could hardly comprehend what was going on around him when a crack sounded through the air. Then, a sting like nothing he'd felt before lashed across his burned and welted back. Had Trylian switched to a whip? Another blow, and then another. Roan couldn't even moan. He didn't move as the flail drew more blood from his bruised and burned back.

It went on forever. He couldn't stand it anymore. He closed his eyes and his legs went limp.

"Please, stop!" Phael begged from behind him. His voice was thick with crying.

"That's enough," Elendir said. For the first time in his life, Roan heard Trylian's Claret speak strongly. "He's had enough, Trylian."

The other three Archon Knights hadn't said a thing. Just watched in silence.

Trylian had raised his hand one last time, but the blow didn't fall. Roan was grateful. His ribs were shattered, and he didn't think he could bear one more hit. His breath came ragged and shallow. Everything hurt and his flesh was searing. He felt hot blood trickling down his back. His long hair stuck to his back from the blood.

"I am satisfied," Gaelin Hamlin said at length. "Let him go. I am off."

Roan heard the man turn on his heel and walk out, the

gravel crunching under his booted feet. He hung there, wondering if anyone would let him down or if he'd have to hang from his wrists until morning. The others retreated as well, and he even heard the familiar gait of Trylian walking back to the keep, whispering softly to Gaelin. Roan stopped himself from crying out.

But then someone scampered up behind him, running full tilt. Cold, lithe hands touched his bruised and burned sides. He hissed at the contact and winced.

"I don't understand," Phael wept, reaching up to untie the leather that bound Roan. He had to stand on his toes to find the knots and untie them.

Roan shushed Phael. "It's all right," he whispered. "I'm... fine. It's all right."

Once the knots gave way, Roan's legs buckled, and he fell to the ground. Phael knelt and wrapped his thin arms around Roan and pulled with all his might. Roan knew he was too heavy for Phael to carry, so he forced himself to stand. He moaned as he stood and leaned heavily on his Claret. He saw his blood seep into the white robes Phael wore.

"To the caer," he grunted.

⁓⁓

PHAEL DID his best to haul Roan to their horses and then lead them back to the caer. Roan appreciated his effort. They got to the caer, and it was late, so no one was awake to see them. Roan guided Phael through the stone fortress and down to the infirmary, where poultices and ointments for such wounds waited.

"I'll do my best," Phael said, sniffling. He went to work cleaning the wounds, which hurt all over again. Roan groaned at the pain but marveled at Phael's light and gentle hands. "Sorry," Phael said every time Roan hissed in pain.

The Claret cleaned the wounds and then applied an ointment to stave off infection before he started to wrap Roan's entire torso in a bandage.

"Roan," Phael whispered, and his voice echoed in the stony underground. "I...That is, thank you for... For saving me."

Roan turned his head to look Phael in the eye and nodded. Phael gently took Roan's long red hair in his hands and pulled it over one of his bare shoulders as he wrapped his wounds. Silence followed. Roan didn't want to speak. He was afraid if he took a breath, his ribs might just shatter inside him. Instead, he watched Phael move around him, his eyes never leaving his Claret's face. He wanted Phael to know he was grateful. He had to say something.

Before either of them spoke again, the door at the top of the stone steps opened and Trylian came down, a spring in his step. He smiled at Roan.

Confused and worried Trylian had come to berate him again, Roan stiffened.

"Roan, you magnificent bastard," Trylian praised him softly. He opened his arms and shoved past Phael to embrace Roan.

Roan's entire body tensed in Trylian's embrace. Trylian squeezed him gently and then stood back. He placed his hands on either side of Roan's face and tilted his head down, kissing him on the forehead.

"You did so well. I am very pleased. And proud of you."

"What?" Roan snapped, jerking out of Trylian's hands. The quick movement ignited the pain on his back and he winced. His voice shook as he spoke his next words. "Why, Trylian? I don't understand. You're pleased with what I've done? I did what you asked and you—"

Trylian covered Roan's mouth with his hand, shushing him. "You cannot know why I do the things I do, Roan, my boy. But you did well to obey. But next time," his face turned dark, and his eyes sparked, "do not implicate me. Ever. Never shuffle blame onto someone else."

Trylian kissed him one more time and turned to leave. Confused, hurt, and not knowing what to say, Roan watched him ascend the steps and go out of sight.

"Why?" Phael whispered.

Roan swallowed and shook his head. "I can't know. I shouldn't know. I am to obey." All thoughts left his head then, and he looked into the middle distance, not seeing anything. All feeling left him. "I am to obey."

CHAPTER XV

"I have placed my own Thane in the village keep," Trylian said. He sat in the window, looking out over the training yard, watching Roan and his fellow Knights spar. He held a tiny dagger in his hand and tapped it against the stone around the opening.

Gaelin Hamlin stood behind him in the library. Trylian felt his eyes on him, but kept his body relaxed. The other Archon Knights were all out except for Baelian, whom Trylian permitted to be with him in most meetings. Elendir waited in the corner.

"I am finding it hard to trust you, Trylian," Gaelin said evenly. "You cannot even control those Knights closest to you. I thought you had that boy under control."

"I do," Trylian said lazily. "What Roan did was part of a plan."

"Plan?"

Trylian nodded, still focused on Roan's form below him. "I ordered Roan to kill the Thane, and he obeyed. I have complete control."

"What?" Gaelin Hamlin stammered. "But you had him beaten before me. You said—"

"I said what I needed you to hear at the time," Trylian mused. "Roan took the punishment you needed him to take in the moment."

"Why did you have your boy slaughter Thane Merdoc on the road? We had a plan!"

"My plan was simpler," Trylian said easily, stopping his tapping of the blade. "I needed you to believe that Roan disobeyed so I could summon Aramis Whitley to me and place him in the village as Thane. Which I have done. I wanted my own man in there and knew you wouldn't allow Aramis."

"Aramis Whitley?" Gaelin growled. "Of course I wouldn't. He's in your pocket, Archon. I wanted a more neutral party installed. Merdoc would have bent the knee eventually."

"I cannot wait for eventually." Trylian's right brow raised in amusement. "And obviously I wanted someone *I* could trust."

Gaelin didn't move from where he stood on the other side of the room. His eyes calculated before he spoke again. "You wanted to show his obedience. To show he'd do anything you said. It was a risk, Trylian. What if I had asked for his death?"

"I knew you wouldn't."

"And why the display of obedience?"

Trylian smiled wickedly. "It wasn't just for you. I have plans for Roan. I needed to know he would do as I asked without question. I needed the others to see his fealty to me."

"Why?"

Trylian's smile never faltered. He shook his head. He'd not divulge his plans now.

Gaelin looked affronted, his lips turning down in annoyance. "I can't trust you anymore, Archon."

Trylian turned and made eye contact with Gaelin. "Are you sure? Who else will you turn to?"

He knew he had the other Archon Knight when he licked his lips nervously and changed the subject. "And the village?"

"The people of the village assume the Thane passed away and gave the land to a relative. We own that village and the farmland around it now. We can trust Aramis Whitley. He's loyal to the Modeus and Aatheria."

"Delsinor will know what you did," Gaelin said. It wasn't a warning; he was simply being cautious.

"They would have found out what you did as well," Trylian shot back. "Sooner, too, since it would have been an all-out battle. This gives us weeks, at least."

"And when the king realizes you've slaughtered one of his most loyal Thanes?" Gaelin stood still, his hand hanging casually on his sword hilt.

Trylian glanced at Baelian beside him. The half-Vyrkarian looked at ease, but Trylian knew he was ready to spring into action should anything go wrong. His brown horns glinted in the midday sun. He looked back at Gaelin. "We will be ready to defend the keep, should it come to that."

"It may come to that before you are ready."

"I am ready. We are ready. Roan is ready." He stood and dropped the dagger on the table before him. "I'm going to make him Archon Knight soon enough. He will be a good and ruthless leader."

"I don't understand," Gaelin said, a slight frown bending his manicured brows. "Why the obsession with the boy?"

Trylian smiled and shook his head. "That's for me to know. You will find out soon enough." He turned and looked back down, tracking Roan's long, bright red hair from the window. The boy moved quickly, easily besting Razvin. They shook hands and embraced before moving toward the smithy to allocate new crystals. His eyes flitted to the Clarets, who waited off to the side in the shade of the cloisters. Phael. That was the name of Roan's Claret. He was thin, slight, and frail-looking. He might not have been the best choice for Roan, but he'd do for now. The weakness just meant the magic was strong with him. He hoped Roan could harness that magic. Their bond needed to strengthen.

He took a deep breath and turned back around. "Your son is interested in courting Eliana, isn't he? Thaniel's daughter?" he asked easily.

Gaelin tilted his head and sighed. "I cannot follow what the young ones do these days. Why do you ask?"

Trylian looked out the window and watched Roan come back with some crystals and start combat once again. "No reason," he said simply.

⌇

ROAN WENT to the bathing room and took Phael with him. He had his Claret help him undress and wash him down, since his ribs were still sore, and the wounds had not all healed. Phael's hands were gentle as he lifted Roan's shirt off and tossed it aside. He reached down and picked up some soap after unwrapping the wounds. Roan groaned as the wrappings fell away, releasing his battered torso. He looked at his reflection in the water in the wooden tub and took in the bruises and burns on his ribs and back.

"Do they still hurt?" Phael asked as he gently scrubbed Roan's shoulders down.

Roan nodded. "Less than yesterday, more than tomorrow." He leaned on the tub and let Phael get to work. He hated that he couldn't raise his arms just right without pain shooting through him, but the Claret didn't seem to mind the washing. Or if he did, he didn't say anything.

"What are we doing now?" Phael asked softly.

Roan shivered as Phael's fingers lightly touched him. "I want to go see Eliana. I heard she's going to be in town today at the silk merchant."

"You have spies looking in on her?" Phael asked, but Roan

heard him smiling. It was the first time Phael had smiled since his capture. It made him grin.

"Razvin has a very loose tongue after three drinks or so," Roan confessed. "And all the women in the city love him. He knows things about them only their handmaids know."

Roan waited for Phael to finish washing his arms and back before they went back to the Knights' quarters. He got changed and put on a green tunic with golden embroidery. He needed Phael's help in pulling it over his head and felt the eyes of the few Knights inside the quarters watching him. They had heard that Roan had disobeyed Archon Knight Trylian and had been punished for it. Only he and a few others knew the truth. He let it go. Let them think what they wanted.

"I'll stay," Phael said meekly once Roan was ready to depart and heading for the stables.

"No, you won't," Roan shot back. "I'm not letting you out of my sight. I can't risk you running."

Phael's eyes dropped to the ground, and he clasped his hands before him in silence at this. Roan wasn't sure if Phael would run, but he didn't want to give the Claret the opportunity.

"You'll come with me," he said.

With his Claret in tow, Roan jogged out to the stables, had his horse saddled, and soon was riding out into the city to find his prey for that afternoon. He'd learned that Eliana was Archon Knight Thaniel's daughter. She was one of the prettiest girls in the western realms. Roan knew others were pursuing her, so he wanted to make his move sooner rather than later.

"What exactly are you planning on doing to woo Eliana?" Phael asked.

Roan shot him a glance, shocked that he'd spoken and that his question was so bold. "We're going into town and going to buy food for a picnic." He suddenly pulled up on the reins of his horse, slowing to a trot. "Is that not good enough? I thought that maybe..." He trailed off.

"That's a good idea," Phael said quickly. "In fact, bring your lute."

Taken in by the idea, Roan turned and quickly fetched his lute from the caer before they were too far. He knew he'd made the right choice in bringing Phael with him. "When we're speaking," he instructed as they galloped to the city square, "I want you to interject with stories about my prowess."

Phael's thin brows pinched in a frown. "I cannot lie, Roan."

"Then don't. Tell her about the way I slaughtered the Thane and how strong I look while I train."

The Claret blinked but kept his eyes focused ahead. "I'll do what I can."

They wound their way around the countryside and into the city quickly. The streets were packed as it was market day once again, and the sun was warm while the wind blew cool. Merchants packed the streets while manservants, cooks, tavern owners, and a few rich lords and ladies buying silks threaded throughout them. The sun shot down onto Roan's head, heating his scalp pleasantly. The smell of a blacksmith nearby mingled with the aroma of fresh baked bread and the dusty smell that only comes from last year's corn being sold in burlap sacks. The cacophony of sound echoed off the stone walls of the buildings and rose up into the blue sky. A stall from the east was selling bright lanterns of green, blue, and red. The sun caught the glass and smattered the entire square in bright, colorful triangles of light. Somewhere, someone was preserving meat. The smell of salt and herbs permeated the air.

"Find a basket," Roan instructed Phael. He handed his Claret a few gold coins and then went to work gathering food. He found a bright block of cheese, as well as a huge bundle of grapes and a fresh loaf of bread. He picked up a few apples that were ripe early and spilled it all into the basket when Phael returned. Then he found a flower seller and bought a large purple lily.

Once they had all that together, he went to a wine merchant and purchased a bottle of wine the color of a sunset. The merchant promised him the ladies liked the sweeter wine and that he wouldn't be sorry he'd chosen it. Roan left it up to the merchant's knowledge and shoved the bottle into the basket.

"I saw her," Phael whispered as they finished preparing everything. "She's at the stall over there, looking at ribbons."

"Good eyes, Phael," Roan praised him. He followed Phael's azure gaze and spotted his prey.

Eliana was tall for a woman, and slender. Her breasts didn't spill out the top of her bodice like other women's, Roan noted. He'd just have to look past her faults. She was the daughter of an Archon Knight and would make any Knight a fine wife. And besides, Roan hoped to elevate her beyond that. He hoped a lordship or maybe even the title of Thane was in his future. If Trylian had anything to do with it, they'd both be lords or Thanes soon.

Roan licked his lips and handed Phael the basket before marching over to Eliana. Her blonde hair was tied in golden ribbons already, and a light veil covered most of it. She wore a dress of blue with gold trim and she smelled of waterlilies. Roan approached her and leaned against the stall when he got close. He looked at the ribbons in her hand. They were green.

"Blue matches your eyes better," he said as smoothly as he could.

Eliana gasped and looked up. "Roan, son of Monguard, one does not sneak up upon a lady like that." Her tone was sharp, but her red lips smiled. She glanced back behind her at her maid, who looked wide-eyed at him.

"I am sorry, my lady," the maid stammered. "I didn't see him approach."

"It's fine, Mila," Eliana said with a wider smile. "As you can see, young man, I am not alone. Don't try anything funny." As she said it, she dropped the green ribbon and her delicate fingers went to Roan's chest, where they traced the embroidery there.

Mila, the maid, cleared her throat and raised her brows. Eliana dropped her hands. A hot wave rose in Roan then, one he was not familiar with. He wanted her fingers back on his chest. The light touches had ignited something deep in his belly.

"Eliana," he said. "Would you accompany me for a picnic in The Humming Meadow?"

It was a well-known spot among the younger folk. The Humming Meadow, so called because of the number of bumblebees that frequented all the wildflowers that grew there, was a secluded little area just outside the Sactrium. A small patch of wilderness inside the city walls. The legends said that if a couple kissed in The Humming Meadow, they'd be bound for life.

Eliana smiled and a light pink tinge came to her face. "Mila, we are going out. Follow at a distance."

Roan smiled and offered his arm to Eliana. He led them back to where they had hitched their horses and helped her up behind him once he'd mounted. Phael did the same with the maid and lashed the basket to his horse's side. The four of them rode out into the city, beyond the market square. They wound their way around the dirt paths and up the hill toward the Sactrium. The city thinned out closer to the holy structure and the meadow came into view. It was to the right of the Sactrium and looked empty. It wasn't very big, but a few trees dotted the meadow to give it some shade. Roan led the way to one of these trees. The bells from the Sactrium rang, calling the Clarets inside to midday worship.

Roan helped Eliana down and then had Phael help set up the picnic under the tree. Mila aided him. Roan took the lily from the basket and offered it to Eliana.

"When I first saw you at the festival," he said, "you were wearing purple. I remember it."

Eliana smiled and took the proffered flower, smelling it. She closed her eyes, drinking in the scent. Roan watched her face and noted her thick black lashes. They were so long they touched her cheek when she closed her eyes.

"Even I don't remember what I wore that day," she said. "I remember how brave you were, though."

She turned and led the way around the meadow in a slow, leisurely pace. Roan walked beside her. Part of him wanted to agree with her. Yes, he had been brave that day. He also had had no idea what he was doing. Just knew he had to defend the people. But she didn't need to know that.

"I was terrified that day," he said instead. Women loved vulnerability, so he went with that. "All I knew was that I had to protect the people standing behind me. I'd never been in battle before. My mind went suddenly sharp. Like I had been doing it all along." It was a lie, but she didn't know that. "I dived into action without a thought for myself. I just thought of you and the others."

"Really?" she asked, her eyes going wide. "You thought of me in that moment?"

"Of course. I knew you were back there. I wanted to keep you safe."

"Oh, Roan," she sighed happily, smelling the flower once again. "You are a great warrior. Everyone has heard that. But father says you're Trylian's favorite. That you're his pet."

He'd heard that before. Alamar said it often. He clenched his jaw tight to bite back the words that wanted to escape his lips. "Everything I have, I have earned," he said as evenly as he could.

Eliana must have heard the edge in his voice because she looked up at him. "I know that. I've heard about Roan Red Mane."

Now he glanced down at her. "Who calls me that?" He knew very well who had started it, but didn't know it was so widely known.

"Everyone—all the Knights—call you that. My father calls you that. They say you are a beast in battle. That you slaughter without thought. That you're a monster."

Something stabbed Roan in the chest. Pet. Monster. Was that how everyone thought of him? He clenched his fists.

"It doesn't matter what everyone says about you," Eliana said, and she touched his hand. A surge of warmth radiated from the touch and he relaxed a little. He wanted her to touch him more. But he wasn't sure in what way. Just wanted to feel her skin. Her soft, pale flesh. His eyes went to her exposed collar bone and roamed over her, imagining her naked. He wondered what those long legs looked like under the skirt.

"A man's reputation is all he has," Roan said at length. "It does matter."

"Not when those who matter most know the truth," she argued back. "Razvin speaks very highly of you."

"Razvin drinks too much," Roan cut back.

Eliana smiled and laughed. "He knows about reputation. He's half-Vyrkarian. They have a reputation he cannot live down. But he does his best."

"He overcompensates," Roan said. "He tries too hard to be humorous, to be liked." He stopped himself there. Razvin was his best friend. He wouldn't speak badly of him. "But he's also loyal to a fault. That's common among Vyrkarians."

"See?" Eliana said with a smile. "There are good things about a bad reputation as well. I know none of the men challenge you, despite you being moved from fourth to first column. They fear you. Because of your brutality."

Roan flushed red. "I'm not a brute."

She pressed her lips together to hide a larger grin. "I like it." Her hands traveled up his arm until she was holding him close. "Means you're strong. I like strong men."

Roan stopped and faced Eliana. She looked up at him, a coy glint in her eyes.

"Kiss me, Roan," she whispered.

Awkwardly, Roan leaned down to her pretty face. He'd never kissed anyone before. Something in him buzzed, and his feet suddenly melted to the ground as he reached for her. She closed her eyes and tilted her head up.

"Ahem," came a disapproving voice.

Roan froze and looked over to see Mila standing there, hands clasped in front of her. "The food is ready." She said it like they had done something to offend her.

Eliana dropped her head. "Coming, Mila."

The maid nodded and turned, eyeing them as she did.

"We'd better go," Eliana sighed. She took Roan's hand in hers and turned, walking back to Phael and Mila.

Roan sighed inwardly. He'd wanted to kiss her. Part of him wanted to pull her back right now and crash his lips into hers, taking his first kiss the way he wanted. But he didn't. Eliana wouldn't like that. And he didn't want to do anything to her she didn't ask for.

They sat under the tree and ate and drank. Phael and Mila kept a respectful distance away as Roan and Eliana talked. Roan was shocked to hear her speak about philosophy, the Winds and their faith, and other matters with confidence.

"I didn't know women studied books," he said with a grin after some time.

Eliana smirked and held her head high. "I am shocking, aren't I?" She nodded to the lute on the ground. "And I didn't know men studied music, outside of bards. Can you actually play, or was that a prop to impress me?"

Roan gave a wicked half-grin and picked up the lute. "I'm as good as a bard, if not better."

"Prove it," Eliana quipped, popping a grape into her mouth.

Roan pressed his fingers into the strings and strummed a chord. He looked up at Eliana and she raised her brows.

"Can you play 'The Fall of Aldir'?" she asked. The way her brows went up told Roan she didn't think he could. It was a complicated piece.

He cleared his throat and strummed the first melancholy chord. Her hand froze halfway to her mouth, another grape held delicately between her pretty fingers.

Plucking the chords, he began to sing. He knew the words perfectly. It had been Father's favorite song. He'd played it a million times since he was a boy. The complicated nature of the music had thrilled him as a child. He'd loved Father's praise when he'd finally finished the song for the first time. He had been so happy. Father had kissed Mother and proclaimed their son a genius. It had been a good night.

When he finished, he looked up. Eliana's mouth hung open a little in shock. She smiled gently.

"Not only did you play beautifully, but your voice," she breathed. "You have the golden throat of a bard, for sure."

Roan looked up at Phael, who also looked impressed, though he didn't say anything. Mila wiped at a tear from her eye.

Roan put the lute aside. It was getting late. "Eliana, may I see you again?"

The girl beamed, her cheeks tinging pink again. "I'd like that."

Happy to have her permission, Roan began to pack up the

picnic and together the four of them walked back into the market square to return Eliana to her shopping.

They were not three steps into the market when a man shoved past Roan, hitting his shoulder hard. The blow sent a jolt down his bruised ribs and he caught his breath, pressing his hands into his chest.

"Out of the way, Red Mane," the man growled.

Roan spun to face him. It was that man, Gaelin Hamlin. "My name is Roan," he snarled, trying to catch his breath in his damaged lungs.

Gaelin Hamlin turned, eyes rolling. "I know it is. Everyone knows Trylian's pet. Though I did enjoy your punishment that day." Something else beside his disdain for Roan fumed under Gaelin's face.

Roan's fists clenched. A muscle in his jaw ticked. He hadn't disobeyed that day. He'd done as he was told. But Trylian had warned him not to implicate him.

"Eliana?" Gaelin Hamlin said, his eyes flitting beyond Roan. "What are you doing with this boy?"

Eliana smiled sweetly. "Having a picnic, if it's all right with you."

Gaelin Hamlin arched a brow. "My son wanted to see you. Shall I have him call upon you?"

Roan jolted upright at this. Another man wanted to see his prey? "As usual," he said. "I got here first."

Eliana giggled. "Two boys in one day? I have to tell Father."

Roan glanced at her, half a glare bending his red brows. She liked that two men wanted to court her at the same time? She smiled at him.

"I had a lovely day, Roan. Thank you. Come and see me again." She turned and vanished into the crowd with Mila at her heels.

"It seems the lady is not satisfied with just you," Gaelin Hamlin smirked. "My son will be calling on her soon."

Roan snarled inwardly as Gaelin Hamlin turned and also vanished into the crowd. Phael appeared at his side, touching his back gently. Roan shrugged him off and marched back into the square, heading to the gate.

THE PAIR of them were just outside the caer's gate when they spotted Trylian and a few other Knights just inside in the ward. Trylian was speaking to them, Razvin among them.

"Roan!" Razvin called, waving his arm. "We're going to battle."

Trylian turned and waved Roan in. Roan and Phael trotted up to them, listening.

"What's happened?" Roan asked.

"The Thane we placed in the village outside Delsinor calls for aid," Trylian said quickly. "The village is rising up against him and we must defend him. We need our reach in that area and cannot afford to let him fall."

A thrill shot through Roan. "A battle? Won't this start a war?"

"We're nearly ready," Trylian said eagerly.

Roan smiled and looked sideways at Phael. His Claret had gone even paler than normal. Roan knew what he must be thinking: he'd have to fight his own people. He might even know a few of the villagers. And they were going to slaughter them. He might even run.

"This could be the start of our conquest," Trylian said, a fire in his blue eyes. "And this is a chance for you all to prove yourselves."

The Knights nodded eagerly.

Roan smiled. A real battle. A time for him to finally show his true prowess to Trylian. To show his strength.

CHAPTER XVI

The weeks it took them to travel back toward Caeth and the small village outside Delsinor grated on Phael's nerves. His stomach tied in such tight knots thinking about the village—a place he knew well—that he couldn't eat. He thought about taking bites of the stew the cook prepared, but every time his stomach roiled and rebelled against him. He wanted to beg to be let go. To not watch the slaughter. He even thought about running away and warning the village that the Modeus Knights were coming. But there was no escape. When Roan wasn't watching him, Alamar was.

The young Knight's gaze was violating somehow. Phael hated it and often hid his face inside the deep hood of his white cloak. No, there was no escape.

"You must eat," Nox whispered as they made camp that night. He brought over a piece of bread and a bowl of stew. "I've been watching you. You are not eating. It's been days since you've had anything."

Alowyn followed Nox. He held three metal cups of spring water and handed one to Phael, who took it and tried to drink. When he did, his stomach bubbled.

"We can't do this," he whispered, his heart breaking. "These are our people. We cannot hurt them. The Elsarius will surely punish us. The Winds will smite us."

Alowyn shook his head, his sheets of white hair rippling. "We are abandoned by the Elsarius. Surely you must know that by now. Have you not felt their absence?"

"Blasphemy," Phael hissed, knowing full well that Alowyn was right. "The Winds wouldn't abandon us like this." Even as he said it, he felt the Modeus' eyes on him. They laughed at the forsaken Claret.

"Then what do you think has happened to us?" Alowyn replied. His eyes shone with unshed tears. He looked desperate, like he really expected Phael to give him an answer. But he didn't have one.

"It's a test of faith," he said, parroting what Lailen had often told him. "We must hold strong in our beliefs."

Alowyn shook his head. "I'm too afraid. I spoke to Veryl. He told me about the Knights. About what they do to Clarets they think are not loyal."

Phael glanced over at Veryl. He was Alamar's Claret and hadn't said so much as three words to him. He was quiet, often with eyes downcast. He looked permanently melancholy. Alamar caught him looking and leered at Phael. The Claret quickly turned his face away.

"One of us could break out during the night," Phael whispered, leaning in close to Nox. "We could warn the village."

Nox shook his head, his black eyes sad. "I won't risk my life like that. And you shouldn't either. What good are we to the Winds dead?"

Phael gaped at his friend. "Don't you care?"

"Of course I do." Nox quickly wiped at his eyes, rubbing away a sudden tear. "But we can do more if we're alive. What if they attack Delsinor? We need to know when they will strike, and then we can warn them."

"Would they do that?" Phael asked. "Overthrow the king?"

"I wouldn't put it past that Archon Knight, Trylian. He seems to be the ambitious one." Nox offered Phael the bread. "Please eat. It's been days."

Reluctantly, Phael took the bread and bit into it. It was warm and fresh, heated by the fire by the cook, no doubt. It was soft and somehow sour, but in a good way. His stomach suddenly grumbled. Deciding it was all right to eat, he devoured the bread and took the stew next.

"Thank you," Nox whispered. He reached up and stroked Phael's arm.

Heat exploded from where Nox touched him and Phael felt his face burn hot. He buried his face in the bowl so the other Clarets wouldn't see him blush. He hadn't thought about Nox in some time, but that one touch brought all the feelings he'd had. He wanted to touch Nox back, to stroke him, run his fingers through his hair. But Clarets had to remain pure. It was demanded by the Elsarius. He could never act on his feelings, no matter how strong they were.

He suddenly wanted Nox to take his hand off him. He couldn't stand the touch without being able to repay the gesture. So he focused on the stew.

"We should pray tonight," Phael said after he was finished. "Pray that we are protected tomorrow. And that our Knights survive."

"We'd be better off dead," Alowyn hissed.

Nox glared. "Enough of that. I won't stand for it. There are other ways. Trust me. We can fight a more silent war on our own against the Modeus. You just have to have faith."

Phael looked Nox in his dark eyes. He couldn't stop his gaze from traveling down to his pale lips and then back up. He wanted to kiss him, to believe in him. He looked away, pushing away his impure thoughts. "I trust you," he whispered. "But let's not fool ourselves; we are alone." He thought back to the night he had prayed over the crystals for the first time. It had been terrible. But ever since then, he'd mumbled prayers to the Modeus. He was a heretic in the Elsarius's eyes. Guilt suddenly filled him. Yes, he needed to pray for forgiveness. Surely the Elsarius would understand that he had to pray to the Modeus to survive.

Nox pushed himself up straight. "We're not as alone as you think, Phael. I promise you will be free of them one day."

ADORIAN, A VILLAGE OUTSIDE DELSINOR. 19TH OF GILDEN, 1217.

Roan was sharpening his blade when Trylian called him to his tent. The mist of morning had not departed yet, and the sun was just peeking over the hills and mountains. Roan laced up his shirt and went to Trylian's tent. Inside were Gareth, Tanis, Razvin, and Alamar. They were all outfitted in their black armor already. Their Clarets were nowhere to be seen. Roan looked around and didn't see Phael. He hadn't come to their tent that night, either.

Trylian stood before a table with a map set out on it. It had a hand-drawn version of the village and the surrounding landscape.

"You five will act as my second-in-command," Trylian said once Roan was inside. "The men know this. You will each have ten Knights and a few soldiers from Aatheria under your charge and we will divide into groups to surround the village. Our spies tell us it is nothing but farmers with pitchforks, but an attempt has been made on Thane Whitley's life. They stormed the keep once and killed several of his guards. He's holed up inside now and we must break the line."

"Peasants," Gareth spat, and Tanis nodded, keeping his eyes on his older brother. "We'll show them."

"We don't need a display," Trylian sighed. "We need results. Roan, take point. You and your group will charge in first and set the stage for the rest of us."

"Will fifty Knights and a handful of soldiers be able to take them?" Roan asked. He saw a slaughter in their future.

"The rebels are merely dozens," Trylian replied. "Once we breach the village, they will fall."

Razvin frowned. "We're killing the people?"

Alamar chuckled. "Careful, Vyrkarian. Your conscience is showing."

"Anyone who stands up to us," Trylian said. "Once they see us heading to the keep, they should leave us be. But if anyone tries to stop us, kill them."

"Understood." Roan nodded. "And the Clarets?"

Trylian pointed to a copse of trees several yards away from the village border. "They will be hiding here. They won't have anyone to protect them, but I doubt the villagers will look for our Clarets."

Roan started at this. "This is *their* village. Some of them might even be from here. They will run if we leave them."

Trylian's brow bent gently at this revelation. "You are right. Very well. We'll bind them."

"What?" Razvin shot. His gray skin paled. "What if someone comes for them? They'll be helpless."

"We'll leave Modeus-raised Clarets in command," Trylian offered. "We'll give them orders to untie the Elsarius Clarets if danger presents itself. Is that acceptable?"

Roan nodded, but Razvin looked worried, his face pinched. He licked his lips and turned away, shaking his horned head.

"I'll bind them," Roan offered.

"You'll need help," Gareth said. "We'll each bind our own once we're there. When do we march?"

Trylian looked the boys in their eyes and smiled. "We march now."

⁓✦⁓

THE ARMY MARCHED from the camp, leaving it behind. With one hundred Knights and Clarets combined, and a few Aatherian soldiers, Roan knew the village would see them coming. They would run and hide. A messenger might even flee to Caeth or Delsinor and bring word. It didn't matter. They'd be long gone by the time either city reacted. He decided then to keep an eye out for a runner. He could stop them.

He checked his sword where a green crystal waited in the hilt. He had a yellow one, and an orange embedded in his vambraces. He noted Trylian wore his on rings and wanted to have some made for himself that way.

Beside him rode Phael. His Claret was quiet. Phael, Nox, and Alowyn had been out in the woods praying, Phael had said when Roan found them moments after meeting with Trylian. Roan didn't know what they'd prayed for, but hoped it was for a smooth victory.

Once they reached the copse of trees, Trylian called for a halt. Roan slid off his horse and walked up to Phael. He raised his hands, motioning for him to come down.

"What's happening?" Phael asked. He braced himself against Roan's shoulders and slid off his horse.

Roan seized his wrist hard and pulled him toward a tree.

"Roan?" Phael gasped, struggling against his sudden grip. "What's wrong?"

Razvin hauled Nox forward and Tanis brought Alowyn.

The Clarets tugged against their Knights, demanding to know what was going on. When the ropes appeared, Phael cried out.

"Please, don't do this," he begged Roan. He dug his heels into the earth, but Roan easily hauled him to a slender tree.

Roan gripped Phael's hands and wrapped them around the tree, pulling them together where he bound him, tying it in place.

"Roan, please," Phael begged. It almost worked. Roan felt a twinge in his chest at the sadness in Phael's voice, but he quickly quashed it.

"It's for your own good," he said.

"Why?" Nox cried, jerking against his bindings. "What are we to do if we're attacked?"

"We'll be slaughtered!" Alowyn cried.

"Athael," Trylian called. Gareth's Claret stepped forward. Trylian looked him sternly in the eye. "You are in command while we're gone. All Clarets will obey Athael. If someone attacks you, unleash the other Clarets and run."

"We trust you to protect us," Athael said with a strong nod.

"Roan," Phael sobbed softly, trying one last time to reason with him.

Roan hardened his heart and turned away. He remounted his horse and drew his sword. Clicking his tongue, he started a trot after Trylian, who had already taken the lead. Phael called out to him again, but he ignored him.

Riding up alongside Trylian, Roan looked ahead into the village. Smoke was just now starting to rise up from it; the people were just waking up. He scanned the horizon.

"Farmers," he said, pointing. Ahead of them, he spotted a small gaggle of farmers in the fields.

The farmers stopped and looked up, seeing the mass of armored Knights and soldiers marching toward them. One's face went lax, jaw popping open in fear and eyes widening. He dropped his scythe.

"Modeus Knights!" he shouted, turning to his fellows. "Go! Warn the village."

"Stop him," Trylian said easily.

Roan raised his sword and thrust it forward. He called on the magic inside the crystal on his sword. A pulse of power went out from him and hit the running farmers hard. The one closest to him was hit the hardest and the force of the magic rent him apart. The other two farmers screamed and fell to their knees. They raised their hands, begging for mercy as the blood and guts from their fellow rained down around them.

"Strong hit," Trylian mused. "Finish them."

Roan kicked his horse and charged down the other two. They stood to run, screaming, but he caught up to them, lopping their heads off with two strong swings. Their heads spun, free from their necks, and landed with a thud among the wheat stalks.

"We ride!" Trylian called. He raised his sword and shouted to the heavens above. Then he kicked his horse hard in the sides, and together he and Roan galloped to the village borders. The other men were just behind them.

Razvin, Tanis, Gareth, and Alamar broke from them and spread out, their Knights and soldiers following them. Soon they were in the form of a massive wave, rushing to the village. The keep was visible on a small hill inside the village. It wasn't a grand keep by any means, with only two towers and a single drawbridge in the gatehouse. The portcullis was open, and Roan could see a few men using a small battering ram on the doors. They were just in time.

Flinging his hand behind his head, readying it to throw, he conjured a ball of flame. He loved the rush in his veins that the magic gave him. It was like pulling on a fountain of elixir. Energy spiked through him, exciting him. He felt the bond to

Phael strengthen as well. Roan was shocked to find emotions coming through the bond. He felt a tinge of sadness and a bit of fear. He knew they were Phael's emotions because he wasn't feeling those things himself. No, he was thrilled. Joyous, even. He loved the fight. He didn't know how to not let the feelings through the bond, so he let them flow easily to Phael.

Roan heaved the fireball at a gathering of peasants who rallied quickly once they saw the Modeus Knights. The people screamed, and some caught fire, their hair burning. The force of the fireball also knocked them back, blowing them off their feet. Roan didn't wait, galloping up into the village and hacking at the peasants.

The wave of Knights and soldiers crashed into the village, fire, lightning, and bits of earth exploding here and there. The peasants didn't stand a chance. Roan watched as Trylian lifted a slab of earth with a wave of his hand, making it explode from underneath the ground. The people standing over it were blown up into the air, screaming as they came crashing back down. That was when Roan saw they were sparing no one.

Deciding he liked fire the best, he arched his hand over his head once more and threw a fistful of fire at a small shrine to the Elsarius near the side of a road. It erupted into flames and a woman quickly grabbed a bucket to douse them. Roan used his lightning crystal then. A bolt arched from his palm and hit the woman square in the back, making her shake and scream before she fell over unconscious.

Then he turned his attention to the houses. They were made of wood and thatched roofs. He flung spurts of fire onto them, catching them alight. The people inside screamed and came pouring out into the streets. When they did, he cut them down, hewing them with his blade.

"Get to the keep!" Razvin shouted from far to Roan's left. "Don't bother with the people. Get to the keep."

A bit annoyed, Roan obeyed. He knew what they were

here for and knew he had a job to do. He kicked his horse and galloped up to the keep where Trylian, his sons, and Alamar had already led their men. They had slaughtered most of the ones using the battering ram and were now forming a protective line around the base of the keep. Roan whet his sword on any who came close to him. He tried once more to fling another ball of fire, but the flames flickered and died in his hand. Checking the crystal, he saw it was such a pale orange that it was almost white. He was out of magic.

He joined the ranks around the keep, ordering his men to do the same. He'd forgotten to give his men orders and had been so taken up in the slaughter that he'd not led them. He'd almost abandoned them. He glanced at Trylian, but he hadn't seemed to notice.

"Listen to me," Trylian shouted, his horse snorting and rearing up in fright. He wrestled it back down and calmed it. The people around them stopped running and looked up at him.

Roan took in their faces. They were terrified. Their dirty faces, cut through with tracks of tears from the smoke or from fear, he didn't know, looked up at them. They begged for mercy with their eyes. Some fell to their knees right away, hands clasped before them.

"We will never listen to a murderer of the Modeus!" a defiant man shouted, running forward. His fists were clenched around a pitchfork that he brandished toward Trylian.

The Archon Knight motioned Roan forward. Happily, Roan raised his other hand and shot a bolt of lightning at the man, hitting him square in the chest. The man crumpled with a cry and fell to his knees, panting. Roan slid off his horse and marched to the man, readying his sword.

"Please don't!" a woman screamed from the small crowd that had gathered. "He didn't mean it. We won't stand up to you again. We swear allegiance." She ran forward, hands held high as she defended the man.

Roan raised his blade, ready to strike them both.

"Don't," Trylian ordered.

Roan stayed his hand, looking back at his commander, confused. "Why spare them?"

"We cannot slaughter them all," Trylian said simply. "Leave them. We are not without mercy, surely."

Roan glared at the man but backed up, dropping his blade to his side.

"Listen to me," Trylian repeated. The smoke wafted around them, obscuring some of their vision, but Roan knew the people watched him. "We have taken the keep. We will defend it. Thane Aramis Whitley is a good and just man and will do well by you, should you obey. You think you are safe this close to Delsinor, but our reach is long. You know now who stands behind Thane Aramis Whitley, and you would do well to remember it. Carry on as normal. We will not interfere with your lives. In fact, be informants for us and you shall be rewarded. The Modeus are inevitable, my people. And we have shown you mercy here today. Remember that."

"You'll spare us?" the woman asked, standing protectively in front of the man.

Trylian nodded.

The woman turned to face the others. "Let us make peace."

A few people muttered and shook their heads.

"We're not lords and Athelings," the woman shouted back. "We're the people of the village. What do we care whose protection we are under? We need safety. Look at your homes. See how they burn."

"Proclaim loyalty to the Modeus and we will pay to have your homes repaired," Trylian offered.

Roan frowned. This wasn't how he'd thought they would take the village. He'd thought they'd burn it to the ground.

"We just want peace," another man called out.

"And you shall have it," Trylian promised. "Fly our flag and be at peace."

A few more rumblings crept through the crowd, but eventually the woman turned back and faced them. "We will pray to the Modeus if you will spare us."

Trylian smiled.

CHAPTER XVII

Roan followed Trylian inside the keep, finding Thane Aramis Whitley holed up inside his upper chambers. The servants went to get him and soon he was kneeling before Trylian, proclaiming his gratefulness.

"I thought I was done for," Aramis said, taking Trylian's hand and kissing his Modeus insignia on a ring around his finger. "Praise the Modeus you came when you did."

"We were fortunate, it is true," Trylian replied.

"Will you please stay?" the Thane asked. "Tonight, we will celebrate. We will drink, eat, and dance, surely."

Trylian looked back at Roan, Razvin, and the others who had followed him into the keep.

"Sounds like a good time to me," Razvin smiled. He elbowed Roan. "We haven't celebrated in ages. What do you say?"

Roan met Trylian's eyes. "We could stay for the night?" he half-asked. He wasn't sure why Trylian looked to him for an answer. Was it another trap?

"Tonight, we feast," Trylian said, turning back to Aramis.

Aramis gave a soft exclamation of joy and raised his hands above his head. "I shall have a feast prepared immediately. In your honor."

Before following the Thane deeper into his keep, Trylian

turned to the boys. "Go back, free the Clarets, and bring them into town. We'll stay indoors tonight. Alamar, inform the camp and come right back."

"Why me?" Alamar whined, glaring at Roan, then back at Trylian.

"Do as you're told," Trylian barked.

The Knight huffed, let his glare sweep over the rest of them, then turned and marched out of the keep.

"The rest of you," Trylian said, motioning a servant over, "get cleaned up once the Clarets are safe."

Smiling, Roan nodded.

He and Razvin turned on their heels and marched out back to their horses. They mounted and began a quick trot back to the copse of trees where the Clarets waited.

"You were rather savage in the fight," Razvin noted.

Roan heard a bit of judgment in his best friend's tone. He arched a red brow. "They don't call me Red Mane for nothing, you know."

Razvin forced a smile. "True. Do you enjoy the slaughter?"

"Why not? It's what we're made for."

"Do you never think about mercy? Like today. Trylian showed diplomatic mercy."

Roan cocked his head. "I can't think why, though. We should have just burned the village to the ground."

The half-Vyrkarian blanched at this. "We need them. They're farmers. They provide the food to the keep. You cannot slaughter everyone, Roan, or there's no one left to support you."

Roan heard the words, but also heard the ulterior motive in Razvin's voice. His friend was softer than he was, perhaps. Wanted to spare the people, to show mercy. He didn't understand that. But he left the conversation there.

When they reached the copse, the Clarets rushed them, asking if everyone was all right.

"We didn't lose one Knight," Roan told them, easing their worry. "And tonight, we're feasting and celebrating."

He slid off his horse and walked to the tree Phael was tied to. His Claret met his eyes and sighed in great relief.

"I was worried," Phael said, sniffling lightly. When his hands were free, he rubbed his wrists, which were raw from struggling against the bindings. "I was afraid something might happen to you. To us."

Roan scoffed and smirked. "Nothing will happen to me. I'm Roan Red Mane. I cannot be killed."

"What a pompous ass," Razvin called from where he freed Nox. He laughed.

"The day I die in battle is the day the Modeus damn me and forsake me," Roan spat back. "It will never happen." Razvin smiled. Roan threw his arm around Phael's shoulders. "Now, let's get back to the keep. Tonight, I am getting you drunk."

Phael blushed fiercely but let Roan lead him back to the horses.

❧

THE FEASTING HALL was huge despite the keep looking so small from the outside. Stone walls arched up into a beautiful wood ceiling of intricate designs. Windows along the walls let in the moonlight. A huge hearth at the end heated the place and lit it up, along with many torches dotting the stone walls. Green garlands with small candles in them decorated the walls, flickering like fairy lights from legend. The room was warm and glowed. The smell of braised meat and honeyed ham filled the room to the rafters, mingling with the scent of fresh bread and the tangy aroma of cheese. Fruits piled high on the tables, a colorful array of foods and drinks.

Servants rushed between the long tables, which were filled to bursting with a few chosen Knights, their Clarets, and a couple visiting nobles that were staying in the keep. Thane Aramis Whitley sat in the middle of the head table with Trylian on his left and Roan to the left of Trylian. The others —Tanis, Gareth, Razvin, and Alamar—were also at the head table. Their Clarets were allowed to join them. Roan sat beside Phael and made sure to fill his goblet with an aromatic, sweet, honey-colored mead. The night was young, but Razvin was already deep into his cups. He swayed to the music and made crude jokes to anyone who would listen.

"Drink, Phael," Roan said, shoving the brass goblet toward his Claret.

"We're not supposed to drink," Phael whispered, his nose turning pink in embarrassment.

"Is this that purity talk?" Roan asked. He picked up Phael's hand and shoved the goblet into his thin fingers, forcing them closed around the base. "The Modeus have no such rules. And you're a Claret of the Modeus now. Aren't you?" He eyed Phael, daring him to argue.

Phael swallowed hard and then slowly tilted the cup to his lips. Roan gently lifted the base of the goblet, tipping the mead into Phael's throat. The Claret drank and then sputtered as too much dribbled down his chin. He coughed and put the goblet down. Then he looked away, his face reddening.

"It's mead," Roan said over the din. "Made with honey." He smiled. "I know you like honey."

Phael's cheeks reddened and he almost smiled.

"Why purity, anyway?" Roan asked, emptying his own goblet. His head began to spin just enough to make him smile. Somewhere, music was playing, making him want to sway to it.

Before Phael answered, a woman passed them by, carrying a basket of fruit. Roan blinked, watching her pass. She was short but lithe. Her long sheets of brown hair hung to her backside, and her skin was like ivory. But she was dirty. A slave girl. When she passed Gareth, he grabbed her and dragged her onto his lap, attempting to kiss her. Gareth was drunk. The girl struggled but was no match for Gareth's strength.

"Have you ever been kissed?" Roan asked Phael.

The Claret blushed deeply. "No," he whispered.

Roan frowned. "I find that hard to believe. Any woman would faun over you."

Phael turned even more red and dipped his head into his shoulders shyly. He turned away from Roan.

"Unless…" Roan said, smiling as the mead encouraged him. "You don't like women." He laughed harshly. "That makes sense. Of course you don't. I'd forgotten."

"What do you mean, 'of course'?" Phael asked almost defiantly. But he still looked scared.

Roan shook his head. "I'm just saying it makes sense." He watched Gareth stand and take the slave girl in his arms. She cried out and hammered against his chest, but he lifted her and carried her out of the feasting hall, no doubt to plow her. Roan watched jealously. He liked the slave girl. She was pretty.

"There's nothing wrong with that, Phael," Roan said with a sigh. "The vow of purity is a shame, though. I could never."

"It's not just purity," Phael argued, finally sounding a bit bold. "It's about self-control and honoring my own body. This is something I want. If I don't want to give my body to someone, that should be respected. No matter the philosophy."

Roan froze, listening. "Yes," he agreed bitterly. "If someone doesn't want to be touched, they shouldn't be."

Phael must have seen the change in Roan's eyes because his went soft then. "Roan?" He gently touched Roan's wrist.

Roan jerked away from his Claret then and turned to face the musicians. They began a sort of jig and a few of the Knights stood, making a line to dance. Everyone smelled of wine and mead now. The entire hall stank with it. The Knights who stood to dance began to sing the song that went in time with the footwork. Razvin leapt up and dashed to the head of the line, leading the dancing. They began to make a circle around the room and the ruckus grew louder.

"Excuse me," Phael whispered and stood from his seat. Roan watched him wind his way around the table and sit next to Nox. He watched as Nox asked Phael a question with a concerned pinch to his brows. Phael mumbled a reply and avoided Roan's searching eyes. A strange kind of jealously rose in Roan. Phael was his Claret. He should be the one Phael confided in.

"Roan!" Gareth shouted, appearing again after some time. He embraced Roan from behind, his chest sweaty and his hair matted up behind his head. "You have got to try that slave girl. Her name is Antinea and she's fantastic."

Gareth sighed and flopped into Phael's vacant chair. He poured himself some mead and downed the entire goblet in one drink.

"You're drunk," Roan laughed, taking another sip himself.

"Not drunk enough to not know a good fuck when I've had one." Gareth stood and heaved Roan up with him. "Come on. You have to have a good plowing now and then, and I never see you at the houses in the city."

"That's how you get spotted dick, Gareth." Roan snickered.

"Not this one," Gareth said, clearly pleased. "Pretty sure she was a virgin. Second place isn't bad. Go on." Gareth led Roan out of the feasting hall and down a regular hall to a bedroom on the west end of the keep.

Gareth flung the bedroom door open. Inside came a small gasp. The girl, Antinea, scrambled to cover herself with the bed clothes. Her long brown hair covered most of her chest, but not before Roan got a good look at her. She had full breasts hidden behind the sheets. He smiled and leaned heavily on Gareth, the wine spinning his head.

"What do you want now?" the girl asked. She looked scared but was putting on a brave face.

"Another round," Gareth chuckled. He shoved Roan into the room and slammed the door shut.

Roan stumbled in and then looked at the girl. Her eyes were a bright, fierce gray. She glared at him, but shrank away at the same time.

"Is this what I am now? To be passed from Knight to Knight?"

Roan shrugged. "Why not just be quiet and enjoy the ride?" He threw his shirt off and kicked his boots off into the pile of clothes in the corner that looked to be her dress.

Antinea watched him for a moment before her eyes went to his boots. With a grunt, she lunged to his boots and unsheathed the tiny blade he kept hidden there. She brandished it at him, eyes wild.

"Don't," Roan laughed. "You cannot hope to take me down."

"My hope is pretty strong," she tried. She lunged at him, swiping the blade.

Roan was slow from the drinking and didn't move in time. Antinea caught his abdomen with the blade and Roan felt hot blood trickle down his stomach. Glaring, he looked down.

"You little bitch," he half-laughed, amused that she'd gotten so close.

"I told you," Antinea quipped. "Now stay back." Despite her brave actions, tears filled her eyes.

Roan scoffed and jumped at her. He was so much taller and stronger than her that he was able to wrestle her down easily. He gripped her wrist and smashed it against the ground until she let go of the knife. The weapon went clattering away into a corner. Roan pinned her under him. She was beautiful and naked. She squirmed under him, trying to pull away. He let his eyes rove over her without any hint of anything but lust.

"Stop resisting," Roan grunted, holding her down.

A fresh wave of struggles made her buck against him.

Smiling, Roan let her slip out of his grip just enough to make them tussle once again. He liked wrestling the naked girl. It made her body shake and shiver in the best ways. Finally, he got her under him once more. He loved how her hair splayed out around her head. It was long and made for pulling.

"Any girl would want to be plowed by me," Roan grunted. "I'm Roan Red Mane, Trylian's pet."

At last, she stopped struggling. "You're him?" the girl asked. She looked up into his face. "You have some influence among the Knights, I hear. They fear you. Do as you say."

Roan wasn't entirely sure about that, but he nodded, grinning.

Antinea's beautiful gray eyes calculated a moment. Her face went taunt and serious. "Have you ever been with a woman before?"

Roan's mouth went dry as a desert in the east. He couldn't stop the paleness that sucked all the blood from his face, or the way his eyes widened. Nerves suddenly filled him. "Of course I have," he lied quickly when he saw Antinea register his fear.

Her eyes calculated one last time before she sighed and nodded. "Fine. Just get it over with."

Satisfied that he'd won, Roan grinned and went to work. He looked down at her beneath him and let his eyes travel to her full, pink lips. He'd never kissed a girl before. This would be the first time. He was sad it hadn't been Eliana, but did it matter?

Suddenly, hesitation hit him. He had no idea what he was doing. He'd never touched a naked woman before. A strange chill halted his movements and cooled his blood. Was that a tinge of fear in the back of his head?

Sensing his hesitation, Antinea went still, a curious look in her eyes. She slipped her hand out from his grasp and gently touched his face. "You've never done this before, have you?" she whispered, catching her breath.

Roan swallowed hard, but didn't answer. He didn't want to admit this was his first time. It seemed embarrassing, somehow. Instead, he tried to grasp her again. She easily slipped his hands, but didn't sit up. One of her hands went to the side of his face and she gently ran her pretty fingers over his cheek. A tingling and somehow searing sensation followed her fingertips. He shivered.

Antinea raised her head and gently brushed her lips over his, kissing him like a butterfly. Another shot of excitement lanced through Roan as she did. He wanted to experience it in full. He dipped his head and caught her mouth with his, kissing her hard. Her hand went to the back of his head, and she pulled him into her harder, opening her mouth to invite him in. Unsure what he was doing, Roan slipped his tongue into her mouth. She tasted like fruit of some kind. An eagerness rose in him now.

Roan let his hands roam over her chest and middle as he kissed her again. He liked kissing her. Liked how her hands clung to him as he did. She was fierce in her administrations, and it frightened him a little. Her hand went to his belt buckle and pulled his belt off quickly. He didn't know how she had undone the buckle so quickly. Then she was running her hands over his chest. He gasped but forced himself to not pull away. She strained to keep her lips connected to his as she slipped her fingers into the top of his pants.

Unsure what he was doing yet again, Roan let her pull them down until he slipped out of them. Both naked now, he suddenly knew exactly what he wanted. But he froze.

His conversation with Phael came back to his mind. No one should be touched if they didn't want to be. Was he forcing her? Despite her seemed eagerness, he couldn't help but wonder.

"What?" Antinea asked, panting. Her hands were around his hips, positioning him. "Why'd you stop?"

Roan swallowed hard and met her eyes. "I don't... I can't—"

"Yes, you can," she whispered breathlessly. "I'll help you."

"You want to?"

She didn't answer. She instead let her hands travel down to between his legs where she gripped him and began to move her hand. "Just follow my lead."

Heat shot through Roan and a rushing filled his ears. He swore fire burned under his skin. It felt like when he cast the magic. He couldn't even acknowledge her. His throat was too tight. He just nodded, panting as she worked. He was entirely under her control, and he couldn't stop her.

"Sex is about control," Trylian used to say.

Roan clenched his eyes tight against the dark memories. He didn't want this. Didn't want to be touched. Not like this... He went stiff and still.

"Good," Antinea breathed. "Just let me..."

Her voice soothed him. She was being gentle. Kind. This wasn't *that*. He could do this. He took a shuddering breath and tried to calm himself.

The next five minutes passed in a heated blur. He felt himself moving rhythmically into her, following her lead. The next thing Roan knew, his body shook, and he felt like he might explode. Antinea's legs wrapped tight around his middle and she held him in place as a wave of euphoria crashed into him, deafening him and making him moan loudly. He wanted to pull away but couldn't. She held him too tight. A sensation washed over him, tight and hot. Then it was gone.

He gasped and collapsed beside her. Only then did she let him go.

He lay there, trying to catch his breath, his face pressed into the bearskin blanket beneath them. Antinea's gentle hand went to his face, and she petted him delicately. Then she ran her fingers through his long red hair.

Somehow, he wanted to apologize. He was the authority in this situation. She didn't have the power to say no to him. Had he forced her? He couldn't speak. His nose tingled and tears blurred his vision. He turned his face away. Antinea cooed and wrapped her arms around him. She gently petted his head, holding him to her chest.

"Remember this," she whispered. "Please. I need protection. Remember how I made you feel."

He couldn't comprehend her words, so he didn't listen.

Roan lay there, engulfed in her naked body, and let himself drift off to sleep, exhausted and melancholy.

CHAPTER XVIII

Roan sat near the banks of the river in deep thought. The morning sun was gently warm, trying its best to heat the cool air around him. A gentle breeze kicked up the scent of wildflowers to his nose as he crouched near the glittering blue water of the river. It rushed, making a nice, soothing sound that helped relieve his anxiety. He kept reliving the night with Antinea. She had struggled, initially not wanting him to touch her. But then she'd given in. She'd taken control. But had she wanted to?

He picked up a smooth river stone and tossed it into the water. It didn't skip; the water moved too quickly to let the stone get purchase on the surface. Roan wondered briefly how deep it was. He couldn't see the bottom, and it was pretty clear. He picked up a stick and tossed it far to a small island in the middle of the river. It landed among the tall grass there, vanishing from sight.

"What's wrong?" Phael's gentle voice asked from behind him.

Roan turned to see his Claret walking carefully over the rocky shore toward him. His white brows were pinched in concentration as he made his way to Roan. "What do you mean?" he asked.

"I can feel your distress in my own head," Phael replied.

So Phael had gotten a hint of that bond as well? That made sense. Trylian had never told Roan about a bond like this before. He would have liked to know that his emotions would be leaked to his Claret. But there was no help for it now. Unless he could find some way to block the emotions. He leaned into it, curious what Phael was feeling. Only trickles of sadness and worry came through. Was Phael always melancholy? Roan didn't like the feeling.

"Can you feel my thoughts?" Phael asked. He gathered his white robes in his hand and then squatted next to Roan, picking through the rocks on the bank.

Roan watched Phael's thin fingers play with the smooth stones. "Yes. I don't know what that means. I was never told about this kind of thing."

Phael hummed in thought, resting his chin on his knees. "What did you do last night?"

"Plowed a girl," Roan said before he could stop himself.

"That slave girl?"

He nodded. Why did he feel like he'd done something wrong? Guilt surged through him and his head started to ache.

"Oh," Phael moaned. "I felt that. What happened?"

Roan glared now. Was he never going to have a private thought again? He tried to stifle his feelings but couldn't manage it. The anger at his emotions being known made them too loud to quiet. Phael would know everything he couldn't get under control in his mind.

He squatted, taking the smooth stone Phael had picked up. He turned the stone in his fingers, inspecting it. If the waters were calmer, it would be a perfect skipping rock.

"I took her against her will," he whispered. "I think she thought she had no choice. I shouldn't have done it."

A rush of sympathy poured in from the bond. Roan felt

Phael looking at him. Knew his white brows would be pinched in concern.

"After what you said..." Phael whispered.

"I know," Roan snapped. "You don't understand."

"Help me understand." Phael's voice was so gentle. "Did something happen to you?"

At this, only rage and anger flooded Roan. He stood, grunted, and tossed the perfect stone into the river, not even attempting to skip it. "It's none of your business," he snapped.

"What isn't?" a snide voice asked.

Roan and Phael turned to see Alamar saunter up the banks, a host of first column Knights following him. Phael stood and took two steps to be behind Roan. Roan let him.

"What do you want, Alamar?" Roan called.

The boys marched up to them, their boots crunching over the gravelly shore. Alamar faced Roan.

"Some of the men have made it known they weren't fond of you leading them during the attack on the keep," Alamar said. Behind him, the other Knights grunted in agreement. Some were much older than Roan; others were closer to his age.

"I understand," he said cautiously. "But it was Trylian who put me in charge. And we won the day, so what's the difference?"

Five of the Knights moved, encircling Phael and Roan. Fear lanced into Roan's mind from Phael.

"Leave us alone," Roan growled. His hand flew to his sword.

Just as he moved, so did the others. They dived at him, gripping his arms and pulling them painfully behind him. Phael cried out as they captured him, too. Alamar reached for Roan's blade and pulled it out of its scabbard. He admired it, reading the inscription on the handle.

"To the stars, through adversity," Alamar read. "What's that mean?"

"Give it back, Alamar," Roan snarled. "That's my father's blade." He jerked against his captors but only succeeded in hurting his shoulders.

"Your dead father," Alamar cajoled. He turned the blade and held it up.

Roan thought for a moment that Alamar was going to run him through. But instead, he spun, heaving the sword with all his might toward the river. Roan shouted and watched as the sword spun and then stabbed, point first, into the earth on the small island in the middle of the river. He panted, relief flooding him.

"Go get it, Red Mane," Alamar sneered. He flicked his head up, signaling to the other Knights to let Roan go. They did. "Go now," Alamar said. "Or the Claret gets your punishment."

The Knights laughed and pulled Phael back from the bank, holding him tight. Roan stood alone near the water. He looked at Phael, whose pale face begged him to do as they asked.

Making sure to keep eye contact with Alamar, Roan tossed his shirt aside and removed his boots. He tied his long hair back with a piece of leather from his pocket and nodded to Phael.

"Hurry," Alamar whispered. He drew a small dagger and placed the tip under Phael's chin. A tear ran down Phael's cheek.

"When I get back," Roan said in a low, threatening tone, "I'm going to beat all your asses."

"I'm sure," Alamar laughed. He roughly took a handful of Phael's hair and pulled, making him whimper. "Get going, then. We won't wait all day."

Roan eyed the other five Knights and nodded. He turned

and took a few steps into the freezing water. He gasped at the cold touch but kept going. The river ran deep, so he'd have to swim. He angled himself for a more still area of the river and walked to it. Once the water was over his middle, he pushed out. The ground disappeared under him, and he sank beneath the rushing waves for a moment. Sheer panic from Phael spiked into the bond, distracting him. It wasn't his fear. He had to remember that. Sputtering and windmilling his arms, he got above the water once again.

Finding a rhythm, Roan made long, strong strokes. He knew he was strong and could fight the river. It pushed him several yards down, but eventually, he made it to the small island. He pulled himself out, walked to his father's sword, and pulled it from the ground. He wiped the dirt off and slid it back into its scabbard. Then he braved the river again. This time, he was ready for the steep drop off and swam over the current more easily, not getting swept off his feet. Once he was back on the shore, he eyed the Knights, unsheathing his sword.

Alamar stammered, looking uncomfortable. Roan didn't waste any time. He swung his empty fist into the first two Knights nearest him. They were clobbered, taken off-guard, and fell easily. The other three scattered, with one running away entirely. Roan grabbed one of the Knights by his shirt collar and dragged him back, hammering away at him with the pommel of his sword. The Knight gasped and pleaded, weakly fighting back.

The second Knight jumped Roan, surprising him from behind. Roan didn't let it rattle him, though. He threw his elbow back, bloodying the Knight's face. He whirled around, throwing the first Knight into the second. They collided hard and fell into the shallows. Tangled in one another's long limbs and hurting, they struggled to get up.

Roan spun back around to face Alamar. The other boy

stammered before shoving Phael hard into Roan's arms. Alamar turned tail and ran just as another form came down the path to the river.

Trylian looked livid.

"It wasn't his fault," Phael called quickly in Roan's defense.

"I can talk on my own behalf, Claret," Roan snapped, shoving Phael away from him.

"What have you done?" Trylian barked, glaring at Roan and the two bloodied Knights behind him.

"They attacked me," Roan snapped, shoving his wet hair out of his face.

Trylian glared at Roan with his blue eyes. The other two Knights stood, holding their aching faces. "What did I tell you about shifting blame, Roan?" Trylian hissed.

"But—" Roan started, anger roiling up inside him.

"Do not argue with me," Trylian snapped. He raised his hand like he might hit him. Roan flinched against his will and felt himself quell. "Follow me." Trylian turned on his heel and marched back up the path. "Both of you."

Roan grabbed Phael by his wrist and marched after Trylian, snagging his clothes from the ground.

⁓⁓

ROAN FOLLOWED Trylian silently all the way through the village and back into the keep. Trylian led them up the stairs and into what Roan would describe as a war room. There were books, a massive, long table in the middle covered in maps and trinkets Roan didn't know how to use. Dust wafted gently in the morning light that shone through the windows in pillars of light. The room smelled of dirt, ink, and parchment. A few candles on the walls flickered, giving off weak light.

Around the table stood men Roan knew to be the other Archon Knights: Mathis, Baelian the half-Vyrkarian, and Thaniel, the father of Eliana. Thane Aramis Whitley stood with them, too, looking down at the maps. He stroked his long brown beard in thought as the others went silent upon Trylian entering again. Roan looked around and spotted Elendir silently waiting in the shadows of the bookshelves. Phael was close behind Roan, pricks of nervous energy coming through their bond.

"Is this the young man who saved my life?" the Thane asked, a small smile spreading his lips behind his beard.

"Roan, son of Monguard," Trylian offered, motioning Roan to the war table. "Yes, he led the charge that liberated your keep from the rebels."

Thane Aramis smiled wider. "Brave and so young. How old are you, boy?"

"Nearly eighteen, sir," Roan offered. "Seventeen and six months."

Thane Aramis shook his head. "So accomplished and so young. And so tall." He thumped Roan's muscled shoulder good-naturedly. "And this is the one you've chosen, Trylian?"

Roan looked from the Thane to Trylian. *Chosen for what?* he wondered. But he kept his mouth shut. He knew not to speak when Trylian was plotting.

"Are you certain?" Mathis asked. "There are other men, first column men, who might do better."

"I am sure," Trylian whipped back. "No more questions on that account. Let's get into it." He stepped closer to the table and looked down at the map, resting his palm against the wood.

Roan felt elated. He'd been chosen for something. What, he didn't know, but it didn't matter. Honor filled him, and all the rage he'd felt from before melted away. None of that mattered. He was in the war room with the Archon Knights.

Phael was so close behind him that his breath gently moved Roan's long hair. He didn't care about that, either. Nor did he care about the pricks of worry coming through the bond. He ignored his Claret.

Trylian tapped Emberforge in Moralan with his finger. "We march on Emberforge," he said steadily.

Mathis sighed and Thaniel shifted his feet. Baelian glared at them.

"Why?" Thaniel asked.

Trylian looked up with just his eyes. Roan knew that look. It was the way he looked before snapping. Before violence ensued. He held his breath.

"Last we knew," Trylian said evenly, "that's where the Scion of the Elsarius was seen."

"Ten years ago," Mathis said cautiously. "How can we be sure he's even still there?"

"When I saw the dragon for the first time, it was young." Trylian seemed to ease a little, looking up with his head now and not just his cold eyes. "Too young. Had to have been maybe seven or eight years old. It lived there. It wouldn't have traveled. That means the Scion is roughly seventeen or eighteen. Just coming into his years."

Roan frowned. "What's a Scion?"

Thaniel rolled his eyes.

"A chosen one," Baelian supplied in his smooth, dangerous voice. Roan could hear his draconic fangs in his mouth just like he did with Razvin. Only with Baelian, they sounded menacing. "A single being blessed by the Winds to lead their people."

"In the past," Elendir said gently from the shadows, "they were the ones to lead worship, to lead conquest. They were righteous and strong with the magic. Where your crystal allows you to throw a single bolt of lightning, theirs allows them to conjure storms. Or so it is said. A Scion has not appeared for the Modeus nor the Elsarius in some time."

Something strange came from the bond at this. Phael had a wash of emotions fill him. Something like hope, then trepidation, then worry. Roan understood right away. Phael was hoping the Scion of the Elsarius was still alive. Hoping this chosen one might rise up and put a stop to the Modeus once and for all. He glanced sideways at his Claret, warning him with a look.

So Phael still held out hope of being rescued?

"And the Modeus have not blessed us with a Scion," Trylian said. "That we know of."

"We would know," Elendir added. "There would be signs. The Arch Claret would know. He would have had a vision."

"The Arch Claret would foresee a Modeus Scion?" Phael asked in a small voice.

"But would he let it be known?" Mathis asked, cocking a brow. "He might keep it a secret."

"Our contacts in the Sanctuary in the capital would have told us," Trylian said easily. "We would know. We have a man close to the Arch Claret who would be his confidant."

A rush of anger came through the bond to Roan from Phael then. He glanced over and saw Phael glowering.

"Olenar," Phael mumbled. "The traitor."

"A trusted Emissary," Trylian smirked. "Know your place, Claret. We are trusting you with this information for Roan's sake. But we do not trust you entirely. Know that."

Phael gulped and his face paled.

"And we will accomplish what by attacking Emberforge?" the Thane asked. "We tried once...and failed."

Trylian visibly bristled at this.

"I know," the Archon Knight whispered dangerously. "I was there. It was *my* failure. But what happened last time will not happen now. I can guarantee it."

"How?" Thaniel asked. "We were overrun. Outmatched. We have no Scion, Trylian. If we did, perhaps he could bless us and we could stand up to them. Wipe them out. But without the dragon…"

"A dragon?" Roan asked, remembering the time before when Trylian had mentioned it. "Are dragons appearing again in Vyrkaris?"

"No," Elendir supplied. "When a Knight is chosen as Scion, his Claret transforms."

"What?" Roan couldn't stop himself. He glanced at Phael.

"Yes." Trylian nodded. "When a Knight is made Scion, his Claret is blessed as well with the form of a dragon. They can transform and do great damage with their breath of fire alone."

"Which is why we cannot hope to stand up to the Elsarius," Thaniel said exasperatedly. "We cannot fight a dragon. Not without one of our own. Unless you are thinking of treating with Vyrkaris and hiring one of their monster slayers. But even then…"

The Thane waved his hand. "Enough of what we don't have. Trylian, what's the plan after Emberforge? If we can find and kill this Scion?"

Trylian smiled. He tapped the map, his finger hitting Delsinor. "The Sanctuary. The throne. We take it all. We destroy the Empyrean Core, taking away the Elsarius's connection to their magic, crippling them."

Phael made a shocked sound at this that drew every eye to him. He quaked under their gazes.

Trylian went on, "Then we kill them all. Even the king and his Elsarius sympathies. I will put myself on the throne."

Roan jolted at this. Not only could he not believe Trylian was laying his plan out so clearly for all to see, but because the thought of Trylian on the throne put ice in his veins. He looked around and saw he was not the only one who felt this way. But the other Archon Knights didn't say a word. They merely glanced at one another. No one would speak up. No one would stand up to Trylian. It was better to be on his side than against him. Everyone seemed to know that.

"We will meet with the Athelings of Sorath and Amril," Trylian went on, resting his hands casually on the hilt of his sword. "They will offer their armies to us. Once the Scion is dead, the Elsarius will fall. It will be a mighty blow to them. Then we gather our armies and march on Delsinor. It's not all that complicated, my friends."

"No, Trylian, it's not," Thaniel whispered. He swallowed hard and nodded. "So it shall be. I am sure of it."

Roan heard Phael gasp behind him and could almost feel the tears prickling his eyes. Phael would be forced to march on his own home. To use his magic to destroy everything he knew and loved. Everything he believed in and served. Roan didn't turn to look at him but let him weep in silence. He wasn't sure what that meant. What Phael would do. He decided then that he'd have to keep a closer eye on him.

"And me, Trylian?" Roan asked. "How do I factor in?"

"I need you, my boy," Trylian said, gripping Roan's shoulder hard. "I need those loyal to me close by." He glanced at Baelian. "I need leaders. Men who can control and lead other men. And you are one of those."

Pride, eagerness, and something akin to joy rose in Roan. They were moving. There would be war, and he was to be one of its leaders.

"When do we leave?" he asked.

Trylian beamed at him. "Give me three weeks, and then... we march."

CHAPTER XIX

The army left the village, taking some spoils of the battle with them. The Thane bequeathed them gold and a handful of slaves to use in the caer. Among them, Roan noted, was the slave girl Antinea. He'd lost her once they were back in Aatheria, but noted she was now close by. He wanted to find her again, though he wasn't sure why.

Once they returned to Aatheria, the entire caer and even the city seemed to be a whirlwind of excitement and movement. Roan immediately went home and spent one night there before he told Mother what they intended to do. Lady Juliana had never been good at taking news like this well. She sank into the plush chair by the hearth, hand to her open mouth.

"Trylian wants to take you away from me," she whispered. "He's not satisfied that Monguard is dead. He wants you, too."

Roan knelt by his mother and took her hand. "I'll come back, I swear. I will not fall to an Elsarius blade. You'll see. We will take Emberforge and return as champions. We will slaughter this Scion, and everyone will know the might and power of the Modeus."

Mother closed her eyes, and a single tear dripped down her cheek. "Competing faiths," she spat. "Who cares what one side of the west believes?"

"They would see us crushed," Roan said with a gentle snarl. "We must strike first, find this Scion and put a stop to them. You can't possibly understand."

"I understand my only son, my only child, is going off to start a war!" she cried, taking his hands in hers.

"They started the war when they tried to create marriage bonds between that Thane from Delsinor and the woman in Duskhallow." He stood, glaring down at his mother. "We will not be subjugated. We cannot be. They would have moved upon us if we didn't attack first."

Mother blinked up at him, nodding. "Of course. We must bring the ways of the Modeus to the world. It is the only way to ensure our survival. The survival of the Modeus's teachings. I believe in you, Roan."

He quickly bent over and kissed her forehead. "I will return. You will see. And I will come back an Archon Knight. And then Trylian will let me take my title as lord of these lands."

Mother beamed up at him. "I believe in you, my son."

Roan left the manor then and traveled through the city back to the caer. It was a cool summer night and rain pattered down in lazy, large droplets onto him. The drops sank through his cloak and slipped under his armor to chill his skin. The firelight reflected off the stony pathways, making the roads look like they were covered in fire. Roan was shivering and wet by the time he reached the caer. He entered the main hall to find a handful of the Knights there, singing loudly as they toasted to themselves. Alamar, Gareth, Tanis, and Razvin were among them. Their Clarets sat nearby, huddled close to the hearth, speaking in soft whispers.

When Razvin spotted Roan, he cried out to him, waving him over. Roan could smell the mead on his breath and saw how Razvin swayed on the spot. He was deep into his cups.

"Roan!" the half-Vyrkarian cried. He raised his goblet. "To Roan, and his new quarters."

Half-smiling, Roan joined them, taking a goblet full of pink mead from Razvin. "What are you talking about?"

"You got private quarters tonight," Gareth said, a smile of jealousy on his lips as he said it. "Father wants you well rested for the march tomorrow. Lucky you. The rest of us are still sleeping in the barracks. Room for your Claret, too. He was here just a moment ago."

Roan raised his red brows. "Private quarters tonight?" What did Trylian have planned for him? What was his game?

"Sounds about right," Alamar slurred, mead dribbling down his unshaven chin. "Trylian's pet gets his own cage for the night." He scoffed, disgusted. "What did you do to deserve his praise?"

Roan burned hot under his collar. "More than you know," he snarled.

Alamar stood, facing Roan.

Behind him, his Claret Veryl stood. "Don't, Alamar," he begged softly. "We need everyone strong and well for the upcoming battle. We cannot risk fighting amongst ourselves."

"Listen to him, Alamar," Gareth warned, going still as he watched Alamar like a hawk.

"Listen to my Claret?" Alamar cajoled. "All he's good for is his magic. I'm not listening to some weeping maid."

Roan smirked at Alamar. "It's not the time to fight. You're drunk. I'd lay you out faster than if you tripped over your own feet."

Alamar set his goblet down and raised his hands. "Come on then, Roan. Show me what you've got."

Roan wanted to raise his fists. To lay Alamar out. It would have been easy. He was as drunk as a Claret tasting wine for market. But he sensed in this moment that it would bring him no pleasure, so there was no point. He stepped back and shook his head. "I don't want to hurt you. Not tonight."

"Ah, come on, Roan," Tanis jeered. "Slap him good."

Alamar turned to Tanis then, his hand shooting out. He grabbed a handful of Tanis's long hair and pulled hard. Tanis cried out and stumbled out of his chair.

"Don't touch my brother," Gareth snarled, leaping at Alamar. A tussle ensued.

Razvin stepped back, crying out as he picked up the bottles of mead, so they didn't get spilled. He clutched them to his chest and looked at Roan. "You sure you don't want a part of this?"

Roan shook his head, watching the other boys roll on the ground like dogs. "Where are my new quarters? Do you know?"

Razvin shook his head. "I think Phael went there, though. You can ask a servant. They should know."

Roan nodded in thanks, glanced once more at the wrestling boys, and turned to leave down a side door out from the main hall. He walked toward the barracks, since even the private rooms were in that direction. He stopped a servant carrying a pail of water and asked where his new room was. The servant pointed him to a spiraling staircase that led to the upper levels. "It's the room with the golden dragon-head knocker," she said after trying to describe where the room was located.

Roan thanked her, then asked, "Do you know a slave girl named Antinea?" He wanted to find her. Private quarters meant no one would watch him that night. He could do whatever he wanted the evening before marching out. And spending it between the legs of the beautiful slave girl sounded like the right thing to do.

The servant nodded. "She's...um, busy this evening."

Roan didn't ask what that meant. He knew. But with

who, he wasn't sure. He didn't want to ask. He'd just hate that man. He nodded his thanks and ascended the steps. The halls in the upper levels were covered in a thick red carpet. Roan had had very little reason to go to the upper levels of the caer. Everything he needed was on the bottom floor or outside. He knew the Archon Knights had rooms up here, but they rarely used them, since most of them had their own land. He passed a few rooms and finally found one with a golden dragon-head knocker. He smiled.

He imagined what it might look like inside. A giant four-post bed with red blankets. A small fireplace all his own. A window. Maybe even a wardrobe. He shoved on the door, eager to see the inside, but it didn't budge. Confused, he pushed on it again. It was locked. From the inside.

Razvin had said Phael had gone up, so he guessed his Claret had locked himself inside. Probably out of fear. He thought Phael had an irrational fear of Alamar and the other more brutish Knights.

He knocked on the door. "Phael, open the door," he commanded. He waited a moment, but no answer came. So he hammered on the door. "Phael, damn it, open the door."

Again, no reply. He sighed and leaned heavily against the door, pressing his palms into the wood. "Phael, please," he said more gently. "I need to get some sleep before tomorrow. We both do."

Maybe his Claret was already asleep?

Roan raised his hand to hammer louder on the door, hoping to wake him, when he heard something inside. A pained, gasping moan came muffled from the other side of the door. Then he heard soft panting, sobbing, maybe.

"Phael," he called, leaning closer to the door now to listen. "Are you all right?"

When only another pained moan answered, Roan pounded on the door. "Winds damn it, Phael, open the door!"

Then he heard a sound he knew all too well. A sharp, metallic clatter of a knife or dagger hitting the floor.

All the blood rushed from Roan's face. His heart raced, beating against his ribs. "Phael!" he screamed. He hammered against the wood once more, guessing at what was going on behind the door. Crying out, Roan threw his shoulder into the door. It didn't budge.

"Hold on, Phael!" he cried. He stepped back, raised his foot, and kicked with all his might, channeling his fear into the attack. The lock broke, flying off, and the door swung open. His eyes went to the white mass of robes lying on the floor.

Phael lay sprawled on the floor, a dagger near his feet where he had dropped it. Blood pooled around him, pouring from his slashed wrists. His face was paler than normal, and tears stained his cheeks. Roan gasped and flew into the room, sliding onto his knees. He gathered Phael in his arms and held him tight. Reaching up to the bed, he yanked the covers away. Then he pulled a white sheet out from underneath and quickly pressed it against Phael's bleeding wrists. He bent his arms, pulling them tight into the Claret's chest and above his heart. He squeezed Phael tight to himself. His robes were red with blood, as were strands of his hair.

"Are you mad?" Roan whispered, pressing his cheek into the top of Phael's head. "Do you want to die?"

Phael gasped a sob, weakly fighting against Roan's grip. "I'd rather die than serve in the Modeus army, marching on my own home."

In a wild move, Phael shoved against Roan and reached for the bloody dagger near his feet. Roan jerked him back, trapping his arms against his chest and holding Phael tight. He pinned his arms down and gripped him. Phael felt so small in his arms. Like his bones were made of glass and Roan might break them if he held him too tight. But he had to. Phael's delicate neck bent, and his white hair splashed over his shoulders. He shuddered as he took a breath and sobbed in Roan's arms.

Roan waited a moment, wondering if Phael had lost too much blood. He had to get him to the infirmary. But he wanted to go there without too many people seeing. He didn't want Phael to be seen in this state. People would ask questions. He might be instructed to stay if his Claret couldn't ride.

"Let me go," Phael wailed, and he struggled uselessly against Roan's grip. "I want to die. I want to escape from this place. This life. Make it all stop."

Roan didn't know why, but his own eyes suddenly pricked painfully with rising tears. He growled and shoved back at them. He concentrated on Phael's body in his arms instead. He tried to adjust his grip so it was gentler, but still firm.

"I can't let you go, Phael," he whispered. "I won't let you take your own life."

"All I am to you is magic," Phael sobbed. "Take someone else. Let me go! I can't do this. I won't attack my home."

"You're useless to the Elsarius dead," Roan snapped. "At least if you're alive, you have a fighting chance. Only the Winds know the meaning of your life, and you cannot throw that away."

Phael went still in Roan's arms, making soft weeping sounds. "Why are you saying this?"

Roan relaxed his grip on Phael then, sensing he had the Claret's attention. He released him but held his wrists. He tore pieces of the bed sheet off and started to wrap his other wrist. The blood had hardly stopped, and he needed to staunch the bleeding better. Phael sniffled but let him get to work.

"I don't want to lose my magic. That's all," he said honestly. "Not the night before we march."

Phael whimpered, defeated.

"And maybe one day, you'll put that dagger in my heart," he went on. "Then you'll be free. But not today. No one is dying today. My Claret must be stronger than that. And besides, you could die soon anyway. Just wait."

Phael's blue eyes went from his bloody wrists to Roan's green eyes. Roan saw only hope and despair mingling in his Claret's eyes. He wanted to comfort and slap Phael at the same time. Something about his Claret made Roan want to protect him. Phael was his. And it was his job to keep him safe.

"I... I can't do this," Phael whispered at long last. "Please don't make me. I've been forsaken by the Elsarius—I have nothing!"

Roan tightened the bindings around his wrists one last time. That would do while they walked to the infirmary. "I have no say in it. I'm just a soldier, doing as I'm told. Same as you. We have to do this. We're followers. It will all be over soon enough and everything will be all right."

"Delsinor won't be," Phael sniffled. "The king will be dead."

He sighed and got to his feet, then crouched. He gathered Phael in his arms and lifted him easily. The Claret was so light, Roan thought he must be made of feathers. Phael's head lolled on his shoulders. He'd lost too much blood.

"We do as we are told," he said with finality. "This is your life now. To survive, just obey."

Phael didn't reply. He closed his eyes even as they rolled in his head and snaked his arms around Roan's neck to help hold himself up. He laid his head against Roan's chest and was silent as Roan marched to the infirmary to get him stitched up and healed.

CHAPTER XX

The road was long and uneventful for days. Roan scanned the moving convoy over and over, watching the men and women with them. The Knights and Clarets and a horde of city soldiers moved like a well-ordered mass. The men unconsciously marched in line, their Clarets by their sides. Roan glanced to his left now and then to watch Phael as they marched over the grasslands and neared the mountain pass. The boy looked ill most days, and Roan knew he was sick with worry. Every night, they had the same conversation. Phael would weep, say he couldn't do it, he couldn't attack Ember-forge and eventually Delsinor. That the Elsarius were his people. Roan would try to ease his mind, but he never had the right words.

Nox was the only one who could soothe Phael's hysterics. Roan would watch them as Nox held Phael's hand, leaning his forehead into Phael's. They'd whisper together and Phael would sob and nod. He didn't know what they were saying, but he let them be.

The nights were the same as most marching nights. Roan would play his lute, Razvin would sing and drink, sometimes dancing a drunk man's jig, and Gareth and Tanis would get into some sort of brotherly dispute and end up brawling. The cooks, smiths, farriers, a few stable boys, and some working women made up the convoy that marched with the army. They often joined in the singing as they went about their duties.

After the mountain pass, though, Trylian insisted they be more silent at night. They had fewer torches lit and often sat in silence around a single campfire. Most men spent the nights in their tents—those who had tents—and the others lay out under the stars.

One night, just on the other side of the mountain pass, Roan spotted Antinea among the women of the camp. The girls were there purely for the men to enjoy, and most of them did their work for a few coins. Roan watched Antinea as she skirted around the edge of the camp, trying to avoid the men. He remembered her well. He'd loved her fiery spirit, the way she'd given in but still struggled, how she'd taken control. She'd locked her gray eyes onto his the entire night, never taking them away. It had been intense.

Antinea slinked to the kitchen wagon and stole a cup of water before winding her way around the camp and back out into the nightly mist. Roan had the urge to follow her, but stopped when Phael approached him, Trylian close behind.

"To the Archon tent," Trylian ordered. "We have plans to discuss."

Roan nodded to Trylian and fell in step beside Phael. "Are you better tonight?" he whispered to Phael. He wasn't sure why he was asking. He didn't care that much... Did he?

Phael took a shuddering breath but didn't nod. "I'm not falling to pieces, if that helps."

Roan gently placed his hand on Phael's back. "I'm glad."

Phael looked up at him, slight confusion swirling in his blue eyes. Something in his face shone gratefully at Roan for his kind words. Phael sighed and looked away as they entered the tent. Roan made sure to stand close to Phael as they entered. Mathis, Thaniel, and Baelian were inside, along with Elendir.

Inside the tent was a square table with a few maps and papers scattered over it. Mathis had been speaking when they entered and stopped to give Trylian a quick nod before going on.

"Amril's army should be here," he said, pointing to the map. "There is a small forest outside the village and their last missive said they'd be waiting for us on the twenty-third of Juniper. That's tomorrow."

"So we're right on time. Good," Thaniel sighed, laying his hand on his sword hilt as he inspected the map. "We made good time."

"Did you doubt us?" Trylian asked. He pulled Roan forward.

Roan noticed Gareth and Tanis were present as well. He nodded to them.

"Never," Thaniel replied stoutly. He pointed back to the map. "Once we meet with Amril's army, then what?"

Trylian stepped forward and placed his finger on the map. "We come around the village. There is a keep there we can take and establish a base. We'll have supplies from the surrounding farms and the support of the village once we take it."

Mathis sighed. "And if they rebel like they did near Delsinor?"

"We'll have a legion of Knights and the soldiers," Trylian said. "We'll burn them alive if they so much as whisper against us. They'll want to live. They will support us."

"And the Scion?" Baelian asked. His brown horns glinted in the firelight.

"Our sources say he's been spotted," Trylian replied, glee making him smile manically. "They've seen him."

"The Scion is real?" Roan asked. "What's he like?"

"He's a boy," Trylian said. "Just as I suspected. About

seventeen. He was discovered in some small village in Moralan when he was young and was taken to Emberforge that day to see the Anakrite and confirm his identity. That's the day we attacked. Unfortunate. He was confirmed as Scion and sent back to his village to be raised in secret. Not even he knew what had happened that day. But he will understand when we attack Emberforge. He's near Duskhallow and we will find him. And we will kill him and everyone he loves."

"He doesn't know he's the Scion?" Roan asked. "What about his Claret? They had to be bound."

"They were born bound," Trylian said, slight disgust in his voice. "When blessed as a Scion, the Winds choose your Claret. You must find one another. He has no idea the boy closest to him is his Claret. His dragon. He believes he has kept his magic abilities secret all these years."

"How do we know this?" Gareth asked tentatively.

"We planted a spy some years ago, when we were first betrayed," Trylian explained. "I cannot tell you all the details, but he was able to get close to the Scion over the years. The boy trusts him."

Roan tried to fathom the Scion's life. Growing up with magic, not knowing everyone around him knew what he was, but trying to keep it a secret. And then there was the betrayal. How would it be to find out that one of his closest friends was a Modeus spy? "What's his name?"

"Cassander," Trylian replied.

So they knew everything about this Scion except exactly where he was now. Roan was jealous of him. "Why haven't the Modeus blessed us with a Scion?"

"I am not an Anakrite," Trylian said. "I cannot know." He glanced at Elendir.

"We cannot know the will of the Modeus in such matters," the Claret replied gently. "But I pray for one every day. Our sources tell us the Anakrite who confirmed the

Elsarius Scion has been gifted the knowledge of the Modeus Scion, but we have not found and captured this Anakrite."

"And the Anakrite is in Emberforge?" Roan asked, understanding dawning on him. "We're looking for him?"

"Her," Baelian corrected.

Roan raised his brows. "She? Elsarius Clarets can be women?"

"The Elsarius do not believe as we do," Trylian offered. "That women should not wield magic. They have female Knights as well. They do not dispose of their female Clarets as we do."

Roan had been taught all his life that women with magic went mad. That was why the Modeus killed any female Claret. He frowned. "Are they not mad?"

Trylian shrugged. "I've met some in battle. They are wild warriors, to be sure. But we will find this female Anakrite and we will learn what she knows."

"And if the Scion is not in Emberforge?" Thaniel asked.

Trylian's azure eyes snapped. "Then we take it anyway. I will blot out the failure from ten years ago."

Roan glanced back down at the map. His nerves bunched under his skin in anticipation and excitement. They were going to sack another village, take another keep, and eventually march on the city of Emberforge. They were finally doing it: they were going to take over the west. Trylian had spoken of nothing else his entire life. Everything had been leading up to this moment.

"Tomorrow," Trylian said, "we meet with the army from Amril. Then, we march on the village and take the keep. From there: Emberforge."

PHAEL'S HEART WAS BREAKING. He watched the men plan out their attacks on the map, making little marks here and there. He caught Elendir's eyes more than once and always looked away quickly. He wasn't sure if the Claret was like him, someone kidnapped and taken away from his life, or if he had always been a Modeus Claret. The more he wondered about it, the more he wanted to find Nox.

The night before, Nox had told Phael not to worry. Said he couldn't explain, but everything would be all right. They had been so close that Nox's sweet breath had touched Phael's cheeks when they'd spoken. He closed his eyes, imagining Nox's black eyes and his gentle touches. This calmed his heart, and he breathed more easily.

"That's everything, then," Trylian said at length. "Get some rest tonight. Tomorrow, we fight."

Roan nodded and turned to leave. Phael followed him closely. They left the tent and Roan started to look around as if he'd lost something.

"What are you looking for?" Phael asked as meekly as he dared. He saw something in Roan he didn't like. Before, Roan had been open and focused on Phael. Now, he had a bloodlust in his eyes and a fire Phael couldn't identify. Phael had to remind himself that Roan was not his friend. Yes, he'd saved him when he'd tried to take his life, but he'd done that out of selfishness. It was hard to see it like that after the words he'd spoken that night. But Roan was a killer. A Knight of the Modeus.

"That girl," Roan replied. "Antinea. I'd like a nice plowing before we go into battle tomorrow."

Phael felt disgusted at the way Roan spoke about women, especially Antinea. He'd told Phael about the night he'd slept with her for the first time, and he hadn't enjoyed the story. Especially after the conversation they'd had. But that had been a night Roan had almost opened up to Phael. He'd wanted to have that conversation again, to get deeper into Roan's mind, but the chance hadn't come up again. Or if it had, he'd been too much of a coward to take it.

Phael sighed. "May I go back to our tent?" He didn't want to watch Roan have sex with the poor girl.

"Fine," Roan quipped. "But don't even think about running. We're watching."

Phael almost rolled his eyes. Of course he'd not run. There was nowhere to go. If he ran now, he'd be killed by a wild beast, or worse.

He broke from Roan and meandered through the large camp toward their tent. Unlike the men in third and fourth column, second and first column Knights had tents. Razvin had pitched his near Roan's, since they were best friends, which meant Nox was close. Phael wanted to see his friend and perhaps find comfort in his arms. But when he found their tents, neither Razvin nor Nox were there. There was no one nearby. Everyone must be around the campfire several yards away. A little heartbroken, and not wanting to join the others, Phael lingered outside Roan's tent before pushing aside the ornate flap and entering.

They had set up their bedrolls before. A barrel of water stood to the right, unopened. Phael vaguely thought about bathing and washing the day's march off himself. Before he could turn, though, the flap whipped open again. Phael gasped and turned.

Alamar and three other Knights stood before him, blocking his way out. Alamar leered at Phael and motioned to the other boys to move. Phael snapped into motion to run, but he wasn't fast enough. The much larger boys grabbed him by his arms and held him tight.

"Don't scream," Alamar warned him, flicking a blade out from his belt and pressing it to Phael's cheek.

Phael whimpered in fear and struggled against his captors. He looked around. Where was Roan? Should he call for him?

"Go on," Alamar instructed the third boy, who didn't have a hold of Phael.

The boy stepped forward and punched Phael hard in his chest. All the wind was knocked out of him, and he gasped in pain. The Knight then backhanded him hard across his face before laying into him. He punched every inch of Phael's body he could lay his hands on, pulled his hair, and smacked his face.

"This is what you get for being Roan's Claret," Alamar said. "Trylian's pets."

"Coward," Phael moaned once the other boy stopped hitting him for a moment. "Come back when Roan's here."

"I'm no simpleton," Alamar said. He sheathed his little blade and motioned for the others to move. "I made sure Roan was occupied before coming in. This may not teach him a lesson, but it will teach you."

Phael's knees went weak, and he almost fell, but the boys held him up. "Coward," he reiterated.

Alamar glared. "Over the barrel." He pointed.

The boys dragged Phael to the barrel and heaved him over it onto his stomach. They let go, but Alamar's hand went to the back of Phael's head, holding him in place.

Phael vaguely wondered what Alamar was doing when he heard a tearing sound. Alamar ripped his robes open from behind. His hands then went to Phael's backside, gripping him hard. Alamar pulled, ripping his pants as well. Phael felt the wind touch his sensitive skin.

"No!" he screamed before one of the boys punched him hard in the face, winding him once again.

Alamar's hand went between his legs, rubbing him roughly. Phael writhed against the touch, trying to pull away, but the Knight was too strong. Then his hand trailed back, a single finger wedging its way into him. Phael sobbed and struggled.

"I hear Elsarius Clarets are pure," Alamar whispered, leaning over Phael's prone body. His finger delved deeper.

Phael whimpered as the finger breached him. Tears instantly spilled down his face. It hurt.

"Look at you," Alamar purred. "There's no way someone hasn't rutted the shit out of you." He forced in a second finger and pulled hard, tearing Phael.

Phael screamed in pain and writhed against Alamar.

"You won't scream for him," Alamar hissed. "He won't come."

Something in Phael broke. He didn't care if Alamar killed him now. He just wanted it all to stop. "Roan!" he screamed with all his might. "Roan, help me!"

Alamar slapped him hard. His other hand went to Phael's backside, where he pulled savagely, opening him up. Phael twisted and finally dislodged Alamar. He threw his head back, making cracking contact with Alamar's face. He heard his nose crunch. He rolled to the side and fell to the ground. Crawling backward away from the Knight, he prepared to scream again. Alamar grinned down at him, motioning to his friends to grab Phael. They did, one covering his mouth before he could cry out.

"Brave little boy," Alamar crooned. "But you'll pay for that."

The others lifted Phael again and slammed him down on his belly over the barrel. They held his arms this time, and Alamar kicked his feet wide apart. He held Phael's legs open with his knees and went to work on the laces of his own pants. Fear lanced through Phael, but something else happened. He froze. Realizing what was about to happen to him, his body locked up.

Just stay still, he told himself. *It will be over soon.* He prepared for the pain that was about to tear him in two. Everything went silent and still.

The tent flaps burst inward. In a flurry of red hair, Roan appeared. His face was twisted in rage when his eyes landed on Alamar.

"Run!" one of the boys holding Phael cried.

They dropped him and Phael fell to the ground, his legs too weak to hold him up. His mind buzzed, making it impossible to see what was going on. He heard the crunch of bones, the slapping of flesh on flesh. He curled in on himself and waited.

Someone came in the tent behind Roan. In a blur of brown, followed by the scent of wildflowers, Antinea flew to Phael and knelt on the ground beside him. She wrapped her arms around his head and held him to her chest. She quickly rearranged his robes to cover him and held him tight. She called Roan's name, begging him to stop.

Phael looked up and his vision was blurry. He saw Roan's long hair whipping about as he pummeled Alamar and the others. Roan then pushed Alamar out of the tent and followed him, dragging the other two with him. Outside the tent, a ruckus erupted. Phael hardly heard it, though.

Roan had come for him.

Tears filled Phael's eyes, and everything came back into focus all at once. He heard Antinea breathing into his hair and whispering kind words.

"It's all right," she said, rocking with him and holding him. "He's gone. Roan took him away."

Phael burst into sobs and pulled his knees together into his chest. He still hurt. Alamar had torn him and made him bleed. He could feel it.

Before Phael could stop himself, he burst, "I was to remain pure! I'm tainted now. He took it from me." He couldn't stop the string of words and babbling that poured from his mouth after that.

Antinea shook her head and shushed him. "No, Phael," she whispered sweetly. "Your purity is not your body. It's not something that can be taken from you. Trust me. You are still pure. You are still worthy."

Not sure what he'd said, these words did comfort him some. But he couldn't stop the sobs. He pressed himself into her and let them come. Roan wasn't there to see.

Roan.

He'd come when Phael had screamed for him. Or did he come because he felt his fear through the bond? Did it matter? He *had* come. He'd saved him. Again.

"It's about power, Phael," Antinea whispered, petting his long, white hair. "It's nothing else. It's all about power. Trust me. You are still righteous and pure."

He wasn't so sure, but he took her word for it for now, allowing it to comfort him. He gripped her arms and let her rock him until calmness started to wash over him. He closed his eyes.

CHAPTER XXI

Roan woke the next morning before anyone else in camp. Behind him, he felt Phael breathing softly. The Claret had lain close to him that night after the incident with Alamar. Roan didn't mind. Part of him wanted to stab Alamar for touching Phael the way he had. Rage ignited in him, waking him up.

The air was cool, and he could smell dew and fog in the air; clean and wet like after a spring rain. He pushed himself up and got dressed quickly. When he went out to the fire to get tea and something to eat, Trylian and Elendir were already awake, dressed in their armor and robes, respectively. Trylian nodded to Roan when he approached. Roan let them alone and ate in silence. The morning was indeed fog-covered, and he couldn't see the treeline just beyond the camp.

Soon, the others woke up and the camp stirred. The Knights donned their armor, and some sharpened their blades last minute.

"Listen to me," Trylian called once most of the Knights and Clarets were awake. He stood on a crate and addressed the army. "I will take a few men, and we will scout ahead. We will meet with the Archon Knights from Amril and then meet you outside the village. Everyone is to remain silent and not light torches this evening. We are to remain unseen. The army from

Amril will strengthen our numbers, and we should take the village easily. They don't know we're coming. Understood?"

The Knights and Clarets nodded and some mumbled a, "Yes, sir."

"Roan, Razvin," Trylian said, hopping down from the crate, "you will accompany my boys and me. It will just be the five of us."

"And the Clarets?" Roan asked, falling into step with Trylian. Razvin, Gareth, and Tanis followed behind them. "Will we be using magic?"

"Shouldn't need it," Trylian said with a wary sigh. "We're meeting our alliance, not fighting them. Leave them behind."

"Nox," Razvin called. The black-eyed Claret trotted up to them. "Watch the others while we're gone. Make sure they're safe."

Nox nodded and turned to leave. Roan watched him wind his way through the men and find Phael. They'd be fine, he told himself. Alamar wouldn't dare try to touch Phael again. At least, he hoped not. He found Alamar in the crowd as they marched to their horses and glared at him, warning him with a glower. Alamar didn't blink, but didn't have his constant look of superiority on his face this time, either.

The five of them mounted up and together they trotted out into the forest. The sun continued to rise as they rode. Roan tried to count the minutes and the distance, but lost track after about an hour. He glanced sideways at Razvin and noticed he looked shockingly sober and not hungover.

"No drinking last night?" he asked with a small smile.

Razvin shook his head. "Need my wits about me today, don't I?"

Roan shrugged. "Never stopped you before. Something wrong?"

His lifelong friend grinned at him. "When is anything right?"

Roan laughed and Trylian hissed at them to remain quiet. He did then, keeping his eyes straight ahead.

It took another hour before Trylian raised his hand in a fist, signaling them to stop. The boys pulled up on their reins, stopping several feet behind Trylian. Roan looked around. It was too foggy to see far. He glanced at Trylian and saw his black brows descend into a confused frown.

"What is it?" Roan whispered. "Where are they?"

Trylian slowly looked around, not answering. Finally, he said, "I don't smell fire. We should be close. Where...?"

Roan saw Trylian tense. Something was wrong.

"Gareth," Trylian called. His son trotted up next to him. "Watch Tanis. Roan, take the lead. Razvin, watch our flank."

The boys moved into formation and then Trylian led the way with Roan deeper into the forest. Roan tried to put his senses on high alert as they made their way through the fog. They couldn't see far, and the fog muffled the sound of their horses' hooves against the earth. They'd not hear anything until it was too late.

Roan's sharp eyes caught something ahead. He squinted and held up his hand to stop Trylian. He pointed ahead.

"What is it?" Trylian asked, looking in the same direction.

"A clearing," Roan whispered. "I think I see tents."

Trylian waited a moment, considering his next move. Then he shouted, "Martin! Are you there?"

Roan gripped his reins tight, sweat beading on his brow.

No one replied.

"Winds damn it," Trylian hissed and kicked his horse in the side. He shot off in the direction of the camp ahead. Roan followed him at a trot.

"Father?" Tanis called softly. "Roan?"

Roan shrugged and went after Trylian. The others followed Roan. They broke through the trees and ended up inside a large clearing. Roan pulled up on his reins hard and froze. His mouth dropped open.

They stood in the middle of a camp. That much was obvious. But no one milled about. The ground was covered in bodies, Knights and Clarets alike scattered over the mud. The tents were torn; no fires poured forth smoke. As far as Roan could see, the ground was covered in bodies and destruction.

Trylian slid off his horse. "Martin!" he called again. His head whipped this way and that, looking for the Archon Knight. Roan watched him walk among the dead, lifting his legs high to step over the corpses. He surveyed from the back of his horse.

"Winds," Gareth whispered when he finally joined Roan. Razvin and Tanis also appeared.

"Are they all dead?" Razvin said in a hushed tone. "Even the Clarets. Every last one."

Roan watched Trylian enter a tent, call for Martin again, then reappear, looking around.

"What happened?" Roan called.

Trylian looked lost. His hands fell empty and useless at his sides. "They're dead. All of them. The plans and maps are gone." His chest rose and fell as he began to pant. "Everything's gone."

Roan noticed no smoke rising from anywhere. The blood on the tents was not wet. This had happened days ago. They were not just moments too late, but much longer.

"The Elsarius did this?" Roan asked. "How?"

"Elsarius wouldn't do this," Razvin said, disbelief making him hoarse. "Surely. Not the Clarets. Some of them were innocent. Stolen Elsarius Clarets like ours. Why would they kill them?"

"Because they are traitors," Trylian said. He still looked around as though he were missing something. "They wouldn't risk taking them back."

"But how did they know they were here?" Roan asked. "How did they strike before us?"

Trylian met his gaze, a dangerous glint in his eyes. "That's the right question to ask, Roan. How did they know Amril would be here?"

Roan exchanged glances with the other boys.

"A traitor?" Gareth asked at the same time Tanis said, "A spy?"

The bottom of Roan's stomach dropped out. "The others," he cried. "They could be going back to the camp."

Trylian's face paled. He dashed to his horse and remounted quickly. "Back to camp," he shouted. "Run!"

Roan kicked his horse and turned sharply. Together, the five of them galloped back toward the camp.

They ran for an hour before Roan spotted a glint in the forest to his right. He turned and saw a man in white armor galloping toward them, bow in hand.

"Scouts!" he shouted, pointing at the man. He saw the golden sun and raven symbol for the Elsarius on his chest plate. "Elsarius!"

Gareth stood in his stirrups, turned, and fired an arrow behind him. It missed the man, but it made him lurch to the side on his horse, almost unseating him.

"In front!" Tanis shouted in his high, panicked voice. "Two more!"

Trylian drew his blade and kicked his horse hard in the sides. Roan followed suit. Tanis galloped after the two, vanishing into the forest. Gareth cried out after his brother, but couldn't follow as two more men appeared beside him, swords drawn.

The one Gareth had shot at turned hard and galloped around Roan, making it hard for Roan to aim any magic at the man. Roan raised his gloved hand and threw a small ball of fire at him, but it missed, hitting the trees.

"No magic!" Trylian cried as he fought on horseback with one of the others. "We'll burn the forest down and alert them to our presence."

"We know you're here!" the Knight of the Elsarius shouted back.

Roan pulled up on his reins and turned to look for the man. As he did, something hit him hard in his front. Roan groaned in pain and was shoved backward. He jerked on his horse and lost control, falling off.

"Roan!" Razvin shouted.

Roan looked up, winded from his fall, and saw an arrow sticking out of his shoulder. It had hit him right in the gap of his armor. It hurt. He felt hot blood seeping out under his armor. He tried to sit up, but any movement jostled the arrow, tearing at his muscles. He groaned in pain again and tried to roll over to get up. All around him, the sounds of battle went on.

One of the Elsarius Knights dismounted and sauntered toward him. He drew his sword.

"No!" Razvin screamed. He ran up behind the man and, with one wild swing, entered combat with him.

Roan blinked and tried to focus on his friend defending him, but the pain made his mind fuzzy. He watched Razvin fight the man for some time before the half-Vyrkarian finally lopped off the Knight's head. The head spun off into the forest and Razvin slid onto his knees by Roan. He picked him up, laying his head on his lap. "Are you dead?" he asked, trying to smile.

"Not yet," Roan moaned, gripping the arrow.

"Don't—!" Razvin started.

But Roan pulled anyway. He regretted it right away. The barbs on the end of the arrow tore his muscles and skin, making another fresh wave of blood pump out of his wound. Roan screamed at the agony.

"Well done," Razvin sighed, a half-smile making his lips crooked. He grabbed Roan's good arm and slung it over his neck. "They got them, I think." He looked toward where Trylian paced, searching the woods. Razvin stood, hauling Roan with him.

"Tanis!" Gareth shouted, fear strangling his voice. "Where is he?"

Trylian looked around. "He went after the other two."

Without waiting, Gareth kicked his horse and charged into the forest to find his twin brother. Trylian shouted for him to wait, but Gareth didn't. Trylian looked at Roan, then off into the trees where his boys had vanished.

"Go," Roan said through gnashed teeth. The pain was tormenting him. "I'll be fine."

Trylian leapt up onto his horse and dashed into the trees after his sons. Seconds later, shouts rose up and the sound of metal on metal clanged through the forest. Razvin walked Roan to his horse and helped him up onto it. By the time he was reseated, the three of them came trotting back into the clearing. Tanis beamed.

"Damn bastard!" Gareth was shouting after him. Roan noticed tear tracks on Gareth's face, cutting through the blood and grime. "You could have died."

"I had it," Tanis said easily, sheathing his blade.

"You certainly did," Trylian offered, though he looked weary and disheveled. He glanced at Roan. "And you? Took an arrow to the shoulder?"

Roan nodded. "Hurts like hell, but nothing that cannot be fixed."

"Keep it clean," Trylian sighed. He looked around as though expecting more men to pop out of the bushes. "Infection is what kills."

Razvin gave Roan a stern look. Roan nodded and rolled his eyes. "I'll do my best," he promised.

"Are we safe?" Tanis asked, looking around.

"For now," Trylian answered. "We need to get back to the camp. Winds know what has happened. And Winds know where the Elsarius army is now. Those were scouts. They were looking for the camp. They must be close."

"Do you think they're at Emberforge?" Roan asked.

Trylian blinked in thought. "I hope not. Now, back to camp."

*

WHEN THEY RETURNED TO CAMP, everything looked to be all right. No smoke rose from the trees. The sound of battle didn't reach Roan's ears. No one screamed. They broke through the trees and beheld the rows of tents and wagons. Everything was fine. He breathed a sigh of relief, but his chest hurt. Blood soaked his tunic under his armor and sweat dribbled from his scalp.

"Roan!"

Phael ran forward, leading the other Clarets behind him. Each Claret went to their Knight, half-inspecting them for wounds and half-eager for news. Roan slid off his horse and his knees bent under him. He'd lost a good amount of blood and everything hurt. They'd been riding for hours, and he was hot and tired. Phael grabbed him and helped support him. Roan watched as Nox embraced Razvin.

"We were so worried," Nox whispered, but Roan heard him. He was intrigued by the interaction. He hadn't known Razvin and his Elsarius Claret had gotten so close.

He glanced back at Phael, who looked worried. "Just an arrow," he said simply. He tried to shrug but that shot a bolt of pain through him.

"I'll take you to the healer," Phael said, and he started to pull Roan into the camp.

"No," Roan sighed. "Just my tent. I'll take care of it myself."

Phael pressed his lips together but ultimately did as Roan asked. He walked before Roan, leading him to his tent. They passed a group of Knights that had surrounded someone. Roan wasn't going to intervene with their cajoling and rude remarks until he heard Antinea's voice.

"Please," she was begging softly. "Leave me be."

Alamar was one of the Knights that had encircled her. He reached out and grabbed her arm, pulling her to him. Roan didn't hear what he said into her ear, but it made her blush and wince. She jerked against him, but he didn't let go. With his other hand, he grabbed her breast and squeezed until she cried out.

"Plow her or let her go, Alamar," Roan barked.

The Knights turned to look at him. Some of them mumbled about him being Trylian's pet, and others suggested he take her to bed. Alamar pushed Antinea away and she ran.

"You in charge of saving everyone, Red Mane?" he sneered. He let his eye fall on Phael, who quelled under his gaze.

Roan let Phael duck behind him. He stood his ground, blood dribbling out of his arm. He glared at Alamar, almost wishing he'd rush him. He wanted to fight the boy again, reminded of what he'd done to Phael. Something in his eyes must have resonated with Alamar because he scoffed, shook his head, and departed.

Together, Roan and Phael made their way to his tent, satisfied. Roan groaned as he sat down, tired, in pain, and hot. Phael went to work and quickly removed his armor, then poured a bowl of cold water from the basin on top of the water barrel. He dipped a rag into the water and wrung it out.

Roan struggled but eventually got his shirt off. It was soaked red with blood. Phael blanched and whimpered silently when he saw the damage. Roan grunted and leaned back.

Before Phael could dab at the wound, the tent flap opened. Antinea stood framed in the doorway. She didn't smile, but her pretty face was placid. Roan frowned up at her. Silently, she entered and took the rag from Phael.

"I've got him," she whispered. "Go find Nox."

Phael opened his lips to speak back but stopped when she touched his wrist. Curious, Roan watched Phael leave and then let his eyes drift to Antinea. He was tired, and she seemed to glow in the candlelight. He sat up, but she pressed her hand into his good shoulder and pushed him gently.

"Lie down," she instructed.

Curious, Roan did as he was told. He watched her hands as she went to work on his wound. It stung, and he tried not to hiss, but couldn't stop the sound of pain.

"I'm sorry," she said softly. She wiped at the blood, then dipped the rag back into the basin, cleaning it. She pulled a small brown bottle out from her simple dress's pocket and emptied it into the water. "Herbal oils. To help stave off infection."

He didn't argue. He was too mesmerized by her smooth, gentle movements and delicate touches. He watched her face as she wiped away the blood. She looked serene, calm. Almost alluring. Like she hadn't been manhandled by Alamar seconds ago.

"You're dirty," she whispered, and her hands went to the laces on his pants.

Roan froze for a moment, then his face flushed. He wanted to know how far she'd go. But he was tired and sore, so he shoved her hand away gently.

"Not tonight," he said, guessing her intent, though he wasn't sure why she was trying to get him into bed.

Antinea licked her lips, thinking. Then she nodded and went back to his wound. She cleaned it well, gently. He loved the feeling of her fingers on his flesh and thought twice about pushing her away now. He'd had her before, but something was different tonight. The way she came to him, the way she moved so gently... Something was far more intimate about it.

"Trylian never says no," she whispered.

Roan frowned, meeting her eyes. She shook her head, clearly thinking better of what she was about to say.

"He's rough with me. Like you were. But I bear it."

Somehow, guilt flitted into Roan's chest. He was like Trylian?

"Men like when I say no," she went on, wrapping his wound now in strips of cloth she pulled from his pack. "It excites them."

But she had stopped when he said no. What was she getting at? What did she want? An apology? He wouldn't give her that. He wasn't sorry.

She gently pulled his long red hair to the other side of his neck and tightened the wrappings. The way her fingers trailed through his hair made him shiver. She finished tying the ends off and stood, then hesitated, like she had something else to say.

"I want to sleep," he said.

Antinea nodded, turned, and went out. Roan took in a deep breath, calming his hot blood. She was gone and he could relax. He closed his eyes, and sleep almost took him at once. He meant to call Phael back but was too tired to even do that. So he drifted off.

But not for long. Gentle hands ran up his abdomen to his bare chest. One delicate finger traced his sharp jawline and pushed his hair behind his ear. He tried to open his eyes but was too tired. His lids felt too heavy. He groaned and tried to stir, but his body refused to move.

The hands moved back down his stomach now, to the top of his pants. They gently began to unlace them.

No! he thought in panic. And he jolted awake. His eyes flew open and Antinea knelt before him.

"What...are you doing?" he asked groggily. "I said no."

"You don't know what you want," she whispered back. She sat up on her knees and ran her hand over him and between his legs. "You saved me. Don't you want thanks?"

Heat pulsed through Roan at her touch. He sat up and, fast as lightning, took her wrist in his hand, pulling her away. She gasped and looked up at him fearfully. That look did give him pleasure, like she'd said. He waited, holding her at bay.

"I'm sorry," she sighed. "I thought that if... Well, that you'd..." She demurely lowered her eyes.

That look of submission sent a wild thrill through Roan. He pulled her hand toward him and bent down, taking her mouth in his. She whimpered and moaned into his lips. Raising her other hand, she tangled it in his long red hair. He let go of her wrist. She immediately went back to feeling between his legs, rubbing him roughly. He moaned as he kissed her.

"Yes," she whispered. She stood and threw her dress off, diving right back onto him.

Yes, indeed. He'd give in to her. Just this once, she had won.

CHAPTER XXII

Trylian sat straight and tall upon his horse, looking over the land. A small hill rose up before the village and that was where he'd perched himself. Behind him, the army marched to catch up. The sound of it deafened him. There was no way a nearby farmer in a field had not heard them by now. But what did it matter? Did the village know they were on their way? Amril had been devastated. Slaughtered. He'd not expected the Elsarius to be so brutal. It was like they knew they were on the move. But they didn't *need* the army from Amril. He would have just liked to have it. He fully believed in his and his army's capability to take the village. It was Emberforge where they would need the assistance. But Sorath would meet them there.

Emberforge had no walls and gates. At least, that was what their spies said. It hadn't had walls the last time Trylian was there, but he suspected that might have changed in the ten years since his devastating loss. They were in the process of building walls, but that took decades. No, it was still open. They didn't need siege equipment to breach the walls. Not like they would in Delsinor. Once they had Emberforge surrounded with Sorath, it would fall easily. Or so he hoped.

But it wasn't just about taking the city. He wanted to find the Elsarius Scion and kill him. While the boy lived, he'd give them hope. And a people with hope were hard to kill. But he wanted to rectify his downfall. The people who followed the Modeus all knew of his failure. Yes, he wanted a Modeus king on the throne of Adorian and to eventually conquer Moralan, but first, he had to expunge the black from his name.

And then there was Roan. His eyes flitted to the red dot among the sea of black armor and white robes that was Roan. He had the reddest hair, and it stood out among his fellow Knights. Roan was obedient, pliant, and able to be controlled. He was a good soldier. He was also strong, ruthless at times, and ambitious. He'd do well for what Trylian had planned for him.

"Trylian?" Elendir's gentle voice broke into his thoughts. "The men are in formation."

He took a deep breath, coming back to the present moment. He looked around. "Have the battering rams move up closer as we charge. We need to enter that keep as soon as we can. I don't want to wait on them. Baelian," he called. He turned to the other Archon Knights. "Have your column come in from the south. I know the village is more spacious there and will give you room to charge in deep. Mathis, follow him. Thaniel, follow me."

The men nodded and muttered some "yes, sirs" before moving to their positions at the heads of their columns.

"Elendir," Trylian ordered, "keep the Clarets back. There's nowhere to hide out here." He scanned the open prairie. The village was nestled by a lake, but there were no forests for the Clarets to hide in. "If anything happens, if anyone comes for you, scatter and ride back toward camp. Get lost in the woods when you reach them, do you understand?"

"But the magic won't reach that far," Elendir protested.

Trylian nodded. "I need you alive, my old friend. I'll be fine. I cannot always depend on the magic."

Elendir nodded, though his face was pinched in worry. He

called out to the Clarets and a sea of white began to pull from the army's ranks and filter back behind them. Trylian watched the separation as he rode to the front of his column. He called his boys, Alamar, Razvin, and Roan up to flank him. He trusted them more than anyone else. Except maybe Baelian. They were the strongest Knights despite not being first column. They were good boys.

He didn't stop riding forward after he called them. He charged, sword drawn. On his left hand was a yellow stone for lightning. In his sword rested an orange one for fire. It would be especially useful here, where the buildings were made of thatch and wood. Even the Sactrium in Emberforge was made of wood. The last one he had was a purple crystal around his neck for the invisible blasts he liked best.

"For the Modeus!" he shouted as he charged. Behind him, the Knights cheered and repeated the charge.

They breached the village's nonexistent border quickly. They dashed in, hacking and slashing at the people. They didn't appear to be ready for them. Peasants walked the streets and screamed as they charged in. He cut the heads off a few before he turned to make sure the men had followed him. Already the streets ran red with blood. Fire and bursts of lightning shot up from the horde of Knights. Little houses burned around him, black billowing smoke engulfing the sky above.

A few arrows flew past him, hitting a few Knights. He turned and reached out, blasting away a small group of hunters who had emerged with bows. They flew back, screaming, into a burning wall of a building. For good measure, Trylian threw a ball of fire at them. The men caught fire and screamed, running around and falling.

Trylian hacked and slashed his way inward, making room for the battering rams. He rode back and called to them, motioning them forward. As they started to wheel their way in, a host of guards poured out of the keep and down the hill into the village. Trylian threw an invisible blast at the feet of one of their horses, breaking its legs and causing it to stumble. The rider went flying and landed hard against the ground.

"Roan, stop them!" he cried.

In an instant, Roan and a small handful of Knights turned and swarmed the keep's guards. Trylian continued to fight, throwing a ball of fire here, a web of lightning there. But he stopped when he heard a string of commands going out among the villagers.

"Get out of town! Get the Clarets! We'll hold them here."

All the blood drained from his face as he turned and saw a horde of ragtag soldiers in armor charge toward the sea of white. Elendir had not gotten far enough away yet. They were too close.

Trylian kicked his horse and galloped back out the way he'd come. "Razvin, with me!" he shouted.

The half-Vyrkarian whirled around and motioned for a small host of Knights and soldiers to follow him. But Trylian knew he was too far behind the militia. The villagers that charged outside the village stopped and they all took out bows.

No! Trylian screamed in his head as he and Razvin charged. They wound their way through the village and past confused Modeus Knights. "Push further up and in!" he shouted as he passed.

He watched helplessly as the horde of militia fired their bows into the scattering Clarets. From where he sat, he could see some of them hit their marks. A few Clarets jerked backward from the impact of arrows and fell off their horses. Trylian scanned the sea of white and spotted Elendir. He was hanging back, calling and motioning for the Clarets to run. He was too separated from the herd.

He spotted a man aim and fire at Elendir. Trylian's heart

skipped a beat before the arrow even left the bow string. The arrow looked like it lodged itself right into his chest.

"Elendir!" he screamed. His Claret teetered on his horse, then fell.

"Sir!" Razvin shouted. "We have to go back. They're breeching the keep."

Trylian looked back. The Clarets were far enough away now that the bowmen on foot could not catch up. But Elendir? His heart torn in two, Trylian nodded. He whirled his horse around and charged back into the village. Rage fueled his strokes now. He savagely hacked the villagers, aiming to maim and harm more than to kill. He threw a web of lightning at one woman and sustained the charge until she stopped screaming, her skin blackening and her hair smoking.

He made it back to the wooden bridge that led to the keep and watched as the battering ram did its work. He looked at Razvin and nodded, silently thanking him for his cool head. He had done the right thing. He still had his magic, too, which meant Elendir wasn't dead. At least not yet. But he could be lying alone in the pasture, bleeding out slowly.

No, I can't think like that, he chided himself. Elendir would make it. He had to.

Behind them, Roan and his column defended the invading army. Trylian watched as Roan gave orders and slaughtered at the same time. He truly was a brilliant little soldier.

The battering ram hammered one last time, an earsplitting explosion of wood cracking through the air. It breeched the keep and the Knights began to pour in. Trylian shouted for the men to go, to not stop until the Thane was dead, and his head was on a pike. He didn't hear the exact words he said, but knew they were good from the way the men cheered.

He reeled back around and began to throw fire into all the structures. "Burn the place down," he ordered.

Other Knights followed his example and began to set the entire village alight.

It was perhaps an hour later that they had dragged the Thane and his family out. They did as Trylian instructed and speared them on stakes outside the keep. He gave orders for more stakes to be erected and for the head citizens to join them, even if they were already dead. He wanted to make an example.

Mathis took to the streets, telling the villagers they were in command now. Thaniel followed suit and rode to the eastern end of the village. Trylian wanted to leave, to find Elendir. But he had to wait until the other Archon Knights were done speaking. Everything had to be in order before he left. Baelian rode up beside him.

"Half the village is dead," he reported. "The keep is taken. No one fights us anymore."

"Are you sure?" Trylian asked. He wiped blood from his face. He was caked in soot, blood, and dust.

Baelian nodded. "We should check on the Clarets. Some may be saved."

Trylian nodded and quickly turned his horse around. He'd done his part. He'd led the men, made sure victory was complete, and now he could focus on Elendir.

He charged back out of the village and into the pastures surrounding it. He slowed when he got to where the Clarets' horses stood, confused and whinnying. He slid off his mount and walked into the wheat field. He cast his eyes around, looking for Elendir. He found two dead Clarets on the way. Not ones he recognized. There were too many to know by name or even face. He stepped over them, knowing he'd have to find more to replace them. He marched closer to the horde of white, calling out Elendir's name.

"Trylian," a weak but familiar voice cried out.

Trylian spun around and found Elendir lying in the grass,

blood blossoming over his chest. His once white robes were now a vibrant red. An arrow stuck out of his chest near his left shoulder. Just looking at it, Trylian knew it wasn't a fatal shot.

He exhaled in relief and knelt by his Claret. He gathered Elendir in his arms and touched the shaft of the arrow. Elendir winced. Looking around, Trylian found another arrow in the ground. He pulled it out and inspected the arrowhead. They were barbed. He couldn't pull it out without severely injuring Elendir.

"I have to push it through," he whispered. "I'm so sorry."

Elendir nodded mutely. He gripped Trylian's arm and closed his eyes. Trylian wrapped his fingers around the arrow and took a deep breath. He counted to three and then pushed. Elendir gasped and whimpered in pain. Tears leaked from between his closed eyes. Trylian pushed and pushed. It felt like hours before the barbed arrowhead ripped through Elendir's back. Trylian snapped the arrowhead off and then pulled the arrow back through. As it slid out, Elendir shivered.

"You'll be all right," Trylian whispered. He lifted Elendir easily and helped him mount his horse. Then he led the steed back into the village where the men waited for him.

"How many did we lose?" Baelian asked.

"Maybe five," Trylian sighed. "Gather the men and let's count our losses."

"Twenty soldiers dead," Roan offered quickly. "Seventeen wounded. Five Knights dead."

"Damn it," Trylian hissed. He looked back out toward where the Clarets had run. Some would be dropping dead any moment. Others might take longer to die but die they would. They didn't have the means or time to bind them to new Knights. The loss would be great.

"It's not as bad as it could have been," Baelian offered. "They could have been waiting for us, slaughtered us."

Trylian looked up at the keep. "True," he sighed. "Baelian, gather the Clarets. We're staying here tonight."

"Sir," Thaniel said, riding up in a cloud of dust. He pulled up on his reins and came to a stop. "We captured some local Knights and an Emissary from Emberforge who knows you by name. Should we kill them?"

"An Emissary who knows me?" Trylian asked. "No, keep him. Lock him up. We'll need to question him. He might know where the Scion is. He'll have valuable information."

Thaniel shifted. "It's a woman. What if she won't talk?"

Trylian scoffed. "I can make anyone talk. I'm not worried about that." He glanced around. "Get the men inside. Tomorrow night, we celebrate our small victory."

CHAPTER XXIII

Roan slipped through the crowds inside the keep's feasting hall. It felt like hundreds of Knights and their Clarets had packed themselves inside. Not only that, but a few wealthy citizens from the village had come by to pledge their loyalty and goods to the Modeus. Phael was close behind Roan, but his face was wrinkled in anxiety.

"I'll leave you to your celebration," he said close to Roan's ear. "I want to speak with Nox."

Roan glanced over and saw Veryl, Alowyn, and Nox at a small side table alone. His gut told him to not let the Elsarius Clarets alone by themselves, but Phael looked so pathetic that he shoved his feelings aside and nodded. He watched as Phael's white head wove through the people to the table.

"Roan!" Razvin called out. "Trylian wants you at the head table. We have a seat for you."

Roan turned and spotted Razvin standing on the head table, a goblet clutched in his clawed hand. Someone had tied ribbons around his horns and placed a crown of leaves around his head. Roan guessed it was the servant girl giggling at his side, clinging to his arm. This reminded him of Antinea. He quickly glanced around to see if they had her working, but didn't spot her.

He wound his way around the people. Some of them

clapped him on his shoulders, telling him he'd fought well. Others shook his hand. A few looked daggers at him, Alamar among them. He ignored them, knowing he had earned his spot at the head table. He pushed through the final line of people and broke out of the crowd, climbing over the table and jumping down beside Razvin. Gareth and Tanis were there as well, both red-faced and laughing. They had had too much to drink already.

Razvin poured Roan a goblet full of a dark red mead and shoved it into his hands. "Drink and forget yesterday," he cheered, tipping the goblet back to his lips.

"Forget?" Roan asked. "Yesterday was a great victory. We won't forget it. We're closer to Emberforge than ever."

"Emberforge, Emberforge!" Razvin growled. "Who cares about taking Emberforge? This is Trylian's personal vendetta. We lost lives today because of him."

"Raz, be quiet," Roan hissed, punching his friend in the shoulder. "You were chosen to lead the men. You did a great thing yesterday. And it was an honor. Don't forget that."

Razvin narrowed his red-rimmed eyes at Roan. "Why do you follow him so blindly? So completely? What's he done for you?"

"He raised me," Roan replied, taking some food and piling it high on his wooden plate. "He taught me everything I know. Has given me everything I have."

"And took your estate," Razvin slurred. "That manor is yours by rights."

"Father wanted Trylian to keep it until I'm of age. Which is soon." He frowned at Razvin. "You've had too much to drink. Otherwise, you wouldn't be questioning me like this."

His friend rolled his eyes and took another drink. "I hear they have an Emissary from Emberforge to question tonight."

"I heard that as well. They said she knew Trylian by name. I wonder what—"

But before he could ask any questions, the great double wooden doors at the end of the hall burst open. A gaggle of guards from the keep came in, leading a woman with long white hair. She wore the robes of a Claret. Her hands were chained before her. Trylian stood, looking curiously at the woman. Roan stood as well, just to get a better view of her. The middle of the hall cleared as the guards brought her forward. He'd never seen a female Claret before. She was not tall and was made shorter by the way she shrank from fear.

"The would-be tyrant," she whispered, her voice quivering. "Tell me, do you kill and maim to recover from your fall all those years ago, or is it pure religious zealousness that drives you?"

"Brave words rippling with fear. Your tongue is why we kill all female Clarets," Trylian sneered. "They are not suitable to hold the magic of the Winds. Drives them mad."

The Claret scoffed. "I am not mad, Knight."

"Your life is in my hands," Trylian reminded her. "I will spare you if you tell me all I wish to know."

The woman's brows dropped, and deep thought passed over her eyes. "You will slaughter me even if I do speak. Your men will see the kind of man you are, Knight. I will prove to them you are not a man of your word."

"You will speak, or I will do unspeakable things to you," Trylian warned her.

"I know you," she said quickly. "I am a friend of Olenar."

Roan frowned, thinking. He'd heard the name before. Trylian looked amused at the mention of the name.

"You are?" Trylian asked. "Then you must know you have no reason to fear me, should you tell me all I wish to know."

The female Claret swallowed and waited a moment before she said, "What do you wish to know? Surely I cannot tell you anything you do not know already."

"Tell me about the Scion of the Elsarius."

The woman nodded in acquiescence. "He is a strong Knight. A good boy. I doubt you can stand up to him. He does not want to attack you, but he will take back the places you have stolen from the Elsarius. We do not want an all-out war, Knight. Soon he will know his destiny and will lead us, rising against you. The king will reach out to him."

A look of contemplation passed over Trylian's face. "The king could move on the Modeus-sympathetic cities. Would he do that?"

"That would be an act of war," Baelian offered from Trylian's right.

"The king has already committed an act of war," Gareth offered, his red face serious now. "When he sent that Thane to marry the noble woman. But we stopped it."

Roan couldn't take his eyes off the woman before them. He saw her trying to remain brave, but her facade was crumbling.

"That was you?" she asked, eyes wide. "You killed that woman on the road. We knew it must have been. The Elsarius should have moved before. Now we must stop you before—" She cut herself off, pressing her lips together tight.

Trylian raised his brows. "Before what?"

She gulped and blinked, eyes watering. "No, I cannot say. What if you—"

"Need I remind you I will let you walk away with your life if you speak?"

"You won't," she whispered back, her voice quivering again. "I know you won't."

"Give me a chance to prove myself," Trylian said. "You said you were a friend of Olenar's. You surely know the deals he and I have had. You can help me. I swear on the Winds, I will let you live. If not, we will see how long you can survive my most unique tortures. I have a few I've wanted to try out."

The woman's face calmed a little. "I fear you. But the Scion will not. Whatever I tell you will be of no use to you."

"Then speak," Trylian urged.

The woman swallowed and stood up a little straighter. "If you act on the information I am about to give you, it will only harm you. It will do you no good."

Trylian sighed and rolled his eyes. "I grow weary of this dance, woman. Shall I have your tongue cut out instead?"

The Claret shook her head. "I heard from Olenar that the Arch Claret had a vision he shared with us. He foresaw…" She swallowed again. "He foresaw the Scion of the Modeus."

At this, Trylian leaned forward. Roan saw a hunger and eagerness ignite behind his blue eyes. He wondered if Trylian thought he himself might be Scion. Surely that was what Trylian wanted. To be the chosen of the Modeus.

"Has the Scion been born?" Trylian asked.

The woman shook her head. "He is not among you yet. What he foresaw was a way to…create the Scion. To take the title for one's self. The Winds will grant Scion-hood to one who can complete the trial, the test, and the ritual."

Trylian pushed himself up from where he had been leaning over the table. "The Scion can be made? Tell me what this trial, test, and ritual are."

"You cannot do it," the Claret said, almost like a warning.

"I am exhausted of your stalling. Olenar would want you to tell me what you heard. Speak and you shall be rewarded just as he will be once we take the power. Deny me now and…" Trylian drew his dagger.

"The Trial of Betrayal," the woman said quickly. "The one who wishes to be made Scion must betray someone close to them. Possibly a loved one, a mentor—in a significant way. This tests the willingness to put power above personal relationships.

"Next is the Test of Cruelty. One must demonstrate their

capacity for cruelty, possibly inflicting pain or suffering on others without remorse.

"Last is the Ritual of the Mountain. The most dangerous. The tallest mountain in Drachen, Mount Ormr, is home to the Blood Spring—a sacred place to the Modeus. A place where the Modeus supposedly sacrificed thousands of their own to give power to a single Modeus follower of legend. The person must bring proof of their cruelty and then drink from the Blood Spring."

Trylian sat, not saying a word. Roan watched him. Surely those things would be nothing for Trylian. He had a lifetime of cruelty and malice to choose from. Roan sat as well, wondering if Trylian would accept the quest to become Scion. Surely that was what he wanted, after all. If he were Scion, every Modeus follower would submit to him. Roan wondered briefly if that was something he could live with. Would he have a choice?

"We must find one among us who is worthy," Trylian said at length. He spoke loudly over the soft din of murmurings.

"Not you, Father?" Tanis asked quietly.

"No," Trylian said. His shoulders fell and he took a deep breath. "I will follow the Scion. Be their servant. Lead their army. But it is not for me."

Confused, Roan looked out into the sea of Knights before them. Who would be willing to do such things? Surely if someone volunteered, they'd not be worthy. It would have to be someone reluctant. Someone who didn't understand their full potential.

"You will do this?" the female Claret asked. "Divide your attention now? The Scion of the Elsarius is on his way to understanding who he is. You don't have time. The Trial of Betrayal alone will sow dissent among your ranks. Is that something you can risk right now?"

Trylian smirked. "I see what you're trying to do, witch.

You thought this would distract me. No. This is what I want. But who among us will—"

"I will do this," a deep, strong voice called out from the crowd.

Both Roan and Trylian looked up. Alamar stepped apart from the crowd. He held his head high and had a confident look plastered over his face. Alamar was almost nineteen, tall, strong, and as far as Roan knew, he was ruthless and brave as well. He'd witnessed Alamar's cruelty firsthand. He was always beside Roan, first in the charge and last in any retreat. Roan understood. Yes, Alamar would make a good Scion, though that annoyed him. He couldn't see himself submitting to Alamar's commands and orders. Disgust filled him at the thought.

Roan glanced at Trylian. Others around the tables cheered for Alamar and banged their cups against the wooden tables. Trylian walked around the table and faced Alamar.

"Yes, my boy," he said with a gentle smile. "You have done great and terrible things. I have seen your fervor. You are a zealot among pagans. You are eager. Willing. I have noted that."

With a move like a viper, Trylian thrust his dagger forward and into Alamar's gut. The boy gasped and doubled over, blood immediately flowing from the deep wound. Veryl screamed and ran forward. Phael grabbed him back, holding him tight. The crowd gasped and whispered as Alamar fell to the ground, moaning. All the blood drained from Roan's face in shock and horror.

Trylian turned back to the head table. "No, it will not be you, Alamar. I need someone who does not know their worth yet." He smiled and faced Roan.

Roan's stomach dropped out from under him. He felt his face go even paler as all eyes went to him now. He didn't know what to say. Fortunately, Veryl drew everyone's attention back.

The Claret cried out loud, pleading for Alamar's life. "Find a healer, please!" he begged. He struggled against Phael's grip, but Phael held on tight.

Roan looked up, eyes glassy, barely seeing Phael. His Claret mouthed, "Please." Conflicted, Roan stood silent. Beg for Alamar's life? He would be Scion? The world spun around him.

"Roan," Phael called, his voice quivering. "Please." Veryl sobbed in his arms.

"This boy?" the female Claret said, eyes wide, her voice raspy. "You would inflict such a burden on a child? I must warn you: the Blood Spring brings with it a bloodlust the likes of which cannot be satiated. It drives one to dark impulses that cannot be controlled. There is a price to pay for being the Scion of the Modeus. Madness, even."

Roan looked from Phael's begging face to Alamar dying on the floor.

"Roan, tell me what to do," Trylian whispered, holding his hand out to him. Alamar's blood shone over his long fingers. "Should he live?"

The pressure in Roan's ears built up until he thought his head might burst. He thought of all the things Alamar had done to him. To Phael. He needed to suffer. To do that, he needed to live.

Roan stood and drew his own dagger.

"No, please!" Veryl cried.

Roan ignored him. He marched to the wounded boy and knelt beside him. "You've made my life a living hell," he whispered to Alamar. "You deserve to live and suffer. No death for you."

He grabbed a handful of Alamar's hair and pulled his head up. He plunged the dagger shallowly into Alamar's left eye. The wounded boy screamed and writhed, but there was nothing he could do against Roan's brute strength. Roan pulled the dagger out and stabbed his other eye. Blood and fluids gushed from the punctured eyes. Roan stood, admiring his work as Alamar screamed, his voice echoing off the walls and around the hall. It was deafening.

"Finish him, Roan," Trylian ordered.

Roan turned to face Trylian. He sheathed his dagger. Veryl still babbled between sobs, begging for mercy.

"I will not kill him," Roan said with a sigh. "Let him live like this. Take him out of here." He waved his hand, and, to his shock, a few Knights rushed forward and pulled the wounded and blind Alamar to his feet. They hauled him out, screaming and bleeding, from the feast hall.

Roan looked over at Phael. He still gripped Veryl, who was still wailing. His face was pale, and a look of horror made his blue eyes wide.

"I spared him," Roan said simply. He turned and went back to his seat. He caught Razvin's eyes, too. His best friend looked terrified.

"Monsters," the female Claret whispered.

"Take her outside," Trylian ordered. "Cut out her tongue and remove her hands. Then send her on her way. I want her to find the Scion of the Elsarius and try her best to tell him what happened. That she has betrayed them and let their secrets slip. That soon they will face a Scion of the Modeus."

CHAPTER XXIV

As the sun rose on the third of Hearthfire, so did Phael. He jerked awake, the remnants of a horrific nightmare clinging to the inside of his skull. The summer heat had given way to a cool night and dew soaked the grass as he woke. He pushed himself up and looked around the tent. Roan was already gone. He was no doubt walking among the men. Trylian had told him to do so every morning. "They need to see you, to respect you," he had told Roan. Phael looked up and saw his armor was still on the stand. So Roan hadn't taken it. Phael's eyes went to the crystals in the armor and in the hilt of the sword. No, he'd not pray over them. He'd not ask even the Elsarius to make Roan strong.

He took a few breaths and exhaled to try to remove the nightmare. In it, he had been a dragon, blowing fire over Delsinor. He'd watched as the people scattered, begging for their lives. As was the way with dreams, he'd just known the Elsarius Scion was already dead. Roan had killed him. In the dream, Roan had been covered in hot blood and had loved it. He had reveled in the carnage.

The door flap to the tent opened and Nox entered. Phael's heart no longer leapt like it used to when he saw Nox. He still loved him like a brother, but something had changed in him.

Perhaps it was the hardship of being bound to a Modeus. He wasn't sure. But he welcomed his fellow Claret, glad to see him nonetheless.

Nox knelt by him and handed him a cup of black tea. "We march today," he whispered. "In a few days' time, we will either have made Emberforge submit, or we will have been killed."

Phael's heart fell. He leaned over and hugged Nox. "I'm so scared," he confessed. "About everything. About what Roan might do to succeed in these trials and tests. I'm afraid of the battle to come."

Nox gently petted Phael's hair and returned the embrace. "They will take care of you. You are to be the Scion's dragon. When a Scion is made, his Claret has the power to transform. That will be you. It is a great power."

"I don't want it." Phael felt a sob rising in his throat. "I didn't want any of this. Why did this happen to us? Why would the Elsarius allow us to be bound to Modeus Knights and endure such a life?"

Nox pulled away but still held Phael's hand. "I do not know. But I know we must be strong. Did you pray over the crystals last night?"

Phael shook his head, a hot tear finally leaking from his eyes. "Every time I make myself do it, I pray for forgiveness. I cannot do it any longer."

"You must, Phael," Nox urged. "Even if you have no love for your Knight, you cannot allow him to go into battle weak. His life is your life." Nox stood and went to Roan's armor and sword. He picked up the vambraces and the blade with the crystals embedded in them. He set them down near Phael. "Pray," he instructed.

Phael looked up, pleading.

"No," Nox said sternly. "Don't look at me like that. You know what you have to do." He sighed. "There are things I wish I could tell you, to relieve your distress, Phael. This all may come to an end. I promise."

"What do you mean?" Phael asked. "What's going on?"

Nox shook his head. "I cannot tell you. But trust me. Now, pray." He pointed to the armor and walked out.

Phael looked down at the crystals. They were pale, almost out of magic. Nox was right; he couldn't send Roan out into a battle with little to no magic to use. Taking a shuddering breath, Phael laid his hands on the crystals and began to pray.

"Winds hear me," he whispered. He closed his eyes tight. This time, he didn't even try to pray to the Elsarius. They had forsaken him, and he needed Roan protected. Safe. Strong. "Keep your eyes on your servant," he whispered. "Fill the crystals with your might. Let them be strong for Roan and may your power flow through me to him."

A surge of something cool, like a spring breeze, shot through Phael's veins and up to his fingertips, where they touched the crystals. He swore he heard whispering on the wind, then felt a wave of approval. When he opened his eyes, he saw the crystals were vibrant and full once again. He stood and replaced the armor where it had been. Then he went to the tent flap and looked out. He spotted Roan's red head easily among the men.

As Trylian had urged, Roan was walking among the men. He inspected the war machines they would use soon. As he passed Alamar's old gang of followers, Phael noted how they bent their heads and averted their eyes from Roan. Alamar and his poor Claret Veryl had been abandoned in the village. For all Phael knew, the villagers had killed them now. He hoped it wasn't true. Veryl was a good Claret. He had been an Elsarius follower, just like Phael. He didn't deserve the terrible fate of watching over a boy like Alamar for the rest of his life. Phael's heart broke and tears filled his eyes the longer he thought about it.

He turned away and went back into the tent to prepare for the day.

***

LATER THAT DAY, they were marching toward Emberforge. Phael rode beside Roan but hadn't spoken to his Knight in some time. He knew Roan had noticed. But now, he was glad to have silence. He wanted to think about what Nox had said about everything being all right. Like he knew something was to come that would save them. He glanced up at Razvin, Nox's Knight, and wondered if he could be trusted. He seemed kinder than even Roan and was usually in a good mood. Did he and Nox have some kind of understanding?

"This Scion thing is good for you, too, you know," Roan said, cutting into his thoughts. "The blessing of a dragon. You get to become one of the most powerful beasts in the world."

A small sob rose in Phael's throat. "I don't want that. I didn't want any of this."

"This is good for us," Roan reasoned. "I need you on my side, Phael. We're going to become the most powerful Knight and Claret in the history of Kelroth. You will have nothing to fear ever again."

Was that what Roan thought of him? That he was just afraid? He looked away, thinking. Roan might be right. He was terrified of everything. Ever since he'd been taken off the road and forced to bind. But he had a right to be afraid.

"I understand you want this," he said at length. He tried to keep his voice even and neutral.

"I deserve this," Roan spat back. "I've worked and suffered my whole life for a moment just like this. You wouldn't understand."

No, he never understood Roan. He didn't understand his

rage, his cruelty. Roan was actually one of the last people Phael thought should get such powers. He'd be unstoppable once he came into his magic and Scion-hood. He'd be crueler and more ruthless than ever. But that was the point, wasn't it? They wanted to overthrow the king and his Elsarius sympathies.

But Roan also had a softer side—Phael had seen it. Roan had saved his life, had saved him from Alamar. He also had a love of music and had shown a softness the day he had courted Eliana. He wondered how he could cultivate that side of his Knight. He liked that side of Roan. Phael glanced up at him and took in his handsome face and long, beautiful hair. Yes, he liked Roan despite his darker ways. But that didn't make serving him any easier.

Phael closed his eyes, fighting to not break apart right then. He had trained his whole life to serve a good Elsarius Knight. But that was all for naught. That dream, that life, was gone. He was trapped and a slave to the whims of Roan and the orders of Trylian, the would-be tyrant. And he was forsaken by the Elsarius. He had no choice but to trust the Modeus. Surely they'd protect Roan in his quest.

"Hold!" Trylian shouted.

The four columns stopped. Phael looked ahead. A small smattering of farms sprawled out over the open plains. Phael's heart broke immediately, knowing exactly what Trylian was about to have them do.

"Gareth, Tanis," he called. "Take fifty men and see to that settlement. Roan, Razvin, you do the same to the other. We'll protect the Clarets."

Roan smiled and glanced at Phael quickly before kicking his horse and riding out with a host of men. They charged down onto the little farms, flinging fire from their hands. He watched as they cut down anyone who came out of the little structures. It didn't take long. Soon the fields, the homes, and even a windmill were ablaze. Bodies littered the little dirt streets that ran through the farms.

The men came back and Trylian praised them. "Onward," he ordered, as if nothing more inconvenient than a fly had buzzed past them.

Phael watched Roan wipe his blade clean of blood and slide it back into his scabbard. Roan always did as Trylian ordered. No questions asked. Phael didn't know why. He'd always been rebellious, much to Lailen's chagrin. But not Roan.

A thought struck Phael then. *That's why Trylian wants you as Scion,* he said to himself. *Because he can control you.* He glanced sideways once again at Roan. He had to say something. Not here, but soon. Roan needed to know he was being manipulated. Would he realize it after Phael explained? Would he even heed his words?

Later that day, they came upon Emberforge. They sat atop a hill and looked out over the plains to the city.

"No walls," Roan noted. "It should be easy to penetrate."

Trylian glowered at this. "That's the simple part, yes. But winning the battle will not be so simple. They can see us. They know we are here. Men, prepare the trebuchets."

Phael watched in awe as the men began to assemble the monstrous machines. They brought out oil and fire and he saw now they were preparing to hurl fire into the city.

"It's mostly made of wood," Roan informed him as they watched. "They don't have the stone structures we do in Aatheria. This will be a slaughter."

Phael gulped and nodded.

An hour later, once the trebuchets were up and ready, Trylian ordered the men to fire into the city. Huge balls of flame launched through the evening sky, black tails of smoke behind them. Phael watched in horror as the fiery missiles landed in flaming plumes in the city. He heard their cries in the night as they struck. Flames immediately erupted. His heart clenched. The night's onslaught had begun.

Trylian had the men sleep in rounds. Some watched for retaliation from Emberforge while others manned the trebuchets. Phael couldn't sleep, though. He lay awake all night, and so did Roan. He saw Roan's eyes reflecting the tiny candlelight all night.

The next day, they woke to find four columns of Knights from Emberforge marching toward them and a handful of the city's army. Phael gasped and ran to his horse.

"Tanis," Trylian called. "Take a host of men and get the Clarets out of here. The rest of you, on me."

Phael did as he was told. "Run!" Roan shouted to him as he mounted up. Phael slung his leg over his horse and turned to gallop away with Tanis and the others. But something stopped him. His heart pulled, and he knew it was toward Roan.

"Roan," he called. His Knight stopped and turned quickly to face him. "Be careful."

Roan nodded and galloped away after Trylian, leading his men. That was when Phael felt it. Something like pleasure came through the bond he had forgotten they shared. He hadn't asked Nox if he and Razvin had a bond like this and thought he should. It was strange to be privy to Roan's emotions, even if just a little. But something in him also liked it. It let him know Roan was alive and what he was feeling. He wondered if Roan could feel him as well.

Tanis led the Clarets away from the battlefield and to a safe distance away. They turned and watched as the columns clashed. Phael felt a surge of anxiety through the bond, but then it turned to rage and anger. Roan was fighting. From a distance, the battle looked intense. Blades shone in the early morning sun and fire and lightning spit back and forth as the Knights battled with magic.

Nox rode up beside Phael and waited in silence as they watched the fight unfold.

"I hate having to sit back and wait," Nox said through gnashed teeth.

"There's nothing we could do if we were up there," Phael replied. "We'd be slaughtered." He looked over at Nox. "Do you ever...*feel* Razvin's emotions?" he asked.

Nox looked at him, slightly frowning. "Like in my head?" Phael nodded. "No. What do you mean?"

Phael trained his eyes on the long red hair in the battle before them, watching Roan. "Sometimes, when things are tense, I can feel Roan's emotions in my head. I know how he's feeling."

Nox's black eyes widened. "A true bond," he whispered. "Could it be?"

"A what?" Phael asked.

"A true bond is a bond that was destined by the Winds," Nox explained. "It means that you were meant to bind with Roan." He looked distraught. "But why would the Winds have destined you to bind to a Modeus Knight?"

Phael's heart sank. This was his destiny? His purpose in life? No, he'd not believe that. Roan was a terrible person and not worthy of him.

"Can you really feel him?" Nox asked.

Phael nodded. "Right now, yes. Not always. Only when his emotions are heightened."

Nox hummed in thought and turned back to the battle. Phael watched as Trylian and his men stormed through the Emberforge Knights. It was a slaughter, just like Roan had said. Somehow, the Modeus Knights ran through the Elsarius Knights, killing them. The army and Knights from Sorath joined them from the east, pinching Emberforge between the two onslaughts.

Hours later, the shining white armor of the Elsarius lessened and the sea of black armor dominated the battlefield. Blood soaked the ground beneath them. Phael felt Roan's joy vibrate through the bond.

"They've won," he said flatly to Nox.

Nox's eyes went from Phael to the battle, then back to Phael. "You can sense that?"

Phael nodded, tears filling his eyes. Now they would charge into the city, decimating the women and children who lived there. He heard Trylian shouting and noticed the men lift a battering ram. Yes, they were going into the city and would storm the caer now.

"Move up," Tanis ordered the Clarets. "Stay a good distance behind but move up. They're going into the city."

⁓

COVERED IN BLOOD, Roan rode after Trylian. The horde of Knights and soldiers galloping made the earth shake. Dust kicked up around them and caked to them, stuck to the blood that soaked them. It had been a quick battle and now they were going to sack the city. Emberforge wasn't large, but it would take a few hours to round up everyone—or most—and get them to submit.

"Razvin, with me," Trylian called. "Take that column and follow me with the battering ram to the caer."

Roan looked ahead at the caer. With its many turrets, it stood taller than most of the other buildings in the city. He looked around and noticed the peasants cowering under their gaze. The bravest ones stood before the women and children, shielding them with their bodies. But they didn't attack.

"And me?" Roan asked, eager to move and act.

"You and Gareth, take your men and round up as many

people as you can," Trylian ordered. "Take them to the Sactrium."

Roan turned in his saddle and looked toward the very center of the city. The Sactrium rose from the buildings, its main spire and banners visible from where he sat. It was beautiful and made of curving wood, and elegant buttresses spidered out from the sides. It had a thatched roof.

"Yes, sir," he confirmed and turned to call to his men. "You," he ordered the small family nearest him. "Tell the others to meet in the Sactrium. The Archon Knights will address you there."

"And if we refuse?" the man asked, still shielding his wife and child.

Roan sighed and pulled out his sword. He thrust it forward and the man was suddenly engulfed in flames. He screamed and writhed on the spot. Eventually his cries died down and he fell to the ground before his wife. The woman's mouth went wide in a silent cry and the child mewled loudly behind her.

"To the Sactrium," Roan ordered.

The Sactrium was huge and Emberforge was small. They were able to gather up most of the citizens and pack them into the wide open space. Emberforge had very few Clarets and only one Emissary, so they were smashed into the Sactrium as well.

Roan rode through the streets, making sure they'd gotten everyone they could find within a mile. He had no doubt that at least half the citizens were hiding in their homes or some other building, but he didn't bother to check. They would burn the city soon enough, no doubt. He killed a few more people that ran from him and then rode back to the Sactrium with the rest of his men. The other Archon Knights met them there and together, the Modeus surrounded the Sactrium, capturing the entire city.

Roan turned in his saddle and looked back at the battle-field. It was red and white. The white was the bodies of the dead Elsarius Knights and their Clarets. They had slaughtered them all. The red was their blood. He turned back to the city and looked up at the Sactrium.

"Emberforge is such a small city," he said. "How did Trylian and my father not take it all those years ago?"

Mathis grunted next to him. "They knew we were coming. Armies from all over converged here against our four columns. And they had the dragon. That thing killed at least fifty men with one breath of fire despite it being young. Just think what your Claret will be able to do."

Mathis's eyes went to Roan, and he looked him over. Roan squirmed a little under the gaze. He hadn't spoken about Trylian wanting to make him Scion in some time, too afraid of what the men might think. If they'd hated him before, calling him Trylian's pet, there was no telling what they thought now. But maybe soon it wouldn't matter. He'd have more power than all of them. He'd be the strongest Knight in existence.

"We were lucky this time," Mathis sighed. "They didn't know we were coming. And Sorath helped a great deal."

They waited almost an hour before Trylian showed up again. He was covered in fresh blood and smiled, but his back was bent. He was exhausted.

"We've taken the caer and slaughtered the Archon Knights," he announced. The men cheered and some raised their swords.

"And the Scion?" Mathis asked.

Trylian shook his head, looking a little despondent. "No sign of him. But that doesn't mean we can't find him."

Razvin rode up beside Roan and sheathed his bloodied blade. His eyes were dull, and his gray skin was flushed. He looked unhappy, Roan thought.

"Were you wounded?" Roan asked. He looked his friend over.

"No," Razvin said flatly. "I'm fine."

"What now, Trylian?" Mathis asked. "Should we address the city?"

Behind them, Tanis led his few Knights and the army of Clarets in. Roan turned and waved to Phael. His Claret trotted up on his other side and looked around.

"What a slaughter," he mused sadly. "So this is a taste of what the siege at Delsinor will look like."

Roan glared at Phael. "It's what we have to do. It's our orders. Remember."

Phael met Roan's eyes, his face sad. He nodded and looked away.

"We're ready to torch the city," Mathis said to Trylian.

An idea hit Roan. "No, wait," he said quickly.

Trylian tilted his head. "Wait? Why?"

He couldn't stop the dark and twisted smile that cracked his face. "Don't burn the city. Burn the Sactrium. Bar the doors from the outside."

"Roan!" Razvin shouted, aghast and horrified. "There are women and children in there. That's most of the people inside there."

"What are you saying?" Phael burst, his eyes shining with tears. "Roan, don't do this."

Trylian, however, shared Roan's evil grin. He turned his gauntlet over and checked his orange crystal. "I have some fire left. You?"

"Yes," Roan said, looking. His crystal was pale, but still orange. "Find some torches."

The other Archon Knights ordered their men to find fire. They rode out and came back quickly with candles, torches, and lamps. Gareth and Tanis raised their right hands, fire already dancing in their palms.

"Light it up," Tanis sneered.

"I bet I throw more fire than you," Gareth laughed.

Trylian waited a moment. He glanced at Roan, then back at the Sactrium.

"Don't, please!" Phael begged. Nox appeared at his side and took his arm, stopping him from riding forward.

"Burn it," Roan ordered.

The men whooped and hollered, riding around the Sactrium. Fire spewed from their hands and ignited the wooden sides and thatched roof. The building went up like kindling. Screams and shouts erupted from the inside. The doors, which the Knights had locked from the outside with a beam, rattled as the people pounded on them.

Roan cocked his hand and rode up to the Sactrium, hurling a ball of fire onto a part of it not yet burning. Smoke billowed from the roof and out the windows. A few people managed to escape, Trylian ordered them to be killed. Soon a small halo of bodies ringed the Sactrium.

Roan watched, backing up as the flames grew hotter. The heat radiated farther out than he'd thought. The mass of Knights moved with him, backing away from the flames. The screams escalated as he heard something crash. The roof must have started to come down. He heard the timber fall and the cracking of beams, then a horrendous chorus of screams. He coughed, the smoke choking him. He backed up more to watch the flames burn. He noticed Razvin. He had no fire. He hadn't moved since Roan had given the order to burn the Sactrium. Curious, he wondered what held his best friend back.

Soon the screaming and hammering died down. Cries started to rise from the rubble, moans and groans. Then, eventually, silence. Only the crackling of the flames echoed through the empty city streets.

"Good idea, Roan," Trylian said with a smirk.

Roan didn't look at his mentor, his eyes glued to the scene before him and all the deaths that now burned in his hands. "That should do for the Test of Cruelty, don't you think?" he asked. "For my Scion-hood?"

Trylian's brows went up. "I am glad to see you taking to the idea of being Scion. Yes, I do believe this might take care of that little test. Well done, Roan."

CHAPTER XXV

Over the next couple of days, the Atheling, several Thanes, and a few lords from the surrounding area came to the caer and pledged their allegiance to the Modeus. Trylian sat in a throne-room-like hall where he had had a chair set up. He received visitors, messengers, and others in this hall. He often had Roan and his boys stand behind him while he held this kind of court. He made them wear their armor and gird themselves as if for battle, but none who visited ever showed any hostility. One lord even offered his five daughters as wives to Trylian's sons. But seeing as Gareth and Tanis were still so young, he denied them and offered the lord his choice of Knights instead. The next day, the women were married to five Knights in first column and given portions of the land around them from the lord.

Roan thought things were moving fast as he watched the nobles come and go in the hall of the caer. He watched as Trylian showed his more diplomatic side and made a note to try to remember how he handled himself in this new situation.

"Do you think we'll be attacked?" Tanis asked one day as another lord paraded himself and his house by the new sitting master of the city. "Word has to have reached at least Redwater or Gornath by now."

Gareth looked at his twin with a strong glance to reassure

him. "They wouldn't dare. We have their people. They won't want to invoke more loss if they don't have to."

"Are you sure?" Tanis gulped.

"They might," Trylian said, waving away the most recent lord to come and promise fealty to him. "But not soon. They will want to look into why we moved. Who are we? What do we want? Then they'll consult their Scion." Trylian scoffed. "He's just a boy. He's not an Archon Knight who knows his way around battle. But they will do as he says." He glanced up and waved his hand to Roan. Roan came around to stand before him. "What about you, Roan? Have you given thought to the ascension?"

Roan glanced at Gareth and Tanis. They kept their faces placid, giving nothing away. "Are you sure you want it to be me?" he asked. "I'm not sure why—"

"If you must know," Trylian interrupted, "I didn't want to risk my own boys." He smiled as kindly as he could. "That's why I chose you."

Roan scoffed at the lie, but realized he'd not get the truth out of Trylian. Maybe he was just lucky to be chosen?

"Are you not satisfied?" Trylian asked, clenching the fist he rested on the arm of the throne. "This is an honor. For you and your Claret."

"No, I am," Roan said quickly. "I'm just...nervous, I suppose."

Trylian clicked his tongue and shook his head. "No need, Roan. You are a great man among the Knights. I've seen the potential in you from the very start. Ever since your father died. I knew I had to bring you up for something greater." He smiled. "I knew I had chosen correctly when you burned the Sactrium. You surely passed the Test of Cruelty then. Don't you think?"

Roan nodded, not wanting to disagree with Trylian. It was

a very cruel thing to do. And it had been his idea. The others had followed his lead.

"Don't worry about us," Gareth said easily. "We're not jealous. We like you, Roan. We'd be happy to follow you."

Tanis nodded, smiling.

Trylian nodded slowly. "And what about the others? The Trial of Betrayal and the Ritual of the Mountain? Do you think you can accomplish those?"

Fear suddenly shot through Roan. "Trylian, I'd never betray you, if that's what you're thinking."

At this, Trylian laughed out loud. His voice echoed off the empty walls of the stone hall. "Never, Roan. I know you'd not be that foolish. I do not fear you. And you will never give me reason to, will you?"

Roan mutely shook his head. Trylian steepled his fingers and pressed them to his lips.

"There is something you can do for me, though."

"What is it?" Roan asked. "I'll do anything you command."

"I know." Trylian smiled darkly. He dropped his hands. "Someone among us is a traitor."

Gareth and Tanis both started at this, and Roan frowned in confusion. "A traitor?"

Trylian nodded again. "I've suspected for some time that someone is passing the Elsarius information on our movements. That's how they slaughtered the army from Amril before we got there. They knew they were waiting for us. Amril was caught unaware and paid for it with their lives. I cannot make that mistake again. We need our allies to know they can trust us. And they cannot so long as we have a rat among our ranks. We were lucky word didn't reach Emberforge. Again."

Roan glanced at Gareth and Tanis, who looked at one another, then back at Roan.

Roan swallowed as his nerves tightened under his skin. "Trylian, it's not me, I swear."

"No, you misunderstand," Trylian said easily. "I know it's not you. I know. But I don't know who it is. I want you to find out and stop them. Is that something you can do?"

Roan blinked and tried to calm himself. "I wouldn't know where to start."

"With the men," Trylian offered. "Most of them respect you. Walk among them. Speak to them. Gareth and Tanis will back you up. Understood, boys?"

"Yes, Father," they said in unison.

Roan licked his lips and then bit his bottom lip. He clenched his fists as his hands started to shake. "I'll do my best." He hoped to the Winds he didn't fail. He didn't want to think what Trylian would do to him if he did. The dark memories were a stern warning.

"Find someone you can confide in," Trylian advised. "Get all the help you can trust. Then, turn in the guilty party once you find them."

Roan immediately thought of Razvin. He could trust his draconic friend to help him investigate. Razvin was good at socializing and conversation. The men would tell him anything.

"That should satisfy the Trial of Betrayal," Trylian offered. "Once you find out who it is, turn them in, or stop them immediately. Do you understand, Roan?"

"Yes, sir," Roan whispered.

⁓⦚⦚⁓

THAT NIGHT, once he was off duty, Roan sought out his best friend and confidant like he always had his entire life. He had to tell someone what he had been tasked with, and Razvin would be willing to help him. He also wanted to speak about the ascension to Scion. What if he was the wrong choice? What if he went up the mountain someday and the Ritual rejected him? What would that even mean? Everything he'd done would be for naught.

He found Razvin outside with a gaggle of Knights drinking around a brazier. Razvin was telling some lewd tale about a barmaid that mostly consisted of bad puns. The Knights were practically rolling with laughter, though. Roan walked up silently and waited until the story was finished.

"A word alone," he said at length, once the Knights had filled their cups again from a jug of Razvin's sweet mead. They nodded to him, thanked the half-Vyrkarian for the tale, and left them alone.

"Where's your lute?" Razvin asked. "Tonight is the perfect evening for some melancholy tunes. You know so many good sad songs."

"It's stowed away," Roan said, taking a proffered tankard of mead. He took a swallow, desiring the liquid courage. It tasted sweet, like flowers and honey. "Raz, I need to talk to you."

"I'm all ears, friend." Razvin sat down and patted the earth next to him. His black horns shone in the firelight from the brazier. "What's bothering you? You look ill. Or scared."

Roan tried to make his face neutral but only succeeded in wincing. "Trylian has given me a task."

"Another one?" Razvin asked. "As if forcing you to be Scion wasn't bad enough."

Roan glanced over at his friend as he sat down. He propped up one knee and rested his elbow on it. "Making me," he parroted.

"You don't want it," Razvin said. It wasn't a question.

"No, I do," Roan insisted. "Think of the power. The magic. The authority."

Razvin's dark eyes blinked rapidly. "That's something you want?"

Roan ran his finger over the lip of the tankard. "It's something I've never had. Trylian would be so proud of me."

"Fuck Trylian," Razvin spat. "Why do you want his approval so much?"

"Because I know what it's like to not have it," Roan said quickly, before he could stop himself. He looked away, his cheeks flaming red under his freckles.

Razvin frowned over the top of his tankard, but didn't ask. Roan looked away, grateful.

"I want this. I *need* this." Roan sighed.

"Do you? Why?"

"What do you mean, why?"

Razvin took a deep breath and held it. "Roan," he started, "you don't need to grovel to Trylian. You're strong. I've seen it. You could be so much more."

"I will be!"

"Not like that." Razvin looked away. "There's more to the world than the zealous and violent nature of the Modeus. There are better ways than the path of blood and carnage. Strength above all," he quoted.

Roan scoffed. "Like what? The passive weakness of the Elsarius?"

Razvin went still before his eyes dropped to the fire before him. "I can't do it. I'm tired of it. I've been done with this way of life for some time. I can't anymore, Roan." Razvin held his breath and looked Roan in the eye. "I need to tell you something. But I need to know you can think for yourself. That you're a free man before I do. I have to tell you soon. Before it's too late for you." He whispered now, eyes locked onto Roan's.

"What do you mean?" Roan asked. Razvin's face was so

serious, Roan thought he might be ready to tell him someone had died.

"Can I trust you?" he whispered. "I love you like a brother. We've known one another our entire lives and I cannot hide this from you anymore."

"Raz, I'm confused," Roan confessed. "What's wrong?"

Razvin looked around into the darkness beyond the brazier to check if they were alone. Then his eyes swiveled back to Roan. "I trust you. I love you, so I have to tell you." He took a deep breath and locked his steely eyes onto Roan. "I'm done with the Modeus. I can't abide the way of life anymore. Do you understand?"

Lightning struck Roan's brain. His breath halted in his chest. His heart pounded suddenly in fear. It rose up in his throat. Slowly, he turned to look at Razvin. "Please," he whispered, his mind racing. "Please tell me it's not you."

Trylian had to have known. He knew Roan would go to Razvin and confide in him. Once again, Trylian had manipulated him. Used him. Roan's blood ran cold.

"What's not me?" Razvin asked. Roan watched him for signs of fear. He didn't give anything away in his face, but his body went stiff as he took a slow drink from his tankard. Then he froze. "What do you know, Roan?"

A lump Roan could not swallow lodged itself in his throat. Images flashed before his mind. What would Trylian do to him? What would the others think? His brain reeled and he couldn't think straight. No single words came to his mouth. Too many fought to be released, and he kept his mouth shut. Then the betrayal stabbed him right in his heart.

"Trylian knew. Knew I'd come to you. You were the traitor," Roan whispered. Tears slowly rose in his eyes, blurring his vision, but he could still see Razvin clearly. "You got those Knights killed. The Clarets."

"I didn't know they'd attack," Razvin spat quickly, his

voice shuddering. "I never wanted anyone dead. I swear, Roan. I just wanted us to stop. I thought if we lost another battle—"

"Losing means death, Raz!" Roan cried. "I could have died. Gareth and Tanis, too. You know us. You know *me*." He couldn't stop the way his voice cracked now. He blinked and the tears fell. "We're friends, Raz. Best friends. And you would have had me killed."

"No, you don't understand," Razvin tried again. This time, he reached out and took Roan's hand.

Roan shot up, stumbling away. "No, you don't! Amril was slaughtered. Because of *you*. Some of those Clarets were inno-cent, Elsarius, even. Did they deserve to die?"

"Ro, stop," Razvin hissed, looking around to make sure no one came around the corner. "Listen to me, please. You don't care about that. I know you don't. You've slaughtered dozens—hundreds here in Emberforge. You burned them alive. I could have stopped that. I could have warned Ember-forge, but I never got the chance. I have to live with that knowledge now. I failed them." He hung his head and shook it.

"Live?" Roan scoffed. He sniffled and ran his hand under his nose. "Trylian won't let you live after this."

"We're friends. You won't turn me in." He met his eyes, pleading. "Don't."

Roan swallowed hard and shook his head. "I have to. Our lives are in danger. What else have you told the Elsarius?"

Now Razvin shook his head, pressing his lips together. He wouldn't speak or divulge any more information.

Slowly Roan backed away from Razvin. He didn't want to fight him, to hurt him. So he'd run to Trylian. He'd tell him what he'd heard.

"Roan, listen, please!"

Roan turned on his heel and dashed into the streets of the caer to find Trylian. He wound his way away from the light of the brazier and up the steps into the caer. He prayed to the Winds no one else had heard their conversation. He'd beg Trylian to spare him. He couldn't stand by and watch his best friend be killed. But he couldn't risk him passing any more information to the Elsarius. What if that ambush had been on them? He'd be dead now. So would Phael. So would all the others.

Panting, he rounded a corner and ran down the stone bridge up to the great oaken doors. He pushed the little side door open and dashed into the throne room. The fire there had burned low and almost everyone was gone now. Trylian stood near the makeshift throne with Gareth and Tanis. They spoke in soft whispers. Roan ran to them, gasping for air.

"Trylian," he panted, pressing his hand into his chest. "I found him. The one who has been passing the information to the Elsarius."

Gareth and Tanis perked up at this.

"You did?" Trylian asked, frowning in surprise. "Well, tell me. Who is it?"

Roan inhaled deeply, his knees shaking. "You have to promise me mercy," he started.

"Who is it?" Trylian shouted, grabbing Roan by his arm and shaking him. His voice echoed around the room.

"Razvin," Roan blurted, struggling against Trylian's grip. "But you cannot hurt him. Please!"

"Razvin?" Gareth breathed in shock. Tanis's mouth dropped open, too.

Trylian looked at his sons and flicked his head. Gareth and Tanis rushed out a side door together. Trylian let go of Roan, shoving him a few inches away. "You did well. I thank you." He paced slowly down the hall to the hearth. Placing one hand on the mantel, he leaned over the fire, thinking.

"Trylian, please," Roan whispered, having caught his breath. "Don't harm him. He's a good Knight. He—"

"He turned over Amril to the Elsarius," Trylian interrupted calmly. "That could have been us, Roan. He could have alerted Emberforge and had us slaughtered. It would have been you dying in flames then. Think about that."

"He must have had a reason," Roan pleaded. "We can hear him out, at least. Please."

"Stop saying please," Trylian growled softly. His soft and quiet reply made Roan shiver. He knew when Trylian no longer shouted, that meant he was enraged. He'd experienced it before. "Justice must be served."

Roan gulped and waited several minutes. He paced back and forth, wondering if Gareth and Tanis would find Razvin. What they would do to him. He didn't want them to fight. Didn't want Razvin to hurt the younger boys, either. He ran his fingers through his long red hair and gripped it tight, panic rising in him the longer he waited.

Trylian dropped his hand and placed them behind his back, raising his head in thought. Roan watched him for several minutes more in silence before a ruckus outside one of the doors on the sidewall erupted. He heard Phael's voice begging and pleading. His heart froze and stopped beating. His Claret had nothing to do with this. What was happening?

The door burst open, and Gareth and Tanis stumbled in, roughly dragging Nox between them. The Claret looked like he'd been roughed up, a black eye already spreading over his slender nose to his left temple. He jerked his arms, each one being held by one of the boys. Phael ran in behind them, shouting for them to stop. He came through the door, spotted Roan, and ran to him, hands outstretched.

"What are they doing?" he asked, worry straining his voice. "They came into the barracks and took him."

"Where's your Knight?" Trylian asked Nox. He glared hard at the Claret.

"He..." Nox stopped, looking around the room. He

panted and fear overcame his black eyes. "He left. Ran. I don't know where he's going. I thought he'd come back."

"He left you," Trylian mused. "He's scared. Ran before he could talk to you."

"What's happening?" Nox whispered, a tear dripping down his pale face. He sensed something was wrong. He pulled against his captors uselessly.

"No," Phael whispered. "What's he done? Roan, don't let them hurt him."

Roan stepped forward. "Trylian, the Claret is innocent."

Trylian laughed gently. "Did you know your Knight was a traitor to the Modeus, Claret?"

Nox froze, the one eye they could see behind his curtains of white hair widening. He gulped.

"He knew," Trylian said bluntly. He reached to his belt and pulled out a dagger.

"Roan, please!" Phael shouted, grasping his arm.

"Trylian, don't hurt him," Roan tried, stepping forward. "Let him go. It's Razvin we need to deal with." His heart raced, pounding so hard in his chest he thought it might burst from his ribs. He'd not stood up to Trylian in years. The last time he had, he'd received a beating so terrible even Mother had noticed. He wasn't sure what drove him to defy Trylian now. Was it Phael? That Claret had a mysterious hold over him he didn't like.

"We will deal with him," Trylian mumbled. "Stand down, Roan."

Roan didn't move. "Trylian, listen to me—"

Trylian lunged forward like a viper. His hand gripped Roan's throat hard and shoved him against the stone wall. He lifted his hand so Roan felt his toes straining to reach the ground. He gagged and panicked as his air was cut off. His hands went to Trylian's wrist as he tried to pry his fingers off his neck.

"*You* listen to *me*, Roan," Trylian growled. "There is no mercy for traitors or those who aided them."

Over Trylian's shoulder, Roan saw Phael panicking, looking around like he might find help somewhere in the walls.

"Do you understand?" Trylian asked, tightening his grip on Roan's neck.

Strangling, Roan tried to take a breath to say, "yes, sir," but he couldn't. When he didn't reply, Trylian pulled him down to his knees and backhanded him hard across his face. Roan felt his lip split. He fell over and Trylian rushed him, kicking him in the face hard to wind him. Roan groaned as the pain cracked through him. His nose bled and his eye blurred and stung from the impact. He'd have a black eye, too. He rolled over onto his back and coughed up blood that ran down his throat. He spotted Phael, hands pressed hard over his mouth, stifling his weeping. Roan stayed down.

"Now, as for you," Trylian sighed, turning to Nox. He looked at his boys. "Hold him tight."

"Wait, please!" Phael begged.

Roan wanted to shout out to him, to tell him to stop. Trylian would break Phael if he interfered. He was sure of it. His head spun and his skull ached, but he tried to sit up anyway. He watched Trylian saunter over to Nox. He held his breath. He saw murder in Trylian's dark blue eyes.

Before either Phael or Roan could move, Trylian stabbed Nox in the throat. Blood spurted from the Claret's mouth over Trylian's face. The Archon Knight didn't even flinch. He ripped the blade out and stabbed him again, this time right into his heart.

Phael screamed and fell to his knees. Roan pushed himself up and sat back on his heels. Nox went limp in the boys' grip and his head lolled backward. Bright red blood soaked the front of his white robes.

"Get him out of here," Trylian ordered the boys. They obeyed quickly.

Phael crumpled to the ground, weeping and wailing. Trylian turned and faced him. Roan gasped, shoved himself up, and ran to put himself between Phael and Trylian. He stood and faced Trylian. Blood dribbled from his face. Trylian's eyes met his, and he looked bored.

"Shut him up," Trylian said softly. He turned and walked slowly back to his throne, his boots leaving bloody marks behind him. "And Roan?" He turned and faced the pair. "I am tasking you with finding Razvin. Find him and kill him. Bring me his head. Now. Do you understand?"

Swallowing his own blood, Roan whispered, "Yes, sir."

When Trylian vanished through a side door, Roan turned and knelt, gathering Phael in his arms. He lifted his weeping Claret and hurried back to the barracks where they could be alone.

CHAPTER XXVI

Phael's wailing turned to soft sobs as Roan hurried through the caer, supporting him almost entirely. He took the long way past the kitchens where he knew Antinea would be. She had been traveling with the camp, and he knew she hid out near the food preparation to avoid the men. It didn't always work. But tonight, she was there. He spotted her sitting on a small wooden three-legged stool near the large hearth fire with her arms crossed and eyes closed. The kitchen was empty save for her.

"Antinea," he hissed from the doorway to the kitchen.

Her eyes snapped open wide, and she paled. Her body went stiff as she waited for the worst to happen. But when she saw Phael, her face softened.

"What's happened?" she asked, standing. She crossed the kitchen and went to Phael, taking his hand.

"Follow me," Roan said. He readjusted Phael in his arms and turned to the stone hallways once again. Everything was dark. Every now and then a small torch lit the way in a soft orange light, but mostly the caer was quiet, empty, and dark. "They killed Nox," Roan began and Phael gasped, tears still streaming from his eyes.

"Winds," Antinea breathed, taking Phael's hand again.

"Razvin has turned traitor," Roan went on. "He's been

passing information to the Elsarius for months now. He's fled and Trylian wants me to find him."

Antinea's long sheet of brown hair moved as she ran to keep up with his long strides. "Will you?" she asked.

He glanced at her through his swelling eye. He could still taste blood in his mouth and feel the bruises on his face blossoming. She hummed and looked away. "I need you to watch Phael," he said. "Make sure he doesn't hurt himself."

She gasped softly and looked up again at this. "Has he...?"

"Yes," Roan quipped quickly. "Stay with him, please."

Antinea didn't even hesitate. She nodded and said, "Of course."

It was midnight by the time Roan found an empty room for him and Phael. He shoved the door to the small room open with his booted foot and looked in. There was a window covered by a thin green cloth, a large bed for two, and a simple wardrobe in one corner. A dirty and warped mirror hung on the opposite wall. Roan entered and laid Phael onto the bed, where he curled in on himself. His weeping had died down to small sobs and moans. Roan knelt near the bed and rested his hand on Phael's shoulder.

"Stay here," he ordered, "until I'm back. Do you understand?"

Phael shook his head, a tear running down his slender nose. "Don't go. You don't have to do this. Leave him be. He's gone now."

Roan glared, the bruises on his face stinging as his muscles contracted. "I *do* have to do this. You wouldn't understand." He rose and turned to Antinea. "Please, watch him. Whatever it takes, just make sure he doesn't hurt himself."

"Of course," Antinea replied. She moved to the bed's side and sat on the edge, taking Phael's hand. She stroked his arm gently and leaned over, kissing him on the forehead.

Roan turned and hurried across the room to the door.

"Roan!" Antinea called. Her face was pale, and her eyes were wide. Her other hand went to her stomach. He waited for her to speak. "Just...be careful. Please. And come back."

He nodded silently and marched out the door.

THE HORSE beneath Roan's thighs heaved in huge, gasping breaths. Once he'd made it to the stables, he'd seen Razvin's horse was gone. He'd followed the tracks outside the city and now galloped in the last direction he'd seen them. He knew Razvin, knew where he'd run. He'd head northeast for Duskhallow and safety. So he rode that way.

His mind raced like the hooves of his steed. The cooler night air helped with the pain on his face. His throat hurt too, now that he had a moment to think about it. He knew a hand-shaped bruise would appear the next morning around his neck. He had had no choice in the matter. He knew if he'd refused Trylian, he'd have killed Phael and then beaten him, or worse.

After several minutes of galloping through the fields, Roan slowed and listened. Sweat beaded on his brow despite the cool night air. He wasn't that far from the city; he could still feel Phael in the back of his head. The sorrow washing into him from the bond almost distracted him. But then he heard it.

Razvin's distinct cry rose up not too far from him. He urged his horse on. He must have heard Roan's horse. Trotting more quietly now, Roan hurried in that direction. He hit a small copse of trees and slowed once he was inside. He perked up his ears and listened and then scanned the ground. The moon was out and helped light the way. Below, he spotted fresh hoof prints. Roan looked up and forward and spotted what he sought. Razvin's dark shape moved among the trees, unaware that Roan was so close.

Roan slid off his horse, took up his sword, and crouched, running after the half-Vyrkarian. Razvin slid off his horse as well and ducked down into the foliage. He hit his horse's flank and clicked his tongue, sending it forward into the night as a distraction. He knew he was being pursued. Roan stopped and let Razvin listen for a moment. It was quiet.

"Huh," he heard his friend whisper. "Nothing."

That's right, Raz, Roan thought. *It's nothing.*

Razvin sheathed his blade and looked around. His horned head turned this way and that, looking and listening for signs of being pursued. When he heard nothing, he sighed and leaned against a tree. He dropped his face into his hands and took a shuddering breath. Then he sank to his knees. Roan knew this was his chance.

He stepped out from the shadows and drew his blade. Razvin shot to his feet when he heard the steel being drawn and raised his hand, a crystal clutched in it.

"Don't," Roan said simply. "It'll be better if you don't try magic."

"Ro," Razvin whispered, almost in relief. "What are you...?" His eyes went to the drawn sword. "No. Don't make me fight you."

"You can try, Raz," Roan said. His heart squeezed and his eyes prickled with tears. Was he really going to do this? Fight his lifelong best friend? Kill him? He swallowed the rising lump in his throat. It hurt.

"I'm sorry," Razvin whispered, and he thrust his arm forward. Nothing happened. "Nox?" Razvin cried. "You killed him?"

Roan shook his head. "Trylian did. I'm sorry, Raz."

His friend gulped and looked around. Roan saw the panic settle in his dark eyes and his gray skin paled. "Ro, you don't have to do this. Tell them you lost the fight. Tell them you killed me on the road."

"I can't," Roan said. "I'm to bring your head back as proof."

"And will you?" Razvin's eyes flitted to his sword quickly. So he was thinking about defending himself.

"I have to."

Roan lunged, sword held high. Razvin leapt back, his tail barely making it out of the way before being sliced by Roan's great sword. Razvin rolled and drew his sword on the way. He rose and faced Roan, sword held at the ready. Roan quickly ran to meet him, their blades clanging loudly in the dark night.

He saw Razvin as a child, back when they first met. They were maybe five. Their fathers had been speaking and the two of them had sneaked off to the kitchen to steal sweet bread. It had been Roan's idea. He'd spotted Razvin from the balcony upstairs in his manor and had been intrigued by the half-Vyrkarian. He'd loved his horns and his tail and wanted to know what his part-dragon flesh felt like. Razvin had been very accommodating. He'd let Roan run his hand over his forearm, feeling his hard skin. Had let him trace his fingers up his black horns and ask about his gray flesh. Razvin hadn't been shy at all. He'd been curious about Roan's freckles in return.

Roan dodged a swing, but it clipped his shoulder and drew blood. Razvin's eyes went wide and he gasped, not having meant to actually hurt Roan. With a snarl, Roan moved in a whirlwind of attacks, each one pinging off Razvin's expertly maneuvered parries.

Roan recalled the first time they'd gotten in trouble together. They'd let the goats out of the pen during some celebration Razvin's father and mother were having. The animals had run into the celebration space and relieved themselves all over the guests and decorations. Razvin had thought it was good fun and had laughed, even as his father had dragged him away by his ear. Razvin had never minded getting in trouble. Never minded a beating.

I wish I had told you more, Roan thought as he shoved hard against Razvin's blade, making him stumble back. *I needed you by my side when things got dark. But I never told you. I bore it all alone. Would you have helped me?*

When he was fifteen, Trylian had hurt him worse than he ever had before. Roan didn't even remember what he'd done wrong at the time. He tried not to think about it. But that was the night Trylian had assaulted him. Had thrown him over a bed and torn his clothes...

Roan cried out as Razvin hit the side of his face with the flat of his blade. He'd been distracted. And now he was on the ground, scrambling backward in fear. Razvin stopped and looked down at him.

"I can't do this, Ro," his friend said, holding his hands out to his sides. "I can't hurt you."

Roan scrambled to his feet and readied himself in a defensive stance. "That won't happen again. Come at me, Raz."

"I don't want—"

Roan lunged and rained blow after blow onto Razvin's blade. He moved quickly, putting all his strength into each swing, making them fast and lethal. Razvin stumbled backward and his eyes widened as he realized he was falling behind. Roan then saw his opening. He feinted a strike from above, then swung his sword in an arc to hit Razvin in the ribs. Blood splashed out and Razvin cried out, gasping. He dropped his blade, and his hands flew to the wound. He staggered on his feet and fell to his knees.

Roan waited, looking down at his friend, sword still clutched in his hand. He gasped, finding his breath. Then he raised his left hand, the yellow stone crackling on his glove, alive with lightning.

Razvin looked up at him through his dark lashes, sweat

trickling down his temple. "Roan," he started, his chest heaving with breath. "It's not too late for you. You can abandon the Modeus and live a good life. You can atone for all you've done. The Elsarius believe in redemption."

Roan glared down at Razvin.

"Underneath all that bullshit," Razvin went on, "all that tripe Trylian has hammered into your head, there might be a good man underneath. I can see it, Roan. I believe in you. I know you're not this man. This is Trylian speaking through you. Forcing you. You have to unleash yourself from him. Leave the Modeus and leave him. Then you'll be free. You don't know the man you could be, set apart from him and his zealous ways. All he wants is power. He doesn't care about you, Ro."

Roan's chest tightened. Something inside him strained, and it hurt. He raised his blade. "I'm sorry, Raz. But you betrayed us. You betrayed *me*. You could have gotten me killed."

Razvin shook his head. "No, I bargained for you. I swear I did."

"That's even worse!" Roan spat, tears heating his eyes. "You knew people would die, and you asked them to spare me? Put me in a cell for the rest of my days rather than kill me?"

"Roan, please," Razvin begged. "You don't understand what Trylian wants. What he'll do to you."

"I know," he interrupted. "I am to be the Scion of the Modeus. Were you jealous?"

"Not even a little bit. I love you. I wanted you to be safe, to be the man I know you can be."

The lump rose painfully in Roan's throat again, choking him. "I loved you, too, Raz."

Razvin's eyes went wide at the past tense. "Roan," he began again.

But Roan didn't want to hear it. He couldn't listen to Razvin anymore. If he did, he'd change his mind. He'd lose his nerve. He screamed, whirled his blade around, and brought it down hard. The great sword cut clean through the half-Vyrkarian's neck. His head fell at Roan's feet with a sick and wet plop.

Roan stumbled backward and cried out, horrified at what he'd done. He dropped his sword and screamed. His hands shook as he fell to his knees, reaching out to the decapitated head, but he stopped himself. Bile rose in his throat and he vomited to the side. Tears ran down his face in hot streams.

Unbelief twisted inside him. He hadn't just killed his life-long friend. He hadn't savagely removed his head from his body. Screaming, Roan picked up Razvin's head. It was heavier than he'd thought it would be. Blood ran from the neck onto Roan's knees as he knelt in the grass. Razvin's eyes had rolled in his head and looked in different directions. His jaw hung open, slack and grotesque. He didn't look at all like the playful and smiling boy he had been just hours ago.

Roan wailed, turning his face to the sky. He held Razvin's head to his chest and screamed with all his might. Something in him was destroyed, broken, shattered. He felt it in his chest. Was it his heart?

No, he had to harden his heart. So he did. Roan gasped and pleaded with the Modeus to take his pain away. To make his heart into stone so he couldn't feel this rage and sorrow anymore.

Let me feel nothing, he begged. *Take it all away.*

And then it happened. In a moment of numbness, everything vanished. The pain, the melancholy, the guilt. His tears dried on his face. Roan went utterly and completely numb.

He sat on his knees for what felt like hours before he stood. He gripped the head by its hair and walked back to his horse. Using some leather rope, he lashed the thing to his horse and rode back out into the night, wanting nothing more than to sleep and be done with the entire nightmare.

WHEN ROAN RETURNED to the caer, he heard Trylian was in bed, so he demanded a servant fetch him. He waited in the makeshift throne room for him. The slow plopping of blood from the head in his hand was the only thing that showed the passing of time as he stood near the smoldering hearth.

After what felt like hours, the door opened, and he heard Trylian enter.

"Roan, what have…"

Roan turned on his heel and tossed the horned head of his dead friend at Trylian. The Archon Knight gasped and stumbled back as he caught it, blood leaking over his robes.

"Winds," Trylian whispered. "You did it. I didn't think you would."

"I know," Roan growled. He glared at Trylian. "I have betrayed over ten years of friendship for you."

"Not for me," Trylian smiled. "For you. This should satisfy the Trial of Betrayal. I did this for you. You will be Scion."

The numbness overtook Roan again just as he thought tears would spill from his eyes. He almost felt happy now, too. Trylian was right. He could bring this testimony to the Blood Spring and surely it would satisfy the Modeus.

"Then I'm ready," he mused, almost asking it as a question. "For the Ritual of the Mountain."

Trylian beamed. "My very own Scion. Yes, Roan, you are ready. You can leave whenever you wish."

Something akin to excitement flared up in Roan. He'd

done it. He'd passed the Test and the Trial, surely. Now all he had to do was climb Mount Ormr in Drachen.

"That journey will take months," Roan said. "And Phael must come with me."

Trylian beamed at him for the first time in years. "Yes. Your very own dragon. Roan, this is it. This is what I've been waiting for your entire life. This is what I've been preparing you for. I can't believe it. Once you are Scion and have returned to us, we can march on Delsinor. We can crush the Elsarius once and for all. Oh, Roan."

Trylian dropped the head and strode to Roan, embracing him entirely.

The praise filled Roan. He'd done it. He'd made Trylian proud. For once, he held him with love and pride and didn't hit him. Didn't hurt him. Warmth and pride erupted in Roan's chest. He'd finally done it. Earned the praise and affection he'd craved ever since his father had died. He let himself fall into Trylian's embrace and hugged him back.

Trylian pulled away, beaming. "Get some rest. Tomorrow, we will celebrate. And soon, you will go out and climb the mountain. Are you ready?"

Roan smiled. "Yes, sir."

CHAPTER XXVII

It was hours past midnight when Roan eventually found his way back to the room where he'd left Phael and Antinea. Covered in blood, he knew he was a sight when he entered the room. Phael was asleep on the bed, and Antinea lay next to him, half asleep. She looked up when he entered, but didn't say anything. Roan thanked her for watching Phael and then ordered her to leave. Her round gray eyes latched onto him for a moment like she might speak, but she stopped herself. She bowed her head and left.

He tossed his clothes aside and crawled, exhausted, into bed next to Phael. He thought he heard the Claret say something to him, but he was too tired to hear or care. Soon, he fell asleep and slept late into the morning. The exhaustion helped him fall asleep but also made the nightmares vivid. He relived the moment he'd severed Razvin's head again and again. He felt the weight of the sword in his hand and wrestled to wake but couldn't. He felt his distress leak through the bond and thought he felt Phael's hand on his shoulder once. When he woke, he found Phael gone. He blinked, trying to wash away the sight of blood and the horrific expression on Razvin's dead face, but couldn't. Every time he blinked, he saw it. The nights would be torment for some time.

Realizing he was still bloody and dirty, Roan went to the barracks and bathed before looking for Antinea. He took his time, staring at his bloody reflection in the water before scrubbing himself clean. There was an odd silence in the barracks as well. As though the men knew what he'd done and were avoiding him now. No one spoke to him. Only Gareth and Tanis acknowledged him.

He asked around and found Antinea once again in the kitchen. She was cutting up some sort of root vegetable when he came in. The other cook, the one from their camp, oversaw the cooks and maids who had initially worked in the caer. They all went quiet when he entered. He looked around and his cheeks burned hot as all eyes fell on him. He caught Antinea's eye and flicked his head for her to follow him out. He thanked the Winds quietly in his own mind when she obeyed.

He walked a few paces down the hall and stopped near an open window that overlooked the city. He glanced out and saw the drop wasn't that far, since the kitchens were on the ground floor. Antinea faced him. Her gray eyes were wide with curiosity and fearful respect.

"What can I do for you, Knight?" she asked in a small but sure tone. "If you want to lie with me, you'll have to ask the cook if I can be released."

"No." Roan shook his head. He became distinctly aware of his own scent. He should have done more than scrub the blood off. "Trylian is having a celebration tonight."

Her face pinched in shock. "After what he's had you do?"

Guilt filled Roan, but he quickly stifled it behind his newfound numbness. Of course, it was obscene to celebrate. They were going to drink to Razvin's death, no doubt. The death of a traitor. He swallowed down his emotions.

"I want you to come with me," he said at length.

"What?" Antinea gasped, her creamy skin flushed red, and she took a step back. "What do you mean?"

"Come with me. All the other Knights will have their

wives, consorts, or ladies with them. I need someone at my side. Walk with me."

Antinea stammered and shook her head, but the fear got the better of her. Roan saw her shudder before she nodded. "Of course, sir."

"Don't call me that," Roan said, taking her hand. He pressed a few gold coins into her palm. "Get a dress. I want you to look the part."

She stammered again, shaking in his grip. She shook her head but then met his eyes. Hers were so beautiful. Like a gray sky after a storm, clear and dazzling, yet dark. He loved her soft hands in his. He remembered those hands on him more than once. She knew how to use them. But that wasn't what he wanted from her now. In fact, he felt ill thinking about how he had treated her. But he shoved that aside as well.

"I... I will," she said at last. She dropped her eyes to the floor and nodded.

He followed her gaze to their hands. He ran his thumb over the back of her hand once before letting go. She turned and practically fled back into the kitchen. He let her.

Then something else happened. In the pit of his stomach, something that felt like the fluttering wings of a butterfly exploded inside him. It felt like nerves, but it made him smile. Made him clench his fists in excitement. Was it her? Had she done this to him? Unsure, he ran back up the stairs, calling for a bath to be brought up.

When he reached the room, he found Phael inside. The Claret lay on the bed, curled in with his knees pulled up to his chest. His long white hair was splayed out over the pillows and his eyes were red-rimmed. The excitement Roan had been feeling dropped out a little at seeing Phael in such distress. He slowed his pace and walked slowly to the edge of the bed, where he knelt. He gently laid his hand on Phael's shoulder.

"I tried, Phael," he said, like he had to defend himself.

"You don't understand how Trylian is. I couldn't deny him. I—"

"I know," Phael cut in. He blinked and a fresh wave of tears silently trickled down his nose. He sniffled and wiped at them. "Nox was my closest friend. With him gone, I don't know what to do. I'm alone. I..." He cut himself off with a soft sob.

A softness he couldn't stop overcame Roan. He gently pulled a long white strand of hair out of Phael's face and tucked it behind his ear. "I'm so sorry. You shouldn't have seen that."

Phael finally met his gaze. He raised his pale, slender fingers to Roan's black eye. "Thank you for standing up for us. I didn't think you would."

"I need you. I had no choice," Roan said. Phael must have heard something in his tone that Roan didn't because the Claret's blue eyes squinted in sadness. Phael turned his face away, burying it into the pillow. "Will you come down for dinner tonight?"

"No," the Claret whispered, his voice muffled.

"You have to eat," Roan urged. When Phael didn't answer, he sighed. "I'll have food brought up. Please try." He stood. "We have to leave for Drachen soon."

This made Phael snap his head around and look up at Roan. "For the Ritual?" He pushed himself up and reached his hands out to Roan like he was begging. "No, don't do this, Roan. Please, don't do this. The Claret said you might go mad. It's too dangerous. You cannot risk yourself like this. Scions are not meant to be *made*."

"I have to," Roan replied, his tone hard. "You don't understand."

"Then tell me," Phael begged, gently gripping the front of Roan's tunic. "Why do you have to be Scion?"

"It's what I want," he snapped. He didn't remove Phael's

hands from him. He stood with his own limp at his sides. "No other Knight can boast that kind of authority. We'll be strong, Phael. Able to make others submit to us."

Phael shook his head slightly in defeat and dropped his hands. "I can't stop you, can I?"

Roan placed his hand on Phael's shoulder. "This is for you, too. You'll be gifted the form of a dragon. You'll be a beast of legend. We don't even know what kind of magic might come with such a title."

"We don't," Phael agreed. His face fell and his red-rimmed eyes turned down in sadness. "Go, Roan. Enjoy tonight."

He knew pressing Phael to join them was futile. The Claret wouldn't budge. And Roan knew he needed time to mourn the loss of Nox. Phael wasn't like him, couldn't become numb. He wasn't strong like that.

CHAPTER XXVIII

Roan stood in front of a mirror looking at himself. He wore a green velvet tunic with gold trim and breeches that hugged his muscled legs. His boots were shiny, and he brushed his long red hair until it also glowed. A few other Knights put the same care into their appearance and filed out one after the other to the feasting hall of Caer Emberforge. He followed the line to just outside the hall, where he spotted Antinea waiting for him. A few of the men passed her and whistled or made lewd comments when they saw her waiting.

She wore a slim brown dress with gold embroidery on it. It had wide sleeves and a low neckline that showed off her perfect, creamy breasts. Her hair was long down her back and had been brushed to a shine. A golden circlet rested on her head and her eyes sparkled. She nervously twisted her fingers, keeping her eyes on the floor as the men passed her. Roan walked up to her and took her hand. She looked up, eyes wide.

"I thought you might not come," she said softly. "Maybe it was a trick. To make me look a fool."

Roan smiled at her, letting his eyes traverse her slender body unabashedly. Her cheeks reddened. "Never," he said. "You're more beautiful than any of the other women in the hall by far."

Antinea blushed deeper and lowered her head. "I'm no lady. Far from it."

"You're enough for me," he said, offering her his arm.

Shyly, she slid her hand over his arm and let him lead her into the feasting hall. There were dozens of tables set up inside. Some were already filled with succulent meats, roasted vegetables, and piles of golden-brown bread. Sweet mead flowed, and Roan could smell the strawberry scent of it in the air over the savory meats. For just one second, his heart broke. Razvin had been a maker of mead and greatly appreciated the beverage. He would have gotten drunk tonight, asked Roan to play his lute, and danced terribly to the tune.

But this night celebrated his death.

Roan shoved the feelings aside and tried to freeze his heart once again. Surely numbing himself would come more and more easily.

Minstrels hovered off to the side and played soft music as no one was dancing right now. Garlands of green and summer flowers hung from the ceiling. The torchlight dotted the hall here and there, making everything glow in a warm, yellow light. Roan smiled at Antinea, and she reciprocated with a delicate grin. He knew she felt awkward. This was not her place. She was a common whore, and she knew it. But he didn't care.

He felt and saw eyes on him and on her as they passed the tables and moved through to the head table. Trylian sat in the middle, with Gareth on one side and Tanis on the other. A seat beside Gareth was empty, and Roan knew it was for him. The other Archon Knights and a few lords and other nobles sat at the table too, across from Trylian. Everyone was eating, drinking, and conversing. This was indeed a night to celebrate. They had taken Emberforge. They hadn't found the Scion of the Elsarius, but Roan had suspected that wasn't Trylian's true intention from the start. No, he'd just wanted to blot out his failure from ten years earlier. And he had done that and more.

Roan led Antinea to the table. She hesitated, seeing there

was no seat for her. Roan coaxed her forward anyway. He tapped the shoulder of the man sitting beside his empty seat.

"Move for the lady," he ordered.

The man, a Knight Roan didn't know, looked up. He spotted Antinea and guffawed. His mouth was full of partially chewed meat. He shook his head. "I will not move for a common whore. I know this woman. No, little man."

Roan gripped the man between his neck and shoulder. He squeezed hard, making the man wince and groan in pain. "Do you know who I am?" he hissed.

As if seeing him for the first time, the man stopped, eyes wide. "Roan Red Mane," he whispered. "You mutilated Alamar."

Roan hated the title but nodded. "Now move for the lady."

The man babbled, shaking Roan's hand off, grabbed his plate and goblet, and hurried away. Antinea quirked a small smile. "I've heard that name before." She shyly reached up and touched his red locks. "I like it."

Roan smiled, though it came out more like a wince, and pushed her chair in once she sat down. He took his seat then, and a servant hurried to get Antinea a fresh plate and goblet. Roan saw Mathis and Thaniel across from him, as well as a lord from Emberforge he didn't know. The lord, a shorter man with a brown mustache, was talking animatedly to the Archon Knights. Thaniel glared at Antinea.

"No need for that," Roan said offhandedly to Thaniel. "You gave your daughter away to another man. I wasn't good enough, was I?"

Thaniel quickly averted his eyes and went back to whispering to Mathis.

After looking over the food before them, Roan served Antinea before piling meat, vegetables, and bread onto his own plate. He poured himself some of the strawberry mead and drank an entire glass before refilling it. His stomach was empty, and the alcohol hit him hard before he was ready. His head spun, but he ignored it, leaning into the hubris and courage it gave him.

Before he could speak to Antinea, Trylian rose from his seat, goblet in hand. "My people," he called, and everyone quieted down. "Some of you are here to grovel for a place among us. Others are conquerors. But tonight, I want that all put aside. We are here because we believe in the teachings of the Modeus, that magic is to be subjugated and used. We know that the weak ways of the Elsarius are not to be followed any longer. Tonight, we are united against Delsinor. I want to thank the nobles who have promised us their loyalty. It will not be forgotten." He stopped and looked around until his eyes landed on Roan. "Loyalty," he repeated. "That is what binds us. We are stronger together. And thanks to Roan, that bond is more powerful than ever. Tonight, we celebrate the death of a traitor, our victory here at Emberforge, and our upcoming battles. To the glory of the Modeus!"

"To the glory of the Modeus!" they echoed, and some cheered. Others raised their glasses and toasted before drinking heavily. Roan raised his glass to Trylian and then took a drink. Antinea did as well, but a look of trepidation crossed her face.

"What is it?" Roan asked. He leaned in close to her so she didn't have to speak loudly.

She hesitated, poking at the food on her plate with her fork before she answered. "I was stolen from my home, Roan. My family worshiped the Elsarius. I am sleeping with the enemy."

Roan touched her other hand gently. "Things will change once Trylian sits on the throne."

"For me?" she asked, raising her brows.

The butterflies returned to Roan's stomach. He got the urge to tell her that he'd defend her, take care of her, protect her. He wanted to hold her and never let another man touch her. The feeling was nice, but it struggled against his new cold heart.

"No," she sighed. "Nothing will change for me."

"What does it matter?" Thaniel shouted to them over the din. He had been listening to their conversation. "You're here for one reason, girl, and that's to make sure we're happy when we're not conquering another city." He laughed. "Roan, don't waste your time with this one. There are plenty of women out there. It doesn't matter who you stick your prick in. The more the merrier."

The lord raised his glass to that and drank deeply. Mathis rolled his eyes. Antinea blushed and turned her face away, trying to hide behind her curtains of brown hair. Roan glared at Thaniel.

"You're married, sir," he said pointedly. "But you have no son. Is that why you sleep with so many women? To secure an heir? Have you so little faith in your own wife? You betray her trust every time you plow a whore, don't you?"

"And?" Thaniel asked, taking a long drink.

Roan glared at the man. "Loyalty," he said, parroting Trylian. "That's the measure of a man, isn't it? Are you not man enough to hold back your desires long enough to see your wife again? Or are you subject to your base desires?"

Thaniel froze, his fork halfway to his open lips. "You little whelp," he began.

"Curve your lust," Roan spat over him. "A real man keeps his wife happy and has no need of whores."

"And you?" Thaniel brandished the fork at Roan and then Antinea. "Can't find a wife, boy? Satisfying yourself with this common slut? We've all had her. She's nothing special."

Antinea's face flared red and her eyes watered before she looked away, hands clasped hard together under the table.

"And yet you must say it," Roan said. "Why? To show

how little she means to you? Feeling guilty, sir? Or are you jealous of my freedom to pick whom I desire?"

At this, Thaniel shifted in his chair and looked to Mathis and Trylian before poking his fork between his lips and chewing in thought.

"You do speak a lot for a man who doesn't think much," Trylian called to him with a grin. "Roan has a point. A man who cannot curb his carnal lusts has little control over other urges. And most likely has a simple mind."

Emboldened, Roan went on. "She was never willing, Archon. She was forced. If she's a slut, a whore—whatever you want to call her—it's because you made her one. She didn't choose this. And now you want to call her names as if *her* integrity is the one in question." Roan glared. "You're a hypocrite."

The table went silent.

Eventually, Thaniel sighed. "I see I am outnumbered here." He stood, nodded to Trylian, and vanished through the crowd that started to form on the dance floor.

Roan watched him go, satisfied. He downed another goblet of mead before turning to Antinea and holding out his hand. "Dance with me?" he asked.

Her gray eyes sparkled, and she nodded, though her shoulders still rose with tension. Roan took her hand and stood, leading her out into the middle of the other revelers. She glided next to him as he moved her in a circle around him before taking her middle in his hand. Her eyes locked onto his.

At first, she moved stiffly, not sure of herself and fighting his lead. She glanced around and swallowed hard as eyes moved onto them.

"People are looking," she whispered, her voice shuddering.

"Let them see," Roan said sternly. He shoved Antinea out away from his body, making her spin under his arm before pulling her back in. She stumbled over her footing as she fought against his commands. "Trust me," Roan whispered. "Let me move you."

Antinea frowned slightly, but looked up into his eyes. He loved the slight defiance he saw there. "I always only do as men say," she replied, a small snarl in her tone.

The excitement and that strange emotion exploded in Roan as he said, "Then only do as *I* say. I won't lead you into a dance you cannot follow. Trust me."

With that, he spun her out once more the same way he'd done before. She glided out from his gentle push, her feet not missing a beat this time. She spun and elegantly glided back into him. Her eyes never left his, and it sent a jolting thrill through him. After that, she moved at the slightest touch of his hand, following his footwork.

His mouth went dry as her hand clasped around his harder than before. As they moved, she inched closer to him until her breasts almost touched his chest. He wanted to feel her against him. He'd had her twice, but in that moment, he'd have sworn he'd never touched her before. He wanted to. He wanted to run his hands up and down her slender sides, to kiss her pale lips, to run his hands through her long hair. Heat rose in him. Not a lust like he'd known before, but something more intimate. Whatever it was cracked through his frozen heart and warmed him.

After several more moves, Antinea dropped her head against his chest and rested it there as the music slowed. Roan's heart hammered against his chest, and he knew she could hear it. Her arms went up around his neck and draped there, clinging to him. She closed her eyes and let her entire body be directed by him, unseeing.

In that moment, Roan swore he could have died happy.

PHAEL SAT on the edge of the bed, his feet dangling above the ground. The caer was quiet. Everyone would be in the feasting hall. His face was sore from weeping and his throat, having been tight all day, hurt. He couldn't shake the image of Nox, throat bloody, falling to the ground. He dared not close his eyes because then it came into view fully, sharp and terrible. He stared into the single flame of the one candle that lit the room. It rested on a table near the bed. He let the light burn his eyes, hoping to scorch the images away.

He'd loved Nox. Or something akin to love. That feeling had been slowly ebbing away over the last few months, but Nox had still been a confidant. Someone he could go to. They had endured this torture together. And now he was completely alone. There was Alowyn, but they'd hardly met before traveling with Olenar. No, he was alone.

He did have Roan. The Knight was a monster, to be sure, but Phael found himself drawn to Roan. It could have been his strength. After all, Phael wanted someone to protect him. He was glad to have seen a softer side of Roan earlier that day. He'd shown compassion and a gentleness Phael hadn't expected. And he'd saved him more than once.

Phael looked down at the scars on his wrists. He'd tried to take his life, and Roan had appeared as if by magic the moment he'd thought it all would end. He'd told Phael his life had value, whether he could see it or not. The words had shocked him.

Then Roan had saved him from the ravages of Alamar. Phael closed his eyes and wrapped his arms around himself, remembering that horrible night. The pain creeped back into him, and he shuddered. Antinea had been there that night as well. She'd comforted him. He'd not expected that from her, either. But she was kind and gentle. She had told him that his purity had nothing to do with his body. He wasn't sure he believed her, but he hoped it was true. It wasn't something he'd chosen, after all. Alamar had tried to force him. To break him and take his purity.

But Roan had saved him again.

Phael gently placed one hand on the pillow where Roan had slept next to him the night before. He touched the indentation where Roan's head had been. What were these feelings he had? They were almost the same feelings he'd had for Nox but were more powerful. They made his stomach flutter, and his cheeks burn.

The door slammed open, making Phael jump. Roan came sauntering in through the door, singing some song in slurred words. He had a wild smile plastered over his face and his green eyes glittered with drink. He spotted Phael and sighed happily.

"She's amazing," he said, his words sloppy in his mouth. "And soon I will be Scion, and she will love me."

Phael's heart fell at the mention of Scion again. "Roan, you're drunk," he said. He stood and caught the Knight before he fell onto the hard stone floor. Roan was heavy, made entirely out of solid muscle. Phael could feel it through his thin tunic.

"Drunk on happiness." Roan slurred. He threw his arm over Phael's shoulder and let the Claret lead him to the bed.

Phael tipped Roan onto it and let him land in a heap. Roan closed his eyes and sighed, already half-asleep.

"I can tell you anything, right, Phael?" Roan asked, his eyes half-closed. He reached up and took Phael's hand.

"Of course, Roan." Phael pushed Roan to the side of the bed and then sat down on the edge, letting Roan hold his hand.

Roan's grin turned even more wild. "Winds, I love her. I know I do."

"Antinea?" Phael asked, a little shocked.

The Knight's cheeks reddened under his freckles. "Yes,

Antinea." He stopped smiling then and looked serious. "She was my first. Don't tell anyone, Phael. I didn't know what I was doing, but she did. She was amazing."

"You're very drunk," Phael interrupted.

"I know," Roan giggled. Then, his face dropped again. "I thought I'd never want to plow someone. It's too... Well, it reminds me..."

The sudden shift in tone drew Phael in. He leaned onto his elbow near Roan's head and whispered, "Reminds you of what?"

Roan pressed his lips closed, shut his eyes, and shook his head. "No, don't make me talk about it. Talk about something else. Anything."

"Roan," Phael whispered, gathering his strength. "Don't take us to Drachen. We don't know what will happen if you drink from that spring." He looked up, but Roan was passed out, breathing softly. "Roan?" He tapped the Knight on his chest, but Roan didn't stir.

He watched Roan sleep. His pale skin glowed with a soft light that only came from men being in love. The freckles on his sharp cheeks and too-straight nose stuck out against his pale flesh. His red hair looked brighter than before. Phael couldn't stop himself. He lifted his hand and ran it through Roan's hair. It was soft and silky. Almost cool to the touch.

"You've saved me more than once," Phael sighed. "I... I have these feelings. I don't know if they're about you. They can't be. I don't know." He sobbed softly and dropped his face into his hands. "I want to leave, to go home, but I know I never can. And something in me doesn't want to leave you." He dropped his hands and looked at Roan once again. "What is this sensation inside me when I look at you?"

Gently, Phael stroked Roan's pale cheek with the back of his fingers. His skin was so soft.

Suddenly, Phael felt an urge rise up inside him. He glanced

back at the open door. No one was out there. Then he looked back at Roan. He slept, peaceful and still. Vulnerable.

Phael's mouth went dry, and his throat constricted. Before the sensation went away, he placed his hands on either side of Roan's face and bent over him. Quickly, he pressed his lips to Roan's. When the Knight didn't stir, he did it again, but slower. Roan's lips were soft as rose petals. Phael couldn't stop himself from kissing him again, deeper and harder this time. He inhaled as he kissed him, drinking in his scent: smoke and amber. His chest heaved as his heart hammered against his ribs.

He tasted the mead on Roan's lips, strawberries and honey. Roan moaned and moved beneath Phael's hands. Panicking, Phael pulled back. He watched in horror as Roan adjusted on his back, his brow furrowing in some kind of worry. Was he dreaming? He didn't wake.

Phael swallowed hard and turned away, pressing his hand over his lips. He cried softly. Why had he done that? What were these feelings of fear? Why did he feel drawn to Roan? Were these conflicting emotions the reason he was worried about Roan becoming Scion?

Unsure, sad, and tired, Phael crawled into the bed beside Roan and covered himself and the Knight with the blanket. He turned away from Roan, not wanting to tempt himself even more, and cried softly as he fell asleep.

CHAPTER XXIX

The month-long journey from Emberforge in Moralan to Drachen in Vyrkaris seemed to take a lifetime to Roan. He and Phael had taken a small band of Knights and their Clarets with them until they'd reached the tiny port village near the edge of the Northern Narrows where the Knights parted from them. From there, they'd taken a ship on a what seemed to be a never-ending journey across the water. Phael, it turned out, got seasick easily and spent a lot of the voyage with his head over the side, vomiting into the water. He slept a lot and turned paler than usual. They sailed north-west at an angle over the Narrows to reach the shores of Drachen in just a few weeks.

The voyage was long and slow. Roan tried to distract himself with the other passengers on the ship. He met a young wool merchant, a master builder, and an old man who wouldn't disclose his reason for travel. The man was ill, though, and coughed up blood. Roan helped him walk around the deck from time to time to get some fresh air. The man rarely talked, but Roan enjoyed helping him. It made the time pass more quickly, though the coughing ground on his nerves.

By the time they hit land in Vyrkaris, the summer had ended, and autumn winds had started to blow. Roan had made sure to pack their horses with winter garments. The mountains of Drachen were tall and always capped in snow.

They had to move with stealth and stay away from the cities and villages as they made their way across the Vyrkarian land. The dragon-like inhabitants of Vyrkaris were not welcoming to those from Adorian or Moralan outside the shore-line settlements. Roan thought if they were seen, they'd be captured and perhaps sacrificed to the Winds on a draconic altar. Vyrkaris wasn't nearly as civilized as Adorian or Moralan.

The land was wild and untamed. The skies seemed to be constantly gray, and the wind always blew. The earth was speckled with rocks that had slid down from mountaintops, and Roan looked for the rare forest to hide in. There were rumors that gryphons and other monsters that they didn't have in Adorian or Moralan inhabited Vyrkaris. Roan wasn't sure how much he believed it, but he'd rather be safe than dinner for a sharp-beaked monstrosity. Vyrkaris was famous for its monster hunters, so that was enough to convince him of the creatures' existence. He just hoped to not meet one.

As they walked over the land that neared Drachen, Roan thought about going in just for a place to sleep for the night. Ever since leaving the ship, he'd not felt quite like himself. His legs shook and his stomach turned in sick knots. He'd thought Phael would be the one to catch an illness, but the Claret seemed fine. At nights, Roan shivered but sweated into his blankets. He felt clammy and his skin was too sensitive.

Rain poured down the day they passed the city. He shivered in his cloak and steam rose from his lips. He stopped a moment as they neared Drachen to look at the great city.

Drachen sprawled out over several hills and didn't have a wall like Delsinor. Its architecture reminded Roan of the wings of a dragon. It had many turrets and rounded roofs with spine-like beams and decor. Some of the buildings were painted black and others were the earthen tones of wood. Moss covered the roofs of smaller structures. Smoke rose from the city, indicating warmth. He glanced sideways at Phael, who shivered under his cloak as well. Roan's nose was stuffy, and he couldn't breathe properly.

"We can't," Phael said over the rain. "Trylian warned us to not mingle with the Vyrkarians. They'll lop your head off for sure."

It was a well-known superstition that the dragon-people were wary of those with blood-red hair like Roan. They said they had no souls and were servants of darkness come to corrupt their people. He'd surely be killed on sight. He sighed and looked to the muddy road ahead. Beyond the city lay the spine of mountains. He could see snow already piling up on the peaks. It would be a long and cold journey. But that was the point, wasn't it? To prove he was worthy to be Scion, he had to overcome the Ritual of the Mountain. It was a test, after all.

They marched on until the night. Roan found them a copse of trees where he could build a small fire and not be seen. They were several miles away from the city now and he thought they'd not be found. Once he had the fire going, Phael cooked the rabbit Roan had hunted and boiled some water for tea. He handed Roan a cup of the fragrant liquid.

"What's this for?" Roan asked through his stuffy nose.

"I've seen you walking, heard you breathing," Phael said. "You're ill. That's elderberry and ginger. It should help you."

"I'm not ill," Roan protested before a coughing fit took him. His chest rattled with every cough and phlegm rose in his throat, choking him. Phael tilted his head and raised his brows. "Fine," Roan mumbled, drinking the tea. "Where did you get it?"

"I brought healing herbs," Phael said offhandedly. "I knew we'd be cold here and Winds know what else might ail us. I wanted to be prepared."

To make himself feel better, Roan pulled out his lute once they were done eating and played a few songs until Phael's eyelids were drooping and heavy. He felt relaxed and his nose had cleared a little. He was just putting aside the lute when something screeched in the sky above them. Phael jolted awake and his blue eyes widened.

"What was that?" he gasped. "It sounded like the screams of a child."

"Wyvern," Roan whispered, scanning the treetops above them. "They have those here."

Phael got up and moved to be nearer to Roan, shrinking next to him. "Do they hunt...people?"

Roan shrugged. "I never learned much about monsters. They can't be big enough to carry you off, surely."

"So they'll just mangle us and eat us piece by piece?" Phael shook.

The dark sky above didn't reveal anything to Roan. They'd have to be careful now. Going up the mountains would bring with it more danger than falling rocks, ice, and snow. They'd have to watch the skies now, too.

≻

IT TOOK them days to reach the mountains. The mountain paths were rocky and steep. The rain didn't stop and continued to pour down on Roan and Phael. Roan shivered under his cloak, but tried to not let Phael see it. Their breath came out in puffs of white steam and the roads tilted up more and more. The higher they got, the more they saw signs of the wyverns. Huge claw marks were scratched into rocks here and there, and piles of fecal matter were splattered over the ground and smelled rank. With the clouds above, they couldn't see if the monsters circled them or not. Roan tried to keep a look out but couldn't see far. He wasn't sure what he'd do if he ran into a wyvern or gryphon, anyway. Try to fight it with his magic? He was no monster hunter, though.

They rounded a bend in the rocks and spotted their first patch of snow. It was accompanied by the grotesque chomping sound of something huge chewing on bones and flesh. Roan threw his hand out, stopping Phael from walking closer, but it was too late. Before them, a wyvern hunched over the carcass of a bear, devouring it slowly. The thing was larger than a horse and had wings in place of forelegs like a bat. A great tail swung out behind it, twitching happily as it ate. Unlike dragons, this smaller creature had no scales. Roan froze, but the thing had heard them approach. The horses snorted and reared up in fright, alerting the wyvern.

"Go back!" Roan shouted, wheeling around. He gripped both sets of reins and hurried back around the corner.

But the wyvern pounced, glad to have more to hunt. It screeched, opened its mouth, and shot its taloned feet out as it rose off the ground. The creature charged with great flaps of its wings and latched its claws onto Phael's shoulder. Phael screamed and kicked his feet as the wyvern started to ascend, albeit with difficulty, with its new prey clutched in its claws.

Roan whirled back around and shot a spear of flame at the wyvern. It hit it, rocking it, but did no damage.

"Not fire, Roan!" Phael cried, struggling as best he could. Blood began to leak down his white robes from where the talons punctured his soft flesh. The wyvern's wings flapped manically as it tried to rise again.

Roan switched to his left hand where a yellow crystal was embedded in his bracer. He hurled a bolt of lightning at the thing and hit it right in its chest, just above Phael's head. The wyvern screeched and vibrated in the air as the bolt ran its course through its body. Its legs twitched and its claws opened, dropping Phael. He landed hard, grunting as his ankle twisted when he landed. He tried to push himself to his feet, but his ankle gave out under him, and he fell in a heap.

Seeing this, Roan ran and placed himself between the wyvern and Phael, brandishing his sword and his crackling left hand. The wyvern screeched and backed away, quivering, seeming to consider the magic-wielding creature in front of it. Testing Roan, it snapped its maw once in his direction. Roan gasped and hurled another bolt of lightning at it. The bolt hit its mark, and the thing screeched again, shaking. It reared up, flinging its arms wide, and flapped its wings. Roan guessed it had decided to leave. And then it did. The monster rose into the air and flew around a spike of the mountain, vanishing from sight.

Roan spun back around and ran to Phael, throwing his arms around him and pushing him up into a sitting position. He unfastened his cloak and unlaced his robes, pulling them down to see the claw marks. Phael shook as the wind hit his bare chest. Roan inspected the wounds.

"They're not deep," he whispered, pushing his hand into one shoulder to staunch the bleeding. "But we'll need to clean them. That thing was tearing into a dead bear before it got its claws in you."

Phael nodded mutely, shivering. Roan laced up his robes again and clasped the cloak around him. He helped him to his feet and supported him as they walked on up the mountain, fetching the horses along the way.

"It's not that bad," Phael said in reference to his sore ankle. "With this chill, it should help keep the swelling down."

"How do you know so much about healing?" Roan asked.

Phael's neck tightened, and Roan could see the vein on the side. Phael swallowed and said, "My mentor taught me. He was always good to me. People said I was his favorite. But I was just a ward of the Sanctuary. I didn't have anyone else, and he knew that."

"What does that mean? Ward of the Sanctuary?"

"It means I have no parents. I was an orphan from a young age. I don't even remember my mother or father. But my mentor took me in. At the time, the Sanctuary was full of wards, and they couldn't take any more. But he convinced them to take me, to keep me off the streets. Without him, I'd be a homeless beggar. Before the magic took me, anyway. I owe him my life."

Roan could see the emotion rising in Phael as he spoke. His blue eyes sparkled with sudden tears.

"He was everything to me," he sniffled. "Taught me everything I know. Let me get away with so much. I knew he loved me, and I took advantage of that. I was a bad child."

"I doubt that," Roan chuckled in good humor. "Let's make camp here." He spotted a small outcropping that would at least keep the rain off. He set Phael down and went about making a fire with the timber they had packed onto his horse before ascending the mountain. Roan then saw to the horses, removing their saddles for the night.

Once he had a fire going, he boiled some water and cleaned Phael's wounds. Then he wrapped them with clean bandages. They had some meat left over from the night before and ate that, as well as some apples Roan had packed.

"I'm almost out of water," Phael said softly as he drank.

"We'll have enough water soon," Roan said. "There's snow everywhere up there. We can melt it and use that."

Phael nodded and looked away. Roan saw he was thinking of something and wondered what it was. He tried to tap into their mental bond and feel his emotions. But he didn't have to wait long. Phael asked, "What were you like as a child?"

Roan chewed as he thought. "I don't remember much. I try not to."

"Why?"

He paused a moment before answering. "My father died when I was seven. Trylian raised me."

"Oh, I see." Phael's face lit up like he understood something now. "That's why you obey him like you do. Was he a good mentor?"

Roan stopped chewing and stared into the fire. Could he tell Phael what kind of man Trylian was as he'd grown up? His hand, which held the apple he'd been chewing on, dropped into his lap. "Phael," he began, not sure how to say what he wanted to. Yes, he wanted to tell someone. But what good would it do? "You wouldn't understand," he sighed eventually.

"You don't know that," his Claret pushed back. His face turned to one of sympathy. "What happened, Roan? Tell me."

The darker memories tried to resurface. This was why he didn't want to talk about it. Speaking it made it real again. He winced as a painful memory rose to his mind's eye. He closed his eyes as tears filled them. "No," he said firmly. "It's nothing. Go to sleep."

He rolled over and put his back to the fire, pulling a fur blanket over himself. He closed his eyes and tried to drift off. *Don't think about it,* he told himself as the quiet brought the images fresh and clear. He felt the pain. Saw his blood. His room. His clothes on the floor.

No! he screamed in his own head. The fever rose in him again and he focused on that instead. He took in the sensation of wanting to vomit and then sniffled to clear his nose. No amount of sniffling helped, though.

A moment later, Phael slipped under the blanket behind him and huddled close against the wind and rain. Roan let him. With Phael's warmth and his own, soon he drifted off to sleep. As he suspected, the nightmares came back. Razvin's eyes watched him from his decapitated head. Fear shot through his mind, and Phael must have felt it because he woke to the Claret's hand on his. He didn't push him off and tried to fall back asleep, knowing he'd be tormented by the dreams every time.

CHAPTER XXX

The next day, they ascended the mountain, and the rain turned to thick flurries of snow they could hardly see through. Wind ripped at their cloaks, letting the snow find its way onto their skin at the wrists and down their necks.

"Are sure we're going the right way?" Phael said to him once they were high up on the mountain.

"Yes," Roan replied. "The scholars Trylian consulted gave him the precise location." He stopped and took out a map of the mountain. "According to legend, it's right in this caldera. We're nearly there."

"According to legend," Phael mumbled. Roan ignored him.

The mountain was too steep now for the horses and they had to leave them behind before they ascended any higher. The air got thinner, and Roan found himself panting later that afternoon. The sun was long gone behind thick gray clouds, but that didn't make it too dark. The light reflected off the blankets of snow all around them, making the place glow strangely white. More than once, Roan had to wait for Phael to catch up to him. His Claret was shorter than him and weaker; he knew that. So sometimes, he put his arm under Phael's and hauled him along.

That night, Roan wanted to push on, but Phael was tired. They couldn't make fire, so they huddled together for warmth and prayed that the wind would stop. It didn't. Roan felt his fever spike that night once again. His flesh grew clammy, and his spine ached. He didn't know what it meant, but knew he felt terrible. His head started to throb as well.

The day after that, he pushed on, determined to reach the top. It proved difficult. His legs burned and his lungs heaved the higher they got. More than once, he wanted to give up. It was too cold, too hard. And he was hungry. They ate the snow as they ran out of water, but that didn't satisfy him. His stomach tied itself in knots, and he wanted to vomit, but he held it down.

Just as he thought he'd gotten them lost, the mountain leveled out. His heart hammered in his chest from the exertion and then excitement.

"Phael!" he called back to his Claret, who had once again fallen behind. "I think I found it. We found it!" He laughed hysterically and ran forward around one last bend of rocks. His breath caught in his throat when he beheld the sight before him.

Rocky walls rose on either side of him, making a huge open circle. In the center stood a colossal statue. The man depicted wore armor, holding out his hand as if to stop anyone who might come near. The statue towered above Roan, reaching up into the dark sky. Roan recognized him as the aspect of the Winds they worshiped: the man who first preached the ways of subjugation of the magic and its sacred nature. He'd read about him many times when he studied history. The statue glared sternly and proudly down at him. In front of it was a huge, round, open pool. But it didn't contain water. No, whatever was inside was blood red and opaque. It rippled softly as he approached. Somehow, it wasn't frozen.

Phael came running up behind him, gasping for air. He stopped just behind Roan.

"Winds," Phael swore softly. "So this is it? I can feel the

malevolence in this place." He swallowed, and then tentatively placed his hand on Roan's shoulder. "You don't have to do this. We can go back."

"Go back without my Scion-hood?" Roan snapped. "Trylian would kill me. No, we've come this far."

The silence was eerie. They could hear the wind, but it sounded distant, like it came from far away. Roan looked around. Nothing else lay in waiting in this place. It was just him and the Modeus. He gulped and walked forward, shrugging off Phael's hand.

"Roan, please," Phael started, but Roan ignored him.

"No," he said. "I need this. I must." His mind was then taken over by a sense of calm. He moved automatically forward like he were sleepwalking. He felt his will dissipate the closer he got. Finally, he stood at the edge of the pool of blood and looked in. He saw himself reflected back.

Taking a deep breath, he stepped into the pool. At first, it came up to his knees. But the deeper he walked, the more it creeped up his body. It was warm, and he now saw the steam rising from the pool. It smelled like heated metal in a forge. He walked in deeper until the blood came up over his hips. He stood directly in front of the statue now. He looked up at it and swore it had turned to glare down at him. He licked his lips nervously. He wasn't sure what would happen if the Modeus didn't accept his deeds. Would he be torn asunder? Killed immediately? Or would he burst into flame and burn slowly?

"I am Roan, son of Monguard," he called out. His voice echoed loudly back to him. He winced, not expecting that. "I have completed the Trial of Betrayal. I turned on my lifelong friend, Razvin, and killed him. I have completed the Test of Cruelty. I locked up many of the citizens of Emberforge and burned them alive in their own Elsarius Sactrium. I have studied and followed the teachings of the Modeus all my life. Am I not worthy in your eyes?"

He waited until the echo died down before he turned back to look at Phael. Phael clutched his hands to his chest, tears freezing on his face. He looked surreal in the snow, dressed in white, with fat flakes blowing around his white head.

He turned back to the statue. "Am I not worthy?" he shouted again.

When nothing happened, he remembered that the female Claret had said they had to drink from the Blood Spring. Roan glanced down and winced. His already ill stomach didn't want to think about drinking blood. The thought made his gut flip and bile rise. He gagged and pressed his hand over his lips. He had to do this.

Taking a deep, calming breath, he dropped his hands and cupped them together. He slowly submerged them into the spring and filled his palms with blood. Then he raised them up to his lips.

"Roan, please!" Phael screamed from behind him. "The Claret said there was a madness that comes with being Scion to the Modeus. I don't... I don't want to lose you."

Surely only weak-willed individuals would let the madness get the better of them. Roan brought his hands to his lips and tipped them back. The blood from the spring slipped past his lips and down his throat. It burned. It was like molten metal in his gullet. He gasped and doubled over, coughing and retching. It tasted thick and metallic. Roan had been hoping it wasn't actually blood, but now he had no doubt. He clamped his lips shut and pressed his hand to his mouth again, forcing himself to keep the blood down.

Then he felt it. Something smiled at him. Approved. He swore he heard the words, *You have done well in my name...*

His ears rang so loudly blood dribbled out of them. His vision turned red. Blood filled his eyes until he blinked, and it streamed down his face like tears. It obscured his vision, but he saw something in his mind as he went blind. A cave. Inside grew thin, long pearly crystals. He was to take one of these crystals, heat it in dragon fire, drive it through his and Phael's hands like before, and he would have dominion over the dragon's transformations.

Phael? he asked. *Phael will be my dragon.*

Yes, the voice in his mind replied. It was the deepest voice Roan had ever heard. It spoke slowly and deliberately. *Without the crystal, you cannot control your dragon. They are binding, like the one you used before.*

Do I have to? he asked. *Phael will do as I say without being forced by the crystal.*

Obey, said the voice. *Be master of the beast. Only your commands will allow him to transform. This is the way.*

Perhaps he didn't have to. But why risk it? He wanted control over the magnificent beast he now saw in his mind. The dragon was white, large enough to ride, and spewed fire from its maw over a horde of Knights. He saw himself on its back, riding into battle. Yes, he wanted control over it. Over Phael.

"I will do as you say," he called into the nothingness he couldn't see through. He blinked again and more bloody tears dribbled down his cheeks.

He felt a divine pleasure from the Modeus. *Then my blood shall be your blood, my child. My Scion. Carnage shall be your faith. Now kneel and pray. Let me see your faith in action.*

His vision came back.

But then something else rose in him. He wanted blood. To spill blood. He wanted to hack and maim in the name of the Modeus. He wanted to destroy. The bloodlust filled his mind and drove him wild. He almost started to laugh uncontrollably, but kept his mouth shut. He turned. Phael stood there. He was beautiful in the snow. He'd make a more beautiful corpse, sprawled out and bloodied on the white earth. The red would contrast with the white so well. It'd be stunning.

"Roan?" Phael whispered. He wasn't looking at Roan, though. His eyes were unfocused, and he pressed his hands into his chest. "I feel... I don't know. I feel so—ah!" He doubled over, groaning.

"Phael, you pretty little thing," Roan found himself saying. He was shocked by his own words. "You'll be more beautiful soon."

Then he ran out of the Blood Spring, unsheathed his sword, and charged at his Claret.

Why do I want to kill him? Roan asked himself.

Because he'll make a pretty corpse, the bloodlust answered. *Your slaughter is a work of art. Always has been. Your art is death, and you shall create a masterpiece.*

Roan found he couldn't argue back. It made sense. And he wanted to see Phael's blood.

Phael screamed when he looked up and saw Roan charging at him, sword drawn. "What are you— Roan, no!"

One moment Phael was there, begging and pleading, and the next something huge and white had taken his place. A white dragon. Wings unfurled and claws flashed. And that was the last thing Roan saw before his vision went dark red again. He felt his body moving, hacking and slashing, but he couldn't see.

Wait! he cried. *Not Phael. I don't want him dead.*

Yes, you do, the bloodlust replied.

Roan was helpless as his body moved against his will, fighting some monster he couldn't see. He prayed to the Winds then that Phael wouldn't fall to his blade. Before he could finish, every sensation vanished and all went dark.

Roan's arms were in pain. His head pressed against something cold and stony. He was struggling like a fish on a line, flopping around and wriggling. He heard himself snarl and felt his teeth grinding against themselves. The rage he'd felt before was still there, but it was like he was watching it from another person's vision. He felt the bloodlust separate from him, but it still raged on. It pulled at the ropes he found around his wrists.

I'm bound? he asked himself. His eyes flew open and a red sheen still spilled over his sight, but at least he could see. His fever had spiked and sweat trickled down his neck. He pulled at his arms and legs but found himself tied at the wrists and ankles. He was lying down in the snow.

He opened his mouth to ask what was going on, but only an animal-like snarl emanated from him.

"Be quiet, Roan," Phael's voice snapped. It was full of authority. He'd never heard him like that before.

Looking around, he spotted Phael's white boots walk into his vision. He craned his neck to look up and saw his Claret looking down at him. Phael's brows were deeply bent in a menacing glare. He'd never seen such a look on his gentle Claret's face. He stopped struggling and tried to speak again. His head was throbbing, like he'd been bludgeoned hard.

"I'll cut out your tongue!" he snarled.

What? No. He'd tried to ask what had happened. But the monster inside him still had hold.

"Will you?" Phael asked, his confidence not waning. "I see your red eyes, Roan. I told you the Blood Spring would bring a madness to you. But you didn't listen."

Phael knelt by him and reached his hand out. As he did, Roan snapped at him, trying to bite his hand. Phael pulled his hand back and looked for a moment like he might slap Roan. But he didn't.

"I don't know if this will wane or not," Phael said. He

reached out of Roan's line of vision and picked up his sword. He held it easily in his hands. "But if it doesn't..." He glanced at the blade.

No, Phael! Roan begged in his mind. *I'm here. I just can't stop myself. I don't know what's wrong.*

"You don't have the stones, Claret," Roan snarled, and he felt drool trickling down his chin. "I've known you long enough. You're weak. A coward. I've seen you weep and shudder. You're useless without me beside you to protect you."

Phael stood and pressed the tip of the sword into Roan's heaving chest. "I'll do it. Take us both. I can't..." His eyes softened finally and something of his old, timid self appeared back in his eyes. "I can't go on without you. I didn't want this. I knew what would happen. Why didn't you listen to me?"

Roan growled slowly, and suddenly, he felt his mind coming back to him. The red over his vision began to vanish. The snow felt cold on his fingers now. His head hurt. The fever came back, making his body shake. Sudden fear at having his father's sword pressed into his chest welled up in him.

"Phael, don't, please," he said with a shuddering breath.

Phael's face relaxed into shock. "Roan?" He dropped the sword and knelt by him, taking his face in his hands. "Your eyes are green again. Has it left you?"

Roan gasped in relief. "Yes, it's gone. I can feel it's gone." He pulled on his bonds again and then went lax. "You tied me?"

Phael nodded. "I had to knock you out. I couldn't do it as I was, so...I transformed. It was something to experience."

"Into a dragon?"

Phael nodded. "It was the only way I could take you on. You'd have killed me otherwise. You said I'd make a beautiful corpse."

"I'm so sorry," he blurted before he could stop himself. "You were right. There is a madness in the Blood Spring. But does that mean... You were a dragon. So I must be Scion." He blinked and looked away. "I am Scion." His eyes moved to the cave behind Phael. "I saw what I must do. To bind the dragon in you."

"What?" Phael asked, his face going pale. "We're already bound."

"There is a way for me to have dominion over your will," he said. "I saw it in a vision when I drank from the Blood Spring. I'll be able to control when you transform. And bend your mind to my will when you're a dragon."

Phael gulped and sat back on his knees. "Must you do this?"

Roan pulled at his wrists again. "Unbind me, Phael."

His Claret hesitated a moment. He didn't like the look in Phael's eye as he finally gave in and cut him loose with the knife from his boot. Blood rushed to his hands and feet, and he sat up, rubbing the part of his wrist that was raw and bloody from his struggles. Standing, he marched to the cave behind them.

"Roan, please," Phael begged, following him. "I've only ever been loyal to you. I've done what you asked. You don't have to do this."

"I feel I must." Roan walked deeper into the cave. The crystals on the inside glowed, and he saw where they waited around a bend. "If I don't, the Modeus might take my Scion-hood."

"That can't be true," Phael tried.

Roan ignored him and found the crystals around the bend. They grew out of the rocks there in white, pearly spikes. They were all thin and brittle-looking. Roan gripped one and used his sword to break it off. Once it was detached from the wall, it stopped glowing.

"We have to make fire," he said. Then he looked at Phael. "You can do that easily now, can't you?"

Phael's shoulders dropped as he realized Roan wouldn't consider not using the extra binding. "Yes," he sighed.

Back outside, Roan scavenged for some time to find something to burn. Once he had a small bundle of sticks piled up, he looked at Phael. "Go on," he said, backing up. "I can't wait to see this."

Phael sighed sadly and closed his eyes. At first, nothing happened. Then there was a bright flash of light and a roar, a rush of wind. Roan stumbled back, shielding his eyes. When he opened them again, where Phael had been standing now stood a massive, four-legged dragon. Its scales were white and pearlescent. Great white spines ran down its neck and tail. Huge opaline horns twisted out of its head. Its eyes were a shocking and glittering blue like a faceted gem. The thing looked down at Roan and somehow he got the impression it wasn't happy.

"Phael?" he asked tentatively.

The dragon lowered its head and opened its great maw. A jet of flame burst forth from behind its teeth and ignited the little pile of sticks. Roan gaped as the heat pushed his long hair back and furled his cloak behind him.

"Amazing," he breathed. He looked up at Phael. The dragon was several meters tall, and it looked like he could easily climb on its back and ride it. He picked up the crystal, balanced it on his sword, and held it into the fire. It heated and a single crack zigzagged down the center. "Turn back," Roan instructed. "I was told to bind like we did before. I need your hand."

He picked up his glove and put it on his right hand so he could pick up the hot crystal. When he looked back, Phael had not changed back.

"Phael," he growled. "Transform."

The dragon's eyes blinked sadly and in another flash of white light, Phael stood once again as a human. Roan walked to him. He gripped Phael's hand and pressed it into the ground, making them both kneel. He held him still.

"I need you to hold the crystal," Roan said. "It's cool now."

Phael's blue eyes brimmed and glittered as he begged Roan with just his eyes.

"We don't have time," Roan snapped. "I want to return quickly. Hold the crystal."

"Roan, I swear," Phael began. "I swear to obey you, to do as you say, just please don't take my will away from me."

Roan met Phael's eyes. Something in him made him consider his Claret's words. That softness in Phael's face made him want to agree, to disregard the words of the Modeus.

No, he thought. *I cannot disobey them. Not now. I am Scion.*

"I'm sorry," he said. "Hold the crystal."

Shaking, Phael took the pearly crystal and pressed it into the back of his hand, which lay atop Roan's. Roan took up his sword and gripped it hard, aiming the pommel at the crystal. He breathed quickly, anticipating the pain that was about to come. With a grunt, he hammered the crystal with the butt of his blade. The pearly thing drove down easily through their hands. Phael grunted through gnashed teeth and closed his eyes tight. Roan moaned and waited before dropping his blade and ripping the crystal out. He clutched it hard in his ungloved hand.

With the crystal touching him, he felt the bond suddenly ignite in his head more vividly than ever before. A tidal wave of melancholy washed over him so hard he almost wept just then. He shoved it aside as best he could.

"Phael," he ordered, "transform." As he gave the odder, a euphoric feeling like none he'd ever felt surged through him. An intense excitement and feeling of power coursed through him, forcing a grin onto his face.

Glaring through his tears, Phael vanished in a white light and the white dragon appeared again. Roan stumbled back at the look of anger on the dragon's face.

"Stay still," he instructed, not wanting the beast to attack him. Phael didn't move. He nodded, seeing the power was real. The bond whispered of rage and helplessness at the same time. He felt Phael struggling against his order, trying to move. Satisfied, Roan ordered, "Turn back."

In another flash of white light, Phael appeared again in his human form. He moaned and his knees buckled, making him fall into the snow. He landed on all fours, panting. Roan didn't go to him, instead looking down at the crystal.

"Amazing," he whispered. "I've used the magic of the binding, but it hasn't lost its color. It's still white and pearlescent."

Phael raised his head, one blue eye showing through his sheets of white hair. "A corrupted crystal," he whispered.

Roan looked at him, frowning in confusion.

Phael shook, pushing himself up. "Corrupted crystals don't need my prayers. They never run out of magic. That means you will always have dominion over me."

"Incredible," Roan gasped. He hadn't thought about that. If the crystal had been a regular one, he'd have to somehow force Phael to pray over it, recharging the magic. But not now.

"It's not," Phael said, a warning in his tone. "Corrupted crystals syphon your life force instead of using the Winds. That's why they never need prayer. They make you addicted to using them, killing you more and more. The more you use them, the more they grow their hold on you. Winds know what they might do to me through our bond."

"I felt so powerful when I used it," Roan said.

"That's what they do," Phael urged. "They make you want to use them more and more. But Roan, they lead to death."

"So I've heard," he said, pocketing the crystal. He'd make

it into a necklace once they were back home so he could have it on him at all times.

Phael looked down, defeated.

Roan took a shuddering breath in. The fever he'd been feeling came back tenfold now and his guts wanted to burst. He needed to get out of the cold. "We need to go home," he said.

Another wave of helplessness surged through the bond, but Phael nodded, averting his eyes and dropping his head.

CHAPTER XXXI

The second harvest was upon Kelroth and Roan still hadn't returned. He'd been gone two months and Trylian was beginning to worry. Yes, the journey was long, but surely, they should have been back by now. He was eager to know if Roan had been chosen as Scion. Did he have his champion now? Was the Claret a dragon? Did they now have the power they needed to take over Delsinor and unseat the king and his Elsarius sympathies?

"Sir?" a voice to his left asked him.

Trylian came back to the room at large. He stood in the war room of Caer Aatheria. The windows were long and narrow and let in the autumn sun to warm them just a little. Banners of various lords and Athelings who had come to swear loyalty to the Modeus now that Emberforge had fallen lined the walls around them. A hearth to his right burned brightly, despite it being the middle of the day. The wind that came in through the open windows was cold. Winter would be hellish this year.

Trylian looked to his left and saw Baelian looking at him expectantly. He glanced around the table. The other Archon Knights, an Atheling from Sorath, and a Thane from Amril stood around the table as well.

"Apologies," Trylian said, rubbing his chin. He needed a shave. "I am distracted as of late."

"We're still waiting for this Scion to appear," the Atheling said. He was an older man with white in his beard, but had the broad shoulders and muscled arms of a seasoned fighter. He'd once been a Knight but had since retired his sword and taken up the lordly title of Atheling.

"He will come," Trylian said. He looked down at the map and spotted Drachen in Vyrkaris. It was so far away. And Roan was alone with his Claret. Could the two of them survive the mountains? Had he sent his one chance off to his death?

"You cannot guarantee that," the Atheling said. "I am going to need more from you. I cannot put my trust in a boy," he added when Trylian opened his mouth to reply. "He's so young, Trylian. What were you thinking?"

"I trust Roan," Trylian argued back. He looked to Mathis and Thaniel. "You've seen him. You know him. Is he not the right choice to make Scion?"

Mathis took in a long breath and slowly nodded. "The boy is extraordinary, sir. Ruthless. Strong. Not too clever, but a good follower."

At this, the Thane scoffed. "Is that why you chose this boy, Trylian? To have the Scion of the Modeus under your thumb? Choosing the Scion was something we should have done together. I am afraid, now, I will need more than your promises as well."

"You have my men," Trylian cut in. "We're pledged to protect Amril and Sorath, should you call for aid."

The Atheling shook his head. "I need more. I need to know the man we are putting on the throne will hear me should I speak."

Trylian straightened up, his eyes quickly flitting to Delsinor on the map before looking the Atheling in the eyes. "What do you want?"

"Land," the Atheling replied quickly, as though he'd known all along Trylian would bargain. "In Moralan."

"Are you mad?" Mathis spat. "How are we to procure land in Moralan?"

"Why?" Trylian asked, narrowing his eyes. "Why Moralan?"

The Atheling clasped his hands before him. "There is a Lord in Whiteforest who owes me a great deal. I've done things for him, and he has not supported me likewise. A traitor, if you will. I want his keep, his land. The forest is bountiful for many resources, and I want to control it."

Trylian blinked and waited.

"Once you have the army of Adorian under your command, and you will," the Atheling went on, "you will march on Moralan and demand the lord give it up or be slain. You can do what you wish with his family and men. But I need the keep and the land."

"I want the same," the Thane interjected. "There is a quarry in Duskhallow that by rights should be mine, but the king has given it to another."

"These are great resources," Trylian said, gauging the men before him. "With Emberforge under our control, the road is open. But even still, it will be perhaps years before I can guarantee anything. The siege on Delsinor alone will take days—weeks, perhaps, if we have an early winter. Besides, striking so deep into Moralan would be an act of war. I am not ready to invade the east yet. But soon. First: Delsinor."

Baelian interjected, "War in winter is not a good idea. We should wait until spring."

"I will not wait," Trylian snapped. Then he sighed. "I am sorry, my friend. But I cannot wait. This year has been long and arduous. It is time we moved. And with Emberforge under our command, we cannot wait. We must take Delsinor and gain control of Adorian before Moralan strikes back."

"And what of Caeth, Veloria?" the Atheling asked. "The other cities to the south? Will you take them?"

"I plan on a crusade, yes," Trylian said. "We will take the entirety of Adorian for the Modeus."

"Then moving on, Duskhallow should be your next plan," the Thane said. "The Scion of the Elsarius is said to be there since the desolation of Emberforge."

"Once we take Gornoth and Redwater," Trylian agreed with a nod. He pointed them out on the map. The cities bordered the line between Adorian and Moralan. "If we can have the border cities under our command, the king in Duskhallow might surrender. If he won't, we will take him as well."

"We're spreading ourselves thin," Thaniel whispered, eyeing the map.

"Not once we have the army from Delsinor," Trylian put in. "They may not be Knights, but they are fighting men."

"The army has four columns of Knights—a legion," the Atheling reminded him. "Just as we do. But we must move carefully. Once we have a city under our command, some must stay behind to ensure their fealty."

"We will only appoint Thanes and Lords who we are sure will guide the people to our ways," Trylian said. "Even now, the villages we took pay us their respect and answer to us. I am not worried. Plus, we have ample resources pouring in."

"And our bargain?" the Thane asked. "Will you give me the quarry?"

"And me the land?" the Atheling added.

Trylian looked both men in the eyes. He hated to be bargained with. But he also needed the loyalty of Amril and Sorath. If they were to march on Delsinor, they needed the biggest army they could muster. Besides, did he really care about the resources from the forest and the quarry? He'd have more than he needed with Adorian at his feet. He could spare one quarry and one forest.

"Of course," he said with a smile. "You may have your pick of any lands we conquer."

The Thane and the Atheling looked at one another and a smug smile crossed both their faces. Trylian bristled inwardly at it. They thought they had the upper hand. But they seemed to be forgetting whose ass would be on the throne. The men of Aatheria already followed him. The entire army of the city did. The men, the Knights, and the Clarets. He had the power he needed to overthrow the king and take the power. Once that happened, those smug grins would be put to the test.

"And the Scion of the Elsarius?" Mathis asked. "What if we never find him?"

"We will," Trylian promised the other Archon Knight. "Once we attack, he will show himself. He may be just a boy, but his sensibilities will force him to emerge and face us."

"How do you know?" Mathis asked.

"We have our reports," Trylian said, glad he'd brought up the opportunity for him to boast about his spies. "He was seen in Redwater traveling with an old Knight and his Claret. The old man is training him, teaching him, since he's not a military man."

"The Scion of the Elsarius is not a Knight?" Thaniel asked, aghast. "But he has a Claret."

Trylian nodded, almost not believing it himself. "It's true. He was the son of a farmer in Emberforge when he bonded with his Claret at a young age. My spies say he and his Claret have no memory of what happened in Emberforge ten years ago. But his parents were killed, and he's been living with his relatives in Duskhallow ever since. His latent bond with his Claret reemerged when he turned seventeen. The Scion said he had been having dreams that were not his own. He saw his Claret's face in these dreams and wanted to know who it was. So he began to look."

"They were separated," Mathis mused. "That's good."

"I agree," Trylian said. "But once that little Elsarius whelp starts to look for his Claret, it will be time for us to move. We cannot let them find one another again. I thought the Claret might still be in Emberforge, but it seems I was wrong."

"What if he was, and we killed him when Roan burned the Sactrium?" Baelian asked softly.

"We'd know, I think," Trylian answered. "I have spies in Duskhallow watching for the Scion and listening for information. The dreams persist. He still sees his Claret while he sleeps."

"If you have spies that close," the Atheling asked, "why not just kill the boy now?"

"My men are not fools, sir," Trylian quipped. "If they had the chance, they'd take it. But they are not willing to give themselves away just yet. Should word reach Delsinor that the Scion of the Elsarius is dead, there would be war on the Modeus before we were ready. As it is, we are going to strike first. But not at the boy. That would be foolish. My spies are not assassins."

The Atheling shrugged, making his many golden chains glitter. "You know best, I suppose."

"Have faith in me," Trylian said. "I have a plan."

The Thane opened his mouth to speak, but the door to the war room came flying open. It banged on the wall behind them and all the men inside whirled around to look. Trylian turned first and found his son, Tanis, in the doorway. Tanis was panting and smiling.

"It's Roan," he gasped, a wild grin pulling on his lips. "He's come back. He's nearly here."

"Your Scion?" the Atheling asked, arching a brow. "This is the moment of truth, Trylian."

"Have faith," Trylian repeated. He couldn't stop the smile that spread his lips as well. "Tanis, gather the Knights. Meet us outside the caer's gate."

"Yes, Father." Tanis bobbed his head in a nod and dashed back out the door.

"My friends," Trylian said, unable to keep the joy out of his voice, "this is the moment you've been waiting for. Let's not keep the Scion waiting."

TRYLIAN LED the line of men down the stairs, through the caer, and out of the gatehouse before Roan, Phael, and the small band of Knights that had accompanied them to the Northern Narrows made it to them. He looked out toward the forest on the Narrows' edge and saw the white of Phael's robes before the black of Roan in his armor. They moved slowly but surely toward them. He knew they'd be exhausted, hungry, and cold. But he wanted a demonstration before they entered the caer. He needed to know Roan was Scion. He wanted to see the dragon that the weak, fragile Claret could become.

As they drew nearer, he saw Roan looked ill. His face was paler than usual. His freckles stood out on his nose and cheeks more than before, and a flush colored his cheeks like he might have a fever. He swayed slightly on his horse as well. Trylian's heart tightened, and worry creased his brow where he'd been smiling only seconds ago.

"He looks unwell," Baelian whispered to Trylian.

Trylian chose not to reply. Behind them, Tanis and Gareth appeared with a swarm of other Knights and soldiers. Trylian's heart beat anxiously now. He stepped forward, finally making eye contact with Roan. Roan pulled up on his reins as they got closer. The boy waited for him to speak. At first, Trylian wanted to spew out a command to show him he was Scion but knew that would only upset the boy. He racked his brain for the right thing to say.

"Are you well?" he asked as kindly as he could.

Roan swallowed and didn't answer. "You want to see, don't you?" he said, his voice weak. Without waiting for an answer, he pulled a white pearlescent crystal out from under his armor and held it in his ungloved hand. He turned to face Phael. The Claret sighed sadly. "Phael, show them," Roan commanded.

Trylian's heart now leapt into his throat and hammered. Had the boy done it? He slowly stepped back, eyes on the slender little Claret that dismounted his horse. Roan pulled up on his reins and made his horse back up as Phael walked a good distance away. Once the Claret was alone in the opening between the caer and the forest, he stood still. Nothing happened for a moment, but then there was a bright flash of light. Trylian closed his eyes and turned his face away, wincing. He heard the rumbling breath of the beast before he opened his eyes again.

A general cry rose from the crowd behind him. Tanis and Gareth cursed loudly, but had wild smiles plastered over their faces. Trylian looked and beheld the dragon. The creature wasn't monumental, but large enough to carry a boy Roan's size into battle for sure. It had four legs and two great wings spreading out overhead as it stretched them to the sky. The white scales glittered in the sun, making specks of rainbow flash over the onlookers. The dragon took a deep breath and then roared to the sky. Trylian flinched and had to cover his ears until it stopped. When it looked back down, its deep, penetrating blue gaze landed on him. A shiver lanced through his body and made it so he couldn't move. He glanced at Roan.

"You have control of this beast?" he asked.

Roan nodded. "Completely, yes. But Phael maintains his

mind." He looked up at the dragon. "Phael, show them how you can fly."

The dragon's face momentarily looked annoyed, but then it spread its wings. The wind that pushed from them while it flapped shoved Trylian back. The dragon crouched and then launched itself into the sky. It rose up and down with the beat of its wings as it ascended and eventually reached a height where it soared, wings outstretched. As the dragon circled them, it looked back at Roan. Roan's face was impassive at first, but then he suddenly burst into a grin and looked up at the creature. Almost like he was speaking with the dragon without using words and he had said something amusing.

"Roan," Trylian called. "Can you hear Phael's thoughts?"

Roan suddenly paled and dropped his grin. "I..." he stammered. "It's not quite like that." He was hesitating.

"But you can?" Trylian asked, excitement welling in him. "There's a bond there?"

Roan's face fell and he looked away, like he'd lost a great secret. "Yes," he murmured.

Amazing, Trylian thought. Roan and Phael having that bond meant they were destined to be bound. Like the Clarets and Knights of the Elsarius. He smiled to himself, knowing he'd done the right thing in kidnapping the Claret all those months ago. It was fate. The Winds had ordained it. "Call him back," Trylian ordered Roan.

Roan looked up, touching the crystal around his neck. The dragon curved around and slowly descended back to earth. Just as it landed, there was another flash, and the fragile Claret stood there once more. He panted, hand pressed into his chest as he doubled over. Trylian watched him until he caught his breath and started to walk back to them.

"Roan, I am pleased," he said simply. "You will train all the harder now. We will—"

Roan tipped in his saddle. His eyes rolled to the back of his head and his body went limp. He slid sideways and began to fall. Trylian leapt forward and caught the boy as he fell toward the ground. Roan was heavy and his body was long, but Trylian was strong and tall. He caught Roan deftly and lowered him to the ground. He cradled him in his arms and pressed a hand to his forehead. He was burning up.

"What happened?" he snapped at Phael as the Claret dashed to them.

"He was ill," Phael said, kneeling by Roan. He took Roan's hand in his and stroked the back of it. "He tried to hide it, but he's been feeling unwell since we reached Drachen."

Trylian examined Roan's face. He hadn't lost any of his muscle and he didn't look weak. Perhaps he'd simply caught the fever from the cold. "He'll be all right," he told Phael, who looked worried. "Gareth, help me."

Gareth ran forward and put one of Roan's arms around his shoulders, and Trylian did the same with the other. Together, they lifted Roan into the caer.

"We'll take him to his own room," Trylian said. Roan deserved his own quarters now. And soon, his own keep.

Pride for the boy flared in Trylian's chest. He'd done it. He'd made a Scion. And best of all, this one feared him and did as he was told. Roan would be a symbol for the people who followed the Modeus. They'd flock to see him, want his Claret's blessings. They'd follow him into battle. He had his prize.

CHAPTER XXXII

Roan woke just enough to know he was lying in a bed in a room alone. He saw the stone walls, the singular window to his right, and the hearth on his left. It was small, but a fire burned there. His body was hot, burning up and covered in sweat, yet he shivered uncontrollably. His spine hurt, and the entire surface of his skin was sensitive to the touch. He'd tossed the blankets off once, dying of thirst and moaning for water, but someone had placed them back over him. Then, someone had cradled his head and tried to give him water. As soon as the liquid had touched his lips, he'd gagged and vomited over the side of the bed.

"You have to drink," someone had said kindly, worry twisting their voice. Phael? It had to be. He'd seen flashes of white.

"Where am I?" he had asked, weakly pushing away the person as they'd tried to cover him. "Too hot," he had moaned.

"No, you're freezing. And we have to keep you warm."

A gentle hand had run down his cheek, feeling his hot skin.

The fever had spiked, and he'd lost consciousness. Roan hated being so weak, so vulnerable. Anything could happen. What if someone came in and tried to kill him? What if

Alamar came and... No, Alamar was gone. Roan couldn't keep his thoughts straight. He didn't know what time it was, where he was, or who watched over him. He wanted to wake up, to protect himself. But the illness held him down.

"Phael?" he called, knowing the Claret was the only person he could trust.

"I'm here," the sweet voice replied, but it sounded so far away.

Then he dreamed. He had nightmare after nightmare as the fever ate away at his strength and sanity. Some were worse than others. He saw a castle—he wasn't sure where it was— and a red haze covered it and the field around it. Bodies littered the field. He stood there, satisfied and joyful. He'd done it. He'd won. Then the dream shifted, and he was inside. Gareth, Tanis, and Trylian stood before him. Was he seated on a throne? Looking around, he saw banners and flags lining a throne hall. Yes, he sat on a throne before a crowd of people. The three before him were shackled.

Before he could stop himself, he stood. Words burst from his mouth, but they were so distorted he couldn't understand what he said. He drew his blade and stabbed Trylian, then cut his throat. Joy filled him, a sense of freedom. He was glad he'd killed the man who had raised him. Then he turned to Gareth. Tanis babbled and begged for his twin's life, but Roan didn't want to hear it. He cut off Gareth's head and watched as it tumbled to the ground. Tanis screamed. Then he ordered Tanis to be taken away and tortured in the dungeon. For what or until when, he didn't know.

Sitting back down on the throne, he smiled, satisfied and glad. He closed his eyes and soaked in his victory. But then someone appeared in the throne hall. Roan's eyes flew open and before him stood Razvin.

"You!" Roan gasped. "Raz, I'm so glad you're here." He

threw himself from the throne and ran to his best friend. But Razvin held up his hand, stopping Roan before he embraced him.

"Are you satisfied now?" Razvin asked. He glowered at Roan, blood spilling from a gash on his throat. "You've done such wicked and terrible things, Roan. How can you ever be forgiven?"

"What have I done?" Roan asked. He looked around. "Where am I?"

"You killed them all," Razvin said, his brows bending harshly over his eyes. "King killer, Wind slayer. No one thought it could be done. But you did it. The world is on the edge of destruction, and it's all due to you."

Razvin drew his blade and launched himself at Roan. Roan gasped and raised his hands over his face, closing his eyes and cringing away—he had no sword at his side. But the blow never fell. When he looked again, Razvin was gone and Trylian, bloody and pale, stood before him.

"I'm disappointed in you, Roan," he said, blood dribbling from his black lips. "How could you do this? What were you thinking? Do you know what happens now?"

"Disappointed?" Roan asked, his spirits falling. "I did everything you told me to do. I slaughtered them all. And not just the Knights. Everyone is dead."

"Tragic," Trylian sighed. "The cost of war. But you failed."

"I'm sorry!" Roan blurted, throwing himself from the throne. He landed on his knees before Trylian, grasping the front of his clothes as he begged and babbled for forgiveness.

But Trylian, as always, was not placated. He reached down, seized the front of Roan's shirt, and hauled him to his feet. As he did, the throne room vanished, and a bedroom appeared. It was Roan's old room in his father's house. Trylian shoved him hard, so the backs of his knees hit the bed and he tipped onto it.

"Wait, Trylian, please!" Roan begged, and suddenly he was fifteen and weaker than Trylian. He tried to flail, to move, but couldn't. He was paralyzed on the bed. Trylian walked toward him slowly. "No, please!"

"Roan," someone whispered softly.

Everything went dark.

Roan thrashed against someone who held his wrists, holding him down. He felt the bedclothes beneath him. A pillow under his head. Sweat soaking his brow. He panted and clenched his eyes shut tight, hot tears leaking down his temples.

"It's all right. You're safe," Phael's gentle voice said. "Roan, calm down. Open your eyes."

He stopped. Phael's soft hands held him down. Slowly, he opened his eyes, after a moment of not remembering how. Sunlight streamed through the window, as well as a frozen breeze. But the fire next to him was bright, large, and hot. He was warm and shivering at the same time.

"Phael?" he asked weakly. He tried to pull his hands free, but he was too weak. His body quaked.

"You're all right," Phael whispered, letting go. He gently touched the side of Roan's face, wiping away a tear there.

Roan burned hot in embarrassment, looking away from his Claret. At least no one else had seen him weeping. "I was dreaming," he said, trying to justify the state of himself.

"I know," Phael whispered with a gentle smile. "But now it's time to eat. You have to try."

The thought of food made his stomach roil with hunger and fill with bile at the same time. He wanted to eat. He was weak, shaking. But food made him want to vomit. He shook his head.

Phael scoffed with a smirk. "Don't shake your head at me. You will eat. You haven't eaten in days and you're weak."

Roan knew this new-found courage was simply because he

was weak from the illness. Phael wouldn't dare speak to him like that if he were strong and healthy.

The door opened behind them and Antinea appeared. Roan's heart fluttered and his breath caught at the sight of her. She wore a faded yellow dress, and her long brown hair hung to her backside. She carried a wooden tray laden with a bowl that steamed and a wooden jug of water with a cup beside it.

"Thank you, Antinea," Phael said, standing.

She brought the tray to the bedside table and set it down. That was when Roan saw her belly. She was visibly pregnant. Her stomach stuck out in a big round bulge. She ran her hand over it when she caught Roan looking. She didn't say anything. Roan didn't think too much about it. She'd slept with everyone in the caer, as far as he knew. The child could be anyone's. And no one cared about a whore's babe.

His mind winced at the thought. She wasn't a common whore. No, she was something else. Something more special than that. He looked into her face and a small smile tried to pull at his pale lips. She locked her stormy gray eyes onto his. She didn't smile, but something pleasant passed behind her eyes as she looked down at him.

Phael's eyes went from Roan to Antinea, then back to Roan. "I'll be right back," he said into the silence and vanished out the door.

Antinea took the seat next to his bed Phael had been occupying and picked up a wooden spoon. "You need to eat. Trylian's orders," she said softly. She handed the bowl to Roan.

He tried to take it, but his hands shook too much and his grip strength was gone. Antinea pulled the bowl back toward herself.

"That's all right," she said when Roan groaned. "I'll help you." She set the bowl down and then leaned forward, wrapping her arms around him and pulling him into a sitting position. Then she sat back down, picked up the bowl and spoon, and dipped the spoon into the stew before tentatively offering him the bite.

Roan's cheeks blazed hot and red at the embarrassment. He wanted to smack the bowl from her hands, tell her to leave. But something stayed his hand. Maybe just the illness. But he couldn't stop looking into her beautiful gray eyes. His stomach fluttered again, and something forced him to open his mouth. She slowly and carefully tipped the stew from the spoon into his mouth. When he chewed, she smiled.

"Good," she praised him when he swallowed. "That's one. How do you feel?"

Nervous, he thought. *But why?* Out loud he said, "Hungry."

Antinea smiled and scooped him up another bite, offering it to him. He took it and his stomach went from roiling and ready to vomit to calmer and hungry. "You're too kind to me," he whispered after swallowing.

She shrugged with one shoulder, looking down into the stew like she was the guilty one. "It's in my nature, my mother used to say. I cannot hate. It's too deadly." She scooted closer, offering him a third bite.

Her knee was so close to his hand now that he could just lift it and touch her. But would she let him? Guilt filled him at what he'd done to her. He'd taken her against her will like all the other men. He wished he hadn't. But maybe he could try to ease that pain?

"I... I'm sorry for what I did to you," he whispered. The fever really was making him weak. Apologizing to a woman? What was wrong with him? "Do you hate me?"

Antinea met his eyes. "No," she said stoutly and quickly. But she didn't look him in the eyes. "Hate is a poison. Besides, I told you to take me that night. I was in command whether you knew it or not. I wanted you to fuck me for... For protection. I thought if I could get you to have feelings for me, you'd save me from the others."

Roan frowned. "You used me?"

She finally looked up and met his eyes. "You are not as bad as the others. I knew if I was with you, I'd be safer than with them. It worked. Fewer and fewer men wanted to lie with me once they knew I was yours."

Roan sensed there was something else behind her words, but he couldn't pinpoint what it was. She had more to her little story, but she wasn't going to tell him. "I've never met anyone like you before," he said.

Antinea smiled. "I know." It was a forced smile. But he appreciated it. It made her pretty face glow.

Suddenly, he didn't care what her ulterior motives were. He didn't care that he didn't know exactly what she wanted from him. He wanted to give it to her, whatever it was. If she asked, he'd say yes. So he'd eat, too. She could offer him a mangled rabbit carcass, and he'd take it from her and say thank you. He just wanted to be near her and her gentle spirit.

⸭⸭

ADORIAN, AATHERIA. 1ST OF SORAMAR, 1217.

The fever broke the next day, and Roan went back to training. Supplies began to pour into the caer from all over Adorian and Roan knew Trylian was preparing to move. Soon they'd march on Delsinor.

Roan and Phael were on the outside of the training yard wall in the grand ward. They needed more room for Phael when he transformed. Roan hadn't mounted the dragon yet and thought today would be a good time. The sun shone and the cold air bit at his face. Winter was well on its way, and he needed to be sure of his place on the beast's back. Getting Phael to transform had become easier and easier. When he was in dragon form, Roan could will him into submission. But Phael didn't like that. Roan had promised not to force him to do anything he didn't want. To an extent.

Roan watched as Phael transformed before his eyes, changing from the slender Claret to the great beast. Roan looked up at Phael's long serpentine neck and his great leathery wings. He wordlessly reached up his hand, and Phael dropped his great head down for Roan. Roan ran his fingers over Phael's maw, feeling the silken yet armor-like scales of his face. His blue eyes were huge and vicious looking, despite him knowing Phael was the gentlest soul to ever walk the earth. He ran his hand up between Phael's eyes and then along the great opaline horns that jutted out from his head. The beast gave a strange, appreciative trill as Roan caressed him.

"You look magnificent," Roan said in praise. "Anyone who saw you lighting up the sky would run for their lives."

Phael made a deep, guttural purring sound in his long throat. Roan didn't know what he meant but felt a wave of pride come through their mysterious bond. He smiled and ran his hand down Phael's neck as he walked to where his neck met his shoulders. There were no spines there, and it seemed to be the easiest place to mount. Roan tapped his great shoulder and Phael crouched for him to climb on. At first, Roan moved carefully, thinking he might hurt Phael, but once he felt the sheer walls of muscle under his hands and the hard scales, he threw caution to the wind and clambered up.

He threw his leg over Phael's neck and straddled him. The spikes before him were not razor sharp, so he gripped them to hold on. Through the bond, he tried to tell Phael to rise. Words didn't seem able to pass through the bond well, so instead, he shot a lance of excitement through. Feeling it,

Phael took a deep breath. Roan felt the inhale under his thighs and gasped when the great wings spread out around him.

"Whoa," he whispered, clamping his thighs around the dragon hard. He'd have to hold on with just his legs if he was to sling magic from the back of the great beast. "Easy now," he called. He didn't want to force Phael to fly, so he let go of the crystal's power and let Phael do as he wished.

Phael made a dragon-like hum and crouched. Roan gripped the spines hard and tightened his knees. "If I fall, please catch me," he shouted. A shot of amusement came through the bond. "What's so funny?" Roan snapped.

Phael didn't answer and leapt. Roan couldn't stop the scream that tore from his throat as the dragon launched itself into the air. The scream quickly turned into a mad laugh as he looked over the side and saw the ground grow farther and farther away. The wind caught his long red hair and whipped it about wildly. He gasped and held on for his life as the wings started to beat a rhythm. The rise and fall of the flapping made his stomach turn at first. Then he lost his seat. His legs gave out and he tilted. His heart hammered into his throat, choking him and making it so he couldn't scream. He knew Phael must have felt his sudden terror through the bond, because he leveled out quickly and drifted on the winds, his wings still as Roan righted himself.

"Thank you," Roan called, ducking closer to Phael's neck. He clamped his legs down tight again and adjusted his grip.

Looking down, he saw the caer far away now. He gasped again and the wind filled his lungs and mouth. A thrill shot through him the likes of which he had never felt before. He thought at first the fear would overcome him, and he'd black out, but he didn't. Instead, his eyes became clearer, his mind steadied, and the joy filled him.

"Take us higher!" he commanded without the help of the crystal. Phael roared to the sky in acknowledgment. The roar vibrated Roan's chest and sent another shock through him. It was loud, majestic, and terrifying at the same time. It nearly deafened him.

Then Roan got a shock. *Hold on*, came through their bond in Phael's voice. He leaned forward and clutched at the spines with all his strength. Phael angled up a little, but not enough to unseat Roan, and climbed up into the sky. Roan foolishly looked over the edge and his heart did a flip in his chest. If he fell now, he'd be little more than human jam on the ground once he landed.

"That's good enough," he called, patting Phael's neck. "Take us around the caer. I want them to see us."

A little joy came through the bond then and Phael obeyed. He circled the caer and dropped a little lower, roaring as he went. One small person in the training yard ran along the wall, waving madly. Roan recognized the Knight as Aryn, a boy a year younger than him who was in third column.

After that, Roan let Phael dictate what they did. They soared over the fields and trees, up and down, but always below the clouds. The joy Roan felt never left, nearly suffocating him as it tightened his chest. There was nothing quite like the joy that came with riding on the back of a dragon, he was sure of it.

He was just getting used to all the new sensations when a horn rang out beneath them. Roan craned around to look and saw Trylian and the other Archon Knights filing into the training yard.

"We have to go back!" he called.

A small sting of disappointment came from Phael. Roan patted his great muscled shoulder. "I know. But we must obey."

Phael circled and came lower and lower before landing gracefully back in the ward. Roan slid off and backed away as Phael transformed. He panted, gasping and trying desperately to catch his breath. Then he doubled over, chest heaving. Roan ran to him and helped support him as they walked to the training yard.

"It knocks the wind out of me," Phael confessed between gasps. He gripped Roan hard and stumbled to keep up with him.

"Very impressive," Trylian called with a smile once they entered the yard.

Aryn, who had been watching them, ran up to Roan, beaming. "That was amazing," he breathed. "One day, I'd love to ride a dragon. What was it like?"

"Aryn," Trylian snapped, handing the war horn off to Baelian, "that's enough. We have business to discuss."

Roan looked around and noticed many of the Knights and some soldiers filled the yard to bursting. They were almost shoulder to shoulder with the training dummies that littered the yard. The Archon Knights looked stiff, and their brows furrowed. Mathis looked Roan in the eye, his gaze unwavering. Roan met the older man's eyes, wondering why he had been pinpointed.

"Listen to me, all of you," Trylian said seriously. "I know you have heard the rumblings of my plans, but it's time I confess to all of you what we're doing."

A tense silence followed as Trylian looked almost every man in the eye as he went on.

"We're marching on Delsinor," he said, and a few men cheered. "You will be briefed in the coming days, but for tonight, we celebrate."

Trylian went on, but Roan didn't hear him. Mathis hadn't stopped looking at him. Had he? Was he imagining the way the Archon Knight looked at him?

Gouge his eyes out.

Roan started at the sudden and violent thought in his

head. Had he come up with that thought himself? It almost felt as if someone whispered it to him.

Kill him. That's what he deserves for staring like that. The prick.

The thoughts came to Roan in his own voice. They had to be his thoughts. Mathis was being strange. Suspicious, even. Roan glared at him. He blinked, and he felt as if the world dropped out from under him. Everything went black.

CHAPTER XXXIII

Roan panted, his muscles straining when he came to. Sweat trickled down his temple despite the cold weather. He opened his eyes and found himself in the middle of the forest. Something wet on his neck, face, and hands made the slight wind chill him to his bones. He looked down and saw his hands were bright red. They glistened in the late-day sun.

Roan cried out and stumbled backward. He tripped over something and turned to see a long-handled shovel behind him. Confused and fear settling in, he spun on the spot, looking around. He turned once and then saw it.

Before him, lying on the forest floor in the dying light, was a mangled, naked body. Roan shouted in fright and backed away, thinking the dead man might be alive. But that was ridiculous. He could see the man's ribs where someone had flayed him down to the bones. Half his face was smashed, as if with a blacksmith's hammer. That was when Roan recognized him.

"Mathis?" he gasped, falling to his knees before the mangled corpse. He reached out and couldn't help but notice the blood all over his hands once again. He cringed away from the dead man and whimpered. "What...?" he stammered, tears filling his eyes.

There was no one around him. He saw Mathis's body was half-buried in the ground. Had he been in the middle of burying the body?

"Hello?" Roan called into the forest. No one replied.

What happened? he asked himself. "Did I do this?" Looking down, he saw his naked torso was covered in blood as well. He turned and saw his things neatly folded and placed on the partially exposed roots of a tree not far away from a small stream.

"Mathis?" he tried again. The man didn't move. Roan knelt closer and inspected the corpse. Whoever had done this had left little of Mathis to be recognized. "How?" Roan stammered.

The cold set in then and he started to shiver. Something in him snapped, whipping him into action. He grabbed the shovel and frantically began to heave dirt onto Mathis's corpse. He moved quickly, whimpering with every shovel full of dirt. Soon, tears leaked down his face and he wept audibly as he finished burying the dead Archon Knight. He wasn't sure how, but something inside told him he'd done this. Was it his familiar guilt? Roan often felt guilty for things he had no control over. Trylian had made sure of it all of his life. But this was different.

I'm sure this was me, he thought bitterly. *But how? Why?* And why couldn't he remember? Had he lured Mathis out into the woods and killed him? He remembered before passing out thinking Mathis had looked at him funny. Like he suspected Roan of something. Perhaps this had happened in self-defense? Had Mathis attacked him? Roan didn't know. All he knew in this moment was that he had to hide the body.

When he was done, he hid the shovel and went to the stream where he washed his hands and then his torso. It was cold, and he was shaking uncontrollably by the time he was done. Either from weeping or from the cold, he couldn't tell. He dressed quickly and ran back the way he thought the caer was.

It turned out he wasn't far from the caer. He broke through the forest and saw the gatehouse before him in a matter of minutes. Slowing his pace, he walked quickly through the gate and up into the caer. No one stopped him or looked at him as he made his way to his new room.

He flung the door open and dashed in, slamming it closed once he was on the inside. Panting, he pressed his back up against the door and closed his eyes. When he did, he saw the mangled body once more, so he threw his eyes open wide to dispel the image. He caught sight of Phael quickly scrambling to hide something behind his back. The Claret had been sitting at the desk and had jumped when Roan entered. Ink spilled over the desk now and a quill lay on the floor beneath Phael's feet. The Claret looked horrified and frightened.

"What's wrong?" Roan asked, frowning slightly. Warmth started to come back to his fingers and toes from the heat of the small fireplace in the room.

"I— Nothing. It's just..." Phael stammered through his words, pale and shaking. Then he looked Roan up and down. "Why are you all wet?"

"What are you hiding?" Roan asked more dangerously than he'd meant to.

Phael had both his hands behind his back, nervously twisting something in his long fingers. "Roan, please listen first," he started.

"Phael," Roan warned, stepping closer.

The Claret backed up until his knees hit one of the beds behind him. He stumbled and sat down, his arms still behind his back. He stammered again, words pouring from his mouth in no cohesive sentences. His eyes flashed to the fire.

Roan saw what he wanted to do before he moved. He spotted the other pages of parchment on the desk, the ink, the quill. Phael had written something and now wanted to burn it before Roan could see it. What could it be? A letter of love? Something else he didn't want Roan to see? "What is it, Phael?" he asked, marching toward the Claret.

"Roan, no," Phael begged, trying to roll out of the way.

"Let me see it," Roan said, half-smiling as he grappled with the Claret. Phael's wrists were thin and felt fragile in Roan's big hands. He gripped them and pulled, easily drawing Phael's hand out from behind his back. He felt Phael shaking under his grasp, trying with all his strength to pull his arm back. Roan laughed at his attempt and snatched the parchment from his hand. "There, got it," he breathed, standing up straight and backing away.

Phael jumped and tried to snatch the letter away, but Roan easily stopped him with one hand, the other flipping open the parchment. Phael struggled uselessly against his grasp. Roan's eyes had a hard time reading the now smudged letters, but he was able to make out the name it was addressed to: Lailen.

"Who's this?" Roan asked, smirking. "A lover of yours, perhaps? Maybe..." He stopped the more he read. The letter was short and got right to the point. It warned this Lailen of the upcoming attack on Delsinor and detailed the little Phael knew of Trylian's plans. It then urged Lailen to flee once the king was notified.

Roan's heart froze and then went still. Phael had turned traitor. Just like Razvin. The hand Roan had around Phael's wrist tightened until he knew he had bruised the Claret. Phael whimpered and pulled uselessly against Roan's grip.

"Not you, too," Roan whispered, turning to look Phael in the eyes. Phael's blue eyes rounded in fear. He swallowed hard. "Please tell me this is the first time you're reaching out to Delsinor."

"Roan, listen to me, please," Phael started again.

"Tell me!" Roan whipped Phael around and slammed him hard against the wall, pinning him there. "Is this the first time you've tried to reach out to Delsinor?"

Phael nodded rapidly, a tear releasing from his frightened

eyes. "I swear. Roan, I don't want to hurt you, I promise. This had nothing to do with you."

"Then what?" Roan barked, shoving his forearm hard into Phael's neck. "Do you know what Trylian will do to you if he finds out what you almost did?"

Phael choked but said in a strangled tone, "Delsinor is my home. I have to warn them."

"No, not anymore," Roan growled. "You have to stop thinking like that. You have to bring your loyalty to us now." He shook his head. Phael would never see things that way. He had to remind the Claret his life was at stake. "Phael, Trylian will kill you. Or worse, have me kill you like he did Razvin."

Phael closed his eyes, weeping silently. "Let go of me," he whimpered sadly, struggling once again.

Roan waited a moment, considering the Claret before he stepped back. Phael fell forward and his legs gave out. He fell down and coughed before looking up at Roan from the ground.

"I'm sorry," he said, eyes bright with tears. "I just have to warn them. I wanted them to know. You have to understand that."

"I do," Roan agreed. He crumpled the letter in his hand. "But you must understand that you serve the Modeus now. That your life is forfeit if you step out of line even a little bit. And I don't want..." He stopped himself. He didn't want Phael dead, but he couldn't admit that to the Claret. Not now. Something about Phael made him want to protect him. To keep him safe. So he'd not tell anyone about what had happened tonight.

Roan stepped aside and tossed the letter into the fire. Phael watched, eyes wide. "We cannot speak of this," Roan said sternly. "This never happened."

Phael nodded. He reached out and gripped the ends of Roan's tunic. "I'm sorry. I don't want *you* harmed. I just..."

"I know." Roan sighed heavily. He watched the parchment burn. If he wasn't careful, this Claret would be the death of him. If Phael faltered in battle, ran, or even gave a small hint that he'd betray Roan, his life would be in danger.

"You won't tell Trylian?" Phael asked in a small voice.

Roan shook his head. "But you have to swear that you won't do this again. That you're loyal to *me*."

Phael nodded. "I swear, Roan."

"Good." Roan took a deep breath and looked down at his hands. He still had blood under his nails. "I need a bath," he sighed.

"What happened?" Phael asked, changing the subject.

"Nothing," Roan snapped. He shoved past Phael and went to find a servant to draw him a bath.

THAT NIGHT, the caer was abuzz with music, chatter, and laughter. The air was stuffy with the smell of sweat, roasting meat, and sweet almonds sizzling in honey. The Knights and soldiers crowded into the feasting hall, making it hot and close. Roan dragged Phael to the celebration, but his Claret departed from him to stand near Alowyn, Tanis's Claret, and Athael, Gareth's Claret. Roan watched them whisper together for a moment. He knew Phael would be loyal to him now. He let them chat. Alowyn was just as meek and demure as Phael, so he had no fear. And with Athael, who was a Modeus Claret, they wouldn't speak of treason.

Roan meandered through the crowd and filled a plate. He was famished. He piled it high with roasted meat and vegetables, stuffing a sweet roll into his mouth before taking a seat among the other Knights.

"Roan!" a genial voice called out.

Roan looked up to see Aryn weaving through the crowd to him. Aryn was a year younger than Roan and in third column. He had lanky blond hair and wide green eyes. He squeezed through the crowd and plopped down next to Roan with a carafe of sweet mead and a plate of his own.

"I saw you riding today," Aryn said with a big smile. "What's it like on the back of a dragon like that?" He took a big bite of a roll and chewed with his eyes glued to Roan.

"It's exhilarating," Roan said over the din. "Makes my heart pound, honestly. I was afraid at first, but I had this feeling Phael wouldn't let me fall."

Aryn nodded, smiling as he smacked his lips. He wiped his mouth on the back of his hand and asked, "When did you get your Claret? I've not gotten one yet. I want one, though. What's it like to throw flames from your hand? Do you have a favorite element? Oh, have you ever used corrupted crystals? They say the Scion can use them without consequence."

Roan blinked at the younger boy, not sure which question to answer first. "I doubt that's true about the corrupted crystals," he said. He tapped the white pearlescent point around his neck. "This one drained me a little when I bound Phael. I feel it every time I try to control him when he's in his dragon form."

Aryn's eyes went wider as he beheld the white crystal. "But you're Scion. Which is amazing, by the way."

Roan scoffed through his nose lightly. "We'll see when we attack Delsinor."

"But you're incredible," Aryn put in. "All the men talk about what you're like in battle. Fierce, brave, always leading the charge, and never afraid."

Roan knew that was a lie. Battle terrified him, just like every man. But he didn't want to ruin Aryn's perception of him, so he just nodded with a half-hearted shrug. "Battle is a terrifying thing, Aryn," he said. "You'll know soon enough. Have you ever fought in a skirmish?"

Aryn shook his head. "I'm new. Sort of. Not like you, raised in the caer. My father wasn't a Knight, but I wanted to be. I joined up a year ago and have been training hard ever since. I swear, one day, I'll be the strongest Knight."

Roan nodded. Before he could answer any of Aryn's numerous other questions, Trylian stood up from the head table and banged his tankard. Everyone eventually fell silent, all eyes on him. Roan adjusted so he could see him, Aryn doing the same beside him, though he was a head shorter than Roan.

"My brave Knights," Trylian started off with a gentle smile. "Tonight, we toast to our departure and to our glorious battle ahead." He turned to the men beside him. Thaniel and Baelian sat there. Trylian looked around. "Where is Mathis?"

Roan's gut filled with ice, and he shrank down a little. He still didn't believe that he had slaughtered the Archon Knight.

"Not among us," Thaniel sighed, a slight frown creasing his brow. "Do you think he ran?"

Trylian's face fell into slight concern. "Mathis never was one for courage. I am not surprised he has left us."

No one spoke, but a few heads turned to look around, maybe hoping to spot Mathis among them. But when he wasn't found, Trylian's eyes fell on Roan. Roan tried to hold his head high but found himself shrinking under Trylian's gaze.

"It seems there is an opening among our Archon Knights," Trylian said, raising his tankard high. "I know just the man for the job. Roan?"

Roan gulped but forced himself to maintain eye contact. Was this really happening? Was he about to be made Archon Knight?

"A boy?" an older Knight from the crowd called out. "He's not even eighteen."

"He is your Scion," Trylian said, his words cutting. "Who better to lead the fourth column than Roan?"

Aryn stood, raising his goblet. "To Roan! To our Scion and Archon Knight!"

Almost the entire crowd stood then, raising their glasses as well. They shouted, "To Roan, our Scion!" and everyone drank in his name. Roan blushed, but felt a rush of pride swell in his chest. This was it. This was what he had wanted. And he'd gotten it. Aryn pounded him on the back and cheered, as did the rest of the crowd.

"Roan," Trylian said, still standing. "Will you take this position? Will you accept the title and be presented to our Atheling as an Archon Knight? Though that may have to wait until after we take Delsinor."

So it wouldn't be official. To become an Archon Knight, one had to be recommended by the others and then taken and presented to the Atheling of Aatheria for a signed document, making it so. Until then, Roan would have no claim to any land and would be in command in word only. But did it matter? The men wanted it. They would follow him. A surge of pride, power, and entitlement rushed through him. A piece of him that had always been afraid of Trylian began to dissipate. They would be equals now. No... He was Scion. And he needed to act like it. Trylian had to answer to him. Roan looked around. All the men applauded him. Aryn led a cheer in his honor. He looked Trylian in the eyes. The Archon Knight, his father figure, his tormentor, looked back at him, waiting. Nothing shone in Trylian's eyes. He was waiting to see what Roan would do.

This is it, Roan thought to himself. *This is my time. I've made it.* Strength flooded him. He'd no longer need to bend a knee to Trylian. And it was all due to himself. He had killed

Mathis. But more than that, he had worked and suffered for this his entire life. *I will suffer no longer,* he growled to himself.

Roan stood. "I would be honored, Trylian," he called.

The men shouted and cheered again, raising their glasses once more and drinking in his name.

"I'll follow you, Roan!" Aryn shouted over the commotion.

Roan took the mead Aryn offered him and drank deeply. He spotted Phael over the cup's edge and was pleased to see the Claret smiling at him. This was good for Phael, too. He'd be promoted to Archon Claret and would hold some authority among the other Clarets. Not only that, but he was Claret to the Scion. Roan would need to have a long talk with Phael about what all this meant. The others would look up to him now. Was Phael ready for such a burden? Could he shoulder the load and remain loyal to Roan and the Modeus?

These new concerns filled Roan. But as he looked into Phael's eyes from across the room, he got a sense that he need not worry. Phael would be loyal to him. He wasn't sure why he felt that way, but he was glad for it. Soon, they would march on Delsinor and the real trial would begin.

CHAPTER XXXIV

Roan, Trylian, Phael, and Elendir rode out in the morning to the Sactrium to get new crystals for Roan. The air had shifted entirely to cool early winter gusts, but the sun still shone down slightly warm. They bundled up in furs and new fur-lined boots now. The air puffing out of their horse's mouths was a testament to how cold it had gotten just over the last few days. Roan pulled the hood of his cloak up, but the air still stung his nose and made his cheeks bright red. He glanced sideways at Phael and saw he too suffered from the cold. They would need more provisions if they were to march on Delsinor in the middle of winter. It wasn't the most opportune moment to wage war, but Trylian wouldn't be argued with. It just meant Delsinor wouldn't be expecting them.

They wound their way around the city of Aatheria and through the streets for some time before coming to the doors of the Sactrium. The bells rang, calling the Clarets inside to worship and sing. Roan could already hear their voices rising up through the stone buttresses and open windows. It was a beautiful, heavenly sound. He wondered only briefly what the Elsarius Sactriums sounded like, with the inclusion of female voices. But that thought quickly left his head as Trylian called them inside.

Roan helped Phael down off his horse and then followed the other two into the Sactrium. The great doors didn't open, but a smaller one within the right side did. A Claret welcomed them with tented fingers and a gentle voice. He quickly ushered them inside and closed the door as the wind picked up, making the candles just inside the door flicker. Once they were all inside, they were led down the nave. Roan looked around, having rarely been in a Sactrium, let alone one as grand as Aatheria's. It made him wonder about the much grander Sanctuaries in the capitals of Moralan and Adorian.

It felt different this time being in the Sactrium than his first visit. Then, all he had cared about was binding to Phael. The nave walls were lined with colored glass depicting myths and legends he knew little of. Windows let in the sun and the cool air, but it was quickly doused by the heat of the many bodies packed into the area. The Clarets stood in rows, singing in unison near an altar at the end of the structure. Fire flickered from a hundred or more candles, giving the colored glass a soft glow. The warmth, the singing, and the fire gave Roan a sense of serenity and peace he'd never felt before. He stood a moment, listening, before Phael gently took his elbow in hand and pushed him down a hallway after Trylian, out of the main room.

The Claret led them through some cold, arched hallways and past a square garden. "The head Anakrite will see you in the library. He's in a conclave at the moment but will join you shortly."

He opened a door to his left and ushered them inside before taking his leave. The library was grand. Bookshelves taller than Roan made up every wall. Desks peppered the area as well, all armed with ink, quills, and parchment. Some desks were occupied by Clarets writing speedily, scratching away at the parchment. Trylian wandered a few steps away, picked up an old dusty book, and began to flip through it, Elendir hanging close over his arm to look at the pages.

Phael's face was pale and sad. He watched the hand of a

Claret move over the parchment, scrawling the histories, no doubt. "To think, if only I had as little magic as they. This would be my destiny. Singing hymns in the morning, writing holy texts, maintaining the orchard."

"Sounds boring," Roan moaned, tired of Phael's melancholy. "I'd much rather seek glory and immortality in battle. Be the one they write about."

Phael met his eyes, arms lank and helpless at his side. "And if that battle and glory leads to death?"

Roan shrugged. "So long as I did something magnificent, I'd be immortalized in the texts."

"Remember," Elendir said gently, looking up from his book, "your life is not just your own. You must protect yourself to protect your Claret."

Phael scoffed sadly. "He doesn't care if I die."

Roan was shocked to find his heart stabbed at this comment. But Elendir was right, he had to think about Phael as well. If he died, so did Phael. Eventually. "What's that death like?" he asked. "Dying from the magic?"

"Terrible," Trylian said, closing the book and setting it back on the shelf. "I'm glad you've never seen it."

Phael gulped.

"But, Winds willing, you will never have to know that feeling," Trylian said to Phael. "Though Clarets don't live as long as non-magical humans."

"But you have many years ahead of you," Elendir said soothingly when Phael's brows shot together in worry. "The oldest Claret lived to be a hundred and one. His Knight died soon after."

"Elemor and Estrid," Phael said, recalling the myth. "They fought against Vyrkaris centuries ago."

Elendir nodded, smiling.

Slightly intrigued by this immortalized Knight, Roan asked, "What made them so special?"

"Elemor was a Knight of the Elsarius," Elendir said. "And Estrid a Claret of the Modeus. But they were a true binding. Destined for one another. They could hear each other's minds and knew each other's thoughts."

Roan glanced quickly at Phael and saw his Claret looked at him, too. "That doesn't mean they were destined to be together," he said offhandedly.

"That *is* what we believe," Elendir said kindly, looking at Roan knowingly. "And for them, it was a miracle, since they came from competing faiths."

Just then, the doors opened with a bit of a flourish. The Claret came back, this time followed by an Anakrite in a gold and white robe. He was older, with slight smile lines around his lips and long, dark brown hair.

"Don't Clarets stop aging?" Phael asked.

The Anakrite looked from one to the other and then back at Phael. "I've walked in on some sort of conversation, I see," he said with a gentle smile. "Don't let my face fool you, boy. I am fifty years old."

"Really?" Roan asked, arching one brow. "I thought Clarets didn't live long."

The Anakrite nodded. "We may not live as long as you, but we age gracefully. Your Claret here will look like a young man when you are old and your skin is sagging." Roan blanched and crossed his arms. The Anakrite laughed lightly at Roan's reaction and said, "This must be our Scion?"

"Sylvius, meet Roan son of Monguard," Trylian said. He laid his hand on Roan's shoulder. "I am very proud of him. He's a great leader, fearless in battle, and as good as a son to me."

The Anakrite nodded and then made a shallow bow to Roan. "I am blessed to have the Scion in my house. Anything you need, we will provide, Modeus willing."

"We need crystals," Trylian said, getting back to business.

He dropped his hand from Roan. "I was hoping you might have corrupted crystals."

"No!" Phael burst.

Roan hissed at him to be quiet, glaring. But he then asked Trylian, "Won't those have adverse effects? I've heard stories of what they do to people who use them."

"You are Scion," Trylian said bracingly. "They will not harm you, surely. Sylvius?"

The Anakrite frowned gently and bit his bottom lip. "We don't know. We've never had a Scion of the Modeus in our lifetime. But there is no harm in trying. If you find they are too much for you, stop using them. Simple as that."

"They are addictive," Phael tried again. "You cannot simply set them aside once you use them. The Modeus will punish you for using them."

"Roan, keep your Claret silent," Trylian barked.

Roan turned and glared harder at Phael. "Silence, Phael. I know what I'm doing."

Phael's face fell, and he lowered his head, nodding in submission.

Sylvius nodded and rubbed his hands together. "Then to the crystal stores." He turned and led them out back the way they'd come. He rambled on as they walked, telling them about the history of the Sactrium, who had built what, and what some of the colored glass depicted. Roan lost interest about halfway through and stopped listening.

The crystal stores were a building detached from the main Sactrium. They walked across a ward to the building, which had a large tower atop it. Sylvius explained how the tower was shaped like it was to symbolize their prayers and how they rose to the Modeus or some such nonsense. Roan just wanted to see the crystals.

The Anakrite opened the door to the large tower and when he did, Roan swore a slight humming came from it.

Inside, the crystals glowed with brilliant colors and vibrations, casting light all over the tower walls. On the other side of the tower, a set of spiral stairs led up to the next level. Roan also spotted a door in the floor that led down.

"We go below," Sylvius said with a smile. "We do have corrupted crystals for study, but I am pleased to hand them over. For a price."

"Of course," Trylian said with a little disdain in his voice.

"How do you get them?" Roan asked as Sylvius opened the door in the floor.

"We have miners in Vyrkaris who work for the Sactrium," Sylvius explained. "We pay them for the work, and in turn, the Knights pay us for the crystals. Once they make it to the Sactrium, we pray over them, bless them, and prepare them to be used, essentially unlocking their power."

They marched down the steps and into a lower, darker level. Down below, the crystal light was the only light until Sylvius lit a brazier in the center of the room and then began to light candles in sconces on the walls. Little alcoves dotted the walls down there, and in each recess was a crystal type. Roan noticed they had that opaline sheen like the one around his neck.

"You said you study them?" Roan asked. "What does that mean?"

Sylvius replied, "We have Elsarius prisoners we force to use them and then study the results. It's a bloody terrible business, but we need to know."

Phael made a soft noise at this. Roan knew he must be thinking about how terrible that was. Like them, he was a prisoner of the Modeus, too, forced to do their bidding. But he quickly tamped down the guilt he felt. He needed Phael. He was a tool to be used.

"I have some rare ones as well," Sylvius said. He looked at Trylian. "What were you thinking?"

"What do you have?" the Archon Knight replied quickly.

"I have…" Sylvius reached into one little alcove and pulled out a dark gray—almost black—crystal with the iridescent sheen.

Roan didn't know what it was, but Trylian's eyes lit up. "How did you— Where?"

"Vyrkaris," Sylvius said with a proud smile. "Killed a draconic warlord in the north and took his horde."

"What is it?" Roan asked. Whatever it was, he wanted to use it.

"You're not ready for this yet, Roan," Trylian said with a malicious smile. "But one day, perhaps. Hold on to it, Sylvius. I'll be back for it."

Sylvius inclined his head in a sort of nod and placed the crystal back in its resting place. "So the usual, then?"

"Fire," Roan said quickly. "It's my favorite."

The Anakrite smiled and moved to an alcove with three orange opalescent crystals. He picked one up and handed it to Roan. "This will do more than throw a ball of fire, boy," he said in a warning tone. "All of the crystals we give you today will. Be aware of that."

He moved down one alcove and picked up a dark yellow one. "This will summon storms. And this," he picked up a light turquoise one, "will make a gale force wind the likes of which you may not escape. Be careful how you use them."

"And the blessings?" Roan asked. "Do they need to be prayed over?"

"Not for recharging," Sylvius said. "But I'd make your Claret pray over them all the same. They need to be familiar with you and your magic. The closer you are to them, the more control you will have. And you, of course, want the Winds' blessing. However, yes, you are correct. Phael need not pray to recharge them. But attunement is always beneficial."

"And you're sure these won't harm me?" Roan asked, Phael's pleas still ringing in his ears.

Sylvius tilted his head in thought. "I am sure they will not whisper to you, drive you mad. Will they syphon your life force? Perhaps. Are you willing to be an experiment, my Scion?"

Roan picked up the fire crystal and turned it over in his hands, thinking. "More than a ball of fire?" he asked, a smile quirking his pale lips.

Sylvius mirrored his grin. "Much more."

Roan took the three crystals, and the troop headed back to the caer. On the way back, Trylian told Roan to practice the moment they got back. "I want to see what you can do," he said.

Roan wasn't sure, but he was excited. He quickly went to the blacksmith when they returned and had the crystals embedded in his sword, his left-hand gauntlet, and right hand as well. As the blacksmith worked, Roan told Phael to pray, and he did. He didn't hear the Claret's words, but watched his lips move in silent prayer as the smith worked.

"Can you feel the Winds when you pray?" Roan asked once he was finished.

"I feel wind," Phael replied solemnly. "Like it's inside me. I know they hear me."

"And the Modeus?" Roan asked as the blacksmith finished. "Do you pray to them now?"

Phael refused to make eye contact with Roan. His eyes clouded over.

"Better start," Roan said. "Winds know what might happen once we take Delsinor."

Phael took a shaking breath but didn't reply.

The blacksmith handed Roan his things and together they marched back outside the walls of the caer. There was a great expanse of pasture between the city and the river to the east.

Roan led Phael, Trylian, and Elendir there. A small host of Knights and soldiers followed them, curious to see the Scion in action. Aryn was among them and prattled on the entire way about how great the magic would be. Gareth and Tanis joined them as well.

Roan rode out a ways from the pack and dismounted. Then he walked a good distance away from his horse and looked up into the sky. The clouds didn't let much sun through. It would be perfect for a storm. He raised his right hand and called on the magic in the turquoise crystal, reaching for the storms.

When nothing happened, Gareth called, "Come on, Roan, show us what you've got," in a jeering manner.

"Don't be shy," Tanis cajoled as well, a smirk on his face.

Roan growled and lowered his hand. It felt harder to reach the magic with the corrupted crystals. Like there was another door he had to go through to find it. He tried again, and this time felt a crackling between his fingers. He'd done nothing different. It just came to him now. A bolt of lightning struck down from the sky, hitting the ground before Roan. He screamed and leapt back as the thunder deafened him. He clapped his hands over his ears and looked up. A swirl started in the middle of the clouds and dissipated the longer he stared at it. Thinking he must have conjured it, he reached up and gripped the clouds with the magic. The rotation moved faster until a small funnel cloud appeared.

Getting an idea, Roan thrust his sword toward the oncoming tornado. The orange stone glowed as he summoned fire from the sky. The fire collided with the rotation and the thing turned into a swirling column of fire and wind. It was wide and wobbled as it touched down on the ground. Even from this distance, Roan could hear the rhythmic roaring of the funnel cloud. It terrified him and made his mouth drop open in awe at the same time. The storm moved along the riverbanks, heading toward the little village just beside the river. Panic hit Roan then. He had to stop it.

"Roan, stop!" Phael urged from behind.

"I know!" he shouted back. He pulled his hands back and released the magic as quickly as he could. The fire and storm immediately began to dissipate. The village was safe.

Like Phael had described before, he suddenly felt a rush of wind inside him. It stole his breath and constricted his lungs, suffocating him. He gasped, trying to breathe in, but the air wouldn't come. The magic had knocked the wind out of him. He tried to breathe, grasping at his closed throat. His legs gave out and he heard the blood rushing in his ears. Falling to his knees, he saw blood leaking out from beneath his fingernails. His heart skipped a beat in his chest and then spasmed painfully.

Finally, as quickly as it had gone, his breath came back. He gasped and coughed, his lungs inflating with the life-giving air. Someone ran up beside him and gripped his shoulders, rubbing his back. He recognized Phael's white boots.

"Are you all right?" the Claret asked. "You're bleeding."

Roan waited a moment as his sapped strength started to come back. He couldn't stop the shaking and trembling, though.

"Roan, please," Phael begged as the others ran up to them. "Don't use them. See what happens?"

Roan shoved Phael off so hard the Claret lost his footing and fell onto the ground. Roan stood up straight as Trylian neared. He checked his master's face. Trylian was beaming. At last, he'd done something right.

"Magnificent, Roan," Trylian said with a smile. "Now all you have to do is get used to the power."

"It hurt him," Phael urged, standing. "Don't make him do this."

"Be silent, Claret," Trylian snapped. "Roan, do you think you can work with these? Harness that power?"

Roan nodded. "Of course. I felt it inside me. The power, the majesty. It was incredible. I felt like nothing could touch me."

Trylian's smile widened. "Excellent. Then practice. Within two weeks' time, we march on Delsinor. I want you ready. Both of you," he said to Phael, glaring. "Your dragon must be in compliance as well."

"He will be," Roan promised. "We'll lead this war from the skies."

CHAPTER XXXV

The following weeks rushed by in a haze of magic and combat training. Roan practiced riding his dragon, holding on with his legs and casting magic with his hands. The first several days he nearly teetered off the dragon's neck, but over time his muscles grew accustomed to holding on tight. The crystals sapped his mental strength and often stole the breath from his lungs, but he pushed through it to reach the utter euphoria that came at the end. As Trylian had said, he got used to it and lasted longer and longer the more he used them. But he couldn't deny that what Phael had said was true: he felt the crystals drain him. When he pushed too hard, physical pain overcame him and he had to stop.

"You won't be casting as much as you are now," Trylian tried to comfort him one day. "Save your power for when we need it. Let the dragon do the majority of the damage."

Roan knew Phael would hate it, but he'd force him to breathe fire down into the Elsarius' ranks. In dragon form, Roan was his complete master. Roan had the power to command him to change at will. The sheer power that came with such command was almost a better feeling than using the corrupted crystals.

As the time drew closer, excitement and anxiety began to settle in Roan. He slept less and less and even Phael noticed. His Claret urged him to try to rest and force him to eat, but his appetite had vanished. He knew he should. It was winter, and it was cold. If he was weak, the fever might come back. Then he'd not be able to fight. Or worse, he would force himself to enter the battlefield and die from not being alert enough to protect himself.

Then, the day of the march came. The Knights, the soldiers, and the Clarets all filed out in straight lines, column by column. Trylian led the way with his first column in the lead. Baelian rode beside him with second column abreast with first. Then came Roan and Thaniel leading their respective columns. Phael rode beside him, stiff and silent. The camp supplies, cooks, blacksmith, and others brought up the rear. Behind them came the makings for the war machines, like catapults and ballistae. Roan had hardly seen those machines in action and was eager to see them from the sky once they were assembled. Along with these came Aatheria's military led by several captains and a general.

Nothing much happened in the first few days. The men were quiet as they anticipated the battle to come, nerves and fear silencing them. But as the days went on and darkness came more quickly, they began to loosen up. Roan played his lute most nights near a campfire and Phael lurked close by. Aryn joined Roan almost every night, asking to hear tales about the battles he'd been in that year. Roan appreciated the boy's attention. It made him feel stronger, like he'd actually accomplished something. He watched Aryn next to him one night and thought how sad it would be if the boy fell in battle.

Roan expected resistance from some of the villages, but it seemed their initial battle and winning over the village had spread to the others.

"They are loyal to us now," Trylian said when Roan asked about it one day. "They may say their prayers in secret to the Elsarius, but they bow to us."

Two weeks of marching later, the snow drifted down

gently with a light breeze and Roan spotted the city of Delsinor on the horizon. Trylian had the camp stop a few miles away and set up, hidden, in a small forest near the river. That was when Roan saw her. Antinea was among the camp people. She had once been shared among the men, but now that she was round with child, no one wanted to lie with her. Instead, she cooked and repaired the under tunics of the men as needed. He wanted to speak with her, to be near her, but knew he shouldn't distract himself with her. She did look up once from a great cauldron of stew she was preparing and caught him watching her. Her stormy gray eyes latched onto him with a kind of warmth he didn't expect. She still looked sad, angry, and distant, but something else lurked behind the maelstrom.

That night, Trylian called the Archon Knights, their Clarets, and the general of the soldiers to his tent. Gareth and Tanis were there as well. Outside the tent, snow fell in thick flakes, and it was dark. Inside, Trylian had carpets under his feet, a few small braziers for light and warmth, and tables set up with maps with little metal figures on them. Roan looked over the map and realized this was their plan of attack.

"There are four main gates to Delsinor," Trylian began. "We're going to hit all four at once. One column per gate with an army of soldiers."

"We're ready," the general said in his deep, gruff voice.

"And what of third and fourth column?" Baelian asked. "They don't have the magic we do."

"They will enter the southern and eastern gates," Trylian said, pointing at the map. He moved a few of the metal figures over to surround Delsinor. "Those gates are the least protected, and they'll have Roan. He's worth a dozen Knights now."

Roan smiled a little and looked away from the others as they glanced toward him. He wasn't used to such praise from

Trylian. It made him feel good to hear it. Like he could do anything.

"And the dragon," Thaniel said, slapping Phael hard on his back. "That beast will be able to burn through the doors, weakening them for the battering rams."

"We plan on having them coming out to meet us," Trylian said, going back to the map. "The Delsinor army and Knight columns will come at us from the northern gate, as they can no doubt see us. We'll have an initial battle there and have to work our way to the gates."

"Once we have that under control, we build the siege equipment," Baelian went on when Trylian stopped to rub his chin.

"That could be days," Thaniel interjected.

"Yes," Trylian agreed. "But we're ready for it."

"And then?" Roan asked.

"Once we're inside," Trylian said with a deep sigh as he mulled over their strategy, "we do what we do best: slaughter those who stand up against us and make our way to the Sanctuary, where we'll shatter their Empyrean Core."

"What?" Phael burst.

"You are bound to a Modeus Knight," Trylian said, waving his hand. "You won't lose your magic."

"What does the Empyrean Core do?" Roan asked.

After a tense moment of silence, Elendir said, "The Empyrean Core is a large crystal surrounded by a stone base within the Sanctuary. The Elsarius believe it is the source of all their power. If it is destroyed, they'll lose their connection to the Winds and thus their magic. But I, like Phael, am bound to the Modeus. We will not lose our connection to the magic."

"But—" Phael stammered.

Roan held up his hand to quiet the Claret. He knew what Phael was about to say. He still prayed to the Elsarius, called upon them to relay his prayers to the Winds. He didn't want Trylian or the others to know that, though.

"Are you sure?" Roan asked Elendir. "You and Phael won't lose your powers?"

"And Alowyn," Tanis interjected. "He was Elsarius, too."

Elendir shook his head. "The binding is our power now."

"But you're not sure," Tanis said, getting hysterical. "What if it does take your power, making us useless?"

"Then pray that it doesn't," Trylian snapped. "Control your Clarets, boys."

"Yes, Father," Tanis said, lowering his head.

Trylian sighed and leaned onto his palms on the table. "Once we have destroyed the Empyrean Core, we'll head to the castle and the king. He will most likely be holed up inside, and that is our last stop."

Roan swallowed hard, knowing the answer before he asked the question. "And what will you do with the king?"

"Kill him," Trylian said simply. "And take his throne. Then the Elsarius will bow to us."

"And the prince and princess?" Baelian asked.

"No survivors of the king's line," Trylian quipped easily. "I don't want either of them having a claim to the throne. That's a rebellion waiting to happen. No, they all die. After we're finished with them." He smirked darkly.

"Wait," Roan asked, thinking. "Where is the Empyrean Core for the Modeus? Won't they just destroy that once they find out what we've done?"

Trylian's smile darkened and widened. "There is no Modeus Empyrean Core. We don't need such symbols to speak to the Modeus. The power is within us."

Roan frowned, not believing that to be true at all. Somewhere, there had to be a Core just like the Elsarius had that gave them their power, surely. Or else, where did it come from?

"Do your Clarets not attune to a Core?" Phael asked. "How do you stop the magic from consuming them if not?"

Elendir answered, "Through faith alone."

There was an odd silence after that in which Roan noted Phael's confused frown. The Claret didn't believe Elendir. He had more questions, but he held his tongue. Roan thanked the Winds he did.

"Now," Trylian said with a deep breath, "we need our rest. Tomorrow, we fight."

The other Archon Knights nodded, and the general raised his fist in a salute. Roan nodded, took Phael's arm, and walked him out of the tent. Gareth and Tanis stayed behind with their father.

"Roan," Phael whispered hysterically as they made their way through the camp. "I'm not ready. I can't—"

"You can and you will," Roan hissed, tightening his grip on Phael's wrist until he knew bruises would blossom. "Your life depends on it."

"What if I don't value my life anymore?" Phael whimpered. "I can't slaughter my own people. I won't do it."

"Don't give up," Roan said, turning to face Phael. "Don't do this again, Phael. I need you. Please."

Phael's blue eyes shone with unshed tears. "I-I..." He couldn't go on. He sniffled and hung his head.

"I'll try to save anyone I can," Roan promised as kindly as he could. He took Phael's hands in his, gently now. "Tell me who to save from the Sanctuary and I will. I promise."

Phael looked up, the tears finally leaking from his eyes. Defeat shrouded his face. "Lailen. My mentor and best friend. He was like a father to me."

Roan nodded. "He won't come to harm. I swear."

His Claret looked him deep in his eyes, searching for truth, a lie. When he didn't seem to detect any malice, he took a gasping breath and nodded. "Thank you, Roan."

It was nothing compared to the devastation that would be wrought, the killing of a king—but he knew it would convince Phael. Even if he couldn't find and save this Lailen, at least Phael was compliant and obedient now. All he needed was the dragon Phael could transform in to. After that, he'd be in total control.

⁊

ROAN LOOKED out toward Delsinor and watched the Elsarius army form ranks to face them. His heart hammered hard in his chest. Several yards behind him and his column, the Clarets waited. A few soldiers and Knights stayed back to protect them. Roan's mind went to Antinea in the camp not two miles away. Would she be safe? Would any of them be?

The sun didn't shine through the thick clouds, making a gray light for the morning. The battlefield was wide open and empty save for the two armies. Roan adjusted in his saddle and looked over his shoulder at the men behind him. Aryn was right there, face eager. Roan turned forward. Trylian was several yards away, sitting in front of his column. He wanted to talk to his mentor, to ask him if everything would be all right. But he couldn't. He was alone. He was in charge of hundreds of men. He swallowed hard and trained his eyes forward.

He blinked and Razvin appeared before his eyes. He gasped and shoved the familiar image away. In times like this, he would have given anything to have his best friend by his side again. But no... He had seen to it that Razvin was gone. He couldn't stop now. He had to finish what he'd started.

"Onward!" Trylian shouted from the front lines. His men broke into a furious gallop and charged into the army of Elsarius Knights and soldiers who had emerged from the city to meet them. Roan kicked his horse and followed suit, calling to his men to follow him. He broke off from riding right behind Trylian to come out and circle around the side of the Elsarius army. His men followed him in a great arcing wave. They drew their blades and others readied their magic. Roan kept his hands on his sword for now. Trylian wanted to wait before Roan used his magic.

Roan watched the first column rush into the Elsarius and swords shone and clanged as fire and lightning began to spit from the clashing hordes. He drew his longsword and readied to hack at the first Elsarius that came near him. He didn't have to wait long. Horses roared and snorted as the armies met in a violent crash. Swords flicked about, cutting and slicing. It was instant, pure madness.

Roan found himself turning his horse, cutting down a man, stabbing another, and then wheeling around to avoid a spear. Some men leapt from their horses and engaged in one-on-one combat. He watched one fight and felt a thrill when the Elsarius Knight was cut down. He shouted praise to the man and charged deeper into the fray. He had to maneuver to miss hitting his own men or trampling down a friendly soldier. He looked for the leaders among the Elsarius and targeted those. One spotted him, recognizing his Archon armor, and charged him. Roan was ready, though. He raised his blade and caught the man's sword on his own, spinning it and sending it flying. He easily stabbed the man and twisted his blade. Blood flooded down the man's armor from where Roan had stabbed him between his breastplate and his pauldron.

With one Archon Knight down, dozens of Knights now had no commander. A wave of pride swelled up in Roan like never before. He'd done something magnificent, and it had been so easy for him. Like he was faster and stronger than the others. Was this what it meant to be Scion? Saying a quick prayer to the Modeus, he charged into the fray again. He lopped off the heads of five men before his shoulder burned with the effort. He blocked two attacks and almost took a sword to his neck but dodged it at the last second.

The fighting went on for what felt like hours. Roan stopped worrying about the Clarets and the camp and his mind just reeled with the blood, mud, and snow around him. The snow made his horse slip more than once and he had to steady it while trying not to get stabbed or struck by a spidering bolt of lightning from an Elsarius hand. Soon, the battlefield turned to mud and the white snow was totally gone from around them. His white horse's legs were covered in it, and it spattered on his face as well.

Roan was fighting with another Archon Knight he'd found when a messenger rode up behind him, shouting his name. He quickly dispatched the Archon Knight and turned to see Gareth riding up to him. His eyes were wild, and his face was spattered in mud and blood.

"Father says to show them your powers now," Gareth panted, weaving around a dueling couple. "He says burn them in their armor."

Roan smiled. "As he commands."

Gareth kicked his horse and galloped back the way he'd come. Roan turned his horse around and charged to the side, getting away from the fighting. It wasn't easy, and he had to cut down several men on his way out. But soon he got a good distance away.

"Phael, pray for me," he whispered as he raised his sword to the sky. The orange crystal flared to life, as did the turquoise one in his gauntlet. His excitement seemed to fuel the magic. The skies above twisted and the wind picked up as Roan raised both hands. Fire erupted from the clouds and crawled down the descending rotation.

The people slowly stopped one by one. Thunder cracked across the sky, which was still raining fat flakes of snow. That was unnatural, and they knew it. The Elsarius looked up and froze. The fiery pillar crawled to the earth, spinning devastatingly. It touched down and Roan gripped it, trying to control where it went. He saw blood start to seep from under his fingernails and felt the wind sucked from his lungs. He gasped, suffocating, but held on.

The pillar of fire crawled over the battlefield, igniting some banners and men as it moved. The wind sucked up horses, Knights, and soldiers alike. He watched as the bodies spun around the outside of the fiery tornado. Never had he seen such a sight. Screams erupted from the back lines, and he guided the abomination of nature there.

Then his strength was sapped. He felt his life force pulled from his body and surge into the fiery storm. He had to stop, or he'd pass out. So he let go. Panting and screaming in pain, he released the magic. The fire vanished into a huge funnel of smoke and the winds died down, but the damage had been done, and the fear had been planted. He fell over onto his horse and panted, clutching his chest. Underneath the pain and suffocation came the euphoria. A surge of something he couldn't identify flowed through him, making him feel invulnerable despite the damage.

Tanis, Gareth, and Aryn rode out to him and escorted him to the back lines where he had a moment to rest and regain his composure. He looked out over the battlefield and saw the Modeus had a numbers advantage now. They were able to push forward a little where the fiery storm had penetrated the masses. Roan took a deep breath and knew that the battle had just begun. It would be days before they reached the walls of Delsinor, but he was ready. He was powerful.

CHAPTER XXXVI

It had been days, and the siege had not moved inside the walls yet. The men fought valiantly, and the skirmishes moved back and forth. Sometimes they would go hours pulled back, no fighting happening. Once, it went on for an entire day. Like both sides had declared an unspoken truce and tended to their wounded and dying. Small convoys of soldiers and Knights from both sides had sneaked out during the nights more than once and had tried to catch the other unaware. But Trylian had seen to them quickly, dispatching the Elsarius factions. The Archon Knights took turns returning to camp to rest and now he walked among the tents of the others, listening to their conversation and gauging the morale of the men. It was a dark, cold winter, and the men missed home already. The stalemate had them nervous. He needed Roan to push harder.

Trylian took long, quiet strides through the rows of tents as the snow drifted down in soft curtains around him. It had been piling up over the last few days, and he knew the front lines must be struggling. Already once they had retreated farther back to regroup. But the Elsarius had fallen back inside the walls once as well. That was how he'd left them. He wanted to go back, but he had to wait at least one more day in case a messenger from Aatheria arrived. He was expecting word from Amril or Sorath and didn't want to miss it. Plus, he needed the break from the constant fighting and bloodshed. He was tired. But his boys, as well as Roan, were still out there. His heart squeezed as he thought of Gareth and Tanis. He hoped they were all right.

He had just opened the flap to his tent when a shriek rent the air. He'd been hearing moaning and gentle cries all night but had had no idea what it was. He'd thought the men must have been plowing one of the girls. But this didn't sound like that. Trylian followed the screams and came around the healer's covered wagon. Lying on the cold ground, almost entirely exposed, was a girl he recalled whose name was Antinea. Gareth had lain with her once, and he was sure Roan had as well.

He looked on in horror at the large wet spot beneath Antinea's legs. She lay on her back, knees bent with the healer between them, the man holding a candle with a brass backing to reflect the light.

"One more push," the healer said, wiping sweat from his brow. His white mustache and beard glittered with sweat and melting snow. "Come, Antinea. He's coming. But you have to push."

"I did!" Antinea growled through gnashed teeth. Her eyes were screwed tight in concentration and no doubt pain.

"Again!" the healer barked.

Antinea screamed and threw her head back, howling to the skies above.

"Shut her up," Trylian snapped, looking around. "They'll know where the camp is. Do you want that?"

"Sir, she's in labor," the healer said, a bit snarky. "It will end soon." To Antinea he said, "One more, girl, come on!"

Antinea shrieked again, straining so hard her face turned bright red.

Trylian, entranced by the blood and violence of it all, watched with eyes wide open. He remembered the birth of his boys. Two at once. His wife, Alyah, had been in labor for hours. When Gareth was born, he'd thought that was it and was happy to have a son. Especially one as strong and healthy as Gareth had been. But then she'd screamed again and held her still-bulging belly. She'd been pregnant with twins. Trylian remembered Tanis as a babe. He'd been small, fragile, compared to his brother. He'd loved him so much. He remembered holding both boys as Alyah panted and cried.

"Two," she had said. "I've given you two sons. Are you proud?"

He'd wept then. Of course he'd been proud. He'd held the boys for hours, not knowing Alyah was breathing her last. He had kissed the boys on their foreheads and when he'd looked up, she was gone. Only days after that, he'd been sent away to Emberforge, where Monguard had betrayed him. He'd not had enough time with his boys and had regretted not being there for the first two years of their lives. He prayed now that they were still alive and that he could hold them once again.

Trylian sniffled and savagely wiped at his eyes as Antinea gasped and groaned loudly. A second later, the babe yowled and mewled at the top of his lungs. He plopped into the healer's hands in a heap of blood and fluid. The boy screamed as the healer quickly slapped him down onto his mother's chest. Antinea wept immediately. She wrapped her arms around the babe and wailed. The child was tiny.

Stunned, Trylian didn't shush her this time. At first, he wondered if the bastard was Gareth's. After all, he'd slept with her months ago. He went around to Antinea's side, knelt, and looked down at the child. He had thick brown hair. He couldn't see the eyes as the child still clenched them tight, but he didn't need to see them to know. The boy had a straight, elegant nose and the long chin of Roan. His heart tripped in his chest.

"Do you have a name?" the healer asked, cleaning up underneath Antinea.

The girl nodded. "Eurion. After my father."

"You must keep him quiet," the healer said, handing her a cup of tea. "We cannot be discovered. We must be careful with him, as well. He's very small. He came too early. I will find blankets for you both." He looked at Trylian, smiled, and said, "I'll be around the back if you need me."

Trylian couldn't take his eyes off the pale babe. The resemblance to Roan was uncanny, and no one could miss it. This—a child—was the last distraction Roan needed. He needed his Scion to be focused and eager for blood. Not cooing over an infant.

"Listen, girl," Trylian said, kneeling beside her. "You don't need this burden. A child in your state, at your age, is a war you cannot win. He will starve. *You* will starve. And out here in the winter—if disease doesn't take him, the cold will."

Antinea, face red and hair plastered to her neck from sweat, looked up at him. Her stormy gray eyes filled with tears and darkened with shock and anger. "What are you saying?" Her grip tightened around the babe. Around Eurion.

Trylian reached out and gently touched the child's head. His hair was wet and cold to the touch. "I can dispose of it for you."

"No!" Antinea gasped, yanking Eurion out of Trylian's reach. She clung to him tighter now. "He is the child of a Scion. What do you think that means?"

Trylian frowned. Could the girl know Roan was the father?

"He could be a natural-born Scion," she said, her words eagerly spilling from her mouth. "We don't know what it means when a Scion has a child."

"How do you know this is Roan's child?" Trylian hissed so no one else would hear.

"I know it," she whispered back. Her eyes pled with him. "He could be naturally gifted in magic. If not that, he will carry on your legacy if you let me tell Roan. You raised Roan. You will live on in him and thus through Eurion. Or he could be used to your political advantage later in life."

"What do you mean?"

"Marriage ties," Antinea said quickly. "He could be useful for a political alliance when he's grown."

Trylian narrowed his eyes at the girl. He knew what she was trying to do. Trying to convince him not to kill the child with promises of power, political ties, and appealing to his pride. But she had a point. The child could be useful. Perhaps.

"You are a wise and just leader," she said, her voice now shaking with fear and weeping. "You wouldn't kill an innocent child. *Roan's child*. If Roan ever found out that you'd killed his son... He'd turn on you, surely."

He considered her words. A natural-born Scion? Or better, what if the boy was one who could use magic, but not have it overwhelm him? He could be a Knight. A man with such powers would be unstoppable. And if he was raised near Trylian, he'd have the same teachings Roan had. The same mentality. The same obedience.

Trylian took a deep breath. "I see what you are manipulating me with, girl. But I also understand. What you say is good and true. Very well. The child may live."

"Oh, Winds, thank you, Trylian!" Antinea wept, tears splashing down her face. She clung to Eurion hard, squishing the baby's face against her chest. "Will you send a runner to the front lines? To tell Roan. I want him to know."

He saw the hope in her eyes. Did she have feelings for Roan? Had she kept the pregnancy to trap him to her? He knew there were many ways for a woman to dispose of an unwanted pregnancy, and most in her line of work did. But she hadn't. He glared at her now.

"Please," she whispered, seeing the change in his eyes. "Roan must know."

"I cannot have Roan distracted by this," Trylian snapped. He stood.

"No, no," Antinea begged, touching his leg. "He won't be. He's strong and wise. He will fight better, be stronger and more determined now that he knows he has a son. You understand, don't you? You remember when your boys were born? How proud you were."

His heart ached again for Gareth and Tanis. He wanted them with him, safe, and away from the battle. He'd do anything for them. Fight a dozen men alone, take on the entire army for them. He'd even go back now and risk his life for them. His eyes floated down to Eurion. Perhaps Roan would be the same way.

He sighed. "Very well. I will send a runner to the front this very moment. Roan will be here before sunrise."

"Winds bless you, Trylian!" Antinea wailed, bowing her forehead to his shin and sobbing. She clutched his pant leg and kissed him.

"Don't thank me yet," he sighed. "We don't know this news will please Roan at all."

༄

ROAN HAD PULLED BACK to let his men take a breath. They had pushed forward and the other columns, as well as the soldiers, kept the Elsarius army at bay. They had been switching out for some days now to keep their men as fresh as they could. The nights were terrible. The Elsarius would pull back inside the city walls only to charge early in the morning once again. Roan had barely slept in the last several days, and his mind was reeling and his eyes stung.

"Sir," Aryn called, riding up to him. "We've chased a pack of the Elsarius to the west. We think they are trying to hide in the trees."

Roan squinted in the direction Aryn spoke of. "Don't chase them. Stay the course. They want us divided. We won't do it."

"Are you sure?" Aryn asked, confusion on his young face.

Roan nodded. "Tell the men to not give chase. We'll move out in the next ten minutes and relieve first column."

"Yes, sir," Aryn said, nodding and dashing off back toward the men.

Behind him, another horse galloped up. He sensed Phael through their bond before he turned to see it was him.

"I've moved the Clarets as you instructed," he panted. "We're now to the north, closer to the river."

Roan had had the Clarets move their position more than once, just in case the Elsarius found out where they were. He needed Phael safe and alive. They hadn't shown their true power to the Elsarius yet, but knew he'd have to soon. They couldn't keep fighting in this stalemate forever.

"Good. Thank you," Roan sighed. He turned to give Phael an approving look. "How are they? How are *you*?"

"We're fine," he said as a way to placate any fear Roan had for them. "No one has even come close to us. I don't think they know where we are."

"Good," Roan answered quickly. "If only we could get ahold of theirs." He glared at the city walls, knowing full well that the Clarets were behind them, safe and protected. They'd never get to the Elsarius Clarets.

"Sir!" a loud voice shouted from behind them. "Roan!"

Roan whirled around at the urgent call, Phael joining him. "What is it?" Roan asked, recognizing Trylian's messenger. "Is everyone all right?"

The messenger nodded and a strange smile spread across his face. "But you must hurry back to camp. It's Antinea."

Confused, Roan frowned. "What of her?" He couldn't leave the front, not now. His men needed him.

"You must come and see," the messenger panted.

Roan glanced over his shoulder at the front where magic flew across the battlefield and the clang of swords still rang.

"Trylian insists," the messenger added quickly.

Roan groaned. "Very well. Phael, you're in command. Stay back. Don't go into the fight. Get the men moving and have Aryn lead the next charge."

"Yes," Phael nodded, his face set in determination. "Be safe. Please."

"*You* be safe," Roan shot back. He nodded to the messenger. "Lead the way."

The messenger shot off on his horse back the way he'd come, and Roan followed him. He wondered what could have happened that he needed to attend to during such a time as this.

They weaved their way through a small forest and back to the camp in a matter of minutes, galloping on their steeds. The messenger pointed to Roan's tent wordlessly. Panting for breath, Roan leapt from his horse before it even stopped and marched to his tent. Trylian stood outside it.

"Are you all right?" Roan gasped, grasping Trylian's arms. "What's wrong?"

Trylian smiled and nodded. "We're fine. Better than fine. Go inside and see."

Confused and hating the secrecy, Roan pushed open the flap to his tent. He glared, looking around, then spotted Antinea sitting atop a pile of fur blankets near the brazier. She cradled something in her arms. She looked up when he burst in and a gentle yet hopeful smile crept over her face. Roan only had to glance at the thing in her arms before he realized what it was. But why did they need him here for a baby?

"I don't understand," he stammered. "What—"

"Roan," Antinea interrupted, her smile turning nervous. "Meet Eurion." She met his eyes. "Your son."

Roan physically felt the blood drain from his face. He froze and his lungs stopped breathing. His mind wouldn't form any words as he looked from the girl down to the babe in her arms. How? When? He blinked rapidly, his lips moving, but no words came out.

"He's early," Antinea whispered. "But I think he's impatient, like his father."

"Stop saying that," Roan burst. "You don't know he's mine. He could be anyone's. He could be Gareth's."

Antinea shook her head. "You're the only one who..." She stopped, biting her bottom lip, trying to think of how to say whatever she was going to utter next.

"Everyone knows you don't come inside a whore," Trylian said, lifting the flap to the tent. "Something I never taught you, I suppose."

Roan exhaled hard and ran a hand through his long red hair. He glanced down at the child. Antinea shifted him so that his face was visible. He had alabaster skin, just like Roan. A long, elegant, straight nose. But he had his mother's hair and eyes. Roan saw himself in the babe now that they'd said it.

"Leave us," Roan whispered to Trylian. The Archon Knight didn't argue. He bowed his head and left the tent. Roan took two cautious steps toward Antinea and the babe she had called Eurion.

"He won't bite," she giggled. "Come here." She held out her long and slender hand to him.

He took it and knelt, his eyes never leaving the child's face. He was enchanted by the babe somehow. The child was the most beautiful thing he had ever seen, he was sure of it. He lowered himself next to Antinea and instinctually held out his arms. She smiled, lifted the little bundle, and handed it to him.

Roan gasped when the weight of the babe laid against his arms. It was a real child. A living, breathing human. And it was his. He set Eurion in the crook of one arm and with the other, he touched his face gently. He wanted to feel his skin. It was as soft as rose petals.

"I don't know what to say," he whispered at length. "What am I supposed to do?"

Antinea looked up at him, her eyes shining, pleading, but he didn't know for what. She didn't answer him. He looked back down at Eurion, at the child in his arms. *His* child.

Suddenly, nothing mattered. Not the war. Not Trylian. Not him being Scion. He didn't care if they took Delsinor or not. He didn't care if everyone was slaughtered on the front. So long as Eurion was safe, he'd be happy. He was so small, so fragile—he needed protection. Roan held him closer, closing his eyes as tears filled them. Antinea put her hand on his arm for comfort.

"Thank you," he whispered after a moment. He opened his eyes, letting the tears fall. He didn't care if she saw. "Thank you for keeping him. For bearing him."

She smiled and shed her own tears. She nodded. "I love him," she choked.

Roan was about to say he still didn't know what to do. But then it hit him all at once. Raise the boy. Yes, he was little more than a child himself, but what did it matter? This was his new reality. He had land in his name, a title soon to come. He was Archon Knight. He had everything he needed. Everything he wanted. Even a son. But no wife...

"Antinea," he blurted, making her jump a little. "Marry me."

"What?" she burst. Her tears dried almost immediately and her eyes rounded.

"Marry me," he repeated. "You'll be a lady. We can live together. We can raise our son together."

"Roan, I didn't— That is, I never—"

"I know you don't want it," he said. "But it's what you need. Let me take care of you, protect you, provide for you. I can do it. Let's live together. A real family."

She stammered some more before going silent. Her eyes trailed down to Eurion and she took a deep breath. "Are you sure?" she asked. "Roan, you heard Trylian. I'm just a whore."

He shook his head fiercely. "I know how you were taken from your home. I know how you've been treated. By me as well. Let me make it right. Once we're married, we can find your family. I want you to be safe, to be happy. Let me do this for you."

Antinea sniffed and looked down demurely. "I never wanted to be saved. I wanted to save myself."

"And you have," Roan said gently, taking her chin in his hand and tilting her head up to look him in his eyes. "Remember? You manipulated me into loving you. You said so yourself." He smirked. "I was easy, wasn't I?"

Antinea laughed through her stuffy nose and nodded. "You were naive, and I knew it."

Roan looked down at Eurion. "I don't care. Look what we made."

She smiled at him, more tears spilling down her cheeks. She sniffled once and then sighed. "All right," she said. "I'll think about it. If I may."

Roan felt his face light up and his eyes round. "You will?"

She nodded again and leaned against him, looping her arm around his to hold him close. "For Eurion."

He didn't care that she hadn't said yes. Satisfaction filled him and he laid his cheek against the top of her head, gazing down at his son.

CHAPTER XXXVII

"We're nearly through!" Baelian shouted to Roan.

Roan glanced up at the city walls. Yes, the battering rams were doing their work. The Elsarius had retreated behind the walls, and the catapults had begun assaulting the outer walls. Perhaps it was time to show them his Scion abilities. Trylian hadn't told him to yet, but did he really have to wait for the command? He was Scion after all. Others should be bowing to him.

"Keep pushing," he urged. "I'll be back."

He turned his horse and galloped back toward where the Clarets now hid. The snow was deep, and more drifted down from the sky as he charged to Phael. He'd soon see to it that most of it was melted away. The battlefield was red with blood and strewn with bodies, both Elsarius and Modeus alike. His horse had become adept at avoiding the carnage and galloping around it.

"Phael," he called as he entered the safety of the trees. His Claret ran up to him, eyes wide. "It's time."

"Roan," Phael started, but Roan leapt off his horse and grabbed Phael by his wrist. He marched him to the edge of the trees.

"Don't argue with me now," he commanded. "Transform and let's finish this. We're so close."

Phael pressed his lips together and his face screwed up in sorrow.

"Remember what I said," Roan reminded him. "We won't harm anyone in the Sanctuary. I promised."

He saw Phael wanted to argue but kept his words behind his closed lips. "Very well, Roan," he sighed.

Roan didn't know what kind of inner turmoil Phael was facing, but he was glad to see it go. He needed his dragon, and it felt right in this moment not to force him to transform. He wanted Phael to do it himself.

Phael stepped apart from him and closed his eyes. He sighed deeply and in a flash of white light, his small, frail body disappeared, and a roar shook the earth as the great white dragon appeared. Roan stumbled back and gripped the crystal around his neck, just in case he needed to command Phael. But Phael didn't attack him. Instead, he stuck out his front leg so Roan could climb up onto his neck. He situated himself at the base of the dragon's neck. Deciding he didn't want to order Phael, he said, "To the front!" and the dragon took off of his own free will.

Roan clapped his thighs down tight around the dragon's neck and hunkered down close to his shiny white scales. He looked down and watched the earth speed past. Before them, Delsinor loomed into view. He knew that those on top of the city walls could see him now, but he wanted everyone to know they were there. Through the bond, he urged Phael to roar.

A great roar, which only a dragon could make, shot out before them and echoed into the distance. Roan trembled at the sound as it vibrated in his chest and sent shivers down every part of his body. Feeling such power beneath his legs gave him a sense of invulnerability.

"Now, show them your flame," he ordered.

He sensed Phael hesitate through the bond. Roan gripped the crystal, sending a warning. He was in command. Not

Trylian. Not Phael. Only Roan. Phael opened his maw then and spewed a jet of flame down onto the top of the wall. The soldiers and Knights screamed and leapt out of the way, not all of them making it. The smell of burning flesh quickly rose to them on the freezing air. A surge of regret and sorrow pulsated through the bond.

The dragon angled his head up and re-ascended into the sky, circling to come back again. Roan held up his hands now and conjured his flaming tornado. The crystals sapped his strength, and his vision blurred for a moment as he rapidly called down the tunnel of flame. He gasped as the wind was knocked out of him and he panted, trying to make his head stop spinning. He just needed to reach that euphoric feeling that came after.

The rotation of flame came down inside the city walls. It obliterated any structure in its path and set fire to anything not made of stone. More screams came up from inside the city, and it was music to Roan's ears. But the toll it took was hard to bear. He fell forward onto the dragon's neck and lay there a moment as Phael strafed the walls once again.

"Take us to the front," Roan ordered. "We need to get the men inside." He shook his head hard, throwing off the last of the fatigue.

The dragon swooped around in the air, turning and heading back to the front. He had to flare his wings out to slow down enough to land with his back legs reaching for the earth to not knock over the siege machines. He landed hard and Roan was pitched forward but held on tight. He didn't fall.

"Follow me!" he called to the army behind him. "Phael, to the front gate. Give it all you have."

With a snarl, the dragon marched forward with huge, gentle strides. He maneuvered through the battlefield easily and approached the great wooden city doors. Once they reached them, he threw back his head and then launched it forward, spewing a jet of flames onto the wood. The wood heated and then crackled, turning a bright shade of orange.

"Again," Roan ordered from the back of the dragon.

The dragon repeated the move, launching flames onto the door until it was smoldering and cracking.

"Now," Roan commanded, moving Phael out of the way. "Bring the battering ram."

Once he and the dragon had cleared the way, the soldiers with the battering ram stepped forward and began their work again. Roan urged Phael back into the sky, where he stopped his fiery tornado now that the men were going to be inside. He looked down at the devastation he had wrought and smiled. Bodies littered the destroyed streets, smoldering in their armor. The euphoria hit him hard then. He felt invincible. In command. No longer did he feel fear.

He flew over the city walls, mapping the way to the Sanctuary in his mind. He found the best route and committed it to memory. Once he was down in the city, it would be harder to find his way, but at least he had a bird's eye view for now.

Looking up, he took in the Sanctuary. It was up on a hill in the center of the city, white and gleaming like a cluster of pearl spears. The colored glass in the windows didn't catch the gray light from behind the clouds, which spewed snow, but he could still make them out. The bells on the Sanctuary rang, calling the people to flee. That was when he noticed a stream of peasants filing out the back of the city.

Let them run, he thought.

He commanded Phael to circle the Sanctuary, looking for the best entrance. It seemed the front doors might be best. Besides, it would open into the main room where the Empyrean Core most likely would be. They'd need to haul their rams all the way there to destroy it. But they could do it.

Once they had the army subdued, they'd have free rein of the city.

Roan flew back to the front of the city and watched his men pour into the gate, led by the other Archon Knights. Trylian wasn't among them as he'd been called back for news from Aatheria.

Reaching his right hand out, he shot a storm of lightning down before the men entering the city. He gasped again and doubled over, blood trickling from under his fingernails. His eyes darkened and he lost his sight for a moment. Panic flared up in him and concern shot through the bond from Phael.

"I'm all right," Roan said quickly. "Just winded." His blood dripped down onto Phael's white scales, bright against them. It was enough, what he'd done. But he got the urge to fling another barrage of magic behind the city walls. He wanted to feel that power again. That might. "Phael, take me to the outer walls, near the gate."

The dragon circled close to the now open gate. It needed to be wider, to let in more men. Roan stood up on his dragon and called down, "Move!"

The men scattered and he had an open target. Aiming at the already weakened walls, he raised his left hand where the wind crystal waited. Focusing all his energy on it, he shoved both his hands forward. A blast the likes of which made Phael flinch emanated from his hands and smashed into the walls. The stones didn't stand a chance. They exploded inward, crushing the city dwellers on the inside. The wall crumbled, widening even more.

Roan moaned loudly as the wind was once again sucked from his lungs. He couldn't gasp and his vision went entirely black. He felt himself fall backward onto Phael's back. He couldn't move. It was like being crushed under a huge weight. Gasp as much as he might, air wouldn't fill his lungs. He felt blood trickle down from his nose.

Phael gave a roar and gently ascended, taking Roan away from the front. The Modeus army cheered enthusiastically and surged forward now that they had a bigger opening. Roan rolled over on Phael's back and tried to sit up, but his arms shook until he collapsed back down. As they flew, breath slowly came back to Roan, and he drank it in ravenously. Concern lanced through the bond from Phael, and Roan tried to speak, to tell him he was all right, but he didn't have enough breath.

The dragon landed carefully on the snow and lowered himself to the ground as close as he could before tipping Roan off. Roan landed hard against the frozen ground and moaned as he lay there. They needed to be less noticeable. So he fumbled with the white crystal around his neck and willed Phael to change back into his human form.

"Roan," Phael's voice said from his right after a brief moment. "Can you breathe? Say something." Phael lifted him and laid Roan's head in his lap. He gently smacked his cheek to get his attention.

"Yes," Roan croaked. He gulped in more air and slowly his vision started to come back. He looked up and saw Phael's concerned face above him. "I'm all right. Just give me a moment."

"That was foolish," Phael chided him, but his hands gently petted Roan's hair. "You don't know what using those crystals will do to you. What if next time they kill you? Or worse. What if they start to drain me once they've taken everything from you?"

"It won't," Roan argued back. "I get stronger every time. That was just too much for now. I feel my strength growing."

More than that, he felt euphoric. The more he breathed, coming back to consciousness, the more the elation and joy filled him. His strength started to come back tenfold for just a moment before he felt normal again. He loved that feeling, that rush. The crystals may have been sapping his strength and nearly killing him, but the sensation that came after was too much to ignore.

Phael looked doubtful, but didn't say anything. He slipped his arms under Roan's and rose, helping him to stand. Roan took a deep breath and looked around, his vision restored. The men still poured into the city, but someone rode toward them. He squinted and saw it was Aryn. The boy was dashing to them.

"I can't find the other Archon Knights!" Aryn shouted, pulling up on his reins to come to a stop. "Roan, I had to tell someone. The camp was attacked while I was there. I just managed to escape and come here."

"What?" Roan snapped.

Aryn nodded. "A small convoy of Elsarius Knights, led by someone we don't know, ransacked the camp and attacked."

"Is everyone all right?" Fear choked him.

"Trylian was wounded," Aryn said. "I don't know what to do."

"And the women?" Roan asked, thinking of Antinea. "The others?"

Aryn shook his head and shrugged. "I didn't look. I came for help."

Roan roared and gripped his hair. He marched on the spot, turning tightly as his mind reeled. "We have to go," he said. "Phael, we can find them. We can stop them."

"Of course," Phael said, his brows pinched. He ran a good distance away and Roan ordered him to transform back into his dragon.

Roan ran to him, mounting him quickly. "Aryn, tell Thaniel and Baelian what has happened. They're inside the city walls. Tell them we went back and to keep pushing forward."

The boy nodded, his eyes wide as they took in the dragon before him. "Yes, sir."

Roan kicked the dragon in his sides and together they flew into the air. He soared over the woods and followed the river back several miles until he saw the smoke from the camp. The distance wasn't far from the back of a dragon. Phael didn't need to be told. He descended and landed just outside, lowering himself so Roan could run to the camp.

The camp was in shambles. Tents were burned, people were crying all around, holding a few dead in their arms. The wagons were destroyed and the cook and stable master lay dead on the ground.

"Antinea!" Roan shouted. "Trylian!" He marched in among the destruction and swung his head this way and that as he looked for them.

"Here, master Roan," the familiar voice of the healer called out.

Roan turned and ran to the healer, who knelt over Trylian's prone and unconscious form. A huge gash on his head showed where a small axe had tried to end his life.

"Is he all right?" Roan asked, shaken.

The healer nodded. "Stable, yes. But, Roan—"

"Roan!" Antinea's voice screamed.

Roan spun and caught her in his arms as she stumbled to him. She buried her face in his chest and wept. He wrapped his arms around her and held her close.

"How did they know where we were?" he asked. "What happened?"

"They no doubt have been searching these last few days for our camp," the healer said sadly. "They just finally found us at long last. But that's not the worst of it."

Roan tried to brace himself but sensed it wouldn't be enough. "Where is Eurion? Where is my son?"

Antinea wailed now, her legs giving out. Roan caught her

and slowly lowered her to the ground. She clung to him, crying. "They took him. They stole him from me!"

Ice filled Roan's veins, the likes of which rivaled that of the chill in the river. "They what?" he growled softly.

"They didn't know whose babe he was," she said. "They just took him."

"They won't harm him," Phael said quickly. "I know they won't."

"They took him!" Roan shouted, rage boiling up in him now, melting the ice. He gripped Antinea hard. "I'll find him. I swear." He hugged her once more, then stood. "Phael, we're going to find them. Do you understand? Not one of them will walk away from me."

Roan saw red encroaching on his vision, but ignored it, thinking it must have to do with his rage.

"Of course," Phael whispered in submission.

"Roan, don't," Trylian's strained voice said from below them. "That's what they want. They want us divided, away from the front. You can't leave them."

Roan quickly knelt by Trylian and touched his shoulder. "I have to find him. I have to find my son. They don't know the life they've stolen, but they will soon regret it. I will destroy them and be back before sunrise." He glanced to the west where the sun was setting. "Phael will carry me."

"Don't," Trylian tried again weakly, grabbing for Roan's hand.

"Take care of him," Roan said to the healer, standing again. "If he's dead when I return, it's you who will pay."

Antinea fell into his arms once again, kissing him passionately. She gripped the sides of his head and pulled him into her. "Please," she whispered once she broke the kiss. "Find him. Bring him back to me."

"I will," Roan promised.

CHAPTER XXXVIII

Phael knew it had to be midnight by the time they finally found the trail of the Elsarius convoy that had attacked the camp. Through the bond, he felt nothing but rage and bloodlust from Roan. He wished he could communicate with Roan when in his dragon form. He knew Roan would force him to kill his own people once they found the convoy, but he was helpless to stop it. Yes, he wanted the child back. The babe didn't deserve to be captured. But he didn't want to slaughter dozens on his own with his fire. If he could manage it, he'd transform before Roan ordered him to destroy them. Could he overpower the binding of the crystal? He wasn't sure that was what Roan had in mind, but he didn't want to find out.

"I see them!" Roan called over the wind. "There, to the east."

Phael turned his great head and was able to spot the fire in the trees. His dragon eyes picked up on even the smallest of embers. He could see the main campfire of the convoy and even spotted a few men walking about the perimeter with torches. He tried to send a warning through the bond, but felt Roan reject his signals. He needed to land, to communicate. He started to circle and found a small opening in the trees he could slip through and land.

"What are you doing?" Roan hissed so his voice wouldn't carry on the cool wind. "We have to attack them."

Phael just cleared the top of the trees when he felt Roan fumbling for the crystal around his neck. He'd grip it and command Phael to fly up again, to breathe fire onto the Elsarius. Roan wasn't thinking. What if Phael accidentally hit the child? There was more at stake than just the lives of the Elsarius.

Listen to me, Phael growled through the bond.

In a fit of anger, Roan ordered him to transform. Phael fell to the ground in a heap with Roan landing hard beside him. They both groaned and waited a moment on their backs for the impact to wear off. Phael was winded and coughed as Roan stood. He marched to Phael and hauled him to his feet by the collar of his robes.

"What the hell?" he growled, shaking Phael. "We need to get to them."

Phael saw Roan's eyes were red. Not just the irises, but the entirety of his eyes had turned to a liquid, blood red. He'd seen this before. Roan was not himself.

"We can't torch the entire convoy," Phael said, shoving Roan away from him. "What if we hit the child?"

At this, Roan stopped for just a moment. He grunted in thought and nodded once.

"But you don't have to kill them," Phael whispered, knowing full well he was putting himself in danger. "We can sneak in, find the child, and bring him back. It won't be too hard. I can cause a distraction in my dragon shape. They'll know it's us and come looking for you and me."

Roan glared sideways at Phael. "I will not spare them. Not after their cowardly display. Not after they took Eurion."

"Roan, please," Phael started, reaching out to grasp at him.

Roan whirled around, an angry, animal-like growl emanating from his throat. He gripped Phael by his neck and shoved him up against a tree. His monstrous strength appeared as Roan lifted Phael with one hand, choking him. Phael kicked his feet, trying to find the ground. It seemed with the Scion's bloodlust came strength he hadn't counted on.

"Do not interfere, Claret," Roan snarled. He squeezed harder and Phael began to panic. "Do not try to stop me, do you understand? I will do this alone if I have to."

"Roan!" Phael gasped, trying to breathe. He pleaded with his eyes, unable to speak more. Roan waited, though, holding him there. Choking, Phael managed to say, "Yes."

Roan dropped him. Phael gasped and collapsed at his feet, holding his bruised throat. He couldn't stop the tears that sprang to his eyes. Roan was a monster sometimes. But this wasn't him. This wasn't his fault. It was the damn Modeus controlling him. Forcing him to follow his dark urges. Roan had a softer side. He'd seen it. He had a sense of loyalty to those around him. Phael had experienced that firsthand when Roan had taken the punishment Trylian had laid on him in Phael's stead.

"If you get in my way," Roan mumbled dangerously, "I won't hesitate to cut you down, too."

Phael covered his mouth to stifle a sob and nodded. Roan turned on his heel and marched toward the convoy.

"Roan, wait," Phael called softly. "They have guards on the border of the camp. Be careful."

Roan didn't stop, though. He marched on, drawing his blade. The crystals in his gauntlets and on his sword caught the firelight and twinkled in the darkness as he got closer.

"Please," Phael prayed, "don't let them see him. Protect him. Let him live. Give him the strength he needs to find the child and bring him home." He closed his eyes and clasped his hands together tight, repeating the prayer. He mumbled a few traditional blessings and begged for Roan to come to his senses.

He stopped. He'd been praying to the Elsarius. He gulped

and clasped his hands tighter, pressing them against his forehead.

"Listen to me," he whispered to the Modeus. "He is your servant. Your Scion. Watch over him, please." A chill ran down his spine as he prayed to the dark aspect of the Winds. His hands began to shake. He felt like the aspect watched him as he prayed. He'd prayed to the Modeus many times now, but this felt more personal. He still felt like a heretic. "Protect him. Give him the strength to overcome them all. Let me watch him. If I need to, I will intervene."

He unfurled his hands and stood from where he hadn't realized he'd been kneeling. He rushed after Roan, knowing he had to keep an eye on him. Prayer was one thing, but the Winds demanded action as well. If he needed to, he'd happily let Roan force him into his dragon form and save him. He didn't want to kill the Elsarius, but they were not so innocent right now. He'd much rather protect Roan. He needed Roan.

Crouching, he slipped between the trees and found his way to the edge of the camp. Everything was quiet and the Elsarius Knights meandered about, completely unaware of the danger they were in. Phael looked for Roan and spotted him several yards away. He knelt behind a tent, drawing a dagger from his boot. Roan slipped into the tent and Phael watched in horror as the silhouettes moved inside. He watched Roan grip the man inside and cut his throat. The blood shot out like a geyser and painted the back of the tent. Phael covered his mouth with his hand to stop the scream.

Roan slipped out and moved through a few more tents, doing the same. Phael watched him closely, his heart hammering in his chest and working its way up to his throat. Roan was quiet, and that was good. But soon, someone would discover the dead bodies and then the plan would be over. What then?

Phael wasn't ready for what happened next.

A man entered the first tent and shouted, "Daren's dead!" The flap burst open, and the man charged out. "Men, to me! Someone's here among us."

Chaos broke out then. The Knights ran from their tents and out into the main circle of the camp. Phael almost tried to transform by himself then, but spotted Roan behind a tree, drawing his blade. Roan leapt out from hiding with a cry and quickly slaughtered two men, one with a swing of his blade, decapitating him, and the other with a pulse of air from his hand. The man who took the magic damage exploded into red pulp. Phael gasped and closed his eyes.

He only heard then. Heard the men shouting that a red devil had appeared. Some thought he might be a ghost, since they couldn't see him. Phael opened his eyes and watched Roan charge out of hiding again and decapitate two more Knights. Blood arced through the air as the heads spun away into the treeline.

Horrified, Phael watched with wide eyes as Roan single-handedly slaughtered Knight after Knight. His eyes, bright red and glowing, made him look like a demon. Soon, his face was painted red with blood and the front of his armor was soaked in it. He moved quickly, faster than he ever had before. The bloodlust from the Modeus and his Scion abilities were finally showing. He was stronger than ever.

Phael couldn't stop the sob that broke from him. This wasn't the man he loved. No, Roan was possessed. Mad. Just like the legends said he would be. And there was nothing Phael could do about it. He could try to stop him in his dragon form, but Roan would just overcome him with his crystal-given will. Phael was powerless. That weakness awakened a kind of anger in him the moment he watched Roan slice his twelfth head off. Phael didn't like being so powerless. So weak. He wished he could find a way to overcome the hold Roan had over him. But what chance did he have? What magic or secret might free him of their bond? Did such a thing exist?

Roan snarled like an animal and killed the last man standing. Phael looked around at the camp before him. A few torches had fallen and caught some of the tents on fire. Somewhere behind Roan, a wagon burned. Blood soaked the snow and mud around him. Everything was gone; everyone was dead. He'd done it. Somehow, he had slaughtered every last man standing in the convoy.

Phael cried softly where he hid, watching Roan look around for more people to maim. He looked lost, confused, and hungry for more. He held two blades in his hands now, both bloodied and dripping. He tossed one aside and gripped something else on the ground and stood up, holding whatever it was. Roan was so different. Ever since he'd become Scion, he'd been more brutal, less careful. Like he'd thrown off some kind of shackle. Phael didn't want Roan to lean more into his violent tendencies. He wanted to see a softer side of him. Something that might show he had a shred of humanity in him. But it seemed to be drifting further and further away. Roan had changed, and not for the better. Phael hung his head and wept.

CHAPTER XXXIX

Roan couldn't hear or see. He felt earth under his feet and the world spinning around him. His breath came muffled and deep within his ears. His face was icy cold, like it was wet in the glacial wind. He held something heavy and balanced in his right hand. His sword? His left clutched something that felt like thread, but it was heavy. He tried to turn around and look, but his sight was gone. He blinked several times and finally an orange glow appeared. As it did, so did the distant and muffled crackling of flames. A wave of heat hit him from the left side, and he turned. Something huge burned there. He blinked again and saw it was a large tent, like that of a general or Archon Knight.

He took a deep breath and looked around. The clearing came into view. He hadn't really seen it in several minutes. He remembered walking through the woods. He recalled arguing with Phael. But then, everything had gone red. He'd seen through the haze but had not been in control of his own body. He felt almost nothing. The one sensation he did sense was glee and joy. Exultation in the killing of the convoy. Roan glanced at the ground. Bodies littered the clearing amidst the smoldering fires. Every last one of the corpses was missing its head.

Roan looked down at his hands. In his right, as he'd

guessed, was his father's sword. But his left... Roan gasped and dropped the head he had been clutching. It splattered into the red mud under his feet with a splash. The head rolled and faced Roan. Its eyes were wide open, its mouth stiff in a permanent scream. Blood pulsed from the hanging arteries in the neck. Roan groaned and stepped back, panting. Where was Phael?

"Winds," he whispered hoarsely, "say I didn't kill him." He glanced around. "Phael?" he called.

Nothing answered him. No high, elegant voice called out to him from the shadows. What about Eurion?

Roan spun on the spot, panic squeezing his chest then. "Eurion!" he shouted, knowing full well the babe could not reply. "Where are you?"

"Roan?"

He spun. A white form cowered behind a tree several yards away. Phael.

"You're all right," Roan burst, tears blurring his vision. "What happened? What did you see?"

Phael slowly came out from behind the tree. "Are you yourself again?" His blue eyes bored into Roan's green ones.

"Yes," Roan whispered, wiping at the tears before they fell. "I don't know what came over me."

Phael swallowed nervously. "The madness. Just as the Claret said. I tried to warn you. I told you it would happen."

"Madness?"

"The Blood Spring infected you," Phael went on. "It's possessed you with a bloodlust you cannot control. It took over you, making you do this."

Roan looked around. Could Phael be right? He had lost consciousness. Almost. It had happened like a dream. He'd seen parts of it here and there, had felt his wild anger for only a moment every once in a while. But the evidence lay before his eyes. The fire burned and the blood flowed. And Phael would not have done it. No, only he could have.

"I did this..." he whispered, his words strangled. "What have I done? Where is Eurion? Have I killed my own son?" He couldn't stop the shuddering gasp that escaped his lips. He turned, looking for any sign of the babe. "Help me, Phael. Help me find him."

The child was innocent of any wrong. Roan knew that. But as they scoured the rubble and flames, he couldn't help but think what a fitting punishment it would be for his lifetime of wickedness if Eurion had been slain by his own hand. The silent weeping crept up on him again and he couldn't stop the soft sobs that slipped from between his lips as they dug through the tents and detritus.

"I'm sorry I hurt you," Roan said as he turned over a burning chest to look inside.

"I understand why you did," Phael said stiffly. "But I hope it never happens again."

"Do you think I can control the bloodlust?"

Phael stopped and met Roan's eyes. "I have to have hope that you can. Winds know what might happen next time. You could kill me. Hurt someone else close to you. You have family now, Roan. You have things to lose."

Roan gulped and prayed that he never hurt anyone close to him. Not Phael, Eurion, or Antinea.

They continued to look, and soon Roan began to lose hope. His heart hammered in fear the longer they went without finding the babe. Until finally, they heard something.

The high, yowling cry that only a baby can make pierced the air. Roan's heart leapt into his throat and he spun to face where the cries came from. Eurion wailed and cried, sounding like he was in pain.

"Where is he?" Roan screamed, wildly looking around.

Phael snapped his head around to listen. "There," he called, pointing to a covered wagon.

Roan turned. The thing was ablaze and Phael was right: the cries came from inside. Roan dashed to the wagon and skidded to a halt just outside the back entrance.

"That's suicide," Phael called, not daring to get closer to the hot, raging flames.

"I have to," Roan gasped.

Without waiting for another word, he leapt up into the wagon. The fire scorched his face, and the hot winds blew back his long hair. The heat instantly overcame him, but he didn't care. He heard Eurion wailing and screaming, and nothing else mattered. He shoved his way through the back of the wagon until he saw a small wooden crate with a pile of furs inside it. He leapt over the barrels and supplies and knelt before the crate. Inside, Eurion waited, kicking and screaming. Part of the blanket had caught fire, and his little arm had blisters all up and down it.

Roan scooped the baby up into his arms and patted out the flames. Above him, the slender beams holding up the canvas that covered the wagon cracked and fell. Roan gasped and used his body to cover Eurion as the flaming pieces of wood fell down across his back. The smoldering canvas fell and touched his cheek, burning him as well. He felt welts and blisters rising on his arms as he used them to protect his face against the flames. Eurion had stopped crying suddenly, as though he understood the situation.

Coughing and gagging on the smoke, Roan leapt over the objects in the back of the wagon, heading toward the exit. His head began to spin again from suffocation, and he lost his balance. He fell but made sure to hold Eurion to his chest.

"Roan!" Phael called.

What felt like seconds later, Roan opened his eyes to someone hauling him to his feet and dragging him out of the fiery wreckage. He heard Phael grunt as he dragged his semi-conscious body away from the wagon. Somehow, Phael held him as he descended. He heard his Claret panting and coughing as he struggled to save Roan and his son.

"I thought the worst when the babe stopped crying," Phael gasped.

Roan struggled to his feet, clutching the precious bundle to his chest. He teetered on his feet and Phael caught him before he collapsed. Roan coughed and gagged, clearing his lungs of the smoke. No sooner were they safe outside then Eurion began to softly cry again.

Phael led Roan and the baby away from the wreckage and then out of the clearing into the woods, where the air was clearer. He walked them to a large fallen tree and motioned for Roan to sit.

"Thank you, Phael," Roan said after a moment of gulping in the clean air. "We would have died if you hadn't pulled us out just now."

Phael nodded and collapsed forward, elbows on his knees. "It wasn't so much for you as it was for the babe."

"Of course," Roan replied in good humor. He reached up with one arm and pulled Phael into a sideways hug. "Thank you for my son's life."

He released Phael and looked down at Eurion. The child grunted but had stopped crying. His eyes were open, and Roan saw them for the first time. They were the stormy, steely gray of his mother. His soft brown hair was Antinea's, too, but the rest, Roan saw easily, was all him. He knew in a year or two freckles would pepper Eurion's face like they did his.

He couldn't help himself. He cradled the boy in his arms and pressed him hard into his chest. Phael smiled at the interaction and put his hand gently on Roan's shoulder.

"Rest a moment, then I'll take us back."

Roan bent his neck and gave Eurion a quick, gentle kiss on his forehead. "Thank you again, Phael."

His Claret's eyes sparkled a little as his hand drifted down to Eurion's head, gently cupping his crown in his hands. Phael suddenly gasped and pressed his other hand into his chest.

"What is it?" Roan asked, his brow pinching in concern. "Are you hurt?"

Holding his breath, Phael shook his head. "A strange sensation just came over me. Like a lance of excitement and familiarity just bolted through me." Phael froze, eyes slightly widening. His cerulean orbs didn't waver from Eurion.

Roan glanced down at his child and then up at Phael again. "Probably adrenaline from your brave act."

Phael finally started to breathe again. "Of course. That's what it was."

THE THREE OF them flew back quickly and made it to the camp in the early hours of the morning, several hours before the sun would rise. It was cold and dark. The little fires in the camp told them where it was and Phael landed gently a few yards out before transforming back into his human form. Roan waited for him and together they walked back into camp.

He spotted Trylian standing—which was a good sign—just inside the camp. A thick white bandage wrapped around his head. He stood over a table with a map open on it and was reading a message on thick parchment. Pacing not too far away from him was Antinea. She had her arms wrapped tightly around herself and tears stained her pretty face. Roan hadn't even called out to her when her head shot up. She looked directly at him.

"Roan!" she cried, and limped toward him. "You found him! Please, tell me he's alive!"

Roan couldn't stop the satisfied smile that broke his face. Seeing her come to him, arms outstretched, with hope and love in her eyes, made his stomach turn in knots. He knew she was concerned about Eurion, but she had cried *his* name.

Antinea reached them and plucked the baby from Roan's arms immediately. He let her. She crushed Eurion against her chest, hugging him and kissing him voraciously. Roan stood by, waiting for her to be satisfied. She looked up at him, eyes brimming with tears.

"Thank you," she choked out between sobs. "Roan, thank you."

He waited, praying she'd embrace him. She gulped in air and then did. Using one arm, she wrapped it around his neck and pulled him into a hug. Between them, Eurion cooed in protest of being crushed. Antinea laughed and pulled away, touching his cheek gently.

Then Antinea licked her lips and her face turned bright red. Roan didn't know what she was about to do until she quickly stood up on her toes, gripped him by the back of his neck, and pulled him down into a kiss. Her lips found his and crashed into them with such ferocity, he thought he might bruise. But he didn't pull away. He let her kiss him, her tongue fighting to enter his mouth as she opened her lips. Roan leaned into the kiss, allowing her inside and reciprocating the gesture. He gripped her face with both hands and dived into her, loving everything, from the taste of fruit in her mouth to her soft lips against his.

Finally, they broke apart. Antinea's nose was bright red, as were her cheeks. Roan swallowed and was about to say something when Trylian's voice cut through the falling snow.

"Roan," he called. "I need you."

Antinea nodded and flicked her head toward Trylian. "Go on," she whispered. "I need to find the healer for Eurion."

Roan sighed in frustration but nodded. He and Phael made their way over to Trylian, who pored over the map.

"This is it," Trylian said once they were present. "Our last push. The city has fallen. We're going back and we're finishing off the Sanctuary."

Roan nodded, excitement building in him. He glanced at Phael and noticed his face was stony and impassive.

CHAPTER XL

"Forward!" Roan shouted to his men behind him. He unsheathed his blade and thrust it before him to command the horde.

Behind him, the column flooded past. They surged deeper into the streets of the city and slaughtered any who stood up to them.

"They're farmers and merchants with pitchforks," Aryn said at Roan's side. He'd hardly left it since they'd returned to the front. Roan didn't mind. He liked Aryn and his little band of friends that followed him everywhere and did everything he said. "Not hard to get past."

"We want no resistance," Roan called to his men and Aryn. "We need the roads clear."

Behind him, Trylian and his band moved forward with the rolling ballistae and the battering ram. This one was huge, larger than the ones they'd used to break through the city's doors. It rolled forward on six wheels over the cobbled streets and the dirt ones alike. It moved slowly. It hung from six thick posts made of tree trunks by chains as thick as Roan's arm. Mord, they called it. It had a dragon's head on the front and fire burned inside the mouth to give it a haunting look. It usually drove fear into the men. It glowed in the afternoon light, which was dim and dark. The clouds overhead cast a dark gray pall over everything beneath them. The snow still fell and piled up around their ankles, almost reaching to their knees now.

"Here comes Mord," Aryn said, looking over his shoulder. "What do we need it for?"

"The Empyrean Core," Roan answered easily. He kicked his horse and galloped further in, Aryn just behind him.

"What happens when we destroy it?" Aryn asked. "Will our Clarets lose their powers? The ones who pray to the Elsarius?"

Roan wasn't sure, but he knew what he'd been told. "No. They are bound to us, and we follow the Modeus."

Aryn frowned and pressed his lips to one side, thinking. "Where is the Empyrean Core for the Modeus, then? Won't the Elsarius just retaliate and destroy ours? Then the entire world will be magic-less. What then?"

Roan didn't know. He wasn't sure where the Empyrean Core for the Modeus was, or if they even had one. "That won't happen," he said, trying to encourage Aryn. He hacked down a man who ran at him with a pitchfork poised to strike his horse. "We won't let anything like that happen."

Aryn, convinced, went back to the battle. He pushed ahead of Roan a little and cut down a woman who had run forward with a small dagger in her hands.

As they went deeper into the city, the people scattered before them more and more. The Knights hurled fireballs and streams of lightning at any who dared get too close. Roan didn't want to use his crystals again. He didn't want to do anything that might trigger his bloodlust and make him black out again. The feeling of being out of control did not appeal to him, no matter the carnage he could pile up. He wanted to be in control.

They pushed in and soon made it to the center where the Sanctuary waited. A line of Knights and soldiers in white blocked their path. Roan stopped and looked into the eyes of the Archon Knight that sat atop his horse before his men. Roan ran his eyes over the small horde. Maybe fifty men. It was all that stood between them and their final victory.

"Move aside," he called, coming forward to speak Archon to Archon. "You do not need to die here today."

"You'll slaughter us no matter what we do," the Archon Knight shouted to Roan. "We'd rather die fighting."

Roan nodded. They would push him to use the magic. "Of course, I leave it up to your judgment." He drew his blade and thrust it up toward the sky, calling down a rain of fire. The little flames ignited on the clothing of the Elsarius Knights. Some screamed and a few scattered. Roan teetered in his saddle but managed to hold himself upright. The surge of desire to use the crystals again shot through him. It felt good, euphoric, to use them, despite the exhaustion.

Phael, he thought as the Elsarius patted the fires out, *you don't have to hurt anyone. I just want them to see you. Come.* He sent a surge of need through the bond, knowing Phael wouldn't hear his thoughts exactly, but hoping he understood.

"Do you know who I am?" Roan asked the Archon Knight.

The man spat at the ground. "You're a Modeus savage! A pawn of the dark powers. A servant of the black aspect of the dark Winds."

Roan felt Phael approach before he heard his great wings stirring the wind around him. He smirked darkly at the Archon Knight. "I am Roan Red Mane, son of Monguard and Scion of the Modeus, Archon Knight of Aatheria, and the man who will hear your last words."

Just as he spoke, Phael broke over the tops of the buildings around them and roared as he shot over the Elsarius Knights and soldiers. The men shrank and looked up at the dragon that soared over them.

"The dragon is here!" one of them shouted. The men

began to scatter. They didn't know Phael would never touch them. That was fine, though. Roan just needed them to know the danger was there.

"You are who you claim to be," the Archon Knight gasped, lowering his blade.

Roan nodded. Behind him, Trylian's band finally made its way there. Mord was in the midst of them, smoldering and smoking, eager to devour the Core.

Not wanting to be at a stalemate when Trylian arrived, Roan thrust his sword forward and screamed, "Charge!"

Aryn led the column, shrieking a battle cry to the sky and shooting past Roan. The others followed him, riding into the Elsarius' meager last stand. Roan joined them and charged the Archon Knight. He called on the wind crystal in his gauntlet and let the blast shoot out from him. It hit the Archon Knight directly in the face, exploding his skull. The blood and matter splattered over Roan as he got too close. He couldn't help but laugh in hysteria as the man's headless body slumped over and fell into the snow at his horse's feet.

He wheeled around and stabbed another man only to take a jab to his left shoulder just below his pauldron. He groaned in pain and wheeled around, making the sword cut him deeper. Blood flooded down his side. The pain was enough to make his eyes water. A surge of worry shot to him from the bond as Phael must have felt his fear and pain.

Roan pressed his hand into his wound and tried to regain control of his horse. As he did, an Elsarius soldier came up behind him and seized his leg from the ground. Roan struggled to pull his leg free, but the man had him in his grasp. The man jerked hard, and Roan fell from his saddle into the soft snow. But the frozen ground underneath knocked the wind out of him.

The soldier that had grabbed him stabbed at Roan with his sword but missed as Roan rolled to the side. He struggled to his feet and shot his hand out toward the man. A burst of fire bloomed from his palm and shot into the man's face. The man screamed and backed away, but Roan stayed on him, burning his flesh until he saw his face melting away and his eyeballs burst from the heat. He dropped his hand and panted. The euphoria and the pain filled him in a mixture of agony and pleasure. He continued to pant and turned.

As he did, an arrow struck his wound on his left side below his pauldron. He screamed and stumbled back, wincing in pain.

"Roan!" Aryn shouted. Using his short bow, Aryn turned on his horse's back and fired at the man who had shot Roan. He hit the man right between the eyes. Roan was impressed by the shot.

He pulled the arrow from his shoulder, ripping his flesh and muscles on the barb. Aryn rode up beside him and defended him from two more attacks while he regained his mind. Roan was able to dispatch three more Knights before it was just him and his men left. He looked around, wondering if any Elsarius Knight or soldier would spring up and try one last desperate attempt to stop them.

"Well done," Trylian praised him when he saw the carnage. He rode up before Mord, Gareth and Tanis at his sides, and looked around. "A clear path into the Sanctuary. Thank you, Roan."

Roan nodded, his face sweating from the pain in his left shoulder. Behind him, Phael appeared.

"Are you hurt?" Phael asked, but then his eyes spotted the dark red making its way down Roan's torso. He gasped and touched Roan's shoulder.

"I'll be fine," Roan grunted. He sheathed his sword and marched to the Sanctuary's doors. "Aryn," he called, "come and help me."

The boy ran to Roan's side and together they pushed open

the Sanctuary doors. The bells on top of the towers had stopped ringing some time ago. Roan eagerly looked into the main room of the Sanctuary.

Inside, the place looked like the Sactrium, but bigger, grander, and more open. The ceiling was tall and arched, with beautiful stonework making intricate knots and designs that covered all the eye could see. Great windows lined the inner room, with colorful glass filling them and depicting scenes from myth and history alike. The air smelled like incense and honey somehow.

Before them, beyond the transept, waited a host of cowering Clarets in white robes. None of them had the white hair that magically-blessed Clarets had. Roan noted one who stood before the others, shielding them with his body. He knew immediately this must be Lailen. Behind the crowd of Clarets, blue and sparkling, perched in a base of white marble, was the Empyrean Core. It rose up out of the ground like it grew there and pointed toward the heavens above. It was about the height of Phael in his dragon form and several feet in diameter. It somehow shot awe through Roan as he looked upon it. A slight humming and tinkling sound came from it.

"Do not harm them," Roan commanded his men as they and Trylian flooded the nave. "We are not here to take holy lives."

"We should slaughter them all," Aryn said excitedly from beside Roan.

"There is no pride in that," Roan shot back. "You," he pointed to Lailen. "Tell them to stand aside."

Behind him, Mord wheeled in through the front door, blocking any escape. The fire from its mouth wafted into the room, filling it with a scent of brimstone and fire and destroying the sweet smell from before. The Clarets gasped when they beheld Mord and some cried out.

"We will not step aside," Lailen shouted. "You'll have to kill us if you want to take our power."

"You have no power," Trylian scoffed. "You are Clarets of the Sanctuary. Your magic is weak. You are here to pray and to serve. That is all. Now, step aside. My Scion has spared you."

"Lailen!"

Phael shot past Roan, but did not get far. Roan knew his Claret too well to let him run to his old mentor. His hand shot out and grasped Phael by the back of his robes, pulling him back.

"Phael?" Lailen gasped, hand over his mouth. "You're alive!"

"Roan, please! You promised," Phael begged, turning and grasping Roan's front.

"Where are the others?" Lailen asked, hope and fear igniting in his blue eyes.

Phael turned back to face him. "Nox is...gone. But Alowyn still lives. He's near."

"Near?" Lailen asked, his face falling. "You are bound? Not to..." His eyes roamed to Roan. "You are the dragon?" he gasped. "Phael, are you bound to the Modeus Scion?"

Phael nodded.

"Enough of this," Trylian barked. "Roan, control your Claret."

"Phael, fall back," Roan urged, pulling him back once again.

Phael jerked himself out of Roan's grasp. "No, I will not stand down! I will not let you do this."

"We talked about this," Roan hissed. "Don't do this now."

"Take the Claret away," Trylian ordered. He snapped his fingers and two soldiers came forward, grasping Phael between them. The Claret cried out and struggled.

"Let him go, Trylian," Roan implored.

"This Claret has angered me for the last time," Trylian snapped. "Make him silent."

The soldiers threw Phael to the ground and began to beat him. Roan watched, wanting to intervene, but valued his own battered and wounded body more. The soldiers kicked the Claret and blood immediately dribbled from Phael's nose and mouth. Lailen shouted for them to stop, but Roan held his sword out to stop the Claret from coming forward.

"Don't make me kill you," Roan warned. He turned to the men who held the pull chains for Mord. "Move in."

"No!" Lailen screamed, running forward.

Roan leapt to catch the Claret before Aryn or someone else put their sword through him. He gripped Lailen and hissed so no one else could hear, "I promised Phael I'd not kill you, but you are testing me."

Lailen looked Roan in his eyes. "You will not keep such a promise." He shoved at Roan and dashed behind him to try to tackle one of the men pushing Mord. Gareth moved quickly and caught the Claret, though. He held a blade to his throat.

"Father?" he asked.

"Please," Phael groaned from where he lay. "Roan, please."

"I've had enough!" Trylian shouted. He drew his sword and charged the little host of Clarets that shielded the Empyrean Core.

Tanis, Aryn, and the others followed Trylian. They dived into the helpless holy men and women and cut them down easily. It took hardly more than ten seconds. Gareth moved to slice Lailen's neck, but Roan held up his hand.

"We might need information," he said to Gareth. "Don't kill him."

Gareth looked to his father. Trylian, bloodied and panting, narrowed his eyes at Roan. "You disobey my orders?"

Roan set his face in a gentle glower, meeting Trylian's eyes. "This is an order from your Scion." His stomach flipped as fear threatened to consume him for standing up against Trylian's orders. Surely Trylian would beat him for such insubordination. He'd fight back if he came for him. No longer would he cower before his mentor. No longer would those memories of fear and pain control him.

He swallowed down the trepidation and strength melted the anxiety away. He held firm, his hand on his sword, unshaken.

Trylian looked for a moment like he might burst into rage, but something clicked behind his eyes, and he nodded. He waved his hand to Gareth.

"Fine." Rather than kill the Claret, Gareth tied his hands behind his back and shoved him to the ground.

Roan watched as the blood washed over the pure white of the Clarets' robes. Soon, no one stood between Mord and the Empyrean Core.

"Roan," Trylian breathed, catching his breath. "Give the order. This is your victory."

Roan glanced from Phael, to Mord, to the Core. "Destroy it," he ordered the men.

Roan stumbled out of the way of the battering ram, his bloodlessness finally catching up with him. The crystals' toll also made his head spin. He fought to stand upright. He caught sight of Phael, who was also struggling to stand. He was in the way of Mord. He'd be crushed if he didn't move. Roan gasped and rushed forward, gathering Phael in his arms quickly and rushing out of the way. He glared at Trylian, but the Archon Knight didn't respond. He simply watched ahead, eyes steely and empty.

Mord made its way to the Empyrean Core, the men shoving the altar and other holy accoutrements out of the way. Candles spilled over and caught the white rugs on fire, but no one paid it any mind. Roan watched in awe as the men holding the pull chains groaned and grunted, hauling the battering ram back. The Knights and soldiers began to chant, "Mord! Mord! Mord!" as the thing was pulled back.

Roan held his breath as the men released the giant beast. It swung forward and crashed into the Empyrean Core with a devastating crunch. The fiery maw of the dragon collided with the crystal and a huge crack splintered up the middle of the Core.

"No!" Phael moaned weakly. But he didn't fight against Roan's hold on him. "Don't do this."

The men pulled Mord back once more and let it swing against the Core a second time. This time, pieces blasted out from the Empyrean Core and scattered over the earth. Roan covered Phael with his body as the sharp shards splattered over his back. When he looked back, the crack was bigger in the Core, white spidering veins crawling out from where the maw had struck it.

"Again!" Trylian shouted.

The third time was all it took. Roan watched in horror as Mord swung forward on its six chains. The fiery maw collided hard with the crystal and sank deep into its center, breaking through like a pane of glass. The men waited as they watched the front penetrate the Core. No one moved and hardly anyone breathed.

Roan sensed it before the others. "Get down!" he shouted.

No sooner had he spoken than the Core exploded. The light that shot out from it blinded everyone near it. The blast knocked Roan back, but he clung to Phael, trying to shield him from any sharp pieces that might want to pierce their bodies. Roan hit a pillar on the side of the nave and his head cracked against it, knocking him out cold.

CHAPTER XLI

After the explosion of the Empyrean Core, Roan had woken up to most of the others unconscious as well. Trylian had hit his already injured head and had taken a few days to wake. Roan had Lailen taken to the city's prison underneath Caer Delsinor and locked away. Phael had thanked him for sparing him, but it was obvious that he was destroyed over the slaughter of his brethren. Roan didn't have time to comfort Phael in any way. He was, being Trylian's chosen successor, immediately put in charge of the other Archon Knights and made to oversee the takeover of the city.

More troops arrived from Amril and Sorath and helped get the massive city under Modeus control. But that wasn't all it took. King Caedric, his queen Mareetha, and their children, Princess Eltra and Prince Valorian, were next. According to those in the city, the royal family had been sequestered in the castle some time ago to keep them safe. Before that, King Caedric had been out amongst his people in the city, commanding his men from behind the walls. Roan admired him for this and thought it was a pity that the great king had to die. But that was Trylian's plan.

Roan waited until Trylian woke and was strong enough to march on the castle. He had guards around it night and day to watch for the royal family in case they wanted to flee. He even had men outside the city and around the walls in case they escaped through the sewers or another way they didn't know about. To make sure the king and his family were still there, he sent an Elsarius Claret ahead to scout. The Claret came back, weeping, and announced that the king and his family were still holed up in the castle.

That afternoon, Trylian, Gareth, Tanis, their Clarets, and Roan and Phael marched to the castle with a small horde of Knights, soldiers, and a single general. They met no resistance on the way to the castle as the city had been so severely decimated. Some of the inhabitants even bowed their heads as Roan rode past and murmured, "Scion." At first, Roan didn't notice, but once he did, he enjoyed the subjugation. Having people bow in his mere presence gave him a sort of thrill and awoke a desire he hadn't known he had. For once, it was nice to not be the one bowing his head.

The castle stood large and faced the southern wall of the city. It was surrounded by a hedge maze and a bit of land where gardens and trees blossomed in beautiful rows. A small stone wall also surrounded it and a black wrought iron gate blocked their way at first. Trylian seemed to have anticipated this and had the men tear it down easily. No one stopped them as they popped the hinges and removed the gate. No moat surrounded the castle and so there was no drawbridge to cross. The portcullis opened for them when they came close.

"Be prepared to use your magic," Trylian had told Roan before they moved out. "You are our best shot at getting in. They will cower before your might."

But Roan was disappointed when they were shown directly into the palace by the scared guards at the gates. "Why are they so complacent?" he asked. "Don't they know their king is in danger?"

"They have no magic," Trylian answered. "It's gone. They are but meager men now. Thanks to you."

But Roan had been wrong. A few Knights appeared in the

foyer of the castle and tried to stop them, but he, Trylian, and the others made short work of them, cutting them open and removing their heads in a few minutes. They weakened the Knights with fire and lightning. To Roan's shock, the Elsarius Knights didn't use magic back at them. So it was true. The destruction of the Empyrean Core really had taken their powers. Roan was glad to see, when he hurled a single fireball at a Knight, that his powers were indeed still intact. Trylian had been right.

A few more valiant Knights appeared as they ascended the castle steps toward the throne room, but they were easily dispatched as well. Two more Knights stood guard outside the doors and demanded they stop. But Trylian had Roan obliterate them with his wind blast. Roan thought it was too easy, and he liked it. They had won. Yes, they had lost some good Knights, soldiers, and Clarets, but they had won. This was what victory looked like.

Trylian kicked the doors open and looked down into the dark, stone throne room. It was lined with small torches on the walls and a deep red carpet trailed from the door to the set of four thrones at the head of the room. The thrones were made of ornate stone and within them sat the royal family.

King Caedric sat defiantly on his throne, which was grander than the others and had the head of a crowned dragon on the back of it. On his right sat his queen, Mareetha. On his left was Prince Valorian, and to the right of the queen was Princess Eltra. King Caedric was a tall man with a golden beard and hair shot through with white strands. His brows were in a permanent scowl. He wore the royal green and gold of Delsinor and a great golden crown sat atop his noble head. His son looked just like him, but was many years his junior, and he had a smooth face. The queen was beautiful, with dark red hair and piercing blue eyes. The princess looked just like her mother.

"So you have come," King Caedric said in a deep, rich timber that dripped with disdain. "I had hoped my men might keep you at bay."

"They cannot stand up to us any longer," Trylian said, a cocky grin pulling at his lips. "We've taken the Sanctuary and destroyed the Empyrean Core. Their magic is gone. They are only weak, frail men now. And women," he added, as if amused.

King Caedric stood and unsheathed a sword Roan hadn't seen. Beside him, his wife gasped.

"Father, don't," Prince Valorian protested softly.

Roan drew his sword, and so did Gareth and Tanis.

"Don't be foolish," Trylian sighed. "My Scion can kill you quick as a wink. You cannot hope to stand up to us."

"Fight me like a man, then, usurper," King Caedric challenged Trylian. "Man on man."

"Is that what you want?" Trylian asked. "Roan, make sure the queen doesn't interfere."

Understanding, Roan raised his left hand and sent a huge, shocking blast of wind from his palm. The blast hit the queen and obliterated her skull. Princess Eltra screamed and stood as brain matter and blood splattered over her.

"Mareetha!" King Caedric shouted in horror. Prince Valorian stood and drew a blade as well, taking two dangerous steps toward Roan. "Don't, my son," King Caedric ordered, reaching his hand out to his hot-headed son. He turned to Trylian. "I understand," he whispered. "What do you want?"

Trylian marched forward, gripped King Caedric by his collar, and tossed him from the little stone dais. The king crashed and clattered down the four steps and hit the stone floor hard. His crown rolled from his head and spun to a stop near Roan's feet. Trylian glared down at the king. Then he looked at Roan and motioned for him to pick up the crown.

Roan dipped and picked up the golden and gilded circle and held it up to Trylian. He took it, admired it for a moment, and then placed it on his own head. Then he snapped his fingers and Gareth and Tanis rushed the prince, grabbing him by his arms and forcing him to drop his blade. They pulled him away from the throne as the other men seized the princess.

Trylian turned and sat on the throne, looking down at the king. He placed his hands on the arms of the throne and looked out. "This is what I want, king. To sit on the throne and never again be reminded of my failures. To rule in your stead. To anoint the land in the blood of the Elsarius and snuff out its reach. The Modeus have blessed me this day and the Elsarius have abandoned you." He drew his sword and stood. "I shall be called Knight King and all of Adorian will bend their knee to me and my Scion." He motioned to Roan. "I am the man who made the Scion of the Modeus. Who fought and slaughtered Delsinor. I have blotted out any failure of my past and have made the Winds proud. I will be blessed, and I am righteous in their eyes. Rise, king."

King Caedric slowly got to his knees. Before he could stand, Trylian lunged forward and swung his blade hard. It erupted into flame and, with a smooth arcing motion, he severed King Caedric's head. Because of the fire, no blood spilled from it. The body teetered on its knees for a moment, then tumbled over.

"Father!" Prince Valorian cried. He struggled against Gareth and Tanis but couldn't free himself. He snarled and snapped at Trylian, "You will die one day. Not from age, but by my blade."

Roan thought then that Trylian would command him to kill the prince, but he didn't. He simply smirked.

"How many winters are you, boy?" Trylian asked.

Prince Valorian glared. "Sixteen." He said it proudly.

Trylian raised his head and inhaled deeply, as if this pleased him. "I am king now and you may beg for your life."

"I will never," Prince Valorian growled.

"I will have my way," Trylian argued back gently. "With whatever and whomever I wish." He smiled darkly.

"Shall we bring the princess to the king's chambers?" Gareth asked, leering at her. "For you?"

Trylian's cold blue eyes roamed to the princess, who wept in the grasp of the men. He looked her over once and then sighed. His eyes then went to Prince Valorian. "No," he said slowly. "Bring the prince. And don't disturb me for three hours."

Prince Valorian went pale and struggled harder, as if his life depended on it. But Gareth and Tanis held him fast. They marched out, the prince screaming his protests the entire way. Roan watched, a dark, remembered fear welling up inside him. He pitied the prince suddenly. The princess wept for her brother.

"Do with her what you want," Trylian said, pointing to the princess. "Just take her away."

The men complied, removing the princess from the throne room.

"Roan," Trylian called, flicking two fingers to gesture him forward. "Kneel before me."

Without asking why, Roan did as he was told. Trylian took up his bloodied blade and rested it on Roan's right shoulder.

"I dub you Arbiter of the Knight King. You alone shall be my right hand, my confidant, and my councilor. The Archon Knights will be second to you and I will heed your words over theirs, though they too shall be my council. Do you accept, my Scion?"

A thrill shot through Roan. He glanced back at Phael, who stood with Elendir and the other Clarets behind the horde of soldiers and Knights. His eyes were pinched in worry and sadness. A wave of anguish came through the bond. Roan didn't understand. He wished they could communicate better through the mysterious link they shared. But all he got was melancholy. Phael looked like he might weep. Roan knew if he were Trylian's Arbiter, he could protect Phael better. Protect Antinea. And now Eurion.

"I want my own land," Roan countered, looking up to Trylian. "A keep in my name, with land around it for use. Or you give me my father's land, as is my right."

Trylian's brows twitched for just a moment like he might frown, but then he said, "Of course, Roan. As soon as I can."

Roan nodded. "Then I accept. I will be your Arbiter."

Trylian smiled and then tapped his left shoulder with the blade before sheathing it. "Rise then, Roan son of Monguard, Arbiter of the Knight King, and Scion of the Modeus."

LATER THAT DAY, Roan found himself in the dungeon of Caer Delsinor. It was bursting with Knights of the Elsarius and their Clarets, not to mention most of the Clarets from the Sanctuary. Aryn, Gareth, and Tanis walked with Roan as he surveyed the imprisoned. A few other soldiers accompanied him as well. Phael walked a good distance behind him, looking like he might weep.

"More are being brought into the castle's prison," Gareth relayed to Roan as they walked. "But we're rapidly running out of room."

"And the city prison?" Roan asked.

"Also full," Aryn sighed. "We don't have much choice."

"Why keep them alive, anyway?" Roan asked. "Let's just have them executed."

"Roan," Phael whispered hoarsely. "Don't do this."

"That will take time," Gareth counseled. "There are many to be dealt with outside the prison as well. Entire columns, the army."

Roan hummed in thought as he meandered down the dank and dark hall of the prison. He stopped when he came to a cell with a Claret inside. He looked in and noticed Lailen. Behind him, Phael gasped softly.

"A guillotine," Roan suggested easily. "We'll have one made. We'll hold executions daily for those who won't swear loyalty to us. Soon enough we'll be rid of all the Delsinor Elsarius Knights."

Phael whimpered and turned away, face in his hands.

"An excellent idea," Aryn praised him, smiling up at Roan.

"Take the information to Trylian," Roan ordered Gareth and Tanis. "Aryn, find a carpenter and a smith who will work with us on making the machine. Then report back to me tomorrow morning."

"Yes, sir," the three of them said, bowing their heads. They turned and left back up the aisle of cells and out.

"You," Roan said to Lailen through the bars. "Tell me, where is the Scion of the Elsarius? He's not in the city."

"Did you think he would be?" Lailen asked weakly.

"Roan, what are you doing?" Phael asked, coming up beside him. "Please, don't hurt him. You promised."

Roan shrugged off Phael as he laid his hand on his shoulder. "Claret," he snapped to Lailen. "Tell me where the Scion is or one of your number dies."

Lailen looked at the cells around him. The Clarets inside cowered into the corners, pleading with their eyes.

"Roan, don't, please," Phael begged.

Roan ignored him. "Well?" he asked, raising his hand with the wind crystal in it. "If you won't tell me, you're useless to me."

"No, Roan!" Phael begged. He fell to his knees before

Roan, gripping the front of his clothes. Tears streamed down his face. "Don't do this. This isn't you. You don't have to hurt anyone." He took a shuddering breath and went on, "You promised me! You swore you'd not harm him."

Seeing Phael on his knees before him, weeping and pleading, hurt. He wasn't sure why Phael had that effect on him, but he couldn't ignore it either.

Sighing inwardly, he placed his hand under Phael's chin and closed his eyes. He nodded. "I did. I won't harm him. But..." He dropped his hand and looked around. "For every day I don't know where the Scion of the Elsarius is, one of them dies." He glared at Lailen. "Think about what you're doing and consider telling me the whereabouts of the Scion. This is your new reality, and it's not going anywhere."

EPILOGUE

ADORIAN, A VILLAGE OUTSIDE DELSINOR. 25TH OF
SELAT, 1217.

The days went by quickly following the fall of Delsinor. Roan was kept busy with executions, interrogations, and the implementing of the Modeus regime. Shrines to the Elsarius were burned and taken down. Anyone who even bent their head in prayer in the streets was taken as prisoner or slaughtered on the spot. Roan had little time to see to himself, to stop and reflect on what he was doing. Until one day.

Trylian approached him and urged Roan to follow him out from the city to a plot of land about a mile away. On a hill just west of Delsinor a small but elegant castle rose to the sky. It was surrounded by farmland, orchards, and even had a mill on it. As they rode to the keep, the farmers and peasants on the land stopped their work and bowed to them as they passed. Roan was confused at first, but once they reached the little moat that surrounded the keep, Trylian stopped and handed Roan a ring of keys.

"They call it Castle Rembram. I chose it for you," he said simply with a wide smile. "As promised. Land of your own."

"This is all for me?" Roan said in awe, taking the ring.

"Of course," Trylian beamed. "I cannot have my Scion, my right hand, the Arbiter of the Knight King, living in the caer's barracks with the others. There are plenty of rooms for you, and anyone you want to bring with you."

Roan understood. "I want to bring Antinea and my son."

Trylian blanched a little. "She's just a whore, Roan. Take your son but leave her."

Roan shook his head. "I want her. I want to provide for her. To take care of her. And Eurion."

His mentor sighed and looked away, a little disappointed. "She's not a lady, Roan. She won't fit in with the others. She will suffer all her days in your circles. Why do that to her?"

"I won't argue," Roan said with finality. "I made my mind up long ago." He smiled. "I'm going to fetch her."

"I'll have her brought," Trylian said instead. "You go inside and be ready to receive her."

So he did. Roan dismounted and went into the keep to explore while Trylian left to fetch his soon-to-be wife and their son. The keep was vast on the inside, much bigger than it looked on the outside. It had a garden square inside with a fountain and many marble statues of heroes past, Modeus and Elsarius alike. He found the kitchens where a handful of servants bowed silently to him as he entered. A few other servants moved about the keep as he explored. He found the stables outside with a small smithy set not too far from it. The land itself was vast and beautiful. He could smell some sort of cider being made near the mill, but didn't find it before he was summoned back inside.

Antinea stood in the entryway, clutching Eurion to her chest. She wore a thin cloak over her brown dress and her ankles were bare. She shivered in the cold winter light. Her gray eyes were wide as she looked around. Trylian stood behind her, looking not too pleased. Roan waved his hand and Trylian inclined his head and left the way he'd come in.

"Roan," Antinea stammered when she saw him. "I'm— That is, I don't want to—"

"Don't," Roan whispered with a smile on his face. "Don't say anything."

"But I'm confused. And scared. Roan, I won't give up Eurion." She adjusted her grip on the babe to something more protective. "No matter what you say, I won't let you take him."

"I'll never ask you to give him up," he said, still grinning. He approached her and touched her hands. She was icy cold. "Where have you been living?"

She glanced around as if looking for a trap. "In the basement of Caer Delsinor. The men will need me soon and I'll—"

"You'll do no such thing," Roan interrupted. "Those days are over. Do you understand?"

Antinea shook her head, tears beginning to form in her eyes.

"This is your life now." Roan touched her shoulder and led her through the entrance and into the keep. "I want you to live here with me. With our son. Forever. As my wife."

"Roan!" Antinea gasped. "I can't. I mean, I'm not free to choose such a life."

"You are," Roan urged. He stopped and took her hands where they clutched Eurion. He bent his neck and kissed her fingers. "I want you to be. You won't be a slave anymore. You'll be my wife, a free woman. We can even find your family, if you want. Whatever you want, I'll do it. I swear."

Antinea gasped and the tears fell. "This can't be true."

"It is," Roan said. Deciding now was the best time, he knelt and clutched the front of her dress. "Antinea, daughter of whoever, I promise to love you, to protect you, to raise our son to be the best man he can be. If you'll have me." Fear lanced through him. What if she said no? Then what? His heart raced and pounded in his throat as he waited for her reply.

She gulped and licked her lips. "Can I say no?" she asked, her voice quivering.

Roan's heart nearly stopped in his chest. "Yes."

"Then what will happen?"

He couldn't stop the tears that sprang to his eyes now. Was she really saying no? "I'd free you anyway. Help you leave this place. Give you anything you need. For Eurion." He stopped himself before he begged her. He blinked and a single tear fell.

"You already asked me to marry you once," she whispered.

"You never said yes," Roan reminded her. "I thought you'd leave. Take Eurion away from me."

Antinea inhaled sharply. "I can't believe you are on your knees before me. Roan..."

"Please," he whispered, desperate and afraid. "I'll do anything."

"Stop saying that," she said, wiping at her own tears. She considered him for a long moment before whispering, "All right. Roan Red Mane, son of Monguard, Arbiter of the Knight King, Scion of the Modeus, I will be your wife."

Joy exploded in Roan, and he leapt back onto his feet. He gripped her face with both hands and kissed her, pulling her into him until the babe was squished between them and started to coo in protest. Breaking the kiss, he then planted one on Eurion's head. He met Antinea's eyes and was glad to find her smiling as well.

"You said yes," he breathed in disbelief, pressing his forehead to hers.

"I'd be a fool not to," she replied with a little grin. "You offer me freedom, all this... Yes, I'd be mad to reject you."

"I love you," he whispered, pleading inwardly that she'd say it back.

Antinea stood up on her toes and kissed him quickly. "Thank you, Roan. For everything."

LATER THAT DAY, they moved into the keep. Phael came as well, since he'd have a room of his own. The keep was large enough that Roan let him have his pick of the rooms. Not to his surprise, Phael picked a room with stained glass windows that greatly reminded them both of the Sanctuary. The windows faced east and west on either side of the room, so it was constantly painted in colorful light. It had a few built-in bookshelves as well as a great hearth.

"It suits you," Roan said as he glanced around the room. "We'll have your things brought up immediately from the caer."

Phael's back was to him, and he looked out one of the windows. "I suppose I should thank you," he murmured.

Roan didn't miss the strange tone in his voice. "What is it?"

His Claret turned slowly to face him. He looked like he might weep. "You've done it. Trylian is king. The Elsarius are falling. You must be proud."

Roan frowned at Phael. "I am. I've risked my life for this."

"You risked many lives, including mine."

"What's wrong?"

Phael met his eyes. Roan saw the dam behind his cerulean gaze break before he spoke. Tears welled up in his eyes. "I hate all you've done," Phael began. "What you've forced me to do. It hurts, Roan. I am in pain. I have been for months. I'm subject to your dark whims and evil doings. And I cannot stand it any longer."

Confused and not sure what Phael was trying to get at, Roan frowned. "We had to do—"

"I don't care!" Phael burst. He whirled around and faced Roan head on. "I can't do this. I can't believe my own traitorous heart."

Roan didn't move. He wanted to let Phael have his

moment. Maybe then he'd feel better. But what he said next stopped Roan's heart.

"What you do—all the evil you commit—it hurts me, Roan." Phael turned and paced aggressively. He gripped his long white hair and moaned. "I wish you'd stop doing all these terrible things. Stop doing as he says. I know there is a good man underneath all this wickedness if you'd just try to stand up to him."

"Phael, what are you—"

"I love you!"

Roan's breathing stopped and he froze. His lips parted slowly as he tried to find the words to reply with. He had none.

"I cannot stop myself," Phael went on. "I was drawn to you because you protected me. You saved me. I needed to be safe and so I stayed near you. But then these feelings grew. All I had to do was not fall in love with you, but I couldn't stop myself. But that just drove me mad. I can see the inner light in you, but you never let it out. You are a slave to his whims. You have no mind of your own. You slaughter, you destroy. And for what?"

Now a rage rose up in Roan. Never had Phael spoken to him like this. "I make my own choices. Everything I've done is for my people, for my faith. And now I fight for my future. A future for my child."

Tears cascaded down Phael's pale face. "I don't know how I love you. But it hurts every day. I want to touch you, to hold you. But I cannot because I must remain pure and all that you do hurts my heart. I cannot love an evil man."

Roan waited a moment for his own breathing to calm before he asked, "You love me?" The confession finally sank in.

Phael exhaled hard and blinked, making more tears fall. He nodded and looked away. "I thought now that we've taken Delsinor, I could tell you. That you might do something about Trylian and his hold over you. I want you to be free of him."

Roan shook his head. "We have too much work to do. I'm sorry, Phael. I really am. I love Antinea. But I love you as well, just not in the same way. I wouldn't have stood up for you if I didn't. I wouldn't have saved you. Protected you. I know I spoke callously before, telling you you're replaceable. But the truth is, I hope to never bind to another Claret. I do love you, in my way."

Phael's cheeks turned a dark pink and he ducked his head into his shoulders, hiding behind his sheets of white hair. "I can't help you if you won't throw off his hold over you, Roan."

"What do you mean? Why do I need help?"

Phael shook his head and marched quickly out of the room, pushing past Roan. Confused, and a little upset, Roan watched him go.

ADORIAN, DELSINOR. 15TH OF AURIC, 1217.

Roan sat on a wooden dais overlooking the city square. The guillotine had been constructed, and executions had been being carried out for a month now. He sat on a makeshift wooden throne, overseeing the interrogations and executions. He alternated between Clarets, Knights, and the common folk who had been arrested. Sometimes they died after some torture and questions about the Elsarius Scion. Other times they held on and were later executed under the silver blade of the new guillotine. He had become numb to the blood and the cries of the people. The public nature of the executions drew a crowd of weeping and begging citizens.

Gareth, Tanis, and Aryn stood behind him as henchmen and protection. On his right sat Phael. He was pale, eyes sunken and cheeks hollow. Roan had decided to make him watch after his little outburst before. He wanted to show Phael that he was the man he was afraid of.

Nothing of note had happened in the hours of executions until one Claret was brought forward. Next to him, Phael jerked forward and squinted at the brown-haired Claret.

"No," Phael whispered. "Not him."

Roan looked from Phael to the Claret being brought forward. He had kept his word to his Claret and not executed nor tortured the Claret Lailen. So who was this? Roan looked on in interest as the older Claret was brought to his knees before the wooden dais.

"Scion," the older Claret called up to Roan. "I have news for you."

"Traitor!" Phael shouted over him. "This man, Olenar, is a traitor. He's the one who set up the ambush and is the reason I am here."

"Phael?" the Claret asked, his eyes narrowing. Then they popped in surprise. "It seems I did you a favor, boy. You are Claret to the Scion. So it *was* you who flew over Delsinor that day."

"You did this to me," Phael growled, his eyes shining in rage. "This is all your fault. Everything that has happened is because of you."

"Silence, Phael," Roan snapped. He looked back at the Claret called Olenar. "What do you know?" he asked.

Olenar's eyes went from the guillotine to Roan's face. He swallowed hard once. "I know where the Scion is. What his name is and what he's been doing."

"Traitor!" Phael shouted again, this time throwing himself from the wooden seat. "Shut your lying mouth and accept your fate."

Roan stood and faced Phael, glaring down at him. The Claret quelled a little under his harsh gaze and closed his lips. Roan turned back to Olenar. "Go on, Claret."

Olenar twisted a little in his bonds, but then said, "His name is Cassander Loneridge. He was born in Emberforge seventeen years ago. He and his Claret were born bound—very rare. They found one another just days before the first attack in 1207 before they were separated to keep the Scion safe. He was so young, he has no memory of who his Claret was."

Roan remembered those days. His father had been gone for the war. Trylian, too. "Go on," he urged again.

Olenar nodded. "His parents were killed, and he was sent to live with an uncle in Duskhallow."

Behind Roan, Phael seethed, but thankfully held his tongue. Roan would deal with him later. He needed Phael's utter submission and loyalty. He'd thought he'd had it after his confession but now saw how wrong he was. Would Phael ever be completely on his side?

"And he's there now?" Roan asked.

Olenar shook his head. "An old Knight, Tamarack son of Glorin, has taken him to train him. Cassander is just a simple farmer, but I fear he will rise up a great warrior soon enough. They travel even now, on the lookout for the Modeus Empyrean Core and honing his skills. Soon they will reunite with his Claret, I am sure. Then he will have his dragon, and the real war will begin."

Roan's brows pinched.

"People are no doubt flocking to Moralan, to attune to the Moralan Empyrean Core," Olenar said quickly.

"There's more than one Elsarius Core?" Roan asked.

Olenar nodded. "But they must make a pilgrimage there to attune to it. Only then will they have their magic again. But you." He laughed nervously. "The Modeus are not so weak. Your power comes from your faith alone."

Roan's brows dipped in thought again. No, he wasn't sure where their power came from. They didn't have a Core...did they? "So no one knows where the Modeus Empyrean Core is. We're vulnerable."

Olenar nodded. "Of course, sir, but I could be useful."

Roan groaned and rolled his eyes. He motioned for his men to move. Once they started to bargain, he knew he'd get nothing else from them.

"Wait!" Olenar shouted as he was pulled toward the guillotine. "I helped you. I can be of more service, I swear."

Roan turned his back on the desperate Claret and watched Phael's face. For once, rage and bloodlust showed on Phael's beautiful face. His Claret glared murderously at Olenar as he was held in place and the blade was raised. Roan liked what he saw in Phael's eyes then. For once, he was enraged. However, he might need more information and Olenar seemed pliable and competent.

"Wait," he called, raising his hand. The soldiers who were about to release the blade stopped. Roan considered the anger in Phael's eyes and the babbled pleas from Olenar. "He may still be of use."

"Trylian promised me!" Olenar shouted from where he bent over awkwardly. "I was to be Anakrite. Who are you to go against his commands?"

Roan blinked and frowned. "Is this true? I've heard nothing."

"It is," Olenar blabbered quickly. "Even Phael knows. Remember, boy, when you first acquired your Claret in the woods?"

Roan thought back. That day and the days surrounding it were a blur. But he suddenly recalled the hushed conversation between Trylian and Olenar. They had promised one another power in exchange for the Clarets. In exchange for Phael. But Trylian had said nothing. Roan narrowed his eyes in thought.

So Trylian had planned to betray Olenar. Or at the very least, had not cared that he might be executed with the other Elsarius Clarets. In that case, he might just be of use to Roan.

Roan looked his Claret in the face. Phael seethed but didn't speak. Roan nodded and looked back at Olenar. "Very well," he sighed, waving his hand. "Take him to the prison below Caer Delsinor. Keep him there, alone, away from the others. We'll deal with him when the time comes."

Olenar babbled thanks as he was pulled from the wooden beams of death that rose up on either side of his head. He was soon rushed away, hands still bound behind him. Roan would use the Claret if he needed. Someone inside the Sanctuary and in the Claret's circle who was desperate for their life would be useful.

When they were finished for the day, Roan pulled Phael aside into the caer's archway, away from prying eyes. He slammed his Claret up against the wall and gripped his throat, choking him hard.

"Never speak over me again," he snarled. "Do you understand? I am in command here and you will do as I say and keep your mouth shut. Remember your place as a Claret of the Modeus."

The rage in Phael's eyes from hours before flared up. He gnashed his teeth and glared at Roan. "Let me go," Phael choked.

Roan tightened his grip until Phael thrashed against him in panic. He knew he'd left a hand-shaped bruise on his Claret's delicate neck, but he didn't care. Phael had almost lost him the most valuable information he'd achieved. "Do you understand?" Roan reiterated.

Phael gagged and eventually got the word "yes" out, though defiance and rage still burned behind his azure eyes.

Roan let him go. Phael fell to his knees, coughing and gagging. Roan watched him, regretting his barbaric treatment almost immediately. He'd never understood Phael and wished he could. He couldn't grasp the trauma that must have come with being kidnapped and forced to bind. He knew it must have been terrible but couldn't understand the way Phael saw it. He sighed and turned to leave.

"Roan," Phael called after him, his voice suddenly desperate and sad. "Roan, please, listen to me."

He turned and looked back at Phael on the ground. Phael looked up, his blue eyes sad.

"Can't you see what he's done to you?" his Claret started. Roan frowned, not sure who Phael was speaking of. "He's poisoned you, hurt you. I see that. I don't know what he's done to you to make you fear him—obey him—but you must overcome it. Break the cycle."

"Trylian?" Roan asked, guessing at Phael's meaning.

Phael nodded. "He's evil. He's twisted you up and made you this way. I told you I can see the light inside you. I still can. But he's made you do so many terrible things. None of them were your idea and you can break free of him if you try." Courage flooded Phael's eyes then. Roan had never seen his Claret so brave. He had changed over the last few months. He was becoming more defiant. Less afraid of Roan.

Roan scoffed. "You have no idea what he's done to me. I have to obey, Phael. Just like you."

"No," Phael growled. "Don't give in, Roan. Stop now."

Roan looked once more at his Claret before turning and marching into the falling snow, leaving behind his pleas. The gray light filtering through the clouds didn't light the way well, so Roan followed the torches to the stables where he mounted his horse to return to his new home.

Perhaps there was some truth to what Phael had said. Trylian had beaten him, had abused him all his life. He shook his head, not willing to entertain those memories. Trylian had been controlling him all his life, but for a good reason. For their faith and fealty to the Modeus. If he obeyed, he'd climb the ranks. He had almost made it, and he was just seventeen. He had land, a home, a wife, and a son. He was an Archon Knight like his father.

"I am doing what is right," he told himself out loud. And now, he was on the trail of the Scion of the Elsarius. He'd find the Scion and stop him before he rallied Moralan against them. He had no choice if he wanted to protect all that was his. Yes, he had come a long way, but there was still so much left to do. And now, he had something to lose.

APPENDIX

Author's note:

   This appendix contains descriptions and information that may well spoil the book for you. It is strongly recommended that you do not look at the character list until after you have finished the book.

THE CLARET CLASSES

SANCTUARIES AND SACTRIUMS

Each capital in the western realms of Kelroth are home to a Sanctuary. Smaller villages and cities contain a Sactrium, which is under the protection and authority of the appropriate Sanctuary. For example, Delsinor, the capitol of Adorian, is home to the the Sanctuary. Smaller cities, like Aatheria, contain a Sactrium.

CLARET RANKS

The Sanctuaries are run by **Arch Clarets** as the head and final authority on all matters. The Arch Claret often councils the king and is rarely seen by any outside the royal court, often attending it himself.

Below the Arch Claret are the **Anakrites**. The size of the Sanctuary dictates the number of Anakrites that work under the Arch Claret. Anakrites are also the head authority within Sactriums. They often use Emissaries to report back to the Sanctuary.

Emissaries are the go-between from the Sactriums to the Sanctuaries. They carry news, reports, pleas for aid, and all other communication. The highest rank of Emissary are Emissaries who speak from the Sanctuary to the Sactriums as they speak for the Arch Claret.

The lower ranks have little sway and are not much more than specific jobs. Such as stable master, scribe, keeper of the wards, and so forth. The lowest rank, of course, are the wards —young Clarets who live in the Sanctuary or Sactirum to train to become a higher ranking Claret one day, or to work the land, or to sing the praises of the Winds.

KNIGHTS

The Knights of Adorian and other lands of the western realms of Kelroth are the elites who bind to Clarets in order to wield the magic gifted to mortal kind by the Winds themselves. The Knights are not the city guard, nor the province's military, though they often work closely with both. They are the guardians of the magic.

The Knights' highest rank is **Archon Knight**. Each Archon Knight is in charge of what they call a Column. There are four Columns and therefore only four Archon Knights.

Four Columns make up a Legion. Each Column contains twenty-five Knights, making a Legion one hundred. But not all Columns wield magic. Only First and Second Column are bound to Clarets and can use the elemental magic of the Winds. Third and Forth Column are Knights who hope to one day move up the ranks and become a Second or First Column Knight. Maybe even an Archon Knight one day. The Archon Knight of First Column is head of the Legion and all other Archon Knights answer to him.

Archon Knights are promoted based on merit, time served, and quality of grit. An Archon Knight may be put forth to the Atheling of the city and must be signed into service by the noble. If anyone in the court objects, then the court will hold council to hear both sides and decide on the promotion. Archon Knights are then presented to the king where they receive their blessing from the crown and the Sanctuary alike.

NOBLES AND ROYALTY

The **king** oversees an entire land. The western realms of Kelroth are Adorian, Moralan, and Vyrkaris. Each have their king[*]. The western realms are patriarchal and pass to the first-born son of each king. However, the **queen** still holds some sway and is second in command to the king, often helping him rule in choices, decisions, and even in battle. Below the queen are the **prince** and **princess**. Often times, the prince will act as a general in the royal army.

Each city in the western realms is overseen by a noble

---

[*] Vyrkaris is a special exception. While they do have a king in Drachen, most provinces only respect and revere their own chiefs. There are many wild tribes of the dragonite people and they often only answer to themselves. Vyrkaris is a wild and dangerous land, swarming with monsters. Drachen is the only place the other western realms might consider civilized.

called an **Atheling**. They often own large tracks of land and live inside a castle. They have many who live on and work their land. They are usually related to royalty somehow and pass down their rank from father to first-born, male or female. Below the Atheling come a rank called a Thane or Maid.

Thanes and Maids live all over the western realms and are closer to the gentry and peasant class. Thanes and Maids can acquire this title in many ways. Often they are Knights who have served valiantly and are of a certain age. They can also become this rank by coming into money and wielding influence. They often own land and live in smaller castles or keeps with their own set of guards and farmers to work their land. Very rarely does a Thane become an Atheling, but it is not unheard of as the king may appoint an Atheling should he feel the desire to do so. If one is not a Thane or a Maid, they may be a Lord or Lady.

Lords and Ladies come by their titles strictly through influence and wealth. They typically live within the city limits and do not own much land. However, they are noble citizens, distantly related to royalty, and are often looked up to by those nearest them. They hold some sway and often speak for their part of the city in the royal court. A low ranking Knight in Third or Fourth Column who is of a certain age and never made it to First or Second Column may be a Lord or Lady. Often Lords and Ladies are promoted through social diplomacy to Thanes and Maids. A spouse of a Knight is automatically considered a Lord or a Lady.

A NOTE ON THE ELSARIUS AND MODEUS KNIGHTS AND CLARETS

The Knights and Clarets operate outside the typical noble ranks and peasant classes. They are seen as holy and blessed and ones who must be adhered to as they speak for the Winds.

However, they hold little sway in court outside of the words of the Arch Claret. While an Archon Knight may come to court (though rarely), his words will be heeded but only just as he is not part of the ruling class. However, the words of the Emissaries, Anakrites, and above all the Arch Claret, are taken very seriously. A Claret bound to a Knight, even an Archon Claret, would not be heeded almost at all, except in the rare cases of prophetic dreams. Clarets and Knights, however, are still very respected among the peasant class.

THE EPOCH OF THE EMPYREAN CORE

The calendar in the western realms of Kelroth started when the Winds gifted mortal kind the Empyrean Core, roughly 1200 years ago. This tale begins in 1207 A.C. (after Core) with the years before being called B.C. (before Core). The new year is the first day of spring. The months have thirty or so days in them, give or take a few depending on the year. The months are:

Spring
   —Borealis (new year)
   —Celestrum
   —Luminaria

Summer
   —Gilden
   —Juniper
   —Hearthfire (first harvest)

Autumn
   —Kronomar
   —Eldamar (second harvest)
   —Soramar

Winter
  —Frostfall
  —Selat
  —Auric

CHARACTERS (IN ALPHABETICAL ORDER)

- **Alamar** - A cruel first column Knight who rivals Roan.
- **Alowyn** - An Elsarius Claret who was kidnapped along with Phael; bound to Tanis.
- **Antinea** - A slave girl who becomes Roan's lover.
- **Aramis Whitley** - A Thane appointed by Trylian to govern the village outside Delsinor after it was conquered.
- **Aryn** - A third column Knight who idolizes Roan and becomes his follower.
- **Athael** - A Modeus-raised Claret bound to Gareth.
- **Baelian** - A half-Vyrkarian Archon Knight of second column; one of Trylian's council.
- **Cassander Loneridge** - The Scion of the Elsarius, born in Emberforge seventeen years ago.
- **Daenys** - Monguard's Claret.
- **Elendir** - Trylian's Claret; originally an Elsarius Claret who was kidnapped and forced to bind to Trylian some years ago.
- **Eliana** - Daughter of Archon Knight Thaniel; courted by both Roan and Gaelin Hamlin's son.
- **Gaelin Hamlin** - An Archon Knight from Caeth who forms an alliance with Trylian.
- **Gareth** - One of Trylian's twin sons; older than Tanis by an hour.

- **Juliana** - Roan's mother.
- **Lailen** - Phael's mentor at the Sanctuary in Delsinor; a Claret who aspires to become an Emissary.
- **Mathis** - Archon Knight of fourth column; one of Trylian's council.
- **Monguard** - Roan's father.
- **Nox** - An Elsarius Claret kidnapped with Phael; bound to Razvin.
- **Olenar** - An Emissary of the Elsarius who betrayed Phael and the other Clarets.
- **Phael** - An Elsarius Claret kidnapped and bound to Roan.
- **Razvin** - Roan's half-Vyrkarian best friend.
- **Roan** - Son of Monguard and raised by Trylian. Eager to become an Archon Knight.
- **Tamarack** - An old Knight training Cassander Loneridge, the Elsarius Scion.
- **Tanis** - One of Trylian's twin sons; younger than Gareth by an hour.
- **Thaniel** - Archon Knight of third column; father of Eliana; one of Trylian's council.
- **Trylian** - An Archon Knight who was a friend of Monguard's. He raised Roan and has great ambitions.
- **Veryl** - Alamar's Claret; originally an Elsarius Claret forced to bind to Alamar.

THE WESTERN REALMS OF KELROTH
WYRMFALL
DRACHEN
THE NOR
SORATH
AATHERIA
AMRIL
DELSINOR
ADORIAN
CAETH
INRAL
N

YRKARIS
Wyvern Shallows
DRAKENHALL
DRAIGMORE
DRAGON'S REST
TIAMAS
RTHERN NARROWS
RIVERHAVEN
EMBERFORGE
MORALAN
WHITEFOREST
GORNOTH
REDWATER
DUSKHOLLOW
SILVERBOUGH
VELORIA
LOSTVALE
AURORASTEAD

About the Author

Abi works part-time as a freelance ghostwriter, editor, audiobook narrator, and is one half of the partnership that owns Altered Reality Magazine. She hopes to one day make these passions her full-time job while she hunts for the next bohemian adventure.

She has published works of fiction, poetry, academia, and even won awards for her short stories in science fiction and horror. Her novel, The Trial of Two, was named an Honorable Mention in the Writer's Digest 2021 self-publishing awards and won first place in the dark fantasy category in The BookFest Awards. Abi is also a proud mom of three ferrets. She currently resides in Kansas.

Abi is one of nine children--all who share the creative spark.

Find Abi online at: www.abigaillinhardt.com

ALSO BY ABIGAIL LINHARDT

Season of the Runer Book I: The Trial of Two

Season of the Runer Book II: Sojourn

Season of the Runer Book III: The Eldritch Hunt

Season of the Runer Book IV: The Father of Monsters

Season of the Runer Book V: A Cure for Fate

Prince of MidWest

Why They Killed: A Waksha Virus Novelette

These Darker Streets

Writing as A.J. Morgenstern

DarkFront Witness: Haunted

DarkFront Witness: Hunted

DarkFront Witness: Free